PRESSED

A NOVEL

SEAN R. CABIBI

PUBLISHED BY GREY WOLF CAPITAL, LLC

In conjunction with THE GUILD BAXTER GROUP

Cover and book design by The Guild Baxter Group.
Cover Photo Courtesy of Nijwam Swargiary, modified by The Guild Baxter Group.

ISBN: 978-1-967544-00-4

Just keep in mind, son, life is unfair…

But every once in awhile, with some luck, this works out in your favor.

My Father

Thanks dad… this one is for you.

Chapter One

It was an unusually cool day in June. A day when all of the talent and potential was finally solidified on a piece of paper. It wasn't easy for E.J. Lockhart to get into Ohio University's E.W. Scripps School of Journalism, or so he would tell people. It wasn't easy graduating from college as the valedictorian, or so he would tell people. He could be brash, cavalier, and faintly egotistical, but he would only selectively let others see that side of him. Despite the occasional pretense, most people knew he would soar, even if E.J. attenuated their praise. He was going to accede. Everyone said so.

"Stop fidgeting so much," Kalea said to E.J. "Sit still."

Kalea was trying to keep E.J. relaxed. She grounded him well, delicately vanquished what hubris he did have during their two years together. He made immense strides from the first time they met… voluminously matured from that night when he beat the shit out of her date at a frat party his sophomore year. They would argue about the exact circumstances of that night because they had both been drinking, but the story would become legend at Phi Cappa Gamma. Kalea's date, a football player, and an extremely jealous one, was hovering around her all night long. E.J. didn't notice them at first, until he saw Kalea talking with Benny, a deaf Ohio University student in the fraternity. As she talked with Benny, he thought to himself what most every guy thought when they first saw her: She was beautiful. Kalea's date was beginning to become upset at the attention Kalea was paying to Benny and how close she was to him… unnaturally close. No one noticed her date fuming at this, especially Benny, who could only read lips. Kalea had to be that close for Benny to understand her. Her date didn't know any of this and when he yelled at Benny to back off, he didn't respond… he couldn't hear any of it. Kalea's date thought Benny was just ignoring him. E.J. took notice of the stocky football player and had seen that look before. He quickly moved to intervene, but it was too late. Before anyone had a clue, Benny was struck in the head and on the floor. E.J. screamed that Benny was deaf, but before Kalea's date could process any of this, E.J. punched him in the face and knocked him down. A crowd of partygoers swarmed Kalea's date, throwing the belligerent football player out of the house. Kalea couldn't help but laugh a little when things finally calmed down and the details of what exactly happened were figured out. Even Benny cracked a few jokes while E.J. took the whole incident in stride, nursing his slightly-bruised hand. He expected Kalea to come over and thank him, but she didn't. Terribly embarrassed and trying to save some face, she apologized to everyone, made some off-color wisecracks about her date, and playfully told E.J. that he hits like a girl just to lighten the mood. When E.J. refuted that claim, she socked him straight in the chest, hard, just like a girl. He took a step back and then agreed with her. For the first time in his life, he was intimidated by a woman, and at the same time, acutely infatuated, so much so that he suddenly became too nervous to approach her. He went into the bathroom and tagged on the wall:

If you need another douchebag knocked out, and don't feel like doing it yourself, call me. 555-3834. E.J.

She smiled when she saw the message.

Their first date happened within a week. Neither had too much to offer the other, besides a love for politics, literature, a passion for knowledge, especially philosophy, Kalea's major. They struggled. E.J. freelanced news articles when he could; Kalea worked at a popular local Hawaiian restaurant to make ends meet. She became a good waitress, but that wasn't the sole reason why the owners liked her. She also was Hawaiian. Very pretty and tall with long, flowing black hair, that had a slight curl at the ends, complete with a beautiful smile. The owners of the restaurant loved all these things about her and hardly ever noticed the rare days she was slow or messed up an order.

"I told you to sit still, E.J.," she exclaimed.

"I'm nervous. It's not every day you speak in front of the entire school," E.J. said as he continued to adjust himself.

"Nervous?" Kalea responded, a bit surprised. "You storm into the university president's office demanding information about professors having sex with students and this makes you nervous?"

"That's different," E.J. said. "I'm supposed to look like I'm super scholarly when I give this valedictorian speech, you know, flawless. That's harder than grilling some scumbag school president. My tuition fees pay his salary and the salary of every teacher that decides to stick it to some incoming freshman…"

"Please E.J.," Kalea interrupted. "This is graduation, not a bar."

E.J. nodded his head, quickly gathering himself.

"I'm sorry, babe. All I'm saying is that these people sitting here owe me nothing. They are my peers and speaking in front of them is, well, intimidating. Can I not be intimidated?"

"Of course you can," Kalea said, running her hand through E.J.'s shaggy blond hair. "Just relax and don't say anything about professors fucking students and you'll be fine."

E.J. smiled and Kalea kissed him on the cheek.

All of this was almost a given, considering E.J.'s perfect grades in high school, all in advanced placement classes, his trophies in track and field, student body president, and a key member of every important club at school that saved something, like a forest or some endangered animal in the Ivory Coast... and of course his journalism classes.

Nelsonville-York High School in Ohio. Nelsonville's finest secondary school... the small town's only secondary school. The burg rested just about fifteen miles southeast of the university in Athens. E.J. had lived there since he was ten. His dad moved the family from Cleveland to take a job as an accountant for the city. Nelsonville still had that quaint small-town feel, the old buildings well kept, lamppost-lighted streets, and people too polite to seem real most of the time. The Lockhart's were well liked, and it was the perfect place to raise kids.

By the time E.J. was in the third grade, he could read and write on the twelfth-grade level. Some would say it was because of his mother. Margaret read to him every night from the day he was born and then, when he was old enough, she would refuse to finish the stories and made E.J. read them if he really wanted to know what happened. Others would say it was the high-priced private school he attended before he moved to Nelsonville. Still, others would say it was because of his older brother, Dennis, who was born with Down's Syndrome. When friends and relatives got drunk at family gatherings, they would quietly whisper that Margaret was overcompensating with E.J. Regardless of why, E.J. never struggled in school. In the seventh grade he wrote his first story *The Seventh Beginning*, a science fiction piece he penned after an argument with a friend about an old episode of Star Trek. It was good. Everyone said so.

He was ready as anyone would be when he took over as editor of his high school's paper, The Searchlight. He and another student, Jim Woodrow, transformed the paper into an award-winning high school publication, despite the deficient resources of the small school and the school's administration that did little to help the program. Jim took a lot of the credit, but E.J. did most of the work. When he got to Ohio University, he was determined to do more of the same. He exposed the university's botch purchase of an outdated security system that cost millions of dollars. The school had to replace the entire system only three years later because replacement parts were no longer being made for the obsolete product.

That was the first huge scoop he got.

Then he exposed the hazing practices of Delta Sigma Epsilon. The sorority would confine and beat new members for three days as a ritual to build trust and commitment. That story sent four girls to jail for a year, suspension of the sorority, and an apology from the organization's national chapter. He took down two adjunct night-school professors that were selling grades. He hammered the school's unspoken policy, a type of "don't ask, don't tell," when it came to professors dating current students. The list went on.

He earned an award... then another... and then three more before the day of his graduation. Amazingly, despite all of the time and the dedication he put into the school's paper, he never got less than an "A" in any class. He was exceptional, and everyone said so.

Pomp and Circumstance began echoing through Penden Stadium, on the south end of the campus. Gordon Klatt, the school's interim president, made his way to the stage, across the green grass that lay perfectly cut inside the school's football field. Everyone clapped while E.J. looked down, removing a few flash cards from his pocket. He went through them as Gordon spoke... followed by the dean of students... and then some other person, and probably a few more, before Gordon's raspy voice returned back to the podium. Kalea commented about the speeches, others whispered around E.J. He didn't hear a word anyone said until he was awakened by the thousands of hands that slammed together and bodies that stood up. It was the end of the ceremonial speeches about tradition, the future, and students, all sprinkled with graduation clichés that flowed and weaved over the stadium's P.A. system.

"And now," Gordon said. "I would like to introduce Ohio University's valedictorian for the class of 2000, Eric Jason Lockhart."

E.J.'s robe made him look thinner than he was. He had always been thin, but during the past six months he had become a bit obsessed with the gym after reading about physical health and its links to mental sharpness. He claimed it was some Zen Buddhism thing, but he really couldn't remember exactly where he picked it up. Maybe it was true, or maybe he just convinced himself that he read it somewhere, but it seemed to work, and that was good enough for him. He had put fifteen pounds on his six-foot-tall frame and looked strong, more muscular than anything else. At the podium he addressed his class: He looked across the field at the students and at his family near the first row of seats as he absorbed the crowd, eventually fixating on Kalea. He smiled.

"First off, I'd like to say thank you to Interim President Klatt for that warm introduction and offer my own welcome to the class of 2000," E.J. started. "I also want to welcome my family, mom, dad, and my brother Dennis, as well as everyone else that made it here today. These graduates are going to need your support because we all know they'll be unemployed for at least six months."

The crowd laughed and then applauded.

"I'll begin with a question. What are we commemorating today? Is it simply graduating? Is it the completion of something that took a lot of time, effort, and dedication? Is it a celebration with friends that we have made here at Ohio University? Is it something more? This question, this crucial question, does have an answer."

E.J. paused and took a breath. The crowd silent as his soft commanding voice paused.

"Most people think college is where our lives are shaped, but it's not true. We weren't shaped here, but rather given the tools to shape ourselves and the humanity beyond these walls, out there, in the real world. That's what we learned here: How to shape ourselves and the lives of people around us. With this realization, the answer to the question of why we are here today becomes clear. Our journey to this day makes us capable of being a more valuable contributor to society than we would have otherwise been. We stand here today with the knowledge and the strength of knowing that we can indeed shape the future and it's now our job to make the largest impact we can on the world and the lives of those around us. Simply being more valuable isn't the end, but rather the beginning. It is our duty, as the class of 2000, to make that difference. If we don't, then the power to shape the world we gained here was wasted."

The crowd stood up and cheered. Like everything else leading up to this point, E.J. was successful, brilliant in his delivery and message. Everyone said so.

E.J. had just gotten out of his graduation gown, putting all the ceremonial trinkets in the trunk of his car. Kalea returned from the restroom having changed as well.

"Can I talk to you about San Francisco?" Kalea asked.

In the parking lot they both stood, an envelope in her hand. She didn't know what the letter said inside, but had a good idea.

"What about San Francisco?" E.J. asked back, seemingly confused.

"This letter that came in the mail this morning. It's from Hurston Newspapers Inc. Why are you getting a letter from them?"

E.J. took the unopened envelope from Kalea and pretended to not know what it was. Kalea was upset.

"I didn't say anything earlier because of graduation, but I want to know why you got this letter."

"I don't know Kalea... uh..." he trailed off.

"Really? You have no answer? Look at the address. How the hell would people in San Francisco know about you if you didn't apply to some job out there?"

"The industry is small... word gets around."

"We talked about this," Kalea said in a heated tone.

"You're being ridiculous," he replied

"I'm being ridiculous? Then open that letter and show me how ridiculous I'm being."

E.J. folded the envelope and put it in his back pocket.

"It's not important."

Kalea turned and walked away without saying a word. E.J. took the envelope back out and ran his fingers across the embossed logo in the top left corner. He knew what it was about. It had been consuming him for weeks. He considered opening the letter to see what it said but started to wonder if he was ready to read it. He took out his car keys and ran it under the flap, tearing it open, and pulled out the one page that was sealed inside. E.J. unfolded it carefully, still unsure if he was ready, but like everything else leading up to this point, he was more than ready.

Everyone said so.

Chapter Two

The ballroom at the Onyx Hotel was magnificent. The high ceiling dawned numerous crystal chandeliers with balconies surrounding the room. A skylight allowed the moonlight to shine through. Maroon curtains with a gold trim hung elegantly from the walls and matched the carpet in the ballroom, which had sewn-in circular patterns of gold leaf. Dozens of spherical tables were covered in angelic white tablecloths with bouquets resting in the center. Champagne glasses were still placed on some of the untouched tables with perfectly folded napkins. Other tables had been rustled by the guests, all of whom were mingling, waiting for dinner service to be announced. Students, professors, and industry leaders swirled around shaking hands, meeting future men and women of influence, offering interviews and jobs, and filling the air with acronyms and trade jargon.

Most of the journalism department attended the event because of networking purposes, but E.J. didn't need to network. By the time he delivered his speech earlier that afternoon, he had been offered a dozen jobs: the Lancing State Journal, the Columbus

Dispatch, the Cleveland Plain Dealer, the Post and Courier in Charleston, West Virginia, and a few other smaller papers he couldn't remember off-hand. But the letter he got from Hurston Newspapers Inc. changed everything.

E.J. hadn't talked with Kalea since she ran off. He saw her with her friend, Rebecca, smoking cigarettes outside the ballroom when he first arrived earlier. He smiled at her and playfully shouted from a distance to quit smoking. She looked back, gave him the middle finger in jest. E.J. knew the next conversation they would have would be rough, but compromise was the center of their relationship. He had it all planned for tomorrow. It was the only way he could tell her about the letter he received. He stayed away from her, as she did from him that night, an unspoken agreement between the two to separate from each other for twenty-four hours after an argument.

E.J. stood near the table he would be sitting at for the graduation dinner talking with Banu Dilshad, a high-school friend who shared editing duties at the school's newspaper with E.J. Banu had skipped out of the party for those graduating from the business department because she didn't like too many of them. She like the humanities and arts folks better. She considered journalism as a major but decided to go into accounting because of the money.

"Why aren't you with Kalea?" Banu asked.

"No reason. She's off with her friends somewhere."

"I haven't seen you two together at all tonight."

"We hung out at my department's party earlier," E.J. lied to stop the line of questioning, hoping Banu would be satisfied with that answer.

Banu kept fiddling with her hair, which cascaded past her shoulders in long dark curls. The blonde highlights she put in a few weeks back were faded out, although E.J. thought they still looked good. She was short and concerned about her weight. She wasn't fat, but she wasn't a petite thing either. Banu often blamed American culture for making her feel this way, saying that she never thought about her looks until she moved from Iran to America as a young teenager. She looked stunning, nonetheless, in a dark blue strapless dress that had a cut down the side of the leg.

"Speaking of department parties, I still think you should have gone to the business department's graduating party, even to just make an appearance," E.J. said. "Contacts Banu, you need to make contacts. I just don't think it is the wisest thing to ditch out on."

Banu took a sip of champagne and nodded with a bit of arrogance.

"You don't need contacts when you have a job E.J.," she said in a smooth and confident tone.

"Serious?" E.J. said surprised. "Who?"

"Kohl Jefferies in New York. One of the largest accounting firms in the nation," she said excitedly with a smile.

"Holy shit! When did you get that offer?"

"Yesterday," Banu answered. "I'm going to be leaving on the first of July."

E.J. sat his drink down on the table and wrapped his arm around her, squeezing tightly in congratulations.

"What about you E.J.?" Banu said, slightly out-of-breath from E.J.'s hug. "Kalea told me you're taking the job at the Cleveland Plain Dealer, but I haven't heard anything from you at all."

"Well, it's a bit more complicated than that. I got a letter today..."

A strong thump on his right shoulder stopped E.J. in mid-thought.

"Excuse me," a man's voice bellowed from behind.

E.J. turned around and smiled at the gentleman, an older man with luxuriant white hair, an imperial moustache, and a heavy Wisconsin accent. He dawned an expensive black suit with Salvatore Ferragamo shoes and a diamond-studded Rolex watch.

"Are you Eric Lockhart?"

"Eric Jason… E.J. Lockhart, sir."

The old man grabbed E.J.'s hand and shook it hard, letting out a mild laugh and smiling.

"I do apologize for interrupting you two, but I had to come talk with you Mr. Lockhart."

His name was Art Bechtel, a well-known venture capitalist from New York who was a legend in Milwaukee for his work in the radio and television business before moving to New York in the early

1980s. During his time in The Big Apple, he helped revolutionize cable television, especially the news, and had become a media mogul. He now owned www.eagleeye.com, a start-up media watchdog website that was designed to monitor news across America. The company's focus was to pinpoint inaccurate reporting, biases, half-truths, lies, and favoritism, to name a few of the things. Art had long been discussing his fear that the newly emerging Internet would spawn hundreds of tabloids and amateur media outlets spreading poor journalism. E.J. was nearly speechless. Art was one of the premier forces in the world of new media and journalism.

"The website is up Mr. Lockhart and we're beta testing it as we speak. I'm forming another news team that would monitor news coming from the Midwest and the Great Lakes, and I want you to help lead it. We already have teams on both coasts and parts down south. This is your chance to do something no one else has ever done. I'm talking about revolutionizing how news is reported and monitored. The wave of the future is with the Internet taking over and our wave is to make sure it's accurate and fair."

E.J. smiled and, for a moment, thought about the job, but would never really consider it. Not for one second. E.J. knew that the Internet could create new media that would be shallow, simplistic, sensational, and even bias or corrupt, but he blamed that possibility on bad reporting, fame seekers in the industry, and money-driven ambitions. That possibility had always existed, and always was going to exist regardless of technology. It didn't matter if it was the

Internet or traditional media. The way E.J. saw it, no one was going to put up with that and allow the Fourth Estate to collapse. In the end, the truth will set you free and everyone wants the truth. That, in and of itself, E.J. was convinced, created a check-and-balance system in the media that technology couldn't change or destroy.

"I do thank you for the offer, Mr. Bechtel, but I have already accepted a job with the San Francisco Press-Journal."

Banu was taken aback.

Art reached into his coat pocket and pulled out his card.

"Well, I can't say I'm happy about that. If you change your mind, call me."

E.J. took the card and slid it into his wallet.

"Thank you, Mr. Bechtel."

Banu grabbed E.J. and pulled him to the far side of the ballroom under the balconies.

"When did this happen?" Banu barked with a tone that demanded an immediate answer. "Kalea told me you were taking the job in Cleveland."

"I got a letter today from Hurston Newspapers. They offered me a job at the San Francisco Press-Journal, their flagship paper. I called them just before I got here."

"You haven't talked with Kalea about this, and you took the offer? Are you fucking crazy!?"

"I know, I know… I haven't said anything to anyone."

E.J. led Banu back to their table and grabbed the bottle of champagne that sat inside the nearby admiral craft wine bucket and poured himself another glass.

"It's San Francisco. It's one of the nation's leading papers. The Plain Dealer is a good paper and all, but the opportunity to write for the Press-Journal is huge. I'll be working under Warren Lippman... two-time Pulitzer Prize-winning Warren Lippman. I would never get this opportunity here in Ohio."

Banu listened somewhat sympathetically but was hardly convinced.

"The way I see it, Kalea and I aren't married, we don't have kids, we're young, and it's a major city. Seriously, what are we really going to accomplish here in Ohio? I wasn't bullshitting with my valedictorian speech. I want to shape the world and the San Francisco Press-Journal is one of the largest daily papers on the planet... I mean, look at you, you're leaving for New York, so you know what I'm talking about."

Banu grabbed E.J.'s hand and sat him down at the table. She took his glass of champagne, sitting it next to her.

"I only have myself to worry about. You don't," Banu said. "Philosophy is not the most marketable skill. Kalea's offer at Cleveland State University is not something she is going to find easily in San Francisco. It's not like they're building philosophy factories everywhere."

"The Bay Area is one of the most philosophical places on the planet and they have a huge job market. I'm sure Kalea can find something."

Banu stood up, grabbed the glass of champagne, and handed it back to E.J.

"When are you going to tell her? Tonight?"

"No. Tomorrow I'll tell her. I have a plan."

"A plan?" Banu asked, slightly confused.

"Yes, I have a plan. There is only one way to tell her without having my balls cut off and fed to me in that moment of frustration."

Banu laughed.

"What do you have planned?"

"It's classified, I could tell you, but then I would have to kill you," E.J. said in jest.

Banu shook her head with a mixture of concern and disappointment.

"Well, E.J., you're going to have to sleep sometime."

Chapter Three

"Congraduations" in large, bright yellow lettering, stretched across a banner that hugged the corners of E.J.'s parent's living room. "Congraduations," their hybrid of "congratulations" and "graduation." Food lined the long tables in the backyard, the grill still letting off waves of heat. The kitchen counter was turned into a makeshift bar, dozens of bottles and mixers huddled close. E.J.'s brother and parents stood in the living room crowded with most of the extended family, including Chris Schofield, E.J.'s best friend from high school and pseudo-brother-in-law, who married E.J.'s cousin the prior year.

E.J.'s father finished his story about Vietnam, 401k plans, and the value of buying stock in banks, making the joke that people need to stop putting so much of their money in the bank and put more money *in* the bank. E.J.'s mother winced at the old joke while the few others that were still listening found his wit amusing. E.J. walked past the group and picked up his champagne that was resting on the coffee table. E.J.'s father politely excused himself and quickly moved next to his son, taking the champagne glass out of his hands, smiled, and evenly tapped the glass with a small dinner fork that was hidden in his pocket.

"Attention everyone," his father boomed across the room. "I would like to make a toast to our son, Eric Jason Lockhart."

The crowd cheered and clapped.

Chris heard E.J.'s father and quickly made his way back into the living room from outside of the house, where he was smoking a joint.

E.J.'s father's hand shot high into the air, the champagne swirling around in the glass.

"To E.J., our son."

The room, spilling over with guests, toasted, glasses lifted in unison across the room, all the way out into the backyard. A raucous gesture from the crowd and the tipping of drinks brought a smile to E.J.'s face as he said thank you, putting his arms around both his parents. E.J. looked across the room at Kalea, beaming, and then blowing her a kiss. Kalea, dead-eyed, was still upset and ignored E.J.'s gesture. Chris stood back in the sliding glass doorway looking at E.J., who avoided eye contact with him as well.

"This is gonna be good," Chris said to one of the dozens of cousins standing next to him, although he couldn't remember the cousin's name.

"Excuse me?" the young man replied.

"Just watch... you're going to love this."

Chris winked at the anonymous cousin and began to make his way closer to E.J.

"You have worked as hard as anyone I have ever seen with more heart than most... I couldn't have taught you all of this, but I'm going to take credit, nonetheless," his dad said, the crowd smiling and laughing. "Your mom and I are proud of you and this is your day."

Everyone cheered: "Speech! Speech! Speech!"

E.J. noticed Chris was making his way toward him and didn't want any more of Chris' distant taunting. E.J. turned toward his mother and wrapped his arms around her, whispering he loved her into her ear. He shook his dad's hand and looked at him strongly in the eyes, something he was never comfortable doing, but today was different. He moved into his father's spot. Chris stood off to the far side, now just waiting.

"Thank you all for such a wonderful party... to be honest, I feel like this is just the next step in a much bigger journey. Rather than a celebration of what I have completed, it's a celebration of what I'm starting."

E.J. paused as the room clapped and shouted a few cheers.

"Where's that taking you E.J.?" Chris shouted with a conniving tone.

E.J. smirked at Chris.

"Yes, I have... well, some news..." pausing to clear his throat.

He looked at Kalea whose contrived smile was beginning to slowly collapse into anger. He couldn't take his eyes off of her.

"I have accepted an offer to work under Pulitzer Prize-winning journalist Warren Lippman at the San Francisco Press-Journal."

Everyone began clapping, but E.J. didn't hear any of it. Kalea's brow tightened and her teeth mashed, livid, she turned away and walked out to the backyard. She was furious, felt ensnared, betrayed, and was embarrassed, partly because of what he just did, but more so because she knew in her heart of hearts what the letter was about, and had convinced herself otherwise. She knew E.J. well enough to know what he was hiding. Chris partly covered his mouth and in the distant milieu screamed "Damn!" as Kalea stormed out. E.J. ignored it for now, smiling blindly and shaking hands of those congratulating him, most of whom remained unaware of what just happened.

It would be hours before he was even near Kalea, who avoided him.

The sun began to dip a bit and E.J. got out of the shirt and tie he was wearing. The crowd thinned out and for the first time since making the announcement, he saw Kalea, calm, talking with a small group near the gazebo on the other side of the backyard.

"Dude, Kalea looked pissed," Chris said while sipping a rum and Coke. "I looked right at her when you dropped that bombshell. It's like you punched her in the face."

"Oh please, stop being so dramatic," E.J. replied. "Believe me, this isn't a total surprise to her, I guarantee that."

E.J. continued to pick at the food on the table, nervous and stressed, not really hungry at the moment.

"I don't blame you for telling her this way, but you have a lot of convincing to do with her," Chris said, putting down his drink and loading a paper plate with chicken and potato salad. "My advice: make it positive. Don't try to convince her this is a good move, but rather act like this is something that everyone wants to do, you know, like you would have to convince her not to go. You come at her like that and she'll fall like a domino."

"Serious? Is that some kind of reverse psychology bullshit? Do you think she is that dumb?"

Chris pulled out a rubber band and tied his long brown hair into a ponytail to get it out of the way before he ate.

"Reverse what?" Chris asked, a bit befuddled. "I don't know what the fuck you're talking about. I'm just offering you some advice as I see things. Don't start pulling that college shit with me."

"I'm not pulling anything with you Chris… I just…"

Chris interrupted E.J. before he could finish his thought.

"Dude, just go talk with her and get it over with. You'll feel better and you'll be able to enjoy the party. Fuck man, you're the guest of mothafuckin' honor! This should be one of the happiest days of your life and you're standing here trippin' the fuck out."

E.J. nodded in agreement and downed his beer.

"You're right. Let's fuckin' do this."

Kalea had her back turned to E.J. as she talked with a friend. E.J. slowly approached from behind and called out her name. Everyone looked over and stared. Kalea excused herself, turned around, her face an emotionless stare. He took Kalea's hand and led her to a quiet spot on the south-side of the lawn.

"What?" Kalea barked. "What else? Are you seeing someone else? No, wait, I know… you're pregnant…"

"Please Kalea, just stop for a moment. I'm sorry."

"Sorry?" she replied, shocked, her voice cracking. "After that all you can say is you're sorry? Why didn't you talk with me first?"

"Look, I should have talked with you first, but I knew you expected me to take the job at the Cleveland Plain Dealer…"

"Damn right!" she interrupted. "You know the only offer I have been given is at Cleveland State University's philosophy department. How could you just do this without talking with me first?"

E.J. began to get upset.

"Kalea, that's not fair. First of all, even if I took the job at the Plain Dealer, I wouldn't plan to stay there forever. I need to get to a major American paper, so we would be moving away at some point, so why not now before you get dug into a job in Cleveland. On top of that, San Francisco has a gigantic job market full of 'independent thinkers.' There has to be plenty of jobs for a philosophy degree."

Kalea stood silent.

"I know I fucked up by not telling you sooner... maybe a bad choice to tell you the way I did," E.J. continued, "but this job is a job that most reporters would have to work years to get. This is what we have been talking about since we met… get the fuck out of this place and do something great. It's San Francisco. What's in Cleveland? Why wouldn't you jump on the chance to go to California?"

Kalea wiped her eyes, a bit saddened about how this unfolded, but knew that E.J. wasn't going to be content in Cleveland. She looked at him and realized how much she loved him, and how much he was reassured by her. Both understood how safe and enlivened they felt with each other, bound together by the infinite trust and devotion they had unified. He smiled, his eyes heartened her.

"Okay," she said, wrapping her arms around him. "I'll be there."

"I promise baby, you'll find a better job than at some university," E.J. reassured. "Everything is going to be absolutely perfect."

Chapter Four

San Francisco is seven miles by seven miles; five bridges connecting three counties north to Marin, south through Alameda, down to Santa Clara County. San Francisco stands prominent with the Golden Gate Bridge and the Oakland Bay Bridge being the main arteries into the city. Tall buildings that stretch toward the sky, lined back to back throughout San Francisco, weaving two major freeways through it. Intriguing, compact and scenic, built on numerous hills, home to sundry neighborhoods that blend together to form an interconnected city. Chinatown sits next to the Italian neighborhood of North Beach, with the affluent Marina District, Pacific Heights, Russian Hill, Nob Hill, and the tourist traps along the Embarcadero. The romantic and revolutionary Haight/Ashbury, resting just east of the slower-moving Richmond, Golden Gate, and Sunset districts near San Francisco State University and the Pacific Ocean. Pushing south sits the working-class Mission District and the careworn Glen Park, Portolo, and Bayview/Hunter's Point neighborhoods.

Everything from hole-in-the-wall ethnic bistros, dive bars, to some of the country's hottest night clubs and highest-rated restaurants all find their home in this space. It's immediacy to Napa Valley's wine country, north over the Golden Gate Bridge, compliments the distinctive Californian approach to its food and drink. E.J. and Kalea had too many experiences with uninspired and pitiable cuisine in Ohio, and although it's possible they could find a lousy meal in San Francisco, it would be entirely their fault if they did.

San Francisco can be a difficult place to live.

One can spend months, years... even a lifetime combing the streets, the establishments, meeting the people, and experiencing the culture, but still not ever know the city fully. It's mellow, but decidedly never idle. Everyone seems accepting of the peculiar, the eccentric, and the unconventional, always appreciating the strange and unusual folks that cover the city. Although tolerant, friendly, and open-minded, people in the city are always "on," representing their job, their intellect, their unbiased views, and extreme tolerance, even if they aren't tolerant. Homelessness drowns most districts, crime can sometimes be frequent. While the rich run to prosperous areas, hipsters and hippies brag of how their sordid and treacherous living conditions in the Mission or Tenderloin districts somehow make them a more enlightened and genuine person. Pseudo-revolutionaries scream for gay rights, legalization of marijuana, and stopping war, but often do little as they hustle past people lying down on the corners of their neighborhoods, or worse, ignore the gang violence that plagues the south end of the city.

Friends are made, but they're often professional friends, not real friends. That takes time and work. It's easy to twist the difference between the people you know at a job with having a concrete network of friends. It could be like this in most settings. Journalists are a particularly ruthless double-dealing bunch. They will be there at your job, at office parties, but nowhere near you when you're ill, moving to a new place, stranded on the 101, or just need someone to talk to without worrying about gossip being spread, leaking a story, or getting scooped.

The city is a cerebral and edifying bubble, both swelling with a greatness and being strangled by the conceited and self-important cultural liberal elites. This would resonate with E.J. and Kalea, both of whom were open and intellectual, but gently skeptical.

Their condo in Hunter's Point was brand new, a contemporary development off of 3rd Street, behind Candlestick Park, up the side of a hill. Although the neighborhood at the bottom of the hill that stretched along 3rd Street was one of the worst in San Francisco, the homes that rested above it on the hill were very nice. The neighborhood was cheap, comparatively speaking, and as long as you weren't at the bottom of the hill after dark, you were unaware of the seedy element crawling the streets. That's the way E.J. explained it to Kalea, and she seemed okay with that, mainly because she was still riding the euphoria of arriving into the city earlier that day.

"Wow, we have a fireplace," Kalea said has she strolled into the living room for the first time. The apartment was large, nice-sized living room, with the kitchen off to the side that featured a long countertop that separated the two rooms. E.J. was in the bedroom and couldn't hear Kalea.

"What did you say, darlin'?"

"The living room, it has a fireplace."

E.J. walked out of the bedroom into the living room and spun around to get the full feel of his new condo. He walked toward the windows that peered out, far over the city, pass the Bay Bridge and Treasure Island, deep into the Oakland Hills, commenting on how beautiful the view was. Kalea wrapped her arms around E.J. and peeked around him, looking out the window, smiling at the view that stretched across the city. For the first time she felt confident that this was where she was suppose to be, in a place that tendered opportunity that Ohio could not weigh against. The breathtaking animation of life that draped the entire distance of the city's terrain imbued her, dissolving any doubt that she would find her opening. All the same, the city of San Francisco can be an inconsiderate place. A city that is swift and delusive, sometimes feral, and often unconcerned or indifferent.

Chapter Five

Kalea first went to every college in the city, then to every college down the East Bay and the San Francisco peninsula. When nothing was available, she tried various high schools only to run into more dead ends. Without a teaching credential, a philosophy degree meant nothing. She could write well, so she tried to get a job in advertising, marketing, copywriting, public relations, and tried to get a job helping a local politician during a campaign. Nothing was offered that was anything more than minimum wage grunt-work. Everyone in the city seemed to have nothing less than a master's degree from schools that had a much nicer pitch when spoken versus Ohio University. U.C. Berkeley, Stanford, Davis, NYU, Yale, UCLA, Princeton, and the list went on. After two weeks of job hunting, with bills due from moving and E.J. still a few days from starting his job at the paper, she took a job at Bookmarks, a large retail chain bookstore located in Foster City, just a few minutes south of where they lived.

The store was three floors, housed thousands of books, DVDs, CDs, a restaurant, and a Starbucks coffee shop on the second floor. The third floor was fashioned for after-school programs, such as reading, writing, and various art classes for children. The programs thrived, but the teaching jobs for these programs were not easy to get and they had very little turnover. Kalea thought she could work her way from behind the checkout counter and the bookshelf stacks into the classrooms upstairs.

"Kalea, darling," a voice shot from behind as she stacked some new arrivals in the psychology section.

Kalea turned and smiled at her boss, Shelia Giffin, a heavy-set older woman with stringy blond hair, deep crow's feet, and dumpy glasses.

"Darling," Shelia continued. "I need you to work Saturday morning. Tina has a situation that came up and she cannot make it."

Kalea's smile disappeared. She had only been there two weeks and it was the third time she was asked to cover someone else's shift. Shelia stared blankly, still grinning, and with a soft laugh, rubbed Kalea shoulders.

"Great. Awesome. Thanks Kalea."

Kalea just stood still as Shelia turned and briskly walked in the other direction.

"That sucks," a voice from behind the nearby self-help section rang.

Audette Murphy popped her head around the corner.

"What's up with you taking that weekend shift without even asking why Tina can't work?" Audette asked. "You have been working non-stop since you showed up and they have you covering everyone else's shifts."

"Well Audette, I've only been here a short time. I'm the lowest person on the totem pole," Kalea answered, reaching up high to get several books on the top shelf. "I'll stick it out… for a little while longer."

Audette smiled and shook her head.

"You should be asking why you have to cover someone else's shift. What if her reason for ditching work is to go to a concert? Are you going to give up your time for that?"

"What if her parents are in the hospital?" Kalea responded.

"Well, that's a good reason," Audette said. "But find out if that is the reason and then decide if you think you should be working someone else's shift."

"I will do that."

"Just don't let her do this to you for too long," Audette said. "You're quickly becoming the 'go to' person around here and you don't want that tag on you. Shelia will ask you to do every fucked up thing because she thinks you'll never say no."

"Well, I'm trying to work my way into teaching upstairs. I do my job well, and with Shelia seeing that, I don't think I will be working all the screwed-up shifts around here forever. I'll be teaching upstairs as soon as there is an opening. It's just a matter of time."

Audette laughed softly.

"What?" Kalea asked with a touch of confusion.

"Shelia isn't going to give you a good recommendation, especially if you continue to do whatever she says. The last thing she wants to see is someone like you going upstairs. Where else is she going to find an employee that will jump anytime she needs you? You think she is going to give that up? On top of that, she doesn't like your type."

"That's ridiculous. She likes me, likes my work, I'm here on time, and I do a really good job. I don't see why you would say…"

Audette chimed in, interrupting her.

"No, no, no," she said. "It has nothing to do with that. She doesn't like people with degrees. It's a jealousy thing, especially those who she feels had their parents pay for it."

"Hating on those that have degrees and family support? That doesn't make sense. She has her degree. She talked about going to San Francisco State University."

"No, she'll tell you she went to SFSU," Audette answered. "She dropped out. She got pregnant her sophomore year, had to quit, and never made it back. Her parents basically wouldn't help her after that."

Audette grabbed Kalea's arm and led her around the back of the store near the small warehouse room where all the surplus books were kept. To the side was the employees' lounge where an older man sat, sipping a soda, and staring blankly ahead as if the bare wall was displaying something interesting. He had a bushy white mustache, wild white hair on a toothpick frame that accentuated his winkled face.

"Have you met Bill, our maintenance guy?" Audette asked. "That's him. He has been working for the company for thirty years. I talk with him all the time. He knows so much shit about this company. He told me all about Shelia."

"I haven't introduced myself…"

 Audette continued.

"You see, Shelia wanted to be a college professor. She writes poetry, or some shit like that. She spent her entire childhood working for that goal and bam! Some flakey frat boy knocks her up at a party, parents cut her off, and she tried to get through school on her own. She took a part-time job here and... well, the rest is history. She has a grind against people like you."

"Come on," Kalea said skeptically.

"You're educated, young and beautiful, with your whole life ahead of you. Shelia was once in the same position and screwed it up. Worst of all, she never fixed it. She couldn't make the grade, pardon my pun."

"You have to be joking."

"You know, you don't need a degree for her job," Audette said seriously. "Which is perfect for her, obviously, but you need a bachelor's degree to work upstairs with the after-school program... no way in Hell will she help you get up there."

"That old man in there that looks like he would have a hard time tackling a tuna sandwich told you this?" Kalea asked.

"He knows a lot of things," Audette replied. "We had this girl Christy working here. She quit last year after Shelia just fucked with her non-stop… she was always a bit mean to Christy, but it got worse as she completed each semester at Stanford. When she finally graduated, Shelia just turned into a total bitch and directed it all at Christy. It never occurred to me what was happening until Bill told me what he told me about Shelia. Then it all made sense."

"What made sense?" Kalea inquired.

"Shelia would always bash Christy behind her back, saying that there was no way she was going to get through Stanford, that she wasn't smart or motivated enough, and just a bunch of other mean shit. This went on for four years. As Christy got closer to graduation, Shelia leaned in on her harder and harder, doubling up shifts, giving her crappy jobs, you know, just making her work like a dog."

"Are you suggesting that Shelia was trying to get her to drop out of school or fail?"

Audette thought for a moment.

"That's what I think. After graduation she ran Christy into the ground completely. I mean, Christy was going to leave in a few weeks anyway because she was getting recruited for jobs, but she quit early after a huge fallout with Shelia. Shelia was screaming at her in the back of the warehouse, saying that she was a dumb daddy's girl that had her parents pay for her degree, and shit like that."

"And you believe this is all about degrees?" Kalea asked, still staring at Bill.

"Everything that Shelia hated about Christy seemed to revolve around her schooling and how much it reminded her of her failures. All the things she said, and all the weird things I saw her do, all pointed in that direction. That's probably why she rides you so hard. You're the only girl on the floor with a four-year degree from a prestigious university."

Kalea didn't agree.

"Like I said, I'm the lowest person on the totem pole, that's why I think I keep getting these crappy shifts dumped on me. I just got hired. That's what happens to those that are new to any job."

Audette laughed at the naivety. Bill got up and grabbed the mop and bucket near him. He finally noticed Kalea and Audette and said hi to both of them, Audette returning the pleasantry.

"That 'lowest person on the totem pole' nonsense doesn't apply at this location of Bookmarks. I've been here five years and all I see is favoritism and power-tripping. It has nothing to do with anything but that... and Shelia is in control here."

Chapter Six

The Press-Journal Tower stretched high into San Francisco's skyline. The peak of the tower lit up, "Press" on one side, "Journal" on the other, with the two words meeting at the corner of the skyscraper's diamond-shaped top. It was easy for E.J. to find it even though he was still just getting familiar with the streets of the city. Off the Montgomery Street BART station, he could effortlessly make his way to work by following the glowing name that stood above the buildings around it.

The streets were littered with people moving up and down the sidewalks like a wave, lightly brushing shoulders and occasionally bumping into each other lightly. Some would be reading papers, some on phones, some eating and drinking coffee, some just avoiding eye contact. Cars clogged the streets, creating a river of metal so close to E.J. he could often hear conversations from inside of them as he glided down the sidewalk. E.J. moved with the flow as he navigated around the street performers, batted away the countless homeless people asking him for money, and the occasional protestors. During his short time in San Francisco, he tried to explore the city extensively, even going down to Pier 39, the tourist area, to make sure there wasn't a corner of the city he did not know well, but it wasn't possible to cover so much ground in the short time he had been there. San Francisco was bigger than him. He had seen traffic, but not like this, not even in Cleveland. Even San Francisco's public transit dwarfed Cleveland's RTA metro system. He had seen homeless in Ohio, but not like in the numbers he encountered since moving to the city. Even in the richer areas, guys stood near corners soliciting charity. Others weren't homeless… or maybe they were. Some played music, some danced, and some did card tricks, but most just had their hands out.

The lobby of the Press-Journal Tower was huge and strikingly empty. Chairs lined the entrance with coffee tables displaying the current issue of the paper for those waiting for some appointment. The front desk was part of the original building, a large wooden structure reminiscent of a bar which curved around to the short hallway that led to the elevators. Most of the interior of the tower looked original, either preserved well or restored. Even the smell was vintage. Not bad, but a scent that E.J. could imagine a building resurrected in the late 1800s would smell like today. A few folks worked behind the front desk, one woman sitting up front. She had a telephone headset and a relatively large computer system to answer and transfer calls throughout the building. A fax machine, copier, a few phones, and other assorted business machines filled up most of the remaining space. A security guard, an older white man, stood near the entrance and greeted E.J. with a smile as he made his way into the lobby.

"Can I help you?" the guard asked.

"I'm E.J. Lockhart. Today is my first day."

The woman at the desk looked up and quickly ended whatever call she was on. She stood, removed her headset, and made her way out from behind the front desk area.

"Mr. Lockhart. We have been waiting for you."

E.J. smiled, meeting the woman halfway in the middle of the lobby. They shook hands, exchanged pleasantries, and she ushered him to have a seat on the sofa that rested against the far wall.

"It'll just be a moment," she said.

E.J. grabbed an issue of the newspaper while the young woman went back to the desk and made a call upstairs. E.J. combed through the paper purposefully, carefully canvassing the articles, especially those written by Warren Lippman. He paused, looked at his fingers, light shades of black covered the tips from the cheap ink. He deliberated silently the semblance of the layout and headlines, appraising the stories.

"Mr. Lockhart," a booming voice called out, pulling E.J. from the private audit he was conducting on the paper.

A large man stood above him, borderline obese. His gut hung heavy over the belt wrapped around the expensive suit he was wearing. The suspenders under his jacket looked stressed. His breath was heavy, wheezing as he struggled to move, his double chin shaking as he spoke. His fat hand with stubby fingers moved toward E.J., who stood up to greet the man he only knew from phone interviews.

"You must be Walter Willieford," E.J. said as his hand sunk into the fat palm of the paper's executive editor. "It's nice to finally meet you in person."

Walter nodded, first asking how his move went and if he was able to settle into his new place, before changing the subject and ditching the niceties behind. He quickly moved E.J. up to the fifteenth floor, into his office, where he sat with the paper's city editor, Noland Slade, and the paper's budding assistant city editor, Victoria Cipriani. Noland was a balding, overweight, middle-aged man, and a typical suburbanite who lived in a small condo near San Francisco's Sunset district. Noland portrayed himself as someone that loved three things: His high school sweetheart, his kids, and God, but all too often that facade cracked under pressure. He was quick to quote the Holy Bible and the importance of family, but often he didn't feel that way, often just going through the motions, acting out a lifetime of swimming in the waves of white middleclass suburbia. Victoria was a young woman that didn't look a day over twenty. She was from New Jersey with long flowing dark hair, a thin frame, and a huge chest that defied gravity. She was a pretty girl that lacked the experience, and in many ways the intelligence, to be in her position, but because she was hot and generally capable, Noland was game to promote her to assistant city editor over others more deserving. They weren't having an affair, but Noland liked to think she was into him. In reality, she was only into what he could do for her, but she didn't mind flirting with him, which played well into Noland's current midlife crisis.

"We really see you as our bulldog, E.J.," Noland said, both Walter and Victoria nodding in agreement. "However, we also know that there is a learning curve in the real world of journalism. We're here to help breed you into a great reporter. That's what the Press-Journal is about. That's why we are going to start you out slow, get you into a position where you can do the paper the most good."

E.J. looked a bit confused, seeing how he was heavily recruited by the paper. He was told during the phone interview that he would be covering city politics, under the tutelage of Warren Lippman, the wily old Pulitzer Prize-winning reporter. This was the main reason he came to San Francisco. The city beat would open doors to break major stories. Go national. Win awards. He was supposed to be the man next in line to replace an aging Warren. That changed today.

"So," Noland continued, "we're going to have you as our general assignment reporter."

"General assignment?" E.J. responded confused. "I was told that I would be the assistant city reporter, covering city issues and such."

"I know, I know," Noland jumped in. "But we need you on this beat. Look, this is one of the top papers in the United States.

You cannot expect to start at the top. The city beat is one of the top spots and we need the best of the best there. That's why Warren is there."

"I understand that. I didn't think I was starting at the top. That's why I was supposed to study underneath him. I thought that's where you wanted me to be," E.J. said, now getting a bit irked at the change in assignment.

"You will. You'll get that chance. I promise," Noland said. "We had some recent personnel changes and we need you in this spot right now. The G.A. reporter is one of the most needed and the variety of stories will allow you to get the most experience covering every type of story. This is just until we get things situated."

E.J. sat back into his chair and held his tongue. He was dismayed that he was being sold the idea that the general assignment position was some sort of great position, when in reality, it was the reporter that picked up the shit stories that other reporters wouldn't do or didn't want. He began to grow unsettled that the editors were trying to bend that truth otherwise.

"E.J., we wouldn't have hired someone straight out of college if we didn't see them as someone that would be a great reporter," Walter said as E.J. sat quietly. "Trust us. Let us lead you into that. You'll get your opportunity. We're here to help you grow into that person who will dominate in print."

E.J. cracked a smile and played up to the editors. He thought to himself that patience was key. He would let them get situated. In the meantime, he would make every move possible to dig up good stories and dig himself out of this position. He continued to nod contentedly as the editors colored the situation a rosier shade than E.J. could see. He quickly stood up and headed for the door once the meeting ended, saying nothing negative, nor questioning the editors as one dreadful piece of news followed the other.

"Oh, by the way," Noland said as E.J.'s hand twisted the doorknob. "The G.A. position is a weekend shift, at least for the next few weeks. It's Wednesday through Sunday, so you don't need to come in until Wednesday."

E.J. just moved out the door trying to escape before any more surprises were thrown at him.

By the time Kalea got home that night, E.J. was nearly drunk. He had been drinking the leftover wine from his graduation party while he sat and read all the local rags that saturated the Bay Area. He needed to study. Learn the ins-and-outs of San Francisco, Oakland, and the dozens of other cities surrounding them, hoping that he could find something to go after, a huge story that he could uncover. Kalea just looked at him and, at first, didn't say a thing as she fixed herself something to eat.

"How was your first day?" Kalea inquired.

"A little surprising."

"What do you mean?" she asked, taking the seat next to him and pouring herself a glass of wine from the bottle that rested next to E.J.

"Well, they changed my position on me. I'm now the general assignment reporter, not the assistant city reporter."

Kalea seemed a bit surprised and was privately upset when she learned what the general assignment reporter does, but she wasn't going to show it. She encouraged him and convinced herself that this wasn't such a big deal, even though flashes of doubt ran through her head, thinking the job E.J. was offered at the Cleveland Plain Dealer now was a better career move for both of them. She smiled, tried to remain optimistic with the few words she spoke, as E.J. vented about the beat and the schedule that included working weekends for the next few weeks.

"Well, honey, just hang in there. No one starts at the top," she said running her hands through his hair. "It's got to be better than hocking books all day long."

Chapter Seven

E.J. sat inside the newspaper's employee lounge, which was dirtier than he would have thought a lounge at a major newspaper would be. The coffee maker never seemed to stop brewing and the counter area around it was permanently stained with brown marks. The microwave was old, a faded pea-green with a dial timer and fake wood trim. The refrigerator was old too and had just as much old food stuck to its walls as the microwave. E.J. realized that nothing could remove the years of filth, even if it had just been cleaned. Everything would still look dingy. The tile floor had obviously been installed sometime during Richard Nixon's administration, along with the table and chairs that looked as if they were retrieved from a hospital cafeteria.

Warren Lippman was eating breakfast that morning, as he always did, while the newsroom sat virtually empty, except for a few administrative support staff, people from the circulation department, and a random janitor that vacuumed the floor and dumped the little waste baskets at each desk. E.J. had been coming in early each morning for two reasons: One, to make a good impression with management so he would get moved from the general assignment reporter beat sooner rather than later and, two, to get to know Warren, the man E.J. was suppose to be working under. For the past two weeks, E.J. and Warren were the only two editorial staffers in the office so early. Every day, 6:30 a.m., the two sat alone, something Warren liked since he grew tired of eating breakfast by himself for the past few decades. Up to this point, the two had made mostly small talk: The current news, weather, living in the city, and terrible television shows, but nothing that was personal.

On this particular morning, E.J. walked into the employee lounge and sat at the table across from Warren with a pile of notes in his journal, his laptop, and a muffin he picked up at the coffee shop next door. He had spent most of his first week writing public notices and announcements. He also juggled a story about a funeral home that decided to increase the amount of bodies it cremated, upsetting people who said it was polluting the air. He had two other weak stories that fell into his lap because someone else didn't want them.

He went through his notes again, his first decent story coming a week earlier, after meeting a local gadfly named Donald Tate at a local city council meeting he decided to attend in hopes of finding a good story. He was an older gentleman that was born and raised in Union City, a small town south of Oakland. Donald, according to Donald, was tied deep into the community and the undercurrent of corruption happening in Union City.

Donald didn't dress like the rich Bay Area heritage his upbringing could afford him and he didn't groom himself well. He wore an old tweed jacket with a faded dress shirt, khaki pants, and black dress-casual shoes that looked as if they had seen their best days months before. His hair was a straggly dirty blonde with an unshaven face. But Donald was intelligent, that was clear to E.J.

Donald claimed that the utilities company, California Gas & Electric, was taxing Union City's customers illegally. He had a sliver of eccentricity, but seemed to know the ins-and-outs of Bay Area happenings. E.J.'s pen noted, marked, scratched, and circled as the pages turned in his journal. Donald told E.J. that CG&E was charging some people in Union City a small fee each month called a Nor-Cal tax. Most people didn't notice it because it was $1.10 and buried underneath a long list of charges on their power bill… just another random charge small enough to go undetected. He said the Nor-Cal tax was a tax given to those who live in Marin County, and, somehow, portions of Union City had their zip codes mixed with Marin County zip codes, applying the tax to them. CG&E either made some mistake, or there was a computer glitch, or they were simply ripping people off. Either way, people in Union City had been calling to have the tax removed and were getting nowhere with CG&E. E.J. quickly put a fire underneath CG&E and, after a few threats with the damaging stories the Press-Journal would publish if CG&E didn't play ball, they suddenly changed their tune, promised to fix it, and reimburse everyone. He was finalizing his story that morning.

"Do you think you'll get promoted by doing this?" Warren asked, running his boney fingers through his thinning gray hair and adjusting his wire rim glasses.

"Doing what Warren?"

"Coming in this early every day. No editors are here to see it."

E.J. giggled.

"Well, Warren, word gets around. News people always find out these things."

"That's true," Warren replied dryly, taking a drink from his cup of coffee. "But that doesn't mean they care."

"Well, I have other reasons for coming here this early, for sure."

E.J. shook a bit of sugar onto his muffin.

Warren didn't ask for the other reasons.

"Asklepios Pyrrhus." E.J. quietly spoke.

Warren was taken aback, surprised.

"Where did you hear that name E.J.?"

"I've followed your career a bit, did some research. After you won the Pulitzer Prize in 1984, you gave yourself that name... your Greek God name, used it twenty-three times on stories as your byline. You know, I don't understand why you stopped using it. It's a cool way to raise your profile even more."

Warren leaned back in his chair and crossed his arms.

"The better question," Warren said, "is why I started using it in the first place."

E.J.'s eyes widened a bit, curious.

"Why?"

"That's a story for another day," Warren replied, moving away from the subject. "You said you come here early to impress management, but you have other reasons. What are they?"

"To learn from the best. That's you. You know, I was hired to work under you, but they stuck me with this shitty general assignment beat."

Warren laughed, took a drink of his coffee and shook his head.

"Let me guess," he said, "you come from back east somewhere?"

"Sure do. Ohio University, E.W. Scripps School of Journalism."

"Well, E.J., you just learned your first real lesson in journalism."

E.J. nodded, acting as if he got a joke he actually didn't understand, too embarrassed to respond otherwise and just shook his head in agreement. He waited for Warren to elaborate, but he didn't say another word. Warren picked up his trash and dumped it in the can next to the door that led to the fire escape behind the building. He refilled his cup of coffee, two sugars, and a bit of half and half.

"If you want to get off that general assignment beat," Warren chimed in, "you need to dig and find a really good story. One that goes beyond this newsroom and pushes your bosses into giving you what you want. That's the only pressure they understand."

"I get that," E.J. replied. "I have been making contacts. I think I got something here that's a pretty good start. Hey, do you think you could help me a bit with it, you know, some suggestions?"

Warren put up one hand as if he was stopping traffic.

"When you finish it, then I'll be happy to take a look at it. Until then, don't even talk to me about it. If you're still in the drafting stage, stuck on what angle to take, or with the direction of the story, ask the editors for their thoughts. Don't talk with me until it's finished."

E.J. was confused by the disinterest and unwillingness of Warren to help, feeling like they had developed a rapport during these early morning sessions. He just let it go and took Warren's offer as he thought he should: One of the greatest reporters on the planet was willing to look at his work. That was more than Warren was doing for anyone else, and that was more than Warren had offered to do for E.J. up to that point.

"You know Warren, if better and better stories keep panning out, they'll be giving the choice beats around here to me."

Warren smiled big and laughed lightly.

"Well… something like that," he commented, still stirring his freshly poured coffee and making his way toward his desk. "I'm here when you have your story done and ready to send."

By the time the editors and reporters filed in that morning, E.J. had been working for well over two hours.

"How's that cremation story coming along?" asked Jeffery Corbett, the education reporter that sat in the cubicle to the right of E.J. "That's a gem of a story."

Jeffery had just arrived to work and was hanging up his wool coat. He dressed casually, a part of his liberal inheritance. He was short with wavy reddish-blonde hair that looked much like a surfer, despite the fact that he was raised in Boston. E.J. liked the fact that Jeffery was genuinely nice, something he did not see thus far in journalism. E.J. may have been new to the professional journalism game, but everyone he had ever met that was a professional journalist, or studying to be one, had a tint of shadiness to them, and he recognized that. Even Warren, as much as E.J. liked him, seemed a bit reluctant and mysterious when they talked. Jeffery was the exception, and his comments about the cremation story weren't sarcasm, but the truth. Jeffery saw potential in every story.

"The story is pretty much done," E.J. replied with a flat tone. "I just wish I could spend more time on another story, but they want this one today."

"Another story?" Jeffery said with some interest. "Got a hot one?"

"I'm not sure yet, but I'm thinking this may be huge."

"Is this the CG&E story I heard about?"

"No, this is a new lead I got last night from the same guy that got me the CG&E story."

As the conversation continued, E.J. noticed Skye Langevin, the reporter that covered Oakland, leaning over and eavesdropping from his desk just to E.J.'s left. Skye was a tall dark-skinned man that dressed impeccably, always in a shirt and tie with expensive shoes. He was arrogant and brash, often flaunting his Cornell University education and his rich upbringing in Dryden, New York, just outside of Ithaca, home of the Ivy League university. E.J. hadn't spoken to Skye that much, even though they sat next to each other, but admired him because E.J. saw a lot of similarities between them: He was a young golden-boy type of reporter that was making waves in journalism. Skye had been at the San Francisco Press-Journal for two years, recruited out of college, and worked the transportation beat until he broke a story about a group of Bay Area Rapid Transit officers that were running a drug operation on the trains. It won Skye a Society of Professional Journalists' award, and it was the reason he was promoted to covering the city of Oakland.

"Are you going to hold out on us every time, rookie?" Skye blurted, still unwilling to address E.J. by his name most of the time, even after being on the job for more than two weeks. "You got some CG&E story you're not sharing with us, now some other story? Give us a head's up, man."

E.J. wanted to say that he wasn't holding out on anyone, just still was getting comfortable with his new job, but Jeffery quickly interrupted.

"Langevin, it's none of your business," he said sharply.

"Corbett, you commie," Skye snapped. "Have I told you before that your mouth is too liberal as well?"

E.J. remained silent, still feeling too new to chime in, joke around, or take sides. He liked Jeffery, but saw potential in getting in good with Skye. He wanted to remain as neutral as possible until he got out of the general assignment beat.

"Fuck off Skye!" Jeffery belted back.

"I'm sorry," Skye replied, swinging his chair around and away from Jeffery. "I couldn't hear you with my SPJ award in the way."

E.J. turned toward his computer and finished his story, letting the exchange die out naturally after a few more barbs were traded between the two. After a few minutes passed, Jeffery left to go to the bathroom. Skye apologized to E.J.

"Hey E.J. Sorry about all that aggressive banter," Skye said with a genuine tone, using his name for the first time in days. "Us journalists are like that. It's all in good spirits. We're all here with the same mission in mind. Even teammates get at each other, you know?"

"Oh, I know," E.J. replied, thinking back on his days at the Ohio University paper.

"Look, if you need some help or any suggestions on anything you're working on, let me know. It wasn't too long ago I was the new guy and if I can help, just say the word."

E.J. smiled a bit. He finally felt like he was moving forward. Between Warren and Skye, he was now tying himself tight with two great journalists, although Warren wasn't willing to help him with hashing out story direction or angles, he was at least willing to look at the story after it was written. Skye seemed more helpful with earlier drafts and ideas.

"The story I was talking about, well, I could use a bit of advice," E.J. said.

"The CG&E one?"

"No, the other one I got last night."

"Sure," Skye said, leaning in with interest.

E.J. told Skye about Donald Tate's latest lead. The Union City chief of police, Charles Pastrana, was promoted to top cop shortly after a deal between Union City officials and the developer of the High Hills Shopping Center, a huge new shopping complex on the city's north side. According to Donald, the developer, Gary Pastrana, Charles' brother, was going to use the complex as a center to run drugs, and all activities would be swept under the carpet by his brother. The deal was this, Donald explained: They were going to pull whatever strings needed to be pulled to make the shopping center project happen in Union City, rather than in Castro Valley, where it was originally planned. Then, Union City gets the business, tax revenue, and Charles, as the chief of police, would allow a ton of illegal drug activity to flow through the shopping center. Charles would make sure that activity went unnoticed with everyone involved getting paid.

"Do you know who I'm talking about?" E.J. asked.

"Yeah, I do," Skye replied. "Good 'ol Donald Tate. The guy does know his shit. He has been around Union City forever and he knows a lot of what's going on."

"Have you heard anything about this?"

"Nope. But if that is true, it's a huge story… a lot of people going down."

"Well, what I would like are some suggestions… maybe where I should start so I can get as much information as I can without raising too much attention. I figure once people find out I'm investigating, they may shut down."

Skye thought for a moment and told him to find out if Charles Pastrana was the most qualified for the chief position, see who else was in line for that job, see what local shady folks might have the money to grease the wheels to get Charles into that position, and then talk to Castro Valley officials to see why they believe they lost the development project.

"Between these two, you might get someone to verify, at least in part, what Tate claims. Just be careful… this could set off a lot of alarm bells. You're dealing with some people that would disappear quick if they thought you were onto them."

E.J.'s heart began to pound hard, adrenaline flowing through him as he saw the look on Skye's face.

"Just a piece of advice," Skye added. "Don't tell the editors that Tate gave you this story. They don't like him."

"Why not? He's the one that gave me the CG&E story."

"Do the editors know that Tate gave you the CG&E story?"

"No... I never told them. It never came up."

"Look," Skye interrupted. "I have been here a long time and I could get into it about why they don't like Tate, but just don't tell them he is your main lead on this, or any story you get from him."

"What if they ask?"

"Tell them it's an anonymous source," Skye replied. "That will buy you time, and their dicks will be so hard for the story, they won't press you about it."

E.J. nodded as a voice suddenly cut through the conversation.

"I swear if she comes at me one more time with these stupid questions, I'm going to throw her out of a fucking window!"

Stone Sledge had a reputation for being a hothead and was known for loud outbursts. He had been covering the San Francisco Giants for the better part of a decade and was one of the most respected sports' reporters in the Bay Area. This was not unusual.

Jeffery quickly jumped into the mix as he returned to his desk.

"Hey Stone, slow the fuck down, bro! What the Hell is going on?"

"Victoria is going on, that's what's going on," he said heated. "This bitch is not only dumb by general standards, but even dumber when it comes to sports. I'm tired of her constantly calling me to her office asking me to explain things she doesn't understand and assumes the rest of the world is as dumb as her. She told me to start writing out 'runs batted in' instead of 'RBI,' as if anyone reading the story needs that spelled out!"

The small gathering of people in the area began laughing, drawing some mild interest from the rest of the newsroom. Sharee, a business reporter, leaned over to E.J.

"Hey, E.J. Do you know what a baguette is?"

"Yeah, it's a loaf of French bread. Why?"

"A reporter one referenced that in a story. Victoria thought it was a small bag."

Stone continued to rant while Jeffery attempted to calm him down. Skye sat silent working, but giggling every few seconds as Stone's animated venting began to draw even more attention from across the room.

"Dude, chill the fuck out," Jeffery demanded. "You're going to get into trouble if you keep bitchin' like this, man. Threatening an editor? Are you crazy?"

Stone took a deep breath and resigned himself for a few moments to collect his thoughts. He continued privately bitching to

Jeffery while Sharee and E.J. looked on. Skye continued to laugh as he worked his keyboard, cranking out another story.

"She's griping about a player profile I did on a new rookie and wants to talk to me about a few things she needs clarified... I'm sick of this."

Stone marched toward Victoria's office, most of the staff either watching or, at minimum, mildly paying attention. Noland stuck his head out of his office when he noticed the gathering by Jeffery's desk and a heated Stone.

"Stone," Victoria said, sticking her head out of her office, her eyes still periodically looking back at the computer screen on her desk, completely unaware of Stone's anger. "This player profile is raising a ton of questions, there's a bunch of acronyms and, what's this? Slugging percentage? What is that?"

Stone smiled devilishly.

"Well, I'm sorry Victoria, this is totally my fault. Scratch this whole thing and let's quickly adjust this."

Victoria walked out her office, pulled out a notebook, ready.

"Go ahead..."

"Okay, so new rookie second baseman Duke Silver grew up in Shillings, Nebraska and decided to major in finance, so he attended Texas A&M because he thought the ATM on the baseball hats meant it was a business school, specializing in finance. He also decided to wear number forty-five, to match his SAT score.."

Victoria jotted away, hanging on Stone's every word.

"What the fuck is he doing?" Jeffery asked.

"Holy shit," E.J. said. "He is fucking with her... and look, she's writing all of this down. She can't really believe any of that is real. It's absurd. No one's that stupid."

Victoria continued to write away as everyone watched her, completely oblivious to what Stone was doing. Laughter started to surface across the newsroom, gradually getting louder.

"And a funny little tidbit... he also didn't eat Taco Bell until he went to college. There wasn't one back home, so up until then, he thought Taco Bell was Mexico's phone company. He doesn't know the meaning of the word 'fear,' or a lot of other words, but that's largely due to the fact that dictionaries were banned in his hometown."

Victoria scribbled away at her notepad as Stone made one outrageous statement after another until she realized that Stone was making fun of her. Noland couldn't take it anymore and stormed out into the newsroom.

"Okay, that's enough," Noland told Stone. "Go back to your desk and get back to work."

Stone walked away without saying anything and disappeared down the hall.

"What Noland? Is there a problem?" Victoria asked.

The newsroom was now laughing loud enough that Victoria took notice.

"What's going on?" she asked. "Is this some kind of prank?"

"It's nothing," Noland replied. "Just erase everything you wrote right now and take the original player profile Stone submitted and go with that. I'll edit it later."

Noland eyed the entire newsroom heated.

"The rest of you... back to work."

Chapter Eight

"What is that you're drinking... and can I get another one for you?"

"What!?" Victoria shouted trying to hear over the music.

"Your drink," the young man said again, his Ralph Lauren Drake wool twill suit flashing from black, to purple, to pink, as he stood under the lights of the club's lasers, trying to overpower the thumping techno music that engulfed the room. Victoria still didn't hear him through the sea of drunk voices and music, but figured it out when the man pointed at her drink a second time. He smiled softly, his chiseled jaw and soft blue eyes piercing. Victoria was immediately attracted to the man, who was much taller than her. She only stood 5' 4", but looked deceptively bigger thanks to her ample chest and thin waist.

"It's a Long Island Iced Tea," Victoria said, finishing the drink and swirling the straw around the highball glass.

"I'll get you another one," the man said, reaching into his breast pocket and dropping a Citibank Visa Black on the counter. The weight of the carbon card landed firmly on the bar, splashing a small amount of liquid that had collected from the drips and condensation.

"My name is Brad, what's your name?"

"Victoria."

"It's nice to meet you. Are you here with anyone?"

"Yeah, my friend Hillary."

Brad looked across the dance floor and saw a gorgeous blond dancing randomly with guys.

"That's her... she's my bestie. We're both from New Jersey."

"Oh, cool. I lived in New York for awhile before coming out west."

"What do you do Brad?" Victoria asked, swaying back and forth to the music as she sipped her drink.

"I'm a lawyer. I work for Bennett and Baxter. We mostly do representation for technology and Silicon Valley companies. You know, dotcoms and venture capitalists. It's new ground with the Internet and we're specializing in it. Everything from day-to-day business operations to defense. I've been there two years."

"Wow, that's interesting," she replied, staring at him. "I like your suit."

"Oh thanks... I really wanted something that had the same style of a Ermenegildo Zegna suit," he said, running his hands down the impeccable bespoke tailoring. "But I don't have the $20,000 for that yet... not until I make partner."

"You have a partner?" Victoria asked, slightly intoxicated and totally confused.

"No, I said 'make partner.' You know, get promoted at my firm?"

Victoria nodded indiscriminately.

"Never mind, it doesn't matter... So what do you do?"

"I'm an editor at the Press-Journal."

"The newspaper?"

"Yeah, the newspaper."

"Cool, what's that like?"

"It's awesome... I mean I get to be right there in the mix of the city, you know, breaking news and a bunch of other cool things."

"I'm sure you have a ton of interesting stories," he said with a cloying response.

"For sure," Victoria replied, gulping down another drink of her Long Island Iced Tea. "I've met a bunch of cool celebrities... like Brad Pitt and Edward Norton. I went and covered the opening of *Fight Club* in San Francisco and they were both super cool."

"Sweet. That's one of my favorite books."

"No, it's not a book they wrote, it's a movie they did."

"I know you're referring to the movie, but I'm saying the book it was based on is one of my favorites."

"It's based on a book? I didn't know that. What book?"

Brad smiled, hiding how dumbfounded he was with Victoria.

"Well... it's called *Fight Club*... by Chuck Palahniuk," he replied with a forged nonchalant tone.

"Oh, okay... yeah.. that makes sense, duh," Victoria smiled.

"I also was one of the first to talk with Sean Parker when Napster got in trouble. That guy was cool."

"Oh really? My firm was involved in that initial lawsuit... It's wild. If two people share a file, is it copyright infringement?"

"Well of course it is. You cannot steal music without paying for it," Victoria said, a bit of agency in her voice.

"Is it stealing? It's not like they are physically taking it... a guy is just sharing a copy with another person... maybe tens-of-thousands of people, but simply sharing it nonetheless."

"How can you defend stealing?" Victoria questioned.

"I'm not necessarily defending it, I'm saying according to what the law says is stealing, it may not be stealing. I'm not sure this is classified as such. In one way it is, but not really at the same time. It's nothing like we have seen before. But technically, they're not stealing anything."

"They are. The bands are saying people are stealing their music. People are getting it for free without paying for it, so how is that not stealing?"

Victoria waved down the bartender for another drink, which was hustled quickly.

"Look at it this way," Brad said. "I have a Metallica album in my car. If I burned a CD copy of it right now and gave it to you, are you guilty of stealing?"

"No, that's not stealing."

"Well, what if you lived back in New Jersey and you wanted it. I couldn't hand you a copy physically, so I decide to load the album on my computer and e-mail you a copy? Is that stealing?"

"No, that isn't stealing either," Victoria agreed idly.

"So, what's the difference if someone in Florida, for example, uploads it to the Internet and shares a copy of the album with you? Just because you don't know him, it makes it stealing?"

"They are loading music online and then thousands download it. That's stealing," she said, reinstating blindly.

"It's sharing... if I walked down the street and handed out free burned copies of a Metallica album, dozens of them, no one would care. But if I put it online, it's suddenly stealing?"

"I guess... I don't know."

"What were Sean Parker's comments to you about all of this... I'm curious?"

"He said, it was just like, you know... freedom and he wasn't doing anything illegal and, like, by giving access to share things really isn't stealing... but... I just don't think people should steal music."

Brad smirked.

"Technically, making any copies is illegal, but the record labels and bands only seem to care if suddenly millions of people have access to it. I wish they would just admit to that. Maybe a solution could be reached. I just don't like the argument that it's stealing when prior to this technology, millions of people burned CDs, and even dubbed their friends cassette tapes back-in-the-day, and no one cared. It's about the argument that suddenly a digital form of an action that people have been doing for decades is 'stealing,' and I don't think it is... You don't agree with this?"

"I don't know... it's crazy with the Internet."

"Yeah..." Brad said, officially over any hopes of an intellectual conversation.

Brad signed the bill, picked up his card, and put it back in his pocket. Hillary, glass nearly empty and exhaustedly stumbling over, hugged Victoria from behind.

"Oh Hillary, this is Brad."

"Hey," she said, smiling. "He's cute."

Brad smiled at the two beautiful women standing in front of him. He knew one of them was going to go home with him tonight, but really hoped to get both. They swayed and hugged, laughing at a stream of non sequiturs that Brad didn't understand, nor care to know about. He chimed in every few seconds, nodding his head, thinking about how he could pull off a threesome, while simultaneously concocting a backup plan to at least get one of them in bed before the night was over.

"Your friend is adorable," Brad said charmingly as he stared at Hillary.

"He's a lawyer," Victoria chimed in.

"Wow... a lawyer. I like lawyers."

"I like girls that like lawyers," he replied, winking with a seizing tone. "Where do you work?"

"I work at Macy's."

"Where did you go to school?"

"Mt. Vista High School in New Jersey. Go Vikings!"

"No, I mean college."

"Oh, no, I didn't really go to a university, I just took some classes at a city college... school isn't really what I wanted to do."

"Oh, I see... okay." Brad replied.

Hillary giggled and sipped the rest of her drink.

"Victoria's the smart one," she said, wrapping her arms around her best friend again.

Brad politely smiled and laughed, feigning interest in what the two inebriated women were saying, occasionally tossing pleasant comments every chance he could, both girls giggling in delight each time.

"Do you ladies want to go to Club 331?"

"What's that?" Victoria asked.

"The hottest after-hours club in San Francisco."

The two girls smiled in enchantment, ready to go.

The weather was brisk with a light breeze cascading across the bay. Brad hailed a cab and the three hopped in, Brad helping both girls inside as the alcohol had taken a much stronger hold of the ladies in the last thirty minutes. He sat in between them, placing his hand on Victoria's knee and his arm around Hillary. The cab driver, who barely spoke English, asked them where they were going. Brad told him 331 Bellair Street. The two girls attempted to make more small talk as Hillary pulled out a mini bottle of vodka and shot about half, wincing, and then sliding the remains of the bottle over to Victoria. Brad smiled. This was looking more and more like the night he had two weeks ago at the Boom Boom Room, he thought to himself. That's where he met two airhead party girls, took them to Club 331, and fucked them both. He began to imagine the night he was about to have with Victoria and Hillary, but was more interested in the story he would be able to tell his colleagues at Bennett and Baxter the next morning.

"It's right here," Brad said to the cab driver, who pulled over.

It was a well-lit street lined with newer remodeled apartment buildings, a liquor store on the corner, a nondescript storefront that looked like a Spanish Harlem bodega, a 24-hour check cashing service, and Masquerades, a high-end costume store that displayed a huge Jack Skeleton outfit from the movie *A Nightmare Before Christmas* and an oversized Lego character costume in the window. The three got out of the cab and the two young ladies looked around.

"Where's Club 331?" Hillary asked.

"Right here," Brad answered smiling, pointing to the address on the apartment building. "My apartment. 331 Bellair Street, or as I like to call it, Club 331."

The two girls began to laugh uncontrollably.

"Nice club!" Victoria yelped. "Do they serve Long Island Iced Teas?"

"They have the finest liquor you can buy... I should know, I bought it."

Victoria sat on the black leather sofa, running her hand across the plush pebble grain, while Hillary headed to the bathroom. Brad commenced to making drinks. Victoria eyed the 50-inch Phillips flat screen plasma television and admired the two-bedroom Victorian-style apartment that sat in the heart of North Beach. The kitchen looked newly renovated with slate counter tops, new appliances, and an aggregate of marble and granite stone coffee table with a fully stocked liquor cabinet off to the side.

"Wow, that's a nice T.V."

"Yeah, biggest you can buy."

Brad handed her a drink.

"Where's your friend?" Brad asked.

"Is she still in the bathroom?" Victoria replied.

Brad and Victoria made their way down the hall. The bathroom door was ajar. Hillary lay near the toilet, her one-piece red dress slightly peeled off the shoulder and hiked up, exposing her white panties, puke dripping from the sides of the bowl. Brad smirked, knowing that a threesome was now out of the question. He looked at Victoria and smiled, wrapping his arms around her in a playful manner.

"Oh my God," Victoria belted. "Get up Hillary!"

Hillary didn't move.

"Don't worry, darlin', my cleaning lady is coming tomorrow. She'll take care of that. Let's get her to bed. She's done for the night."

Victoria helped Brad pick her up and take her into the spare bedroom.

"Geez. I don't drink Long Island Iced Teas and I just made a top-shelf one for your sleepy friend."

"Don't worry, I'll finish that one too," Victoria said with a smile.

Victoria and Brad went back into the living room. Victoria rambled on about her career, her goals, New Jersey, her love for San Francisco, and dozens of other topics that Brad simply smiled through as she downed Hillary's drink. He leaned in and kissed her. She grabbed him by the back of the head and pressed hard. They played on the sofa for a few minutes, before Brad led her into the bedroom.

As the sun crept through the window the next morning, Victoria woke up. Slightly hung-over, minimally embarrassed that she slept with a man she just met, and still worried about Hillary, she stumbled out the bedroom telling Brad she had to go to work. Brad mumbled some partly inaudible response about calling her soon, but he never would. The spare room was empty. Hillary had already left. She looked at the clock.

"Fuck, I gotta be at work in two hours."

Chapter Nine

Kalea had been working almost every day for the past three weeks, covering Shelia's shifts the last few days. Shelia had asked if Kalea could do it, in a way that wasn't really asking, but rather demanding, just demanding in a saccharine-sweet passive-aggressive way. She hated it. She and E.J. hadn't really seen each other in what felt like forever. The only time they had been together was when E.J. crawled into bed late and the rattle of another body rustling the bed woke her. E.J. had the same story. When they did see each other in the morning, it became an intense session of trying to figure out when they would actually have time together as they both rushed to grab a bite to eat, drink their morning coffee, and hustle out the door to beat traffic or make the BART train.

Kalea was becoming frustrated and angry as each day went by. She felt a drift between her and E.J. developing. E.J. felt it too, but was handling it better, convincing himself that this was all temporary and as soon as he broke a major story, he would be in a better position to adjust his schedule. The city was permeating their lives. Time never slowed down, but nothing moved quickly. The life of hurry up and wait... and then hurry up and wait some more. Kalea stuck on the freeway to Foster City. E.J. stuck on a BART train or fighting his way down crowded streets walking to work, whichever seemed faster on any given day in San Francisco. They both saw each other less and less, bickered more and more.

Kalea was the first at Bookmarks, the store eerily silent and still. The delivery crew had stacked hundreds of boxes off to the west-side of the building, piled high next to the almost empty bookcases that encompassed a sizable portion of the store's bottom floor. Most of the books had been pulled and moved upstairs, some stacked on the ground ready to be loaded onto carts, while others still sat on the shelves. It had been four of the longest days, fourteen-hour shifts for most of the employees to get the area clear. They had only a few days before the fall semester of school started.

"College At The Marks," an idea Shelia had for the new school year. Create an entire section on the bottom floor dedicated to text books, both new and used, to draw in students. Extra staffing to move students through quickly, books being sold, books being bought back, then re-sold. Faster and cheaper than any school bookstore. The project requiring an extensive restructuring of the store's first floor.

Kalea walked past the yellow tape that was being used to block customers from wandering over to the mess. She was tired, overwhelmed, and didn't know where to start. Shelia, although technically heading the project, was nowhere to be found, having her subordinates cover her shifts. Kalea had taken six of them, Audette two, with a scattering of other employees covering another handful of them.

Kalea started stacking books on a rolling cart with no particular starting point in mind. She looked at the clock. It was 6:15 a.m. Audette came through the door... late.

"Where have you been?"

"Sorry," Audette replied a bit rushed. "Traffic got me."

Audette dropped her stuff behind the counter and immediately helped Kalea push the cart to the elevator.

"How long until you think we finish this shit?" Kalea asked.

"Well, if that bitch Shelia would quit dodging her shifts and stopped making us work double, I'm sure we would be closer. I've been a fucking zombie the last few days."

"Me too," Kalea replied.

"It was her God-damn idea to do this fucking school textbook thing, but we have to do all the work. If you want to get rid of her, start a huge undertaking like this and that cunt becomes a ghost."

"Yeah, she dumped her night shift on me today," Kalea said.

"What?"

"Yep... I'm here until eleven."

Audette shook her head and quickly became angry.

"You know, I asked her why she's skipping so much work and she gave me this attitude like it's personal and I have no right to ask," Audette snapped. "Fuck her! She's telling me to pull a fourteen-hour shift to cover her Monday and gets offended if I ask why?"

"She did the same thing to me when I asked why I had to cover her night shift today," Kalea responded.

"You know Kalea, if you told her to cover one of your shifts, she would make you provide written proof of why you're even asking."

Kalea softly nodded in agreement, too tired to get fired up over it.

"I once saw her drop a shift on someone so she could go to a Seals and Crofts concert... Can you believe that shit, Kalea? Seals and Crofts? At least pick a band that doesn't suck."

By ten o'clock in the morning, Parker, Tina, Dayana, and a handful of other part-time workers showed up. The day dragged on. More books moved upstairs, more books re-shelved, back downstairs, unpack, sort, and shelve textbooks, reorganize sections, breakdown and fold boxes, all the while dealing with customers who got impatient with the skeleton floor staff in charge of running the store while the new textbook section was put together. Shelia popped in sometime during the day, the same as she had before, to check out how progress was going. She'd ask questions, get curt answers, and then leave.

Kalea got home at midnight. E.J. was asleep. A note left on the kitchen sink read: "Sorry, babe. I couldn't wait up any longer... I'm exhausted from work."

Kalea crumpled up the note and threw it away in the trash. She laid down on the sofa and whispered to herself "Me too..." before falling asleep.

75

Chapter Ten

E.J. was hitting dead ends at every turn, and despite the great reception from the CG&E story that had ran a few weeks before, the editors were becoming restless and impatient with this new story. E.J. was frustrated too. Getting information about the other candidates for the Union City chief of police position were considered "personnel matters" and wasn't required to be released. He attempted to talk with police department staff and officers, willing to go off the record, but none of them would budge, mainly because they didn't know E.J. that well and didn't trust him with their jobs if their name leaked out, assuming they had any information at all. There were no signs that anyone knew anything about any drug ring conspiracy with the High Hills Shopping Center. Officials in Castro Valley weren't much help either. No one seemed to think anything illegal or underhanded happened with the shopping center development that was taken away from them and given to Union City. Union City officials and landowners simply offered a better deal, which included free land and a location near the BART station.

E.J., at one point, decided to go undercover, combing the shopping center trying to buy drugs, hoping to unearth any illegal activity happening at any of the shops, but found nothing. Police records were no help either, only revealing a small drug bust at a Thai restaurant that was unraveled a few months prior, but it seemed to be nothing more than a waiter that was running cocaine and marijuana through his job to random patrons that came through. No conspiracy, no cartels. When they raided his house, they discovered the main flow of his drug sales were done from home. The owners of the Thai restaurant knew nothing. The kid was arrested and that was it. Days were going by and no story was materializing. Donald Tate also was becoming less helpful as the new leads he gave E.J. ended up being dead ends. Donald kept telling E.J. to find a man named T. Wayne Hammett, but would not tell him anything more than the name... calls were made, public records were accessed, more days went by and nothing was turning up.

Both Victoria and Noland were marginally assured something was going on in Union City, or so they convinced themselves, despite E.J. keeping his source secret from them, as Skye had advised him to do. Whether they would admit it or not, the editors went along with E.J.'s pursuits in the dark because they knew that failure by E.J. would not result in accusatory or invective attacks on them, while, at the same time, if E.J. was successful, it would be easily filched and annexed by the editors. They had nothing to lose and everything to gain by having E.J. pursue the story. Walter was less than impressed at the progress. The meeting was heated and strained, but the bantering was mostly a back and forth between editors, with E.J. saying very little about what to do with the story, rather offering what he had turned up and allowing the editors to decide where to go.

"We have spent a lot of time on this and we don't really have anything beyond some accusations," Walter said, his voice teeming.

"You're being short sighted with this Walter," Victoria replied strongly. "This is huge. Do you think they are just going to admit to this stuff? I say we run with this until the end of next week and see where we are…"

Walter interrupted, screaming.

"The end of next week?! Days and days of straight reporting hasn't produced shit and you think we're still onto something?! This fucking story has wasted enough of our time, Victoria!"

E.J. continued to sit silent while Noland jumped into the conversation.

"Whoa, Walter, slow down a bit. E.J. still has a name we haven't been able to track down. There is a lot of information that we haven't seen and if we can get a break, all that information becomes open to us. Fact is, we haven't seen enough to know either way."

"Jesus Christ, Noland," Walter shouted. "A fucking name! Why haven't we gotten in touch with this fucking name?!"

E.J. remained quiet, not realizing the question might be addressed to him.

"Well, Lockhart!? Are you going to answer or sit there wasting more of my fucking time!?"

"Well sir," E.J. said with confidence, trying to ignore the uncomfortable feeling racing through him. "I just got the name and there is no reference. T. Wayne Hammett, it's just a name... I don't even know what the 'T' stands for. I was told to find this guy and the answers would come clear."

"And your sources aren't telling you what the 'T' stands for? This is ridiculous... Who is this source?"

E.J. almost blurted out Donald Tate's name, but bit his tongue and dodged the question.

"If you want to drop the story, then I say let's drop it," E.J. said. "Admittedly, I'm running into walls. It's the source that gave me the CG&E lead, which was solid, so I went with it. But that doesn't mean this is a solid lead."

"That CG&E story was a good lead," Noland said. "I mean, if it's from the same source, I think we're stupid to just abandon this."

E.J. waited for the editors to ask again about the source, tempted to tell them it was Donald Tate, but decided it was probably best to not say anything until the story came through. As the editors continued to debate, E.J. stayed quiet, ready to again dodge any questions about the source if necessary.

Both Noland and Victoria began coaxing Walter into sticking with the story, neither of them asking for a source name, seemingly satisfied with E.J.'s answer.

Walter thought for a moment, he himself realizing he had nothing to lose, and everything to gain. He too owned E.J.'s success, and none of the backlash of failure.

"Okay, but you better be aware E.J., we have allowed a lot of leeway with this and it's taken a lot of our time. Get your ass in gear and just get it done."

"You and the editors are sure about this? It's your call."

"I'm not here to debate, Lockhart!" Walter belted.

E.J. walked out straight to his desk and began to make some phone calls. One after another, more names, places, and possibilities. He pressured Tate, who became even more disconnected, but eventually gave him another name... that led to another name... It took two days of more investigation, but E.J. found his man.

Everything hinged on a bar in Niles, a small district in the southern Bay Area city of Fremont that was made famous by Charlie Chaplin, whose films were shot there in the 1920s. The place was dark, mostly bikers and a few women that looked like aging groupies for heavy metal rock bands. He was looking for the man that would be "out of place," as described by one of his contacts. He was looking for Thomas, the name behind the "T."

The bartender was quick to notice E.J., asking him if he would like a drink, even before he sat at the bar.

"A vodka tonic," E.J. replied.

He scanned the bar, but no one looked out of place.

"Do you know a man named Thomas Wayne Hammett?"

"Thomas," the bartender said with a smile. "That's him right there."

The bartender pointed to the backdoor where a tall black man was entering, ashing a cigarette outside. He wore a suit with a bowtie, clearly out of place in the dive biker bar. E.J. thanked the young lady and made his way over to the table where T. Wayne sat alone. T. Wayne was more than willing to talk with E.J., and told him who he was: A former lieutenant with the Union City police department.

"You're a hard man to find," E.J. said, feeling relieved that he had finally solved the mystery.

"Well, I go by Thomas, and when I worked for Union City, most people called me Bubba... not sure how many people in that department even knew my real first name, and if they did, it was Thomas they would know, not T. Wayne... and that was many, many years ago. I have never been called T. Wayne, not by anyone that knows me."

E.J. pulled out some information, a notepad, and the few documents he had about the shopping center development. He told his story hoping that T. Wayne would be the missing link that would lead him to some answers. The former police officer gave E.J. all the information he needed, but it wasn't the answers E.J. was hoping to find.

"You see, the idea that Charles Pastrana was promoted because of shady dealings between Union City and the developer just isn't true," T. Wayne said. "Charles was promoted months before that deal went through, and even years before that, Charles was being primed for the job. Hell, he was being primed for the chief of police job when I still worked there, and I retired six years ago. His brother Gary wasn't even around then."

E.J.'s heart sank into his stomach. He realized that Donald Tate probably had created this conspiracy from that kid being arrested for peddling drugs at the Thai restaurant. Mix this with the fact that the chief of police and the developer were brothers, and it began to make sense. T. Wayne agreed. He knew Donald Tate well and let E.J. know this type of behavior and conspiracy theorization from Donald wasn't unusual. For the first time, E.J. had come up empty.

Chapter Eleven

The screaming during the meeting echoed loudly in the newsroom, right through the thick glass wall of Walter's office. Victoria and Noland quickly downplayed their role in the continued support of the story, as Walter's anger shot directly at E.J.

"Nothing!" Walter screamed. "What the fuck have you been doing with this story!?"

E.J. attempted to defend his reporting, revealing Donald Tate's name, but the backing he had received earlier from Noland and Victoria to continue investigating was no longer there, both now criticizing E.J.'s news judgment in trusting what Donald had to say.

"You need to wake up," Noland said strikingly. "Donald Tate is a noisy gadfly who is half out of his mind and I would expect you to recognize that. How the Hell could you have just gone balls out on something he said? Do you realize how much time we lost, and other stories we could have been working on?!"

Victoria didn't say anything, just agreed as Noland and Walter laid the entire blame on E.J., trying to erase the fact they had defended the continuation of the story just a day earlier. E.J. became angry at the assault.

"What the fuck are you talking about?" E.J. said, firing back at Noland. "Yesterday, what the source of the CG&E story said was legitimate, but now he isn't a reliable source? You all knew I had the same source for the High Hills Shopping Center development... on top of that, I was willing to let this story go, and you and Victoria pushed it. This isn't entirely my fault."

"But you didn't mention that this was coming from Tate," Noland belted. "That's an important key fact you left out!"

"This is the big leagues, and we expect more from you," Walter continued. "If you cannot get this stuff right, you won't be here much longer."

E.J. walked out of the office and passed Skye who launched into cadence with him, both headed down the hall, pass the employee lounge, out the door to the balcony. E.J. stared straight ahead while Skye tried to keep up.

"I heard that," Skye said as they both made their way outside. "That was fucked, but don't worry, they're not going to fire you... they never fire anyone here. It makes the editors look bad and the company doesn't want to have to pay the unemployment. Also, that crap about wasting time, give me a break. This happens all the time. You think you're the first reporter to come up empty?"

Skye pulled out his pack of Nat Sherman cigarettes and offered one to E.J.

"I'm not worried about getting fired," E.J. said, lighting the cigarette. "You know, I was just following what they said, and then they fucking lay every piece of blame on me... maybe I should have told them about Donald Tate from the beginning."

Skye shook his head.

"No, that wouldn't have made a difference. They would have told you to go for it since the CG&E story he tipped you off on panned out well. Don't let them make you believe this is about Tate. They would have said the same shit and then found some other way to blame it all on you."

"I don't think so."

"Well, E.J., I have been here long enough to tell you that editors won't take the blame for anything. They'll screw you at every turn. They'll take full credit for the stories that hit it big, and they'll take no blame for the stories that don't pan out... even if they assign the story to you."

"What are you talking about?" E.J. asked with a plume of smoke flying out of his mouth.

"I've seen it dozens of times. The editors will get a tip on a story, send you out to find out about it, and if there isn't anything there, you'll get the blame."

E.J. laughed with a confused tone.

"How can they blame you if it was their tip and nothing panned out? That doesn't make sense."

"Sense?" Skye replied. "This is journalism. All the editors want is for you to 'get it done.' It doesn't matter if it 'can't be done' just because there isn't a story. That's not a good enough excuse. You must break your own leads and get good stories any way you can. It doesn't matter who you step on because there are no friends in this business. That's how it works, so you're either the predator or the prey."

"You're being a bit dramatic Skye, aren't you?"

Skye laughed in jest.

"I'm just saying it's cutthroat and that's the way they roll in this business. You need to get used to that fact. You have one good hit so far with that CG&E story, but you'll need more."

"Well, I'm not telling any of those assholes anything about any story I'm working on until I know I have a story. They can be pissed at me now, but I got another story in the works. I'll just keep my mouth shut until I know it's coming through. If this hits, then all will be forgotten."

Skye smiled, intrigued.

"I'm not an editor, so tell me what you have cookin'."

As they both headed back to their desks, E.J. told Skye about a man he met while covering the debunked Union City story. His name was Glenn Flannery, a local contractor and concerned member of the PTA, whose son went to school in Fremont.

Glenn told E.J. about a man named David Finch, who was just hired as the Fremont Unified School District's superintendent.

Glenn claimed that Finch was recently fired from a school district in rural central California for abusing his power and may have spent some time in a mental institution. If these things were true, Glenn wanted them exposed.

"If this guy is correct, then you may have a good story there. No one here covers Fremont schools. That's more of a job for the Fremont paper, but it could be a decent story," Skye said sliding his high-back leather chair up to his computer. "I don't think it's a blockbuster, though."

E.J. popped a few raisins in his mouth from the box he bought at the vending machine on the way back to his desk.

"I know," E.J. replied with a bit of arrogance, realizing that Skye did not catch the other angle of this story. "It's not about David Finch at all."

Skye turned back around, waiting for the mystery to be uncovered.

"This guy, Finch," E.J. continued. "Who cares if he abused power and was in a mental institution. It's not about him. The real question is why did the district hire him, assuming they knew this information, which they should of... how the fuck do you become a superintendent without a thorough background check?"

E.J. explained that he was going to get every other application for that job, comb through them, expose whether Finch was the best person for the position, and uncover if the district knew of his past. He was going to go after the district to find out how this man could have possibly gotten hired to be the superintendent.

"I don't know if I'm going to run into walls all day long. I don't even know if these allegations about Finch are true, or if the district knew about them... but if they didn't, shouldn't they have found this out doing their background check?"

E.J. continued to rattle on and on, hashing out every scenario until Skye stopped him.

"Look, when you put it that way, you're onto something. I didn't see it like that," Skye said.

E.J. sat back and marinated in his swagger.

"Come on, you didn't catch that," he said, slightly arrogant, but jokingly. "We're in the big leagues here, right? Gotta catch those angles."

Skye turned back around, a bit perturbed, and ignored E.J.

"Lighten up."

Skye shook his head like an automatic clock's second hand.

"Okay, I didn't see it. Are you happy?" he said.

"I'm just fuckin' with ya, Skye."

Skye let it go, although he was a bit disappointed with himself.

"I know, no worries. Let's get back to work. This paper isn't going to print itself."

Chapter Twelve

"Pete, can you tell the driver that I need to be there by nine?"

The young executive sat up straight, nodded affirmingly to his boss, and tapped the privacy window of the limousine.

"Can you hurry it up a bit," Pete said. "We only have forty-five minutes. Mr. Goodman needs to be there by nine."

The Bay Bridge was jammed at the maze and Cornell Goodman was worried he would be late for the quarterly meeting of executive editors. He sat atop a newspaper empire. A mysterious man that started his reporting career in the early 1950s, but quickly moved up the chain at the Des Moines Register to become its executive editor by 1960. He was savvy with business, and a man that knew who to make friends with. He also was ruthlessly cunning, keeping his enemies close as he positioned himself to be more than just a man that worked in media. He wanted to own it and control it. In 1962, he noticed that a small newspaper, the Springville Gazette, was struggling. He partnered with two other associates, and they bought the paper for pennies on the dollar. It didn't take long to turn it around. This was done by firing most of the staff, and then rehiring them at a fraction of their pay. He quickly consumed two other neighboring small-town papers and consolidated the printing and management operations of all three at a single location. Again, he fired most of the staff, only rehiring the minimum needed at a lower pay rate. By 1966, Cornell and his company, Media Connections Inc., had bought a dozen small and medium-sized papers that were struggling, all turned around by his consolidate, slash, and rehire model, while also bringing in hungry young inexperienced reporters, editors, and artists that would work for much less to get their first opportunity in the business.

By the 1970s, Cornell had forced his partners out of the business when their visions of the company's direction began to differ from his, assuming total control of Media Connections Inc. His ability to "save" struggling media outlets got him top positions on various media boards, earned him awards, and showered him with accolades across the media world for his business model. Unions became outraged, but were ineffective in stopping the juggernaut that was Cornell Goodman. Over the next two decades, like a vulture, he would attack newspapers, radio stations, and television outlets that were failing and turn them around. Long hours, low pay, and mostly staffed with inexperienced skeleton crews, often pulling double duties as he continued to consolidate operations when possible. In the 1990s, with the advent of Internet technology beginning to hurt major media outlets, he made his biggest move and purchased dozens of struggling big-city papers across America. The San

Francisco Press-Journal was one of them, along with six other smaller and medium-sized Bay Area papers. As one of his flagship papers, the price for ads in the Press-Journal were outrageous, and it became a cash cow for the model he had created. It was brilliant in design. Under this new Bay Area subsidiary, called SF News Consolidated, all stories written for every paper he owned in the Bay Area were shared, all sent to a central location outside the city of Martinez, just northeast of San Francisco. All the various newspapers were laid out with many of the same stories running in every paper, placed in different sections depending on its importance to the community the newspaper served. The Martinez location would then print and distribute the papers across the Bay Area. With this consolidation model and running skeleton staffs at his papers, he was focused on three things: Reduce cost in every conceivable way, while keeping ad prices as high as ever, and retain just the minimum staff so all daily papers would still successfully make it out each day. If costs got too high at any one of his papers, Cornell would terminate the executive editor. That was success in journalism, and nothing was more important to Cornell... and Walter knew this.

"As a group, you guys are doing a wonderful job," Cornell said looking across the conference table, his tall frame blocking part of the PowerPoint presentation behind him. Seven executive editors, Walter included, nodded in approval. "We're on a path to surpass our profit margins by more than fifteen percent."

The group clapped.

"Don't get too excited," Cornell interrupted. "Percy, what is the deal with the Hayward Register? I'm seeing some numbers that don't make sense."

The editor, Percy Pivins, a small older man that had been in control of the Hayward paper the past two years, shuffled through some paperwork in front of him. Hayward had struggled since Cornell's company took it over. Percy was the third executive editor that paper had seen in five years, all of them fired for failure to keep profits high.

"What do you mean they don't make sense?"

"It's not making me enough money and you keep getting scooped... that doesn't make sense to me. This is still the one paper in the group that can't seem to get out of the basement."

The group chuckled.

"Well, ad revenue has been down for all of us smaller papers," Percy said. "We're not pulling the same circulation numbers anymore. This Internet thing is kicking our asses."

"I get that," Cornell replied. "But that means you must find new ways to reduce costs and boost sales. Part of the is not getting scooped by other papers. You're getting killed out in the field.

"Well, we have been struggling big time with keeping good reporters. These upstarts are paying people three times what we pay to produce content for websites. I just lost three reporters in the last two months to dotcoms. I also lost a great young reporter even before he stepped in for his first day of work."

"Are you serious, Percy?" one editor chimed in.

"Yeah... this guy goes through two interviews with us, drug test, written test, the whole process, and on the first day of work, he calls and says he took a job at some fucking website called Google."

"Google?" Walter interrupted. "What the fuck is a Google?"

"Some search engine? Doesn't matter. Obviously got a better salary, which isn't hard to surpass. This is why when that Hayward cop got nailed for selling drugs last month through his youth charity, we got our asses handed to us by the San Jose paper... I had no one. It's hard to even keep anyone with what we pay."

The editors in the room began mumbling, side conversations erupted, as Cornell became slightly irritated.

"Also," Percy added. "One thing I think we're all forgetting. Since these websites can be updated immediately and accessed just as quick by anyone, we look like a slow turtle at a NASCAR race. We get scooped all the time and the lack of resources make it hard to stay ahead of the competition. I know I'm not the only one that is experiencing these challenges."

"Percy is right," said Quinn Cole, the editor of the Alameda Union-Press. "This has been hard for most of us. Ad sales down, employee retention harder, getting scooped by other papers and the Internet. None of the smaller papers are doing as well as they did five years ago."

Walter sat silent. He rarely said much because he knew he was in the best position compared to everyone else at the table. The chain's smaller papers from Fremont to Marin were just steppingstones for any writer or journalist. The San Francisco Press-Journal was a behemoth. Despite everything else, it was a major paper and people wanted to be a part of that, even if every dotcom offered much more.

"I just want everyone to understand we're approaching the Internet with the same force as others, so I get the current challenges," Cornell said. "But that's why you have to find those reporters that believe the story is what matters most, over anything else. Money... not important when you get those guys that live and breathe this life. They're out there. You need to find them."

Percy leaned back in his chair and nodded agreeably. It's just hard to find those reporters that think like that. He went over in his head again all the things he had done to keep reporters on staff, and profits high, but none worked. He was tired.

"Walter, what do you suggest?" Percy asked. "Your numbers are outstanding when it comes to hiring and retaining reporters and your bottom line with expenses is the strongest here. Any suggestions?"

Walter cleared his throat and sat up.

"Well, I think as we all know, we want to hire those that want to do real news and willing to devote themselves to the craft, so that money isn't their first concern."

Everyone gave an artificial nod.

"So, when you're up against the fact we pay less than others, you have to first think about bringing in people any way you can, keep them there as long as you can, and when things get a bit contentious, you remind them of the opportunity. In your situation, Percy, and for anyone else at this table, my suggestion is to tell new reporters and editors that they have a direct line to the San Francisco Press-Journal... if they keep doing good work, they will end up at the flagship paper. That's one approach."

Everyone agreed and followed along.

"One of the things I do, and this has been discussed in here before, is changing the pay structure and basing the pay on the job, not the reporter. Let's say, the city reporter would make $20,000 more a year than other positions. You hire someone for the city reporter position, then move that reporter to another position just before they start, promising it's only temporary. It helps control what you're spending with the greatest flexibility in keeping people."

"Sounds like bait and switch to get them to take a job," Quinn joked and laughed.

"I call it being flexible," Walter maintained.

The group laughed as Walter continued.

"And, of course, this type of model can cause issues with upset employees, but make sure you don't fire anyone without due cause. Unemployment comes out of your budget."

The group nodded.

"And Percy," Cornell interrupted. "You've fired two people this year, all without due cause. This is a huge expense and one of the easiest expenses to avoid."

"Mr. Goodman, with all due respect," Walter edged in, "the Press-Journal is a much bigger paper... getting top talent to Hayward and retaining it is a bit more difficult."

"I realize that Walter," Cornell replied. "But this has nothing to do with anything other than simple ways to avoid firing people without cause. If how we operate doesn't work for them, we can get rid of them. It's easy to make sure they understand where they belong in this world, and if it's not with us, they can leave on their dime, not ours. Do you all understand and agree?"

The whole room acknowledged.

The rest of the meeting editors offered more suggestions to improve bottom lines and outcomes, mostly discussing hiring more inexperienced people, cutting staff that makes too much, having reporters do at least three stories a day, and going after college students as stringers paid on a per-story basis.

"Hey Walter," Quinn nudged. "What are you and Carol doing tonight? Summer and I are having Frank and Hilda over. You should join us. Seven?"

"Sounds great," Walter said with a smile. "Carol's been nagging me about getting out ever since Summer told her about your view of downtown. She is dying to see your new place."

"Perfect! Yeah, you'll both love the view. It's amazing."

Chapter Thirteen

Quinn and his wife Summer diligently worked in the kitchen while Frank and Hilda sipped wine in their living room with Walter and Carol. Frank worked in pharmaceutical sales and Hilda was his trophy wife for being a success. The condo, which had been built the year before, was cutting-edge for the new millennium. The living area was open, endowed almost entirely with luxury furniture, from the Regina Andrew leather sofa and chairs, to the elegant glass Shahrooz butterfly coffee table. The Moondust monorail tracked lighting stretched across the sixteen-foot-high ceilings and natural bamboo flooring opened up to a deluxe chef's kitchen, equipped with Viking Monogram stainless appliances and a ten-foot island constructed of quartz embedment. The sliding glass doors led to a balcony that sat high on the twenty-third floor.

"We're almost ready for dinner," Quinn said, stepping into the living room.

"This place is amazing," Carol said. "I love the design. I've been trying to get Walter to do similar upgrades to our condo."

"So much time involved with that," Walter chuckled.

"I love your guys' condo too," Hilda said to Carol. "It's just as nice as this one."

Carol smiled.

"Don't get me wrong, it's beautiful, and we're lucky to have it, but we bought it ten years ago and I think it's due for an upgrade."

Quinn pulled out three Cohiba cigars.

"Gentleman, would you care to join me on the balcony?"

"Holy shit, are those Cubans?"

"Frank, you know I would never do anything that violates laws... so... I plead the fifth."

Walter and Frank smiled, following Quinn out to the balcony while the wives sipped wine and gossiped.

"So, what did you think of the meeting today? I feel bad for Percy."

Walter took a long drag off his cigar.

"Well, I know most of the smaller papers are hurting because the Press-Journal is hurting too. Quinn, I know your job is no walk in the park, but what are you going to do? You're going to do what must be done to protect your family. I know you have made some hard decisions too. More than me, I would guess. Percy needs to do the same and play the game a bit better, that's all."

"Geez," Frank belted. "You guys are really making journalism sound like an assembly line these days. I know it's been a long time since I was in the newsroom, but it couldn't have changed that much."

"Frank, you were smart to get out a long time ago," Quinn said. "It's more of an assembly line now than ever before. I've never really thought too much about anything other than being the best in the business, but times have changed, and upper management doesn't see journalism the same way it was seen twenty or thirty years ago... by the time you get into our positions as executive editors, you're doing whatever it is you have to do to keep your job. It's a challenge."

Frank laughed.

"I love that word: Challenge... all that means is that your bosses are demanding you to find a way to do the same quality work without the needed resources and support, or you get canned."

Both Walter and Quinn laughed, sipped their drinks, and took another drag from their cigars.

"During my years in the business," Walter began to say, "thousands of people came across my path. Editors, reporters, staff that ran the paper, and hundreds of people just coming to visit the paper... teachers, kids, professionals, and the curious that just wanted to see what a real newsroom was like. I wanted that. I wanted to make a great newsroom that would 'wow' people when they came in and looked over our shoulders. They knew when they read the paper, they were reading the finest newsroom journalism had to offer."

"Yeah, me too," Quinn chimed in. "I always saw the newspaper as a living, breathing entity, that was real... it has heart. Somewhere, though, that changed a bit. It's the Internet... this is what's been altering the business for the last few years, and it will continue until it sinks print journalism permanently. It's clear ownership knows that. We're bleeding and I don't think it's going to stop. Still, news is important, and media is important. We cannot lose sight of that despite the situation at SF Consolidated or the state of journalism now in the age of technology."

Walter and Frank agreed.

"You know, the first few years I ran the Press-Journal, we had so many people come through to see the paper and all of them left impressed. Not just a little bit, but honestly affected by what they saw. I was proud of being on that level. It's definitely changed, and it's not ever going back to that. It's sad, but you push forward and do what needs to be done. This is your life now with technology killing your career. You adapt and change. You must do that. You have a responsibility to your job and your family."

Frank sipped his drink and thought for a moment.

'There is a business model BMW employs," Frank said. "They emphasize quality over quantity under this idea: If you have a brand that is cheap and all costs are cut to maximize profit, it's true you will make a lot of money immediately, especially in the short term. However, as the product sells, it eventually is seen by consumers as cheap, and sales go down in the long term as customers don't return, nor recommend the product to anyone. No one wants to buy crap. BMW focuses on the long-term reputation, which in turn allows the product to have more inherent value, thus worth more with returning customers and reputation that attracts new customers. Profits come in the long run versus being immediate, but profits become sustainable."

Walter laughed.

"This isn't a car company, my friend," Quinn quipped.

"That isn't happening in journalism," Walter said. "New readers aren't picking up a newspaper as much anymore. They're going online. Newspapers now have to be flashy, sensational, and shallow to even compete. Either that, or breaking major stories, but those also are picked up quickly by the Internet. Yeah, some still read the paper, but it's losing money big time. The model now is minimum staff, minimizing any unnecessary spending, surgically striking every little expense you can, and not fostering integrity or commitment, but rather minimizing the damage the lack of those things cause. All the while, still maintaining the high standards. That's the mindset nowadays. My job is to make that work at any cost... and I refuse to let anyone ruin what I have built for myself. No one would allow that."

"Preach it brother!" Quinn exclaimed as they all raised their glasses and toasted. "And look at what we have done in our careers... thirty years ago we were all broke reporters that decided we weren't going to just be a part of something, but rather create something. We all did this and look at the beautiful rewards we amassed and the beautiful families we have. Now it's just a race to retirement before this whole thing falls apart. We're almost there."

"It's coming to an end, but even with the industry changing and our own struggles keeping this ship afloat, it's nice to be us," Walter said. "There are a lot of sharks swimming in that ocean and you're less likely to be eaten if you're a bigger one."

Chapter Fourteen

Bookmarks would open early Monday to accommodate the rush of students, most of whom attended nearby community colleges, but some were willing to come up from Stanford University and over the San Mateo-Hayward Bridge, from Cal State East Bay, to find a book they needed. "College At The Marks" looked like a success even before the store opened. The line stretched down the block for what seemed like miles as Kalea gazed out the locked doors just minutes before opening.

"Jesus, look at that," Audette said, standing behind Kalea.

"This is going to be a rough day," Kalea answered.

"Are you okay?" Audette asked.

Kalea looked at Audette and smiled, her eyes just a bit low and slightly bloodshot.

"Well, I'm here… just like last night, and every other day for the past millennium."

Audette smirked, sympathizing, and feeling much the same, sharing many of those late-night shifts with Kalea.

"I'm okay Audette, just fucking tired."

"Did you hear about the spot that opened up in the after-school program? They lost a guy this week?" Audette asked.

"I did... I talked with Matt and already applied."

"Did you put Shelia down as a reference?"

"I did," Kalea said. "I didn't want to, but do I have a choice?"

"Shhhhiiissshhh... Good luck with that."

A disenchanted feeling swept across Kalea. Too much rested in the hands of a woman that clearly didn't like her too much.

The echo of a door shutting, coming from the back of the store, and the sound of someone humming Bob Dylan's "I Shall Be Released," reverberated through the room.

"Unbelievable," Audette spitted out with distain. "What a bitch…"

Shelia strolled through the main floor, her frequent absence from work during the past two weeks leaving her rested and smiling. As the rest of the staff began to show up, Shelia gathered everyone for a briefing before the doors were unlocked. The speech was a mix of protocols and a self-congratulatory ego-fest, ending with Shelia announcing that she was giving herself the "Employee of the Month" award for coming up with the "College At The Marks" idea.

The group of exhausted employees reacted stoically while Audette excused herself in disgust. Kalea snickered with contempt.

Within minutes, Bookmarks was the center of organized chaos. Shelia had developed the system to handle the huge rush they got, modifying what the store normally did during Christmas, and other times, when buying books became fashionable.

Shelia had three staff members work the foyer. Today it would be Audette, Tina, and James. Tina rarely engaged anyone other than another part-time worker, Dayana. Kalea thought it was a "goth" thing since both girls dressed that way. The three in the foyer would ask customers what they were looking for and then direct them to one of the wings. From there, the people working in each of the wings would help the customer find the book. Kalea was put on west wing duty, handling classic literature, with Parker underneath her, a young hippie that claimed he had no last name… just Parker. He was tall, thin, and pale, with long dirty blonde dreadlocks that he kept tied into a ponytail.

Kalea was tired, but still maintained her tempo with the coffee that was racing through her veins. Sumatra, the strongest she could find at the grocery store across the street from Bookmarks, is what was keeping her going all week. She thought about her last day off, but she wasn't sure if it was a Tuesday or a Wednesday, which didn't really matter since it seemed so long ago. Kalea had become so familiar with the sophomoric job of retail book sales that she no longer had to think about it anymore, operating on autopilot, even during times like these.

Kalea had tried all week to talk with Shelia about the teaching program opening, but she couldn't get a hold of her. She had talked with Matt, head of the after-school program, about the position during her late shift the previous Monday. Matt liked Kalea, probably more so initially because she was pretty, but when she told him she was a graduate of the University of Ohio, he was drawn in completely. Matt had attended Michigan State University nearby. She offered him a cup of coffee and they talked about their time in college. Matt wanted to hire her, but it had to be cleared with Shelia. Kalea would still have to split shifts with the after-school program and working the floor, because the only people that worked the after-school program fulltime were credentialed teachers. Matt informed her that working the floor would be minimal, just to bypass the rules about having the proper credentials. Kalea would make more money and spend 95 percent of her time teaching.

"Kalea?" Parker said, knocking her out of her current train of thought. "Did we run out of new copies of 'Candide'?"

"They'll be here tomorrow," she replied.

Kalea saw Shelia come out from the back and walk towards the front of the store, noticeably a bit flustered from the rush of customers. She sat behind the register and took a deep breath.

"Parker?" Kalea called.

"Yeah."

"Can you cover me for about five minutes? I need to talk with Shelia, and she looks like she is on a break."

Parker nodded and quickly flipped around to help another customer. Kalea made a quick move across the floor, weaving in and out of traffic. Shelia rested on a stool and yawned.

"Shelia? Can I talk with you really quick?"

Shelia smiled big.

"Why sure, darlin'," she said, her voice carrying an overly sweet drawl.

"I talked with Matt upstairs about teaching. He has two classes with a bunch of fourth, fifth, and sixth graders, and no one right now to teach them contemporary literature. Did he talk to you?"

"Well, yes, he did. I'm sorry I couldn't give you a recommendation."

Kalea was shocked.

"What? I don't understand…"

"Well, outside of the fact you didn't ask me for a recommendation first, which is not professional at all…"

Kalea interrupted.

"I've been trying to get a hold of you all week. You're nowhere to be found and you didn't return my phone calls."

Shelia just ignored Kalea and continued talking.

"I'm also not sure you're ready to teach and work the floor at the same time. It's one of those things that's tough to juggle… not sure you're ready for that."

"What do you mean? I'm your best worker down here, and I have been working nonstop to help organize this back-to-school event while you have been dodging every mothafuckin' shift since you came up with this idea. How dare you say I cannot handle working down here and upstairs!? You're the only one around here that probably couldn't do it."

"Darlin'," Shelia jumped in. "You need to calm down... let me explain... you have a degree in philosophy. I'm not sure that will help you with little kids. I wouldn't…"

"Wouldn't what!?" Kalea screamed over Shelia. "It's clear you have some fucked up grudge that has nothing to do with me! I'm here, every shift, everyday! I have been a fuckin' beacon of light for you! Never fail! Never die! And you tell me I can't handle this!? Absolute bullshit!"

Shelia stepped back and got defensive, panicking as the entire store began staring at Kalea while she ripped through her tirade.

"You listen," Shelia snapped back. "You better apologize to me, these customers and, if I were you, I would change your attitude with me if you ever want to see any opportunities here."

"I can't believe this. Apologize to you? That's the biggest load of shit that has come out your fat mouth since I stepped into this place. I have done everything, and more, and all you do is drag me around like some piece of garbage. I don't need some idiotic college dropout telling me anything about what I'm capable of doing!"

Shelia stepped forward to the counter, her face quickly shaded from pink to red.

"You listen to me you immature, pretentious, little bitch!" she screamed. "I run this place, and as long as I'm here, you will do as I tell you. Do you understand?"

Kalea punched a stack of books on the counter, knocking them over, and startling Shelia. She quickly ripped off her apron, throwing it in Shelia's direction as the stack of books continued to slide down off the counter.

Kalea took a moment and centered herself.

"I feel sorry for you, for whatever happened in your life, the choices you made, and whatever mistakes led you here," Kalea said assured. "But I'm not the one that owes you an apology, nor am I the one required to suffer the consequences of your life choices. I suggest you find some peace before you find another employee to take it all out on."

Before Shelia could respond, Kalea was gone out the door.

Chapter Fifteen

The streets of San Francisco were wet, rain still dripping from the buildings that recent storms dumped on the city. It had been like that for a few days. Kalea didn't mind the rain because she hated snow so much, a product of growing up in Ohio. Snow was always in the way and so hard to get through. It caused problems, frustrated people, and could be dangerous when traversed. Yet, every day, during winter, people braved the snow and pushed forward. It's part of the reason why those from the Midwest and East Coast are so tough. As the drops of rain ran down the bus window she was looking out of, she smiled. It would probably rain all week, but it would never turn into snow. For a moment, though, she thought to herself that wouldn't be so bad. She wouldn't mind once again hearing her father complain about having to get to work after a huge storm dumped hordes of it onto the driveways and streets. She smiled thinking about her family having to adjust moving from Hawaii when she was eight, so her father, an architect, could take a job at Archway City Design, Inc. He had never seen weather like Ohio. He designed, and built, the house they could never afford in

Hawaii and provided a world for Kalea that exceeded her life on the islands. He was home more, was paid more money, found delectation in the community, and spent every extra moment with Kalea. She casually reminisced about high school, her years as a cheerleader, serving as vice president of the student body, Drama Club, K.E.Y. Club, and even the rough junior year playing softball when she had zero skills on the field. She mused over college and her classes. Her naïve approach to studies during her freshman year and how books by Friedrich Nietzsche and Søren Kierkegaard changed her forever. How much she was looking forward to working in Cleveland State University's philosophy department. As the bus pulled to a stop in front of Kerney's Coffee Shop, Kalea looked long through the wet glass, and for a moment, wished it would snow.

Kalea stared at the tip jar sitting on the counter. It was loaded with bills and a sprinkling of change at the bottom. The barista stood relaxed as she filled the cup of coffee Kalea had ordered, rotating her head back and forth and humming a light melodic tune. She was fixated on that jar until the young woman turned around.

"It's a high school football song we sang back in Texas," the barista said.

"Excuse me?"

"The song I was just humming… it's a song we used to sing before our high school games back home."

Kalea smiled and again looked at the tip jar.

"Can I ask you a question?" Kalea inquired.

The barista smiled and gave an accepting nod.

"Do you make a lot in tips here?"

"Sometimes… but it depends on the day. Friday's are good… Saturday too… Sunday doesn't do too bad… and most mornings… come to think of it, it isn't too bad on any day. Just better on some others."

"Are you hiring?"

The barista was genuinely disappointed.

"No, we're not… and that sucks because you probably would do well here. You're pretty. I know a lot of tips in that jar are because of the cute ones. Who doesn't like a pretty face?"

Kalea thanked the young woman and made her way to the patio.

The sun came out and was beginning to warm the city. Kalea sipped her coffee and opened the book she stole from Bookmarks before she left. "Bagombo Snuff Box" by Kurt Vonnegut Jr. As she began to read, a wave of smoke crossed her face, making her wince.

"I'm sorry," said a young black woman, thin, but shapely, with cat-like eyes. The long, slim cigarette, dangling between her elegant red fingernails. "Did I just get smoke in your face?"

"It's okay," Kalea said. "It just makes me want one right now."

The young lady quickly reached down into her purse and flung out a cigarette from the leather case that rested inside the front pouch.

"Take one, sweetie," she said, handing it to Kalea.

She put the cigarette in her mouth, lit it smoothly, and blew out a long thick plume of smoke.

"Thanks," Kalea said, as the wave of a nicotine high rushed through her. "Wow... that's nice... I needed that. I just walked out on my job."

"That's always a great feeling."

Kalea smiled tepidly.

"Well, it only feels good until the bills show up. I need to find something new."

"What are you looking for?" the young lady asked.

"I'm thinking of something with tips involved," Kalea said. "I used to work at a Hawaiian restaurant in Ohio. Tips were crappy, but I'm betting they would be better in San Francisco. Big city, big tips, you know."

"It's true," the young lady said. "I used to work at The Cliffs, and I got great tips there, but you have to be at a nice place to get the top-tier folks that drop a lot of money on the table."

"I better start looking."

The young lady took a sip of her coffee. Suddenly, a thought dawned on her.

"You know, my cousin works as a dishwasher at The Pennington. Ever heard of it?"

Kalea shook her head no.

"It's a really popular place out near North Beach, just south of Washington Square in the Financial District. It's off Montgomery Street and Pacific, I believe. One of the finest restaurants in the city, easily. My cousin was just complaining about a waitress that walked out last night. If you go there today, you may be able to get the job even before they start looking."

Kalea pulled out her guide to San Francisco and looked it up. She thanked the young lady, picked up her bag, and jolted to the bus stop before the MUNI could pull away from the curb. It didn't really take too much to get prepared as she usually wore nice clothes every day. She stopped into a coffee shop just across from The Pennington to clean up a bit, adjusted her white blouse and black skirt, touched up her make-up and hair, and then headed over.

The place wasn't open, so she went around the back and asked the three kitchen workers smoking in the alley if they would let her see the manager. They had no issue with this request at all, and, in fact, were quite happy to help. Inside, she put on a smiling face and amped up her charm factor well above normal to hide her exhaustion, the weight of walking out of her job just a few hours before, and the stress of her whole experience at Bookmarks, all of which still rested on her mind. She couldn't have been more cordial and pleasant as she went on about her work at the Hawaiian restaurant back in Ohio, how it ran, her experience serving, her skills helping manage when needed, and a few stories that illustrated her leadership ability when things weren't going well, such as when co-workers walked off in the middle of a shift and when patrons complained or became combative. No talk of Bookmarks or her philosophy degree. It didn't take too much to convince the manager that she not only knew what she was doing, but was perfect for the job and their upscale clientele. She was qualified, professional, exuded discretion, was no nonsense, but cordial and sweet when required, pretty, and, most importantly, could work immediately. They needed her tonight.

Chapter Sixteen

"Did you talk with Pastor Teddy?"

Noland was attentively washing the oil off his hands, rubbing Gojo fiercely into his nails. He whistled the melody and mumbled the lyrics to Bob Segar's "Night Moves," completely unaware of Claire and the white noise that was coming from her direction.

"Noland, darling, do you hear me? Have you talked with Pastor Teddy?"

Noland looked up, his eyes reflecting lassitude.

"I'm sorry, what did you say?"

"Are you losing your hearing or something?" she asked sarcastically. "That's what happens when you spend all your time in the den blasting that old rock 'n roll. I asked if you have talked with Pastor Teddy about the homeowners' association board position?"

Noland picked up a towel and began to dry his hands.

"Noland!" Claire belted. "What have I told you about drying your hands on those towels? You're getting oil on them!"

Noland quickly put the towel down.

"Well, I'm sorry. You interrupted my washing. If you would just let me finish without badgering me about Teddy, my hands wouldn't have any oil on them to soil the towel in the first place."

Claire baulked.

"And no, I haven't talked with Pastor Teddy yet... ran into a small issue changing the oil on the Mustang. It took longer than I thought. I'll call him today."

"It's 2:30. A bit late, don't you think? I know Barbara and Jeff are trying to get his endorsement for her to be on the board, and I'll be damned if I let that crazy woman get a vote. You know she hates me. I want that garden in our backyard and she will vote it down just to spite me."

"Honey, don't worry. I'll call him in a minute. Remember, I'm an editor at the Press-Journal. I can get a lot of publicity for his church."

"Well, how nice is that?" Claire said with indifference. "You can get him in the paper. You know Jeff's bonus from TelCorp was $500,000 this year? Can you imagine what kind of donation he could make to the church? We can't bribe the man with a newspaper clip, so we must schmooze him and start schmoozing now. Got it?"

Noland nodded with a vanquished grin as Claire began to walk away.

"If we would have just bought a house, we wouldn't have to deal with all of this homeowner association bullshit," Noland said to himself softly, but loud enough to make sure Claire heard it.

"Did you say something, dear?"

"I did... you heard me... I said if we would have bought a house instead of this condo, we wouldn't have to deal with this, and you could plant any garden you wanted in your backyard."

"And live where? In the East Bay? In Oakland? I did not raise three children, bust my ass keeping this household together for twenty-five years to live in Oakland."

"Well Claire, maybe if you kept that job at the elementary school when we first got married, we would have saved enough money to buy a house in San Francisco instead of this condo."

"Well, if you wouldn't have lost that public relations job with the San Jose Shockers, we would have all the money we need instead of that pile of pennies you get each week at the newspaper."

"I didn't lose that job. The league went under... that wasn't my fault."

"Not your fault? You were poised to become an executive editor at the San Jose Union News and quit for that job... a minor league professional football job. Who watches minor league football? How is that not your fault?"

"That job paid nearly twice what an executive editor makes and, as I recall, at the time, I didn't hear you complaining about that. You weren't stopping me from taking the job. In fact, if memory serves me, you encouraged me to take it. Now, you're complaining about my pay at the Press-Journal? It's the same complaint you had about the Union News years ago. Did you forget about all of that?"

Claire quickly shifted the argument.

"I should have stopped you from buying that Mustang."

"It's a classic car, not a toy... it's an investment. You know how rare a completely restored 1965 Mustang is?"

"Really? An investment? Maybe if you didn't invest in that car or filled out our closet with those ridiculous Armani suits and designer sunglasses, we would be able to buy a house. Did you ever think of that?"

Noland stepped back, provoked, but too tired to continue.

"I'm sorry. I don't want to fight over this. I'll give Teddy a call right now and we'll fix it, alright? No worries."

"I don't know what's wrong with you. You better start acting your age. We have a lot of work to do to make sure I get that seat on the board, and this attitude you've developed, or whatever the heck it is, needs to take a back seat to getting the support of this entire neighborhood."

Noland acquiesced

"Got it."

Noland disappeared into the house to make the call, returning a few minutes later to resume his weekend "honey do's." Noland stood high on his ladder, scraping out the gutters with a small hand shovel as the sun speared down on him. It was a bright and clear afternoon in the mid-seventies, but warm in the sun. With each scoop he sang along with Kiss' "Rock and Roll All Nite," which was blaring from the car stereo in the driveway. Two teenagers on bikes rolled up to Noland.

"Hey Mr. Slade. Can Billy and I borrow your Mustang this weekend?" one of the boys shouted to Noland.

"Ha Ha, Derek... Very funny."

"Come on Mr. Slade. You know Britney down the street? Mr. Edwards' daughter?"

Noland paused and smiled. He knew who Britney was... had seen her dozens of times walking to school, fantasizing about her.

"Yeah," he said. "I think I do."

"Man, she told me she loves this car, Mr. Slade. If you let me take her out in it, you know I would be hittin' that sweet ass by the end of the night."

Both Derek and Billy began to thrust their hips and laugh.

"Knock it off boys. You're not getting my car.... and don't talk about her that way. It's disrespectful."

Both boys shrugged their shoulders in disappointment.

"She really likes the car, huh?"

"Yeah," Billy said. "She says she sees you driving it all the time."

Noland smiled wide and closed his eyes, envisioning the beautiful young blonde riding next to him.

"Hey Noland," a voice shrieked from across the street. Noland opened his eyes and saw Billy and Derek riding off in the distance, while Preston Wilcox, the neighbor who lives caddy-corner from him, walked up to his driveway.

"Hey Preston. How's it going?"

"Good," Preston said with a huge smile. "I got a chance to talk with your daughter before she headed back to school. I didn't know she was already a junior. Seems just like yesterday she headed off to Fresno State University. What an awesome young lady she is becoming."

"They grow up fast," Noland said, with a slightly deflated tone of happiness.

"How's Noland Jr.?"

"Doing good. He just took a job in Seattle."

"Wild," Preston said. "I look at my little girl Suzy and tell my wife, we better enjoy these years, because before we know it, they're off to college."

Noland continued to scrape out the gutters, nodding blindly as Preston talked.

"You know what I got at Home Depot yesterday? Check this out."

Preston pulled out a spray nozzle for a hose. Noland looked over and smiled with mild interest.

"It's the new True Tuff 200. It has ten settings on it, from mist to rotating timed spray optimization."

Preston's voice began to sink deep into the back of Noland's brain as he began to focus on Boston's "More Than A Feeling," which was now playing from the car stereo. The song got him thinking of Julie O'Bannon. She was the young lady who lived across the street from Noland's family growing up. He put down the small shovel and began to squeeze his hand into a fist, feeling the intense emotion of the memory. He smiled as Preston's voice completely disappeared. He remembered throwing the football back and forth with Julie some thirty years ago, something the two did almost every day. From across the street, the ball would be passed as the two smiled, laughed, and had those "serious teenage conversations" about school, parties, and their friends.

He stopped, looked at his right hand intensely. He squeezed it one more time into a fist, harder than he ever had. Preston continued to play with the features on his spray nozzle and babbled on, unaware that Noland had forgotten he was even there. Noland remembered one fateful day they were throwing the football across the street, and one of Julie's throws did not quite make it, bouncing violently off the pavement as he reached for it, knocking his middle finger out of the joint.

For years, the finger would act funny, sometimes popping out at random times... sometimes every week, sometimes every few months. He would just pop it back in and go about his daily business. Two years ago, it popped out while he was in a tirade at work, yelling at Aubrey Worton, the health reporter, about her continued failures on the job. He kicked her desk, buckling the leg and tipping it. In a flash, her computer, her phone, paperwork, and dozens of other trinkets slid violently down to the ground. He jumped back, accidentally banging his hand on a chair. He tried to pop it back in, but he seriously damaged it this time. The choices were either fuse the bones, which would make the finger immobile, cutting it off, or risky surgery that may or may not work... the surgery was a gamble that could have resulted in the finger being removed. He took the surgery. That gamble was the only thing in the last thirty years that worked in his favor.

"And I got this alligator hose... not actually made of alligator, as my wife thought, but that's what it's called.... women... what do they know about tools? Anyway, this thing will never kink up or fray. It's the best hose I have ever seen."

Noland continued to squeeze his fist thinking deeply about the loss of motion in his finger from the accident. It took thirty years for the finger to finally fail on him completely. It was a reminder of the loss and failure of much more. Things just never worked out with Julie. Time passed, things happened, and she faded away.

"The hose, Noland... have you heard of this hose? Hello?"

"I'm sorry, what?" Noland said, snapping out of his daydream.

"Ever heard of the alligator hose?"

"Is it long enough to throw around our necks and hang ourselves from the roof?"

Preston began laughing uncontrollably.

"Noland... you are so ridiculous. I love it!"

Noland didn't respond.

"Are you and Claire coming over this weekend to play cards? Dennis and Patty are coming over and we need a full crew. You guys in?"

"I'm not sure. I'll have to ask Claire. She is all obsessed with getting on the homeowners' association board, so she may not want to do it. We'll probably be scouring the neighborhood trying to get people to vote for her. I just called Pastor Teddy to try and sway his support... whatever, it's not important, but you know how Claire is when she gets her mind set on something."

"Well, let her know she has our support, for sure."

Claire was content that Preston and his wife were supporting her and welcomed the opportunity to court Dennis and Patty as well, figuring that playing cards would be a requirement to keep these people on board with the campaign. She agreed to play, but only if Noland dressed well for the game. Noland attempted to convince Claire that dressing nice would make no difference in how Dennis and Patty felt about her as a board member and reminded Claire that they are friends. This charade was not necessary. She reminded Noland that appearance is fifty percent of any battle and that makes appearance always necessary. She ignored Noland's continued requests until he gave up, sat down, and stuffed envelopes with campaign flyers.

Chapter Seventeen

The Pennington's shift schedule and service areas had not changed since the first day Kalea worked. The restaurant had three areas: the upper deck, which was the south-end of the restaurant where the best tables were located, thus where the richest customers and celebrities were sat. The main floor was the second area of the restaurant where everyone else would be placed, unless they wanted to go outside, which was the third area, the patio.

Kalea quickly learned of this division, and who got the serve the nicer tables, by listening to the other workers talk. At first, she didn't realize how shifts in these various areas were scheduled. Jean-Louis Capelle, the manager, didn't do the scheduling, or much else Kalea would learn, but rather put Jacquelyn Chavis in charge of that duty. She was the most senior of the waitresses, having been at The Pennington for six years. She carried herself professionally with a touch of sexuality, always wearing her long, thick black hair down, shorter skirts, and expensive high heels. Although she never claimed nor admitted her sexuality was anything other than straight, she favored females, especially the girls that showed her the most attention. Those who flirted with Jacquelyn, or possibly did more, were always working with her in the upper deck. Those girls made huge tips. Kalea hadn't realized this about Jacquelyn yet. As with most places that carried an upper class, celebrity, or influential clientele, matters of indiscretion were well hidden.

Kalea moved swiftly, still trying to get the hang of the restaurant's speed. The Hawaiian restaurant was never this quick or this dark. The Pennington always had its lights low with small lamps on the tables, making it hard to see when you entered through the front door and stepped down the small set of stairs into the huge dining room area. The hostess, a young blonde woman named Michelle Dupree, was always at her post near the entrance and took special requests when it came to seating, as long as it was the right people making the right request. Most wanted to be near the Elizabeth Peyton paintings that lined the bay windows across the restaurant's upper deck. Some requested the more intimate area, just off to the side of the paintings. The rest were left to Michelle's mercy.

Jean-Louis, a man who flamed brightly, had worked in the service industry his whole life. Now, in charge of The Pennington, he was adamant about making it the best restaurant in San Francisco. He was a chubby man in his early thirties with a slight French accent, which Kalea thought was phony. His parents brought him to America when he was a baby and raised him in Boston. A Boston accent can destroy any other accent and Jean-Louis had no trace of Boston in him.

He also didn't like what he perceived as slow or sloppy service. He carried himself in an elitist fashion, even though he spent most of his days catering to every whim of any customer that flopped down a gold card. However, with the clientele of the restaurant being San Francisco's upper middle-class and elite, he didn't see it as "serving," but rather he saw himself as an integral part of the social circle that frequented the restaurant. Kalea, as well as most everyone else, just pacified him, thinking to herself: Whatever gets you through the day.

Into her third week on the job, she started to see some payback for her work. She was falling into the groove, masterfully handling more and more tables. She did her studying of cuisine at home and was rapidly becoming a quasi-expert in food pairings, as well as an expert of the Pennington's menu, which was short enough to make quick decisions, yet appealing enough to push customers into taking another look.

Customers were becoming more familiar with Kalea too, so tips got larger, and, in turn, she memorized what they wanted. The tender bread with a delicately brittle crust and feathery white center was always ordered first when regulars Travis and Christina came in. For Dale Shillens, a lieutenant with the San Francisco fire department, it's always the calamari with cannellini bean salad sheltered with a tomato-caper dressing, but the chef had to make sure the calamari was crustless, not a fried tentacle, but chewy, which is often less enviable, but that was the way Dale liked it. Although she was doing well, she didn't get the premium tables. Girls working those were making five times what she did in tips.

Kalea also began to clue in on the restaurant and its ownership, mostly because the owner, Liam C. Walsh, talked loudly on the phone. The nosey gossips at the restaurant filled in the blanks left open by Liam. Kalea heard him tell the story of his grandfather, the owner of DeLuca's Italian Restaurant, a hot spot in the sleepy town of Modesto, California, during the 1930s. One night, without notice, the restaurant closed down and his grandfather ran off to San Francisco, laying low for a while. No one knew where he went or what he was doing. Months later, his grandfather reemerged and opened The Pennington, named after his deceased wife Penny, who died just days before he left Modesto. How she died was still a mystery, never solved, but Liam's story left little doubt as to what happened. The story proved two things, Kalea thought: The Pennington comes from old money, and two, family drama makes for good Italian food while a juicy story with tons of history and exaggeration makes for interest. This place was popular.

Chapter Eighteen

The Pennington was swamped. A line stretched and weaved around the corner of Union Street toward Washington Square, mixing with the dozens of people that were walking up and down the sidewalks of North Beach. It was odd to be this crowded in early December. The bitter wind pushed itself hurriedly against the current of people and a light trickle fell from the sky.

The Pennington was never really crowded during Christmas season, but it was a trendy place for celebrities, politicians, and those who could afford to rub elbows with them. It was Friday when San Francisco Mayor Gavin Newsome and his wife made their way into the restaurant, both looking like they stepped off the cover of a magazine. Michelle, the hostess, smiled, her deep brown eyes widened with a flair of happiness while she escorted the mayor and his wife to their table.

In the back, Kalea hustled to get a drink from the bartender, who seemed to be blowing her off while he got drinks for Jacquelyn and Renee. Andy Taber strolled up next to her and grabbed a few needed cocktail napkins from the bar. Andy was an older man that had been bussing at The Pennington for several years and worked in restaurants most of his life. He was graying a bit, but had a full head of hair and kept in good shape.

"Why does Michelle always sit those people in Jacquelyn's section?"

"What do you mean by 'those people,' Kalea?" Andy asked.

"I mean the rich, famous, and influential. Since I have been here, Jacquelyn's section gets all the motherfuckers that leave insane tips. I haven't seen anything different. It's always the same. When Arnold Schwarzenegger came in the other day… Robin Williams the other week… Sean Penn a couple of nights ago… and now the mayor, not to mention the people who are obviously rich. Michelle always sits them in Jacquelyn's section."

Andy nodded his head and smiled.

"Kalea, Jackie has the most desired section in the restaurant. She sets the schedule and always has the upper deck area. Those are the best seats in the house. Where else would you sit those people?"

I understand that, but it's every time. When someone of notoriety or wealth comes in, she sits them in Jacquelyn's section, even when Jackie's section is crowded. It's no longer the best section when it's overflowing with people. She's forcing those customers to sit at worse tables. I know it's a nicer spot in the restaurant, but when it's overcrowded, my area is nicer… but she still tries to squeeze them in there."

"You really are asking why," Andy replied with a touch of surprise and humor.

"Fuck yes," Kalea said sharply. "It's total bullshit. I need to start getting some better tips. I know Jacquelyn makes more in one night than I do all week."

"Michelle and Jacquelyn… well… have a thing going. Michelle is the hostess, she is getting fucked by Jacquelyn, so of course she is going to make sure that the best customers are in her section. This is why all the girls that are special to Jacquelyn get picked to help serve in the upper deck. What can you do? She sets the schedule and the assignments."

Kalea's heart sank a bit.

"And it becomes a domino effect. They get more tips, they tip the bartenders more money, gets preferential and speedy treatment from the bar, which in turn results in better tips from the people that tip well to begin with…"

Kalea interrupted as she put her drinks on the serving tray.

"I get it, I get it. This is why she schedules herself and her special friends into the upper deck, why I've been standing here for five minutes waiting for drinks to be made, and why I'll get a shitty tip from someone who tips like shit to begin with."

"Now you're catching on."

Kalea turned around and stuffed her check presenter into her pants.

"Just be willing to go down on a girl and things will change."

She waved off Andy playfully and quickly moved to the next table, continuing her shift with a facade of interest and dedication, mulling the rest of the night that a woman with her intelligence and education didn't deserve this... and certainly didn't need to go down on another woman to get a few good tips.

Chapter Nineteen

It was raining hard outside, whipping against the window of the apartment. E.J. sat quietly, focused on paying bills with only the chandelier's light above the small wooden table, which was centered in the apartment's small dining area. He usually had the moonlight as well beaming over his shoulder at night, but clouds had blanketed the city for the past two days. Kalea hummed Aloha Nu`uanu, an old traditional Hawaiian song, while she continued to wash dishes and clean up the kitchen. E.J. recognized the song and knew what it was, although he never fully understood what it was about… a journey of some sort to the island of Ohau.

"Honey, how much did you make in tips this month?"

Kalea dried her hands on a dishrag and drifted into the dining area.

"About $1,000."

"That's all?" E.J. said surprised. "I know you're only part time, but that place is loaded with the richest people in town."

"Well, it should be a lot more, at least double. But I don't get the premium slots or areas yet… I'm going to do my best to change some things at work with shifts and such."

"Well, you've only been there a few weeks… It takes time."

"True," Kalea said. "But there are some horribly slow waitresses that get those shifts and I've been doing my homework as to why they do. It's a fucked situation I don't want to get into… I know my job better than some of these so-called veterans."

E.J. looked back and forth through his finance ledger, an old yellow notepad that was marred with chicken scratch. The numbers at the bottom of the notebook didn't look right. E.J. added again, his fingers moving swiftly over the calculator.

"You know, I make $52,000 a year at the paper, but I think there is something wrong."

"What's wrong?"

E.J. didn't respond. He picked up his pay stubs, a pencil, and began scrawling down the numbers off of his check. The calculator again was smothered hurriedly with his hand, his eyes shifting back and forth for a few moments as numbers flashed back at him, reflecting in the lenses of his glasses.

"E.J.?" Kalea asked again. "Hello? What's going on?"

E.J. stopped hammering the calculator and wrote a few final numbers on the notepad, circling the last one: $41,500.

"If I add up my gross pay from my past paychecks, it comes out to just over \$40,000… \$41,500 to be exact. There is something wrong."

"Are we okay?" Kalea asked with concern in her voice.

"Well, we're fine right now, but without your tips, I think we would be headed for some real trouble."

"I thought you figured out that we would be okay with your salary."

"Well, we would be okay with the \$52,000 a year I supposedly make, but they have my salary wrong."

E.J. lifted his head, leaned it back with his eyes shooting into the ceiling. He wiped his mouth, biting down on his thumb hard with frustration as he rested his hand on his chin. Numbers coursed through his head, along with the details of the continuing battles at work, the failed stories, the never-ending days in the newsroom, and the strain of barely seeing Kalea. Exhausted from long hours, and now facing a new problem, frustration consumed him.

"Jesus-fucking-Christ! I'm going to have to talk with human resources in the morning. This is wrong."

Kalea wrapped her arms around E.J. from behind, saying nothing and giving him a kiss on his cheek.

"I'm sorry I'm dragging you through all of this," E.J. said. "I knew it would be a difficult transition coming all the way out here, but it's a bit more than I thought it would be."

Kalea remained silent and just hugged E.J. a bit harder. She had nothing to add.

The human resources' office was located on the tenth floor of the Press-Journal Tower. It was remodeled into an updated office: a very typical bland, cubicle drenched, square space with a lot of shirts and ties wandering around. It was the only floor in the tower that was stripped of its original character, mainly because the floor was damaged during a fire in 1968. They tried to restore what they could, but when it got too expensive to update the space to modernize it for the Internet age, while still keeping its original look, they just remodeled the entire floor as cheaply as possible, something the owners of the paper were good at doing.

E.J. sat in the office quietly while Angelica Grayson looked over the top of her glasses, which rested on the tip of her nose. E.J. could see the reflection of the computer screen in the lenses which flickered every few seconds as she continued to punch information into the computer.

"Well according to my records, your salary is $41,500 per year."

"There must be some mistake," E.J. replied kindly. "I was hired at $52,000."

Angelica lifted her brow and stared at E.J. with cold, dead eyes. With no emotion existing in her voice, she told him he would have to talk with the editors.

It took two hours to track Noland down. He was only where he was suppose to be and was a ghost the rest of the time. Some rumors claimed he would just disappear to get away from the place. Others said, despite his outward appearance of being a family man, he would frequent a call girl he saw regularly. E.J. didn't have a hard time believing either one. The Press-Journal could drive anyone to hide, and Noland was the model for the midlife crisis. He drove a 1965 Ford Mustang, always sported dark aviator glasses, and wore clothes more fitting of someone half his age. E.J. waited, knowing that Noland had to be back at the office by 4:00 p.m. to edit stories.

A knock on Noland's door broke him out of his concentration. He shook his head, irritated that he was being bothered while trying to finish editing a story for the Sunday edition. He picked up the half-filled ashtray and the Marlboro Reds on his desk, quickly slipping them into the top drawer of his desk.

"Can I talk with you?" E.J. asked as he slid his body halfway through the door into Noland's office.

Noland reached into his sports coat and removed a pack of mints, popping one into his mouth and faking a smile while offering E.J. a seat.

"What can I do for you?"

E.J. sat down on the small leather sofa that rested next to the desk in the modestly-sized office. The room looked like a treasure trove of bad knick-knacks, silk plants, and old newspaper articles that had been framed and hung on the wall. E.J. adjusted his jacket, pulling out the employment contract that Angelica Grayson had given him earlier.

"I discovered that my salary is wrong. Mrs. Grayson in human resources gave me this."

The printout with salary and terms of employment passed from E.J.'s hands to Noland's. He quickly scanned the document, flinging a few pages, and then handed it back to E.J.

"What's the problem? This is correct."

"No it isn't. Look on page three. It says I make 41,500 a year. I was hired at $52,000 a year. Remember? That's what we agreed upon when I accepted the job. I guess it was just printed wrong on the contract I signed."

Noland thought for a moment before reopening the pages of the contract, trying to figure out where the miscommunication happened.

"Oh, I know what's going on," Noland said brightly. "The general assignment position starts at $41,500. That's why it's different."

E.J. curled his eyes, confused, but aware that something wasn't right. What he thought was a mistake began to appear as a "don't ask, don't tell" situation. Noland put the contract down with a completed look on his face.

"Is that all?" Noland asked.

E.J. sat up a little higher.

"No, that's not all. This isn't what we agreed on," E.J. said with a rise in his voice. "We agreed that I would start at $52,000. I don't understand. You see the $41,500 salary on page three. That wasn't our agreement. Why don't you understand that?"

Noland raised his hand up slightly a nodded, acting as if he just figured out where the miscommunication happened.

"Oh, I see. I'm sorry... you're confused. We agreed on your position, not a salary. When you came in on your first day of work, we assigned you a new position as the general assignment reporter and you accepted. That position just happens to have a lower salary than the assistant city reporter position."

E.J. coiled back in his chair. His heart began to race and his hands became warm, tingling at the fingertips. He was angry, not just at the fact that he was not getting the salary promised, but more so at the reality that Noland was acting like nothing was wrong, as if E.J. agreed to all of this. Noland just sat in his chair, staring at E.J. with gentle disregard, as if he didn't understand what E.J.'s problem was.

"That's bullshit!" E.J. belted. "Part of the reason I took this job, in good faith, is because it paid just enough to live in San Francisco. I can't live on this."

Noland straightened up in his chair, mad at the swift realization that his reporter was accusing him of something he didn't do, or at least had no proof of doing, which was the same in Noland's mind. His temper quickly took over, but not to defend himself from any accusations, not to defend his, or the newspaper's honor, nor to defend his honesty, but to protect his own ego from taking any damage from a young punk green journalist. He was a small and petty man and it whistled clear in the irate tone of his voice.

"I'm sorry you misunderstood, but that's not my problem! That's yours!" Noland shouted. "You better realize that you're in a position that every first-year journalist would kill to be in. Remember where you are at, but if that isn't working for you, then leave!"

"I moved 2,000 miles to get here! You know damn well I just can't get up and leave!"

"Then suck it up and grow some balls! Stop whining about the money and be grateful for the opportunity!"

E.J. jumped up, clenched his fist, and for a brief moment, thought about hitting the man. Noland stood up, ready for a confrontation. E.J. stepped back and nodded his head, silently staring hard into Noland's eyes, letting him know he was aware of what was going on. He turned and stormed out of the office. He complained to Walter, but Walter offered nothing, because there was nothing he would offer. E.J.'s pay would not budge. When E.J. told a group of senior coworkers what had been going on, and how he was going to fix it somehow, they all laughed a bit on the inside. They had been at the paper a long time and knew the game, but none of them would say that openly. E.J. would find out on his own that everyone understood, everyone was sorry, but nothing would ever change.

Chapter Twenty

It was New Year's Eve. E.J. and Kalea found themselves at Colston's Restaurant, near Marina Street and Fillmore in the Marina District. It was an upscale place, but delicately cozy and unpretentious. The sky was clear and the biting cold wind was stronger than it had been the past few days. E.J. wore a thick car coat, black sports jacket, slacks, and black Ralph Lauren shoes. Kalea wore her little white off-shoulder dress with a sleek, cream faux fur stroller jacket. Audette had just shown up, coming to the bar from a late shift at Bookmarks. Kalea looked at her watch realizing that Andy, her favorite busboy, was now thirty minutes late as well. He probably got tied up at The Pennington, she thought. He wasn't answering his phone. Audette kissed Kalea on the cheek, said hi, and headed for E.J., who was at the pool table with Jeffery. He didn't see Audette come up from behind him, screwing up his shot. Jeffery smiled as her and E.J. embraced, introducing himself to Audette after E.J. put her down from the twirling hug he gave her. Kalea giggled at the two as she ordered another strawberry margarita. Audette came back to the bar, looking for Andy.

"Where is that little son-of-a-bitch?" Audette asked.

Kalea explained his schedule, but Audette didn't seem to care too much about why Andy wasn't there, just irritated that he wasn't there.

"That bastard still owes me fifty bucks from the 49ers' game last week," she said, wiping off the cue stick's blue chalk that scraped her pants when she hugged E.J. She was casually dressed, nice jeans, Romanstii shirt, and a baseball cap.

"I think he is a bit wounded emotionally that you called that game so accurately. A girl beat the self-proclaimed guru of football," Kalea responded. "He isn't happy about losing."

"Well, I don't care if he is emotionally wounded. My cell phone bill is emotionally wounded too, so I need that money."

Kalea laughed and entertained Audette's playful tirade, never faulting Audette for not telling Andy that her two brothers played briefly in the NFL, and that football was in her DNA, even though she was "just a girl."

"So, how's work? Getting better tables yet?" asked Audette.

"No, not yet... still working on that... it's better than Bookmarks, but it's not without its issues. Is Shelia still pissed off?"

"Well, I still hear rumblings every so often... rumors others share, but that's been going on for months. Shelia still won't talk about it directly. She has been acting like you never existed. You really embarrassed her."

"She can go fuck herself," Kalea said, swigging down another drink of her margarita.

"I heard about E.J.'s pay."

"Audette, I'm so sick of that newspaper. He never stops working. He doesn't make shit and I have to double-up shifts at work to cover the difference, which means I'm never around. I never see him anymore... it's almost like I'm forgetting why I'm with him, why we're here, what we're doing."

Audette put her arm around her.

"I know, but give it some time... things will get better."

"You know Audette, E.J. never makes mistakes... but moving out here, I think may have been one. You know what I gave up to come here? Everything. But in exchange I would have E.J... I don't even have him anymore."

Audette hugged her harder, told a joke to lighten the mood, and assured her that she would be okay.

"Enough of this buzz kill," Audette said. "It's New Year's Eve and all problems must stay home for tonight."

E.J. and Jeffery finished their pool game and headed outside. They talked mostly about work. Jeffery offered his condolences about E.J.'s pay, but he wasn't surprised. He himself had only received minor raises and those only came after winning major awards. He wouldn't tell E.J. this, but he always thought the paper did these types of things on purpose. They did something very similar to him when he was hired three years ago. They also did the same thing to Kenny Wallace, a reporter they had hired a year earlier. The paper offered him a certain job and did the same type of bait and switch, knowing that was the only way they would get the kid to accept the position. Kenny lost $15,000 a year accepting a different position. It took him six months to realize it and Kenny quit when the editors played dumb: They too acted like it was a big misunderstanding and changed nothing. Jeffery knew it was a dirty move the company routinely did. It happened to him, he saw Kenny go through the same thing, and now witnessed it happening to E.J. Although Jeffery refused to fully acknowledge this, even to himself, because he would also have to admit he was duped too, deep down inside he knew what had happened to E.J.

"It's a tough business, not meant for the weak," Jeffery exclaimed, as he made his way with E.J. to the far table that sat near the end of the bar's patio, which overlooked the marina. "You have to make your own opportunities. That's why it's so cutthroat. Everyone is out for themselves... how is Kalea handling all of this?"

"Not really good," E.J. answered. "This is the first night in a very long time we have been out and in good spirits. Even Christmas I had to work... it's been bad. Between her job and my job, we hardly see each other. Now with my lower pay, she has to pick up even more shifts to cover our bills. We're bickering a lot more and fighting."

"Man, I'm sorry to hear that. You have to hang in there. Do everything you can to keep it together and take every opportunity that comes your way."

E.J. nodded, unsure.

Jeffery put down his cigarette and held his glass up to the moonlit sky. The night's illumination danced off of his martini glass. Jeffery looked over to E.J.

"See that light E.J.? Beautiful… The Bay Area has to be one of the nicest places to live on this planet."

Jeffery put down his glass and picked his cigarette back up.

"Look at the job this way," Jeffery continued. "Fuck the newspaper. Who cares about them? They don't care about you. The only thing you should care about is their circulation, their penetration, and their reputation… and the opportunity to break a huge story. Just one huge story… then you get the national coverage, you get the book deals, and television appearances. In the end, this is how you get a premier job, guaranteed… guaran-fuckin'-teed. It can be done at the Press-Journal. The opportunity is here."

"I'm learning that," E.J. said. "I just thought there would be more altruistic reasons to do this type of work. Media is still very important."

Jeffery laughed softly.

"Maybe at one time it was, but not so much anymore. Don't get me wrong, there are some great people in media doing good work… that's how I see myself. However, I don't want to stay at the

Press-Journal indefinitely, unless I'm the head-honcho and can call the shots. Turn that paper into what it should be. Either way, there are bigger and better things."

The two paused for a moment.

"You know, Jeffery, I have a huge story in the works. A major story that's been grinding me for weeks, but I've been having a hard time getting my hands on some documents."

Jeffery nodded, but said nothing.

"There is this school district in Fremont that hired a new superintendent back in September. This guy has a history of abuse and mental issues…"

Jeffery pulled back and immediately interrupted in a hard tone.

"Whoa, slow down boss, don't say anymore. I don't want to know. Talk to the editors about your stories."

E.J. was taken aback. Warren did the same thing, refusing to hear about a story.

"I don't understand," E.J. said. "Why don't you want to hear about my lead?"

Jeffery smiled.

"Around here… probably at most major news outlets, it's bad to tell other reporters your leads. Someone could steal them. At the Press-Journal, they will steal them."

"Are you planning on stealing this?" E.J. asked jokingly.

Jeffery laughed.

"No, I'm not stealing anything, but it's best to practice restraint at all times. The vultures are out there and you never know who is listening. You can't get comfortable, even with those that you know would never do that."

E.J. blindly agreed, but wondered: How could someone steal your story and then face you the next day? Maybe if the story was big enough they would, ultimately resulting in what Jeffery said would happen, moving up to the national news in some other big-time place. Not a bad exit strategy. It's not like anyone is particularly close to anyone in the newsroom, E.J. thought to himself. The newsroom was almost always void of any real personal conversation. There was a lot of talk, a lot of camaraderie, a lot of noise, but it always boiled down to just business. Everyone moved alone, sifting through each day, waiting, mining, and hoping to strike gold… and maybe, according to Jeffery, steal something huge from others if given the chance to do so.

Jeffery nudged E.J.

"Let's find the girls. It's going to be midnight in ten minutes."

The two disappeared into the crowd. The rest of the night was a blur.

Chapter Twenty-One

The Pennington was crowded and Jean-Louis was frantically trying to keep everyone happy. Jacquelyn had called in sick, presumably from drinking the night before. It was her birthday. Michelle had called in sick too… they were out together. Kalea and Andy had a laugh in the kitchen while talking about the two women, mostly about their affair with a string of dirty jokes about them going down on each other. Diane, another waitress that was known to sleep with Jacquelyn when she and Michelle were fighting, made it to work, even though she went out with them as well. She looked hung over, which upset Jean-Louis. Short-staffed, Jean-Louis took over some hosting duties and tried to rearrange the sections to cover the absences, a hung-over employee, and a new girl, Mayra, who was still learning the ropes. With heavy traffic during the dinner rush, Kalea became one of The Pennington's only hopes for a successful service.

Kalea, for the first time, had Jacquelyn's section, as well as her own, and was making more money in the first hour than she had made all week. Jean-Louis made his way around the tables, a nervous wreck. He kept encouraging the waitresses and the bartender Kevin, a yuppie-type with a nice smile and sharp wit, to make sure motivation stayed high.

"Kalea," Jean-Louis said, stopping her in mid-stride. "Make sure Mr. Arrington at table six is taken care of, okay? He is good friends with the owner."

"I know, I know. Jean… stop and let me do my job, okay? We're short-staffed. Service is going to be a bit slower." Kalea replied with a softened assertive tone.

Jean-Louis smirked.

"I don't want to hear any excuses, just get it done. Make it happen, okay?"

"Look Jean," she said, her voiced raised. "You could clean a floor with a toothbrush just as well as with a mop, it's just going to take a lot longer. Understand? We're short-staffed and we're moving as fast as possible."

Jean-Louis just stood silent.

"Now, if you don't mind Jean, I'm busy…"

The front door opened and Jean-Louis lost eye contact with Kalea, her voice instantly disappearing from his head when he noticed who it was that walked in: It was Bailey Walcott

"Are you okay?" Kalea asked.

"Look Kalea, We'll talk about this later," Jean-Louis said, snapping back from the distraction. "Look at the man that just walked in."

Myra, not seeing anyone near the gentleman, rushed over to seat the man.

"Good, good," Jean-Louis blurted. "Mayra is putting him in the nicest section."

Kalea looked across the room as Mayra led him to his seat. He was a middle-aged white man with salt and pepper hair, perfectly cut, wearing an expensive Armani suit, Rolex watch, and black-framed Versace eyeglasses. She recognized the man, but couldn't exactly place who he was.

"Who is that? He looks familiar."

"That's Bailey Walcott. He is the food critic for *The Napa*. He also has a show on the Food Network. We're being reviewed, I'm sure. This is huge for the restaurant."

Jean-Louis began to lightly shake, and sweat started beading-up on his forehead when he realized that tonight's service could make him or break him. He took a deep breath and calmed down. Kalea told him to relax. Jean-Louis sat on a barstool and collected himself for a few seconds.

"Look Kalea, I need you to make sure that man over there is taken extra special care of, okay?" Jean-Louis said. "Just be delightful, cordial, and don't do, or say anything to upset him. For the next hour, you're the best waitress in the world."

Kalea nodded, gathered her check presenter, and made her way toward Walcott's table. Jean-Louis jumped from the stool and gathered the rest of the staff for a quick rally before going into the kitchen to talk with the chef. Kalea composed herself while Walcott thumbed through the wine list that was sitting on the table.

"Good evening sir. My name is Kalea and I will be your server tonight."

Kalea sat the food menu down on the table while Walcott continued to stare at the wine list, never making eye contact.

"Can I get you something to drink before you order?"

"Is this all the wine that you have?" he asked dryly, still staring into the wine list.

"I believe so," Kalea said with a soft tone.

"You believe so?" Walcott replied condescendingly, quickly shifting his eyes into Kalea's. "Are you not my server? Shouldn't you know what you serve?"

Kalea smiled despite her immediate irritation at Walcott's comment. She tried to respond affably and respectfully, but her mildly insolent personality would shine through the cracks of that feeble facade.

"If you wish, I can ask if there is other wine available, but I believe that if we had other wines, they would be on the list, otherwise, why would we have the wine?"

Walcott simply turned his head away and ordered a glass of GuillonMazis-Chambertin Grand Cru, 1994.

Kalea excused herself and headed back to the kitchen where Jean-Louis waited for her. He was nervous and became a bit angry when she called Walcott an asshole, recounting the exchange the two had moments earlier. Jean-Louis reminded Kalea that she needed to do whatever it would take to make him feel like a king.

"I hope you understand what this means to the restaurant," he said, nerves racing through his voice.

"Look, I'm a damn good server and have worked in a restaurant before," she snapped. "I treat everyone kindly and with respect. I don't care who anyone is. But keep in mind Jean, my job is not to be talked to like a member of some subhuman race and I won't stand for it. If that's a problem, get someone else to serve him."

Jean-Louis considered it, but realized that switching servers might look bad. He had been waiting for a moment like this since he took the manager's job two years ago and felt that his career was hanging on the words that would be printed in *The Napa*. For Jean-Louis, this was the biggest night of his career and he could do nothing as his fate, and the fate of The Pennington, sat in Kalea's hands.

"Just don't say any more than you have to, okay?"

Jean-Louis made his way to the table to introduce himself while Kalea got Walcott his wine. Jean-Louis was smiling and laughing, nervously forced, as Walcott remained stoic and flippant as the exchange dragged out. Kalea made her way back to the table where Jean-Louis attempted an awkward introduction between the two before excusing himself. Walcott sat the menu down while she gently placed the wine on the table, smiling, and mentally preparing herself to be as pleasant as possible.

"What would you recommend to go with the Grand Cru?" Walcott asked.

"It pairs well with the grilled breast of duck, roasted rack of lamb, venison, as well as any of the earthy cheeses," Kalea responded confidently, using the knowledge she gained from growing up with an uncle that had an enology degree, along with the knowledge she gained with her time in restaurants.

"Venison? You would recommend this with venison?" Walcott responded coldly.

"Sure," she replied. "The dark berries, griotte, vanilla, toast, and smoky bacon hints of this wine's vintage are great with venison."

Walcott did not react to the statement.

"I'll have the red salmon," he said, putting the menu down.

"Although that's a fine dish, and not too bad with your wine choice, I would go with one of my recommendations, sir. May I suggest the lemongrass-grilled rack of lamb with tamarind sauce? It is superb with the Grand Cru burgundy."

Walcott looked at Kalea coldly.

"I believe I ordered."

Kalea headed back to the kitchen and was stopped by Jean-Louis as she passed through the double doors and hung up the order for the cooks. Jean-Louis started to ask her a bunch of questions, one after another in a slight panic. Kalea pulled him aside to escape the banging of pans, the clamor of cooking, and the white noise that filled the kitchen as orders were put in and filled.

"How did it go?"

"He asked me about recommendations and what wine goes good with what dish. He's an asshole, but… whatever. He ordered the red salmon."

"You didn't have any type of exchange, did you? Straight forward, right?"

"He challenged me a bit on meals that go with the wine he ordered. I corrected him. Other than that, it was fine."

"You corrected one of the country's most respected food critics?"

"Being a well respected food critic still doesn't make the wrong answer right. He wanted a burgundy with salmon and he was asking for my opinion, and I told him it wasn't the best choice. He got a little upset and tried to correct me. That's all."

Jean-Louis's mouth dropped open and his face became red. His voice hit Kalea like an earthquake.

"I told you not to say anything unless you had to! Why are you correcting him!? Are you fucking deaf or just stupid!?"

"Look! Even though I don't think this job will change the world, it's a job I take seriously because I take all my jobs seriously. I serve, so I do it to the best of my ability. I was trying to be a good server by offering suggestions that would give him the best meal experience! This is the crap you told me to do during orientation, so I'm just following procedure, as I see it, you jackass!"

Jean-Louis stormed the other direction and began to stand tall over the cooks as they prepared Walcott's dinner, barking at them as he saw fit, randomly picking them apart as they hustled to get all of the food out to the tables. Kalea continued to serve people, returning to Walcott's table with his food. Walcott looked somewhat disinterested in the meal, poked around it with his fork and knife for a moment, before putting the utensils down.

"Is there anything else I can get you, sir?"

Walcott sat back in his chair and sighed.

"You can replace my order. This food is cold. You waited too long to get this out to me."

Kalea stared at the steaming mound of food, her hand still very warm from carrying it out. She took the food right out from the kitchen the minute it was done. Walcott hadn't even physically touched the meal.

"Maybe you should actually taste the food before you say it is cold," Kalea said in an assertive tone, still trying to remain friendly.

Walcott turned his head and curled his brow with a bit of shock in his eye, stunned that anyone, especially a waitress, would question him about anything at all, let alone the one thing he considered himself the premier expert in.

"Maybe you should take it back now while this restaurant is still open," he replied angrily.

"Look, sir, the only difference between this dish and another is about 10 minutes," Kalea said, her patience wearing thin. "They don't get any warmer without being overcooked. We don't serve overcooked food."

Jean-Louis saw the exchange from the kitchen and quickly made his way to the table, fearing the worst.

"Is there a problem here?" Jean-Louis asked, his voice uneven.

"I complained about the temperature of my meal and your waitress assured me that it is, in fact, perfectly cooked and that replacing it was only a waste of time... she also suggested I taste it first before I judge whether it is of proper temperature."

Jean-Louis began to breathe heavily, sending Kalea back to the kitchen for a break and apologizing profusely to Walcott, who sat with little reaction. When offered to replace the dinner, Walcott declined and ate the meal.

Outside, behind the restaurant, Andy cussed up a storm after Kalea told him what happened.

"Bullshit!" Andy screamed as Kalea nodded and continued to smoke a cigarette. "Who the fuck does he think he is?!"

Jean-Louis came barreling out the back door, ordering Andy back inside.

"Do you realize what you did in there?!" Jean-Louis shouted rhetorically.

Kalea continued to smoke as her boss ripped into her about the incident, most of which she tuned out as she finished smoking, the white noise of Jean-Louis' screaming passed through her with little impact.

"If I had my way, you would be fired tonight! This incident will be noted,"

Kalea threw down her cigarette and mashed it into the concrete.

"Go fuck yourself Jean..." she said, as she walked toward the bus stop.

Chapter Twenty-Two

Jean-Louis came rushing into the restaurant like a screaming bullet into the wind, waving a magazine in the air, and babbling some inaudible chatter. Kalea and the rest of the staff crowded around the bar, quietly talking about Liam Walsh, The Pennington's owner, who had stopped by the restaurant on his way home. Liam, casually dressed in blue jeans and a white button-up shirt, sat at a table in the back going through some paperwork. He had just returned from Paris. Jean-Louis had just returned from the newsstand.

"Mr. Walsh, Mr. Walsh," he belted as he whizzed past everyone else standing at the bar.

Liam lifted his head out of the paperwork, unmoved by Jean-Louis's excitement. He smiled and put everything down.

"Yes Mr. Capelle?"

Jean-Louis handed the magazine to Liam who raced his eyes across the top. In large black bolded print it read "The Napa." Below the mast was a stirring, bright picture of North Beach's landscape, with the Coit Tower standing in the background. Settled in the right margin of the magazine was the cover story: "Bailey Walcott Tastes the Best and Worst of What North Beach Offers." Liam flipped the magazine open.

"Are we in this?" Liam asked.

"Part of the cover story, sir."

Kalea and the rest of the staff gazed upon the two, eavesdropping on their conversation.

"What the hell is that about?" Andy asked.

"Holy shit," Kalea let out. "That must be Walcott's review. Fuck, if it's half as bad as the exchange I had with him when I served that son-of-a-bitch, I'm going to get fired."

"Well it can't be a bad review," said Marco, a busboy that had become Kalea's favorite smoking-break buddy since she started working.

"Yeah, right. Do you not remember that night?"

"No, I remember, but why would Jean-Louis come running in here shoving the magazine in Walsh's face if it was a bad review?"

Marco grabbed a few napkins from the plastic container over on the far side of the bar.

"Think about that missy," he said with a laugh as he headed to set some tables.

"I… don't… know… why…" Kalea trailed confusingly as she attempted to figure out what was going on.

Liam began reading the article out loud as Jean-Louis stood close by, smiling and nodding his head in an approving fashion. In striking detail, The Pennington was praised by Walcott. Kalea became confused, wondering what had happened between the time Walcott left seemingly angry and frustrated to the time when his fingers hit the keyboard. It didn't make any sense. As Liam read, the fog of confusion began to lift off of the story. Walcott had faked the whole thing.

"He did it on purpose," Kalea said out loud, but not to anyone in particular.

"Who did what?" Andy asked confused, still filling out his time card.

"Walcott. He acted like an asshole just to test the service here… he purposely ordered a bad combination to see if I would correct him, like I'm supposed to do… he was acting like a dick to test us… we passed… I passed."

Andy looked over at Liam and Jean-Louis as they read the article. Kalea smiled knowing that Jean-Louis was going to eat crow for the things he said to her that night. He was going to apologize. He was going to recognize what she did for him and for the restaurant. He was going to tell Liam everything that had happened. But as Kalea listened, Jean-Louis said nothing about her. He began telling a dramatic story of his management, his hands and face animated, as he recounted all of the things he did to make sure Bailey Walcott's experience at The Pennington was extraordinary. He went on, never mentioning Kalea, taking all the credit. Liam simply smiled more and more as Jean-Louis conveyed his spurious conversation with the award-winning food critic and lied about how Bailey Walcott praised him, the restaurant, and the food.

"Mr. Walsh, he was one extraordinary man and we shared so much that night… but you can read all about that in the review," Jean-Louis continued.

"You know Jean, this is something that is really going to finally solidify us as the premier restaurant in San Francisco," Liam said joyously. "I mean we already are one of the top spots, but this validates everything that we are doing, and validates that we are doing it better than so many others."

"I know Mr. Walsh and I'm happy to be leading that charge."

"I knew you were the right guy to manage this place… I think you may be seeing a bit more money in your checks."

"Really sir?" Jean-Louis asked. "Thank you so much."

Kalea stood staggered as Andy looked on.

"Wow, that doesn't sound like the story I heard," Andy said.

"That pompous son-of-a-bitch…"

Kalea stared at Jean-Louis, refraining from doing or saying anything in front of Liam. Liam graciously gave Jean-Louis the magazine back and he headed for the kitchen. Kalea followed him, stopping him just as the kitchen doors swung closed.

"Excuse me Jean, do you have a moment,"

"Sure," Jean-Louis said happily, not knowing what the conversation would be about.

"How dare you take credit for what happened with Bailey Walcott."

Jean-Louis's smile dropped instantly.

"That's right," Kalea continued. "I heard everything you said to Mr. Walsh. Would you care to explain?"

Jean-Louis stumbled out a few words, trying to soften the blow that was being thrown at him.

"I'm not sure what exactly you're referring to…"

"Don't even start, you degenerate piece of shit! You're a lying, self-serving coward! How the fuck can you stand there and try to act like this is something other than what it is!?"

Jean-Louis interrupted, trying to calm the situation down.

"Hold up there, I think we all were a bit stressed out that night… it was heated, but that's restaurant work when you're short-staffed and busy, and yes, a major food critic coming in, I mean… no big deal."

"Fuck that!" Kalea screamed. "You just took all the goddamn credit knowing damn well I'm the one that made the right calls, handled the situation, gave him exactly what is expected, and what's deserved by a professional: Good service! If I would have listened to you, we would have been fucked in that article… and if that was the case, you would have laid that failure on me! Are you going to tell me to my face otherwise?!"

Jean-Louis tried to talk calmly.

"We're a team here…"

Kalea cut him off.

"You should be ashamed of yourself... I don't know how you could take the credit, never mentioning what I did, what really happened. You're fucking shameless. At least have the balls to say it to me now, in private. We both know the truth, so admit it."

Jean-Louis said nothing, his face dipped down slightly, his eyes away from Kalea.

"I figured as much," Kalea said sharply. "Now, if you'll excuse me, I have to get back to work."

Kalea tightened her apron, grabbed her check presenter and quickly left to a table where a young couple had just sat down. With a brilliant smile and a soft, pleasing voice, she asked if she could take their order.

Chapter Twenty-Three

E.J. sat at his desk, staring at the phone. It hadn't rung all morning. For the past few days he had been lucky enough to only get superficial filler stories assigned to him, so they were easy to finish. He had the afternoons to go after the new Fremont school superintendent David Finch, but hadn't been able to track down anyone he wanted to interview. He called the school district's human resources office and David Finch himself. Nothing. He went to the school twice and everyone seemed to be avoiding him. It's like they knew he was coming, seemingly disappearing at all the right times. He kept thinking about the dead ends as he stared at the phone.

"Is that phone talking to you or something? You've been looking at it for a long time," said Skye as he sat down, popped the lid off of his coffee, and dumped two packs of sugar into it.

"I'm hitting dead ends on that story about David Finch."

"Oh fuck… been there and done that," Skye said with some sincerity. "No one's getting back to you?"

"It's weird. I'm not telling them what I want to talk about, just leaving messages that I want to talk to them. I mean, I know a few people may not call back, but all of them? I've called ten people in that district… not one call back. Every time I go down to their offices, they're conveniently not there."

E.J. leaned deep into his chair, tilted his head back, and sighed.

"I don't get it."

Skye sat silently for a moment.

"You haven't heard anything from anyone, at all?" he asked E.J.

"Not one call back."

"What about the editors? Have you talked with them about it?"

E.J. sat up.

"Are you kidding? After that debacle with Donald Tate and the illegal Union City shopping center deal? I'm not going to tell them anything until I have something solid."

Skye quickly shook his head approvingly.

"I agree, I agree…"

Skye swung around back to his computer.

"Well, keep trying there champ. That's all you can do."

E.J. picked up the phone and called Glenn Flannery, the contractor and PTA member who gave him the initial tip about David Finch. Glenn's son was a football player at Mission San Jose High School, nestled at the base of Fremont's rolling hills in the Mission San Jose District. Glenn was very active in the school. He never told E.J. how he found out about David Finch, just gave E.J. some direction. When E.J. explained to Glenn what roadblocks he was running into, Glenn wasn't surprised. He knew something was happening and told E.J. they should meet up for lunch.

Cornerstones was a popular place at night, but was slow during lunch and close to Glenn's job. E.J. wondered why it was so abandoned since they served good food for relatively cheap prices. He ordered a Portobello mushroom hamburger and washed it down with a beer, sitting on the back patio waiting for Glenn to arrive. There were only two other groups at the restaurant. It was a ghost town. When Glenn showed up, E.J. bought him a drink and the two began to talk, retracing the steps that E.J. took while combing through the sources Glenn had given to him. It began to become clear what was happening.

"I'll tell you this," Glenn said swallowing a drink. "I talked with a teacher friend of mine and he told me that he thinks Finch has already been contacted by somebody. There are some strange rumors running through the district as well as the PTA. No details, but it sounds like something is up. I'm sure that's why no one is calling you back."

"Ah fuck! Did another reporter get to these people?"

"I don't know. I assumed it was you, otherwise I would have called and let you know someone else was snooping around. I have been laying low because my son is the starting running back and if he does well, he will land a college scholarship… I didn't want to get involved, you know, in case the district retaliates against my boy."

E.J. snuffed out the cigarette he was smoking.

"Well, it wasn't me. Probably somebody from the San Jose Union News," E.J. said.

"I couldn't tell you E.J. All I know is something is brewing."

"Did you tell anyone else about Finch?"

"No, I didn't say shit to anyone... I mean, other people may know, but I don't know anyone that has gone to the media," Glenn said. "As far as I can tell, you're the only reporter that knows anything about this. That's why I assumed it was you causing a stir."

E.J. shook his head.

"I'm so fucking close and then this shit happens. I know it's the San Jose paper that's on this… I'm sure of it."

Glenn took another drink and sat confused..

"I'm sorry. I don't know anything else."

"Well, it's not your fault, Glenn."

E.J. finished his food and lit another cigarette, his face drawn with frustration.

"Things haven't been going well at the paper... or at home with my girl. I really needed this story. It's huge. I can't get beat."

Glenn took the last swig of his beer.

"Sorry to hear that," Glenn said sincerely. "I wish I could help ya."

E.J. headed back to work to finish the two other bullshit general assignment stories that were facing deadline. When he got home at 11p.m., the apartment was empty. Kalea was still at work so he went to bed, but didn't sleep well. All he could think about was trying to find a way to get this story before it was published elsewhere.

The conference room at the Press-Journal was unusually quiet the next morning. Except for Noland softly babbling about baseball to one of the sports reporters, all you could hear were people sipping coffee, jotting down notes on their pads, and the occasional yawning. E.J. sat quietly going over the Finch story in his head, despite the fact that he was in the middle of trying to finish two other stories: One about the BART train extension into San Jose and some random story about a UC Berkeley professor who powers his house on solar energy and recycled fast-food grease. He was becoming frustrated and worried. He wanted to tell the editors what he was doing, but was afraid if the San Jose Union News published the story first, then he would get reamed for getting scooped. He was tired, spending a large portion of the night tossing and turning, going over every possible scenario in his head. He talked about it with Kalea at breakfast that morning, but she said very little, pissed-off that E.J. didn't seem to care about the Bailey Walcott incident. He could not get it out of his head. He thought about it on his way to work, when he stopped by the store to pick up coffee and donuts, thought about it when he hung his jacket on the chair at his desk, and was thinking about it as he sat at the conference table listening to garbled trade rumors concerning the Oakland Athletics, the sips of beverages, chicken scratch, and yawns.

"What are you working on today?" asked Walter as he sat his large frame into the chair at the head of the table. Noland and the sports reporter ended their conversation while others gathered their notes.

"I'll have the follow-up on the bus wreck from yesterday," Jeffery volunteered, "Plus the story about Union City's misappropriation of Measure V funds... there wasn't a whole lot there, but none-the-less, that's in the can by two 'o clock."

"I thought we were onto something big with that," Noland said, a bit concerned.

"I'd explain it, but it's a long story. You'll read it and see," Jeffery responded. "I want to get out of here, so let's just get this meeting moving."

"Great. We'll be waiting for that one. I'm happy that giving the BART story to E.J. freed up your time to finish that, blockbuster or not," said Walter. "Are you going to have the BART extension story done E.J.?"

"It will be in the system by noon," E.J. said flatly. "The solar-powered college professor will be in by five for the weekend paper."

Walter nodded and continued on.

"Skye, where are you with, eh... the story we have been working on?"

E.J. took notice of the tone in Walter's voice, a type of secrecy that he had heard a number of times when reporters were working on huge pieces.

"Well, I would like to talk with one or two other sources, but, seriously, it's pretty much done," Skye responded with hesitation in is voice. "You saw some of the rough drafts. It's your call on this."

"What do you think Noland?" Walter asked, ignoring Victoria, who was nodding like she had any real say in the matter.

"I don't think we want to get beat on this story and with amount of snooping around that Skye has done, we should run it, unless the people Skye is still wanting to interview will make or break this story. I don't want the San Jose Union News to beat us on this."

Skye shook his head no.

"I say we run with it then," Noland chimed.

The crowd at the table whispered to each other about the story, which no one seemed to have any clue about. E.J. leaned over to Jeffery and asked if he knew what Skye was working on, but Jeffery was clueless. He told E.J. it was rare that Skye would be so secretive about his stories because Skye's ego made it hard for him to keep his mouth shut.

"What's the story?" asked Shane Strickland, one of the sports reporters.

The crowd agreed and nodded their support.

"It's about Fremont hiring a superintendent with a long history of mental illness and abuse, and why they hired this guy over other candidates," Noland said.

E.J. was shocked.

Skye quickly got up and exited the room, but E.J. wouldn't let him get away that easy. He jumped up from his seat a darted after Skye, the rest of the room left confused as Noland and Walter asked where the two were going.

"Hey! Hey!" E.J. shouted as Skye ignored him, still walking briskly down the hallway to the main newsroom.

E.J. started a slow sprint, grabbing Skye by the shoulder and swinging him around.

"What the fuck was that about!?" E.J. belted with enough force that the few employees hanging around turned to listen."It was you that took it... I told you about it and you stabbed me in the back, you son of a bitch!"

"Look kid, it's the way things work around here… sorry you had to learn it the hard way. It's really no big deal." Skye replied with a content, matter-of-fact tone to his voice. "There will be plenty of other stories."

E.J. grabbed Skye by his collared shirt, both hands clenched, and shoved Skye hard against the wall. His voiced dropped to a low tone, angry and cracked, his body tensed and shaking with violence. Skye tried to move, but was pinned, E.J.'s mouth an inch away, his breath popping against Skye's face.

"Hey, what the fuck do you think you're doing?" Skye said, frightened.

"You set me up. You've been setting me up since I got here. The only reason I don't put your fucking head into this wall is I would go to jail. You knew what was at stake for me with this story! You knew what this meant! You knew everything and you sat there and lied to my face, you motherfucker!"

"I told you this," Skye snapped back. "There are no friends in journalism. You step on anyone you have to step on. You're the predator or the prey. Now let me go or you'll be sleeping in a cell tonight. Got it?"

Skye relaxed and smiled.

"I better never see you outside of this job, you understand?"

Skye stayed silent.

"Understand!?" E.J. screamed, pushing off Skye so hard that he fell down to his knees, along with two framed prints that hung from the wall. E.J. stormed toward the elevator, looking at the city desk secretary.

"I'm going... tell Noland I'll e-mail my stories by deadline."

Chapter Twenty-Four

"Are you going to get fired for this?" Kalea asked with concern.

"Probably not," E.J. replied. "He isn't going to say anything to anyone because he would have to tell them why I slammed him against the wall."

Kalea was beside herself, unsure of how someone could steal a story like this and simply get away with it.

"I don't understand. If this guy is a story thief, why didn't he go after your story about the High Hill Shopping Center. You told him everything about that story. Why didn't he try to steal that one too?"

"I think he set me up from the beginning. He knew it was a bogus story... he knew Donald Tate's reputation. He acted like I was onto something and used it to gain my trust."

"So what now?" Kalea asked.

"What can I do? Just move forward. Keep my mouth shut when I get another lead. This is exactly what Jeffery warned me about on New Year's Eve. This is the reason why Warren wouldn't help me with my leads or my story's angle when I asked him. He only would help me edit it after I wrote it."

E.J. got off the couch and poured himself another glass of wine from the half-empty bottle he and Kalea were drinking. They both bitched about their circumstances. As the wine bottle emptied, another was cracked... and then another. Both were frustrated with their situations. They were besieged by their bills. They only saw each other in passing most of the time and the distance was growing, both noticeably disgruntled with each other. The bickering turned into fighting about money, their jobs, the move to San Francisco, the fractured promises while blame spilled out as more fingers were pointed. Kalea blamed E.J. for dragging her out west, leaving a real opportunity behind to work at a book store and to wait tables. E.J. blamed Kalea for not being more patient and trivial. Kalea attacked E.J. for his failures at work. E.J. attacked Kalea for giving up too easy at her jobs and at her attempts to find "real" employment. As they drank, their sparring turned into disputation about each other and unavoidably into another shouting match. It wasn't the first, but tonight was a notably bad engagement.

The next morning, E.J. drug himself out of bed, remorseful. He was hung over and upset at himself for last night's fight... and the endless fights him and Kalea seemed to be having over the past few months. As the coffee brewed, E.J. looked at a picture on the wall of him and Kalea. Smiling. Happy. He thought about where things were going wrong as he sipped his coffee and downed an aspirin for his headache. Prior to moving to San Francisco, the two seemed to have it quite easy, but neither one could own this new city. Ohio was easy. School was easy. Opportunity in average towns was easy. San Francisco wasn't any of this. The speed... the competition... the expectations... E.J. sat on the train and glared at the sea of suits, the built-in calmness of some who were either born to live this way, or had lived this way for so long they were beaten into submission.

E.J. sat silent at his desk working on whatever worthless story was handed to him that morning. He hadn't even looked at Skye since the incident, and hadn't really talked with anyone about what happened. He even was being short with Jeffery, who ultimately decided to give E.J. his space after a few failed attempts to engage him. Jeffery didn't know what happened, but figured it had to be one of a number of things. He had been through so much during his first few years as a reporter himself, he knew the signs of someone that wasn't looking to talk with anyone.

E.J.'s phone rang.

"E.J. Lockhart speaking."

The voice on the other end was shy, a bit dark, with hesitation. He asked if this was the guy that was nosing around about the High Hills Shopping Center development and the one that talked with T. Wayne Hammet. E.J. confirmed his identity.

"Can I trust you?" the voiced asked.

"I'm the only one at this paper that you can trust."

"Look, I have some information about something huge, but I need to talk with a reporter that won't say anything to anyone. It's a big deal... are you this man?"

"Sir, if there is anyone on this planet that won't say shit to anyone, it's me... you don't even know how silent I am today."

Skye, eavesdropping, looked away as E.J. lifted his head in his direction.

"Do you know where Shaggy's Pub is in Oakland?" the voice asked.

"Lake Merritt and 18th," E.J. confirmed.

"Meet me there tonight at nine. I'll be wearing a black jacket and a Pittsburg Pirates' hat."

The phone went dead.

Shaggy's was a small bar just off Lake Merritt. Established and a bit worn, but quiet with lounge chairs at the rear of the bar. E.J. walked in and immediately saw the man sitting far in the back. Black jacket and a Pirates' cap. He was a light-skinned black man, young, in his twenties.

"You lookin' for a reporter?" E.J. said softly, slightly sneaking up on him.

The man looked up and nodded his head, no smile, no discernible expression.

"Have a seat Lockhart."

He didn't give E.J. a real name and E.J. didn't question it. He called himself Heist, told E.J. what he did for a living, and how it all came crashing down just two days before.

"I was arrested on Thursday in a drug sting. Mothafuckas' raided my house. Five pounds of marijuana, a bunch of cocaine, and crack... not sure how much, but I'm sure I'll hear about it in court. I just bailed out this morning."

"So what do you want from me?" E.J. asked.

"You know Russell Graham?"

"Yeah. Mayor of Oakland."

"I have been dealing coke to that motherfucka' for about three years. Big purchases too. Mostly half ounces... sometimes an ounce or more, and even broke off pounds to him a few times. I'm afraid as soon as he finds out I've been busted, he may make me disappear in fear that I'll rat him out to cut a deal. You know how it works. You give up names, they'll cut deals."

"Are you planning on ratting the mayor out?"

"Nah man... that would get me killed for sure," Heist said. "But regardless if I do or don't, do you think Graham is going to take that chance? I ain't trying to find out."

E.J. took a moment to process this.

"So, why don't you just go to the cops. I'm sure you can cut a deal with that information, they'll provide some protection, and Graham would be in so much shit that he wouldn't be able to touch you anyway."

Heist shook his head in disagreement.

"Hell no. He's connected in Oakland deep. I can't rat him out. I'm sure I'll be killed... plus I deal to T. Wayne. That's how I got your number and why I contacted you. He said you are the man that can help me. I mean, I just sell pot to T. Wayne, but I'm afraid if I go to the cops, he'll get wrapped up in this as well. He used to be a cop, you know. I can't do 'em like that."

"So what are you proposing? I'm not sure I can help you with anything."

"Look, Graham and I set up a deal last week. He's supposed to meet me tomorrow at the lawn bowling greens, near Adams Point by Lake Merritt. Two ounces of cocaine. I want you to call the cops, tell them you have a lead, and sting him. Put all that shit in the fuckin' papers. And I have to do it now before Graham finds out I was arrested. I don't have any time. Once he finds out I got arrested for this, I'm done. It has to be tomorrow before word gets out."

"You're crazy. You just bailed out. You'll get busted again and be looking at twice the time you are now. It's suicide."

Heist leaned back in his chair, a bit frustrated.

"Mothafucka, I'd rather commit that suicide than get killed... I ain't even worried about some other charges. I'm interested in livin'. I got two baby girls and if I'm dead, what good am I?"

"More prison time isn't going to help with your kids."

"Yeah, but I'll get out eventually... can't wake up from death. If it's done this way, I won't be a rat and Graham will know I didn't go to the cops, because I didn't. You did... You understand?"

"I get it," E.J. answered. "You never go to the cops, so as far as they're concerned, it's just a drug bust that I gave them the tip on. You won't be suspected because you went down too, and went down twice in less than 72 hours."

"Exactly. I'll just look like a crazy mothafucka' that don't give a shit. If anything, it will raise my street cred to crazy levels. No one will ever even think I snitched."

Heist got up and put a fifty-dollar bill on the table next to his empty glass.

"Eleven in the morning tomorrow. You call the cops. You know where I'll be. You want the story that brings down the mayor? It's yours... I hope to see you."

Heist made his way out just as the waitress came up to E.J.

"Would you like another drink?"

"Make it a double..."

When E.J. got home, Kalea was still at work. It was 12:30 a.m. She wouldn't be home until later, so he wrote her a quick note about the story that was going to bring down the mayor and apologized for everything. He hoped it would begin mending some walls. When she got home, E.J. was asleep on the couch. She looked at him, crumpled it up, and threw it away, too tired to care about any of it.

Chapter Twenty-Five

The conference room was bouncing with chatter and talk of stories as E.J. sat quietly in his usual chair on the far side of the long wooden table, which stretched the length of the room. He had become more impassive than ever, answering questions with one word, wearing sunglasses indoors, and dropping them down on the bridge of the nose only to make eye contact with Skye every so often, just to let him know nothing was forgiven or forgotten. Even Jeffery had all but stopped hounding E.J. about what happened between him and Skye. E.J. only talked at length with Warren, in the early morning, as he had done since arriving at the paper. Even then, he couldn't tell Warren exactly what had happened. As reporters went one by one, talking about their stories and leads to the editors, E.J. sat emotionless.

"So, what are you working on Lockhart?" Noland asked.

E.J. stared forward.

"The mayor of Oakland is going down today," he replied in a matter-of-fact tone, with no elaboration.

The room bubbled with whispers. E.J. said nothing else.

"Care to explain further?" Noland asked.

"No... but if I were you, send a photographer with me at 10:30 and clear the fuckin' front page."

"Are you serious?" Noland asked as the other editors and the rest of the room either sat quietly or mumbled incoherently.

Walter sat up and demanded more information.

"Lockhart, what exactly is going on?"

"Just trust me on this. Have a photographer ready to go with me and by deadline tonight, you'll have the biggest story you've seen in a very long time... Am I clear?"

Walter curled his brow, a little upset at E.J.'s tone. He leaned over and whispered in Noland's ear while Victoria struggled to get in between them.

"We would like to have more information about what's going on," Walter said.

E.J. looked at the clock. It was 9:00 a.m. He had two hours. He got up and headed for the door.

"No time to explain," E.J. said as he headed out the conference room on his way back to his desk. "Get a photog ready in fifteen minutes."

The rest of the room excused themselves as the editors looked at each other totally dumbfounded.

"What do you want to do?" Noland asked.

"Send a photographer with him. Let's see what happens," Walter said. "I think we'll know what the fuck he is talking about soon enough."

E.J. rolled with Stevie, the paper's head photographer, who was chatty. E.J. said very little until they pulled up about a quarter-mile away from the lawn bowling field at Lake Merritt. They both jumped out of the car.

"You see that black guy with the Pirates' cap and the red backpack?"

Stevie looked across the field.

"Yeah. The one standing in front of Gold's Gym by the bike rack?"

"He's about to sell cocaine to the mayor of Oakland."

"How the fuck do you know this?"

"Just wait..."

A man appeared from the trees that lined the outer area of the lawn bowling field. He was wearing jeans, tennis shoes, dark glasses, and a hat with a cheap green backpack across his shoulder. It was Russell Graham. E.J. noticed two other men, both at a park bench carefully watching.

"There he is," E.J. said.

"Who?"

"Russell Graham, the mayor."

"You sure?"

E.J. focused on Graham and noticed the green backpack looked virtually empty, except for something loosely banging around in it as Russell walked. He figured it was the money wadded up at the bottom. He looked across the street at Heist, who quickly made his move toward Graham.

"I'm sure that's him," E.J. said. "That backpack has the money in it. They'll make a quick switch."

E.J. eyed the two men sitting at a bench, both of whom were covertly looking at Russell as he made his way toward Heist.

"See those two guys at the bench?" E.J. asked.

"Yeah."

"Those guys, I'm pretty sure, are cops. They're about to bust them."

Heist and Russell met at the exact spot Heist had talked about the night before. They shook hands and began to walk toward a small wooded area. The two men on the bench got up and began to follow, far behind, but with the two in sight. E.J. smiled, nudged Stevie, and began to lead him toward the spot where the deal would go down.

"Get your camera ready."

Stevie chuckled, his camera already out, having snapped a few long range shots while E.J. wasn't looking.

Within minutes, the park was a hail of flashing lights just as Heist handed the red backpack to Russell in exchange for the green one. They both tried to run, Heist making a valiant effort to look as shocked as Russell as he attempted to bolt toward the center of the park, only to be cut off by a patrol car. Stevie ran around the scene, his camera firing off as Oakland police tackled Russell, the red backpack falling to the ground with cocaine spilling out of it. Heist took a few swings at the cops before being slammed against the ground as bystanders gawked. E.J. stood in the short distance taking notes. Crowds of people swarmed the scene to see what was going on while cops secured the area. He took out his cell phone and made call-backs to the editors' desk to inform them on what was happening. More police cruisers showed up and began crowd control, including E.J., who flashed his press pass and asked to talk with someone as soon as possible about the incident. He screamed over the commotion demanding more access to the action, waving his credentials, as the editors shouted over the phone trying to make sense of what was happening. The police allowed E.J. through the makeshift police line to be closer to the scene as the mayor and Heist were pulled aside for questioning. Heist quickly glanced at E.J. as he was held against a police car, quietly cracking a small smile while cussing out the police, his lip bloodied and eye beginning to swell from the collision with the ground. As he was hauled into a police car, E.J. smiled back, praying that Heist was going to be okay.

Chapter Twenty-Six

The next day, the San Francisco Press-Journal had the front page dominated by pictures of the bust as it went down, while other papers simply had a stock photo of the mayor or shots of the aftermath. E.J. spent the morning writing about the details of the sting that no one else could even touch as a follow-up story. The newsroom was on fire and the other reporters tried to uncover how E.J. had figured it out. The editors hounded E.J. for a minute about how he knew, but the deadlines moved so quick that they dropped it to let E.J. finish his work. In the end, they didn't care how he got it. They just wanted the story.

The newsroom was abuzz with every reporter trying to find an angle on Russell Graham. CNN, FOX News, and MSNBC had sent reporters to Oakland. The Associated Press was robbing the details from E.J.'s story and plastering it across every paper and website in America. The Los Angeles Times, The Washington Post, The New York Times, and a half-a-dozen other major papers had satellite reporters all over the bay. The O'Reilly Factor, Countdown

With Keith Olbermann, and a few other news programs also had been in contact with the editors. E.J. took it all in.

Every reporter in the newsroom, even Skye, had congratulated E.J., although he said those words from a distance. Warren offered his first concession that E.J. had outdone the rest, telling him that he scooped everyone else so badly, they would be chasing his story for weeks.

"So... how'd ya do it?" asked Jeffery.

"Do what?"

"Invent the fucking Volkswagen! You know what the Hell I'm talking about. It's a done deal, so it's not like I can steal the story."

Skye attempted to move in on the conversation. E.J. shot him a look that made him quickly rethink any comments.

"Just good reporting, Jeffery."

"Fuck that bullshit! Good reporting is breaking a story, not being there a half-hour before the story goes down. Fuck dude, if you were there any earlier, you would've been buying that coke... so fuck all this 'good reporting' shit."

E.J. laughed and smiled whimsically.

"Well, Jeffery, if you just listen to what people are telling you, you may miss something. You cannot just listen to them... you need to hear them... understand? The difference is hearing and not just listening."

Jeffery rolled his eyes.

"Great... thanks for the advice," he said sarcastically as he walked away.

"You need to hear, Jeffery!"

"Fuck off!"

Hope rained down on E.J. and Kalea. As the news spread across the nation, every media outlet scrambled to get the story that E.J. broke wide open. He made quick moves to corral several high-ranking police officers that he could quote off the record, securing information the others would not be able to get. He went directly to the Alameda County jail and talked with Russell Graham, using his original article's balance and objectivity to persuade him that every media organization was going to crawl all over him for interviews, and then slam him publically for their own gain. He was the only one that could give Graham a fair shake in the public print. Russell was skeptical, but after E.J. finessed him, he realized that media agencies from other parts of the country had no stake in him, his city, his mayoral track record, or any positive contribution he had made to the Oakland community. Russell agreed to only talk with E.J. Within hours, E.J. had already saved the outline of the exclusive interview with Russell Graham in the Press-Journal's computer system, while others were still waiting for representatives of the city or Graham's lawyers to call them back. E.J. already had the man in his own words.

The next few days E.J. dominated the Bay Area coverage of Russell Graham, appearing on CNN, MSNBC, and FOX News, coupled with interviews on local news stations giving discussing exclusive information as the story continued to unfold. Every other news agency either chased him or his leftovers. After two weeks, the Russell Graham story began to die off with only court appearances, pleas, and other peripheral pieces still being written. Following the long and exhausting run, E.J. felt vilified. Kalea, as upset as she had been for a long time, shared in his joy. They finally had a reason to celebrate with an evening of drinking and dining. For the first time in what seemed like a lifetime, they didn't end up in a fight. Kalea was reassured that the big break E.J. had fought for finally came through. Rumors of awards were circulating and a book deal was even mentioned. As they rejoiced, he promised to her that this was just the beginning. The darkest of times suddenly lightened.

As the weeks went on, the Russell Graham story began to evaporate from all national media outlets completely and the world moved on. New stories surfaced while the old news faded into the distance. However, in the Bay Area, the story had a longer shelf life. While the papers covered the court proceedings and the hearings, most reporters had abandoned trying to find any new angles for a story that now was slowly disappearing. Talk of it in the morning meetings almost stopped completely, with it only being brought up occasionally by the editors when it was a slow news day and they were desperate for a story that might light a bit of a fire. When the news came out that E.J.'s initial story and his subsequent exclusive interview with Russell Graham was nominated for both a Society of Professional Journalism and a California Newspaper Publishers

Association award, the editors privately boasted to their bosses and competitors, but were lukewarm to E.J. in the newsroom. They simply moved on, wanting everyone to be on top of what was next and not rest on their laurels. When E.J. eventually won the awards, the Press-Journal editorial staff gloated publically and passed a few verbal congratulations to E.J., but what he accomplished amounted to very little in the eyes of the editors. It was E.J.'s job. This wasn't special, it was expected. Nothing more. Only their success really mattered to them. For E.J., nothing had changed in their minds. No new beat, no offers for a better schedule, and no raise. When E.J. approached them about some possible changes, the editors blew him off. Warren wasn't surprised.

"I told you, they'll take full credit and high-five you for doing a good job, but when you go into that office for a raise, they'll tell you how you misspelled someone's name in some random story. They'll never acknowledge that you brought down a mayor for buying drugs in that conversation."

E.J. listened and asked a simple question.

"So what do you do to get anywhere in this industry if the editors always take credit for busting a huge story, but turn around and treat you like a dog that did a cool trick for the first time?"

"Trust me, others know you now... This was a major story and you just nailed down two huge awards. So now, you wait... work any national coverage, make more connections, and hopefully move up the ladder of journalism. You never know, you may have your own talk show eventually."

"Yeah right," E.J. chuckled. "All off of busting the mayor of Oakland buying cocaine."

"Look at Marion Barry... he gets busted smoking dope and that became a national story. Some journalist made a career off of that guy."

"We'll see about that," E.J. said.

Warren got up to get another cup of coffee.

"This story looked as if it was going to save my relationship. A better schedule, a better beat, some more money… something. Boy, Kalea needs to see something for all the crap I have been putting her through. When this story broke, I was sure all of our problems were solved, but I feel like I'm right back where I started."

"This job is not designed for long term relationships most of the time. I'm on my third marriage. Is she still working as a waitress?"

"Yep... still hasn't found another job."

"Well, don't expect any changes in your schedule or beat here."

"I know… but I have to have some pull now. At least some."

"I've seen this a million times. Don't bet on much changing from one huge breaking story."

E.J. attempted to retort, but couldn't get a word out of his mouth.

"Seriously, E.J., haven't you picked that up already? They may initially treat this story as something special, but it quickly dies out with them. It becomes nothing but another story. Secretly, they're bragging about this, shoving it in the faces of their competitors, and getting raises from their bosses, but that doesn't mean you'll get anything at all."

E.J. nodded with a disappointed acceptance and a growing bitterness.

Chapter Twenty-Seven

E.J. woke up earlier than he usually did, which didn't really spark any curiosity from Kalea who had seen this every day for the past eight months. E.J. always made a point to get to work early to have coffee with Warren. She quickly extinguished any odd thoughts knowing tonight was their anniversary and since they had begun fighting again, E.J. would either keep things simple or do something extravagant to try and reconnect. Much of it didn't matter at that moment because she didn't get home from The Pennington until 3:00 a.m. She mumbled some inaudible term of endearment and went back to sleep.

The Russell Graham honeymoon was over between the two and the paper's failure to recognize any of it in E.J.'s favor eventually surfaced. It made Kalea more downhearted than ever before. She was convinced that nothing would change. The same arguments returned as the two barely made rent, struggled to pay bills, and forcing them to count pennies each week. Kalea was miffed at why E.J. wasn't getting a raise, a better beat, or a better schedule because of this story, and questioned whether he was really demanding it or letting the editors walk all over him. He argued that the dotcom boom had made it tough for newspapers and raises were not being handed out. E.J. asked for patience, but it was clear that patience wasn't going to happen with Kalea much longer. He talked about getting another job, somewhere else, that was a move up the ladder, which just infuriated Kalea even more... asking her to move again for E.J.? She wasn't interested in his wild goose chases and the thought of having to relocate to another city, another place, another set of issues to deal with, made her ill. She was tired and fed up.

E.J. promised to make it up with their anniversary dinner. He promised a new start. He assured her of more stories like Russell Graham that would make up for the struggles they had endured... he told her he loved her and needed her for this journey. He argued his case, showed the evidence, and Kalea always just smiled with skepticism. She knew, in many ways, he needed her, that she was his rock, but that wouldn't change anything. She didn't want things to be this way, but she couldn't do anything to make it better and E.J. was failing at that as well. He never failed at anything, and this failure was becoming harder each day for Kalea to swallow.

Within moments of opening, the doors of Hayes Valley Floral swung wide. E.J. was on a tight schedule and needed to arrange the flower delivery. He thought about just calling the order in, but this needed to be timed perfectly. He had the night planned down to the minute. At 9:30 p.m., the flowers would be delivered to their table at Acquerello, about the time him and Kalea would be finishing their dinner. He explained this to the florist and slipped an extra $100, which he couldn't afford, to make sure the flowers arrived on time.

Kalea had the day off, thanks to a blackmailed Jean-Louis who had still been feeling guilty about taking credit for the positive review in *The Napa*. Kalea had let it go, but was using the incident to get some perks… and this perk was the most important: Getting the night off on her anniversary with E.J. She wanted to talk, start fresh, and figure out some way to make their relationship work. In her mind, this was her raison d'être. Although inside she refused to fully admit it, Kalea was at her breaking point.

E.J. skipped a long breakfast with Warren that morning, which was odd. The two had become close during the past eight months and Warren's empathy deepened as he grew closer to E.J., almost fatherly. Warren let down his rules of interaction with colleagues and helped E.J. with the ins-and-outs of story angles, leads, sources, and how to get people to talk. He always offered advice through his journalism experiences with constructive praise and criticism of E.J.'s work. E.J. would finally talk about Skye, to which Warren nodded with expectedness and comforting guidance, offering the same sincere counsel when E.J. talked about Kalea and other personal matters.

By noon, E.J. had done two bullshit filler stories and needed to finish a weekend piece before deadline so he could be out of work by 6:00 p.m. He had two meetings, which were done by 3:00 p.m. At

5:30 p.m., he sent his final draft to the editors and started to pack up his stuff.

"E.J., I need to see you for a moment," Noland said, sticking his head out from his office.

The two had barely spoke since the fight over E.J.'s salary and more animosity was built after Noland, and the rest of the editors, quickly downplayed E.J.'s success in bringing down the mayor. E.J.'s disillusionment from the river of failed misconceptions, the false impressions, and forged judgments of the business had fully surfaced, fully entangling itself with too many deceptions. Feeling deceived, he was left cynical and overly critical of everything in this building, this business, and those that ran it.

"What do you need?" he asked coldly.

"Look, there is a huge event at the Julia Morgan Ballroom so clock in the overtime because we need you tonight at the event."

"Noland, tonight's my anniversary and there is no way I can miss this. I have reservations, flowers... I'm locked and loaded. You need to get someone else."

"Scott was going to cover it, but his kid is sick and they went to the hospital this morning. Everyone else has other stories they need to finish and I have no other options. You're the general assignment reporter and this is your gig."

"No way! No way! I don't care if you have to go cover it yourself, I can't do it. Things have not been going well with Kalea..."

Noland interrupted.

"Look, I know, and I wouldn't be asking if this wasn't huge..."

Noland paused for a second.

"Look, Mayor Gavin Newsome will be making an announcement. I have some insider info and this is going to be huge. It's exclusive and you'll be the only reporter there. You think Russell Graham was big? This may be bigger."

"I doubt that it's bigger, as if it would make a difference to you," E.J. said with contempt.

"We care about this one a lot."

"What's the announcement," E.J. said with curiosity.

"Don't really want to say here..."

E.J. thought for a moment, pride and ego conflicting with the bitterness that had taken root. He realized what a huge favor he would be doing for these people, regardless of how big the story may be, and what this night means to Kalea... and what it would mean if he canceled on her. He also refused to believe he could be defeated by anything or anyone. He recognized that opportunity, even if it was mixed with a favor to the editors, was still an opportunity. Another notch in the post and another whisper that would spread throughout the media landscape would only bolster his reputation. He knew this would piss Kalea off to no end, but he also didn't think it could get much worse, and another big story could only make things better for him, for her, and for them. Despite these thoughts, his jaded heart could bleed no more, not for them, no matter the prospect.

"Can't do it," E.J. said.

From the back of the room a booming voice rang out.

"We're not asking, Mr. Lockhart."

Walter stood in the doorway of Noland's office.

E.J. became respectfully defiant.

"What are you going to do? Fire me? After the Graham story? Really?"

"You walk away from your assignment and don't bother coming back in the morning," Walter said.

Noland tried to calm the situation down.

"Look E.J., we need you. If this wasn't an important story, we wouldn't be pressing you like this. I know it's your anniversary and my wife would be fuckin' raging if I missed my anniversary too, but this is huge. We know what you're capable of... and I know we've had our disagreements, but look at the work you have done. We told you when you got here it would take time and you're showing us what we knew you could do. This is equally as important and all the work you have put in is paying off, even if you do not see the full picture right now. Agree?"

E.J. thought for a moment. He thought about walking out, but mused again, arrogance and attitude overpowering his disgust for these people. He had never quit, never been fired, never removed or kicked out of anything, and always rose above everything. He knew this moment was a defining space of decisions. If he was fired, everything that he had been put through would be for naught. He also knew the firestorm that would follow with Kalea by vanishing. But two back-to-back blockbuster stories would be the Godsend that would forgive all. He contemplated if this story would be the answer to an intricate puzzle that had corroded his personal and professional existence.

"This is important?" E.J. asked for confirmation.

"Yes, this is huge to us," Noland said.

"Big announcement?"

"Gigantic announcement."

"I want tomorrow off. The whole day. No surprise calls, no nothin'. Otherwise I walk right now."

Noland looked at Walter, who confirmed the conditions gently.

"It's yours," Noland said.

E.J. nodded his head and walked over to his desk, grabbed his notepad, the directions to the event, and his cell phone. On the road he called Kalea and explained the situation. He told her he had tomorrow off and that the entire day would be for them. Not just dinner, but anything and everything that could be done in twenty-four hours. Kalea said very little, her voice light and shallow. He promised to make it up to her, something she reminded him he said too many times. She told him to really consider what he wants in life and then hung up. E.J. knew this wasn't going to blow over easy, so he began planning the day. All stops had to be pulled out. Money became no object. As he hashed a basic idea out in his head that included boat rides, limo service, a parade of flowers, and expensive meals, he also began to focus on this story and its midnight deadline, hoping that it was big enough to add an award to the collection. Get it done and then get home to tell Kalea his grand plan for the next day... he would never get that chance.

Chapter Twenty-Eight

The Julia Morgan Ballroom was one of the nicest ballrooms in San Francisco's financial district. Its Beaux-arts design was reminiscent of Hearst Castle's style, resting fifteen floors atop the Merchant Exchange Building. E.J. made his way down the barrel-vaulted lobby, lined with marble, gold leaf, and bronze. In the ballroom, it was floor-to-ceiling arched windows that opened to a magnificent straight view into the heart of San Francisco's skyline. He stood near the twenty-foot cream-stoned fireplace and looked high above into the honey-combed ceiling, constructed of chestnut octagonals, before resting his eyes out the window onto San Francisco's horizon, dancing with lights, seemingly burning through the darkness that never took a hold of the city.

The place was packed with local politicians, Bay Area financial bigwigs, anonymous suits, and other hanger-on's that seemed to always be around these types of events. E.J. made his way to the long mahogany bar and introduced himself to Alex Tourk, Gavin Newsome's deputy chief of staff. He was a middle-aged man, who could easily be Caucasian, but with a shade of color that made it hard to tell. He was distinguished, tall, well-spoken, with a nearly shaved head that loosely camouflaged his thinning hair.

"E.J. Lockhart. The San Francisco Press-Journal."

Alex put down his glass of wine and shook E.J.'s hand.

"So good to meet you," Alex said. "Where's Scott?"

"I'm covering for him tonight... where is Mr. Newsome? I would love to get an interview. I have a midnight deadline."

"He is unavailable right now, but no worries. He speaks at nine and should be ready for a quick interview shortly after that. We can have you out of here by ten."

E.J. nodded with acceptance.

"So, Alex, what's the big news? I hear it is huge and it seems to be a bit of a secret. I was told I would be the only reporter here, although I did see Vince Green... one of our company's vice presidents."

Alex looked at E.J. with a bit of confusion.

"You don't know?"

Alex pointed to one of the banners that stretched across the ballroom's walls. The banner read: "Newsroom in the Classroom," with Hurston Newspapers Inc. and the San Francisco Unified School District logos prominently displayed underneath.

"I don't understand." E.J. said. "What's this 'Newsroom in the Classroom' deal."

Alex explained that the Press-Journal's parent company, Hurston Newspapers Inc., finalized a deal that would partner schools with local papers, and this idea would then be taken to California's governor as part of a partnership initiative, encouraging all papers and media outlets to come together with their local schools across the state. The mission was to set a new standard in education, blending expository writing, literature, current events, and the emerging computer and Internet technology that was becoming the norm.

"That's the big deal?" E.J. said with displeasure.

"We think it's a big deal," Alex said. "Hurston Newspapers also thinks it's a big deal, and we're happy to be partnering with them."

E.J. walked away, cursing the editors under his breath. He spent the rest of the evening at his table, taking notes, getting quotes, and transcribing Gavin Newsome's speech. He didn't bother to interview the mayor and quickly hammered out a story before heading back to the newsroom.

When he arrived, he walked into Noland's office unannounced. Noland looked up from his monitor and didn't have a chance to even move. E.J. slammed his flash drive into Noland's computer, pushed him aside, and pulled up the file containing the "Newsroom in the Classroom" story.

"There it is you asshole!"

Noland jumped up out of his chair.

"What the fuck do you think you're doing?!"

E.J. pointed to the computer screen where the story was on full display.

"A fucking PR piece! That's what that is right there! A fucking PR piece promoting your program!"

Noland's face showed a bit of forged confusion, as if he had no clue what E.J. was talking about.

"You told me that this was some huge story, but it's nothing more than a PR piece promoting your program and your fucking company."

"Hold up," Noland busted in. "I told you this was huge, and it is huge. We're talking about a major change to the education system and this is the first announcement that it's being supported by one of the most influential people in politics… and being adopted by one of the biggest cities in America."

"Look, you can peddle your bullshit to someone else. You purposely didn't tell me what the announcement was because you knew what it was, and you knew I would shove it back in your face. You sent me to do a PR piece! It wasn't news! It never was!"

Walter came out of his office after hearing the screaming match and quickly broke up the argument.

"Lockhart, I don't know what your problem is, but this is unacceptable!" Walter belted.

"You too Walter!" E.J. screamed. "You knew damn well what this fucking story was about and you lied to me! This was my anniversary night, for Christ sakes!"

Walter moved his enormous frame over E.J., shadowing him and quickly quieted the rookie reporter.

"You listen here. You do the stories we assign you. I don't care what you think is news, a PR piece, or anything else for that matter," Walter disseminated with authority. "You came into this business thinking it was just about 'being a voice for the voiceless,' a steward of your community, stopping corruption, or some other bullshit that was handed to you in college. This is a business, first and foremost, before it's anything else. This is my business. My paper. This story involves a lot of people, a lot of money, and it's our baby. You either do your job or get the fuck out of this building. Are we clear on this?"

E.J. stared up at Walter, his eyes beaming, red-faced. Walter showed nothing.

"I'm going to ask one more time, Mr. Lockhart. Are we clear?"

E.J. nodded in silence and then headed for the office door.

"Thanks for ruining my anniversary," he said with a sarcastic tone as he headed out the door. "You two are real class acts! I hope you have an amazing evening!"

Noland and Walter said nothing back, both just staring at E.J. walking away with slight looks of disgust on their faces.

"That wasn't too pleasant," Walter said.

"That's the business. With the amount of money on the line for this company wrapped up in that partnership, we had no choice. We got the story."

Walter walked back into his office while Noland sat down with indifference to edit the story. E.J. headed down the 101 hoping to make it home soon enough, and praying Kalea was still awake, to make up for what happened. She wasn't there. Long before he arrived home, Kalea had packed a few necessities, booked a flight, and left back home to Ohio. A note rested on the bed when E.J. arrived.

E.J.,

This is not the life I want to live with you. I'm sorry, but I can no longer handle not having a career and not having you either. I'm going home...

Kalea

E.J. crumpled up the note and threw it across the room in a fit of frustration and anger. He tried to call her. No answer. He punched the walls enough times to get an angry visit from his neighbor who didn't seem to care about his girlfriend leaving him. He went to the kitchen, grabbed a bottle of Jack Daniels, and quickly put a dent into it. He spent the rest of the night thinking and venting. One drunken fit after another. One angry rant after another. Little did he know that one random idea passing through his head that night would be his master plan. He didn't know it just yet, but it would be his way to correct the mistakes he made with Kalea, to correct the mistakes he made with his job, but more so, to make The San Francisco Press-Journal regret they ever hired him in the first place.

Chapter Twenty-Nine

"So she left... just like that?" Warren said with a content tone.

"Yeah. Packed up a few essentials and caught a late night plane back to Ohio."

"Did you call her?"

"Called a few times and got nothin' but voicemail. E-mailed her and got nothin'... I thought she loved me. I guess for better or for worse doesn't apply anymore."

E.J. got up and grabbed another cup of coffee. He didn't look well and Warren could see it. His hair was disheveled, his face unshaven, and it was clear from his blood-shot eyes he was hung over. His clothes were the same he wore the day before, wrinkled as if he had slept in them. Warren was a bit fuddled that he still made it to the office, like clockwork, at 6:30 a.m.

"I'm surprised you're here," Warren said. "Looks like you had a long night... not much sleep."

"Who said I slept at all?" E.J. replied with a soft tone of contempt in his voice.

Warren smirked.

"Warren, I need to ask you a question."

"Shoot."

"These prick editors destroyed my relationship over a public relations piece and didn't seem to care one bit. They also don't care when I bust a major story. They don't care when I win awards. They don't care if this job burns my relationship to the ground. They surely don't care that I cannot pay my bills or if I can eat tonight. They have ruined me. What's stopping me from kicking the living shit out of Noland and Walter? I mean, just fuckin' them up!"

"Jail, lawsuits... and you're smarter than that."

E.J. nodded and sipped his coffee.

"Plus, E.J., you don't seem like a tough guy."

"Yeah..." E.J. replied as he slightly drifted.

"Why don't you quit? Go back to Ohio and make up with Kalea? I'm sure you can get a job at any paper you want. I mean, if you give your two-week notice, be nice to the editors for a few days, you know you'll get a decent recommendation. You also have two major journalism awards under your belt. You should be fine."

"And let them win? Fuck that! Why don't I just get fired... make these son-of-a-bitches pay me some unemployment at least. I mean they fucked me out of the higher-paying assistant city reporter beat under you. Even after the Graham story, no raise... nothing... they owe me some money, as far as I see it."

Warren sighed.

"E.J., can I tell you something?"

"Sure."

"You have to promise not to get bent out of shape."

E.J. looked at Warren a bit worried.

"Great. What is it?"

"You have to promise not to get upset."

"Warren, what could you say that is going to upset me any more than I already am, considering the past twenty-four hours."

Warren nodded in agreement and leaned back in his chair.

"I don't know this for sure, but it seems clear to me, there was never a position underneath me for assistant city reporter. Never has been, as far as I can tell."

"What the fuck do you mean?"

"I have been here thirty years, twenty of those in my current position. I would say in the last ten years there have been about five guys hired to be the assistant city reporter under me, but it's never happened. Jeffery was one of them. He showed up and they gave him the same general assignment beat you got when you showed up."

E.J.'s brow curled, his eyes fixed on Warren.

"I noticed that they would go after high-profile college graduates with huge potential, like yourself, and offer this assistant city reporter position under me. When those folks finally arrived, settled in, they would stick them on another beat... and here is the kicker... that position was never offered to anyone from U.C. Berkeley, or Stanford, or any other California college that's relatively close by. Not even really any school on the west coast. It was always some guy from back east."

E.J. began to assemble this information, as if the missing fragments of a complex design were coming together, and the omitted shades of distant colors were suddenly revealing themselves. Clarity took over. The San Francisco Press-Journal would have a hard time competing with other papers to get him if they offered him the beat they ultimately bestowed on him. Counterfeiting the assistant city reporter position under a distinguished writer was their carrot. With their hook-in-mouth, the bait perfectly implanted, the net undividedly caught its pigeon. They altered what they offered, eased into something less with the promise that it would be temporary, that the course would change. They knew all along they could pull any string they wished because it would be too hard for E.J., thousands of miles from where he started, to simply go back.

"They lied... they fuckin' set me up!"

"Calm down," Warren said softly. "I don't know this to be fact, but that's the pattern I've seen."

E.J. sat back down at the table next to Warren, his face finally showing defeat.

"They fucked me."

Warren got up and put the remaining leftovers from his breakfast in the fridge. He took his cup, refilled it with coffee, and stood tall, sipping the hot liquid. The room was silent, only a scattering of noises could be heard in the building from the over-night janitors finishing their cleaning.

"Do you remember when you asked me why I stopped using my Greek name as my byline?"

E.J. sat up, a slight look of confusion on his face.

"The first day we hung out in the morning, you asked me why I stopped using my Greek name as a byline after I won the Pulitzer Prize. Do you remember what I told you?"

E.J. thought for a minute.

"Um, yeah, something about the real story being why you started using that name in the first place."

"That's right."

"So, what's the reason?"

"After I won the Pulitzer Prize in 1984, I asked for a raise. I didn't get it. The old editors pulled much of the same shit they pulled on you, the same shit they have been pulling for the thirty years I have been here. A million excuses, zero raises. I was pissed off. I realized that they were selling papers, in part, because my name was on the bylines. I had a huge fight with the editors that lasted weeks. I woke up one morning, looking a lot like you, and decided that until they gave me a raise, they couldn't use my name. Asklepios Pyrrhus was born. After a few weeks, the paper found some loophole to force me to use my real name, so I stopped after twenty-three stories... still never got that raise."

"Why didn't you quit?"

"My family is from San Francisco. I grew up here. This is the premier paper in the Bay Area and one of the top in the nation. I had a wife, had kids in schools here, and had inherited my house from my mom, so I didn't have the insane rent people pay in this town. At the end of the day, where was I going to go, and what point would I prove at the expense of my life, and the life of my family?"

"Well I'm not fuckin' quitting shit! I'll make them fire me before I quit."

"You'll never get fired from here without cause, not in a way that would allow you to collect unemployment. They never fire anyone because they don't want to pay for that, and the owners of this company will come down hard on editors that cost them unnecessary money... and unemployment is one of the most unnecessary. That's how cheap they are here. If they don't want you, they'll just make your life miserable until you quit."

E.J. thought for a moment.

"So what happened to all the others they've done this to?"

"Well, some quit, while others just accepted it, like Jeffery, and hoped for the best. Others just put up with it until they got a better job or left the profession. I've seen a handful rebel against the editors here and they just drove them out... made 'em quit or dumped so much on them that they eventually screwed something up and were fired with cause. They're good at this. Walter has been with this company over twenty years. He's perfected getting rid of those he doesn't want."

"Well, I've definitely been defiant. Some major fights... but I also have won awards. I've done some amazing things here. Do you think they want me to quit?"

E.J. looked at Warren for an answer, but he didn't reply. He simply smiled at E.J. with nothing to say.

"I guess they want the best out of me as long as I'll do that, and when I become too much of a pill, then I'm done no matter what I've accomplished for this paper." E.J. said with a dejected tone in his voice. "They get what they want... they got my stories and the accolades, and that's only worth what it's worth in the moment. This company is a 'what have you done for me lately'-type of business. That explains a lot about the way they treat me."

Warren got up from his chair and dumped his coffee, cleaned his cup, and gathered his papers. E.J. sat quietly at the table thinking, mulling his options.

"Why don't you go home, E.J. You need to take a day off. You look like shit."

E.J. got up and went to the sink. He quickly washed his face, running the dripping water from his cheeks through his hair.

"Warren, I'm staying today. If they think they are going to make me quit, they have another thing coming. I'm gettin' fired without cause, whether the editors like it or not."

"How do you plan on doing that?"

"I'm not exactly sure, but I know I'm going to make them regret that they ever hired me... and make them regret even more that they can't get rid of me."

Chapter Thirty

"What If You're Fired?" was the title of a relatively thick pamphlet that sat on E.J.'s desk, resting next to a manual titled "Hurston Newspapers Inc. Policies and Practices," the company's doctrine on conduct, performance expectations, and rights. It became E.J.'s Holy Bible. It outlined everything an employee is expected to do and consequences for undesirable actions. E.J. put in a request for the booklet, having lost the original he was given when he was hired. He spent two nights combing through the pages, highlighting every word that had a loophole in it and every policy that was poorly worded or incomplete. He made notes in the margins, prepping to figure out what he can and cannot do to infuriate the editors without doing anything that would get him fired with cause.

Jeffery noticed the Hurston Newspapers Inc. Policies and Practices manual and asked E.J. why he had it out. E.J. blew it off as something he found in his desk while cleaning. E.J. quickly learned exactly what cause meant under the employment contract. There were five main categories:

1.)   Failing a drug test: E.J. was clean and the company didn't drug test unless you had an accident on the job.

2.)   Theft: E.J. didn't steal.

3.)   Committing a crime: E.J. wasn't a criminal.

4.)   Violating safety: He had to be irritating as Hell, but not dangerous.

5.)   Not performing to minimum expectations: E.J. did more stories than anyone and rarely made big mistakes.

However, the pamphlet also outlined state laws about employee contracts, and how an employee's misconduct can render the employee ineligible for unemployment benefits. There was this gray area. An employee who is fired for being a poor fit for the job, lacking the necessary skills for the position, or failing to perform up to expected standards might be able to collect unemployment, but an employee who acts intentionally or recklessly against the employer's interests will likely be ineligible for unemployment benefits. E.J. had carefully highlighted this information, realizing that as long as he stayed within the Hurston Newspapers Inc. Practices and Policies, then regardless of what he does, he technically never violates the company policies, practices, and thus is not working against the company's interests.

"Did you ever tell a boss to fuck off when you quit or left a job?" E.J. asked Jeffery, who had his nose deep in a story and wasn't paying attention.

"I'm sorry, what?" Jeffery answered, turning his attention towards E.J.

"Was there a job you left or quit, and you got that chance to tell your bosses to fuck off or some other variation of that?"

"I think most people at some point look back at old jobs and say to themselves: 'I wish I would have told my boss this or that,' but that's just one of those fantasies that probably sounds good in theory, not really worth it in reality."

E.J. thought for a moment.

"Maybe so… but I would like to find out one day."

Chapter Thirty-One

E.J. packed up his laptop and exited the San Francisco Botanical Gardens newest exhibit, one of the first stories the editors handed him following their confrontation days earlier. Although cordial with each other since, the constriction between E.J. and the editors was only thinly veiled. Management, of course, was denying anything that resembled E.J.'s accusations, while E.J. discounted both overt and cloaked threats of dismissal. Knowing what he now knew about the paper, they weren't going to fire him without cause.

The story was a puff piece about a project the gardens was doing in honor of some famous horticulturalist. At first, E.J. was upset at the string of lousy stories, but realized that stories like these were quick and easy to put together with little or no resistance from sources. The more he cursed the editors under his breath about these types of assignments, the more he realized that weaker stories meant more time to execute his plan, although he had yet to actually figure out what exactly the plan was going to be.

E.J. stood on the corner of 9th Avenue and Irving Street talking on the phone, pleading with Kalea's mother to get her to talk with him, but it seemed like that wasn't going to happen.

"Look, I really need to talk with her. Are you sure you cannot convince her? Just a few minutes."

"E.J., I think she is done with you for the moment. I've called her twice in the last few days myself and she hasn't even returned my calls. She got that job at Cleveland State University, the one she was offered before you two left. She is moving into a new place, so she is busy. I don't know what you want me to do?"

"Wait, that job was still available?"

"Yes, the one in the philosophy department... I'm really not exactly sure, but it was waiting for her. Some connection she had. They never filled the job and when she came back, they hired her."

E.J.'s heart sank.

"Well, tell her I miss her, I love her, and that I'm going to make things right."

E.J. hung up the phone and stared at the building in front of him, noticing the girl in the window that was sorting boxes of shoes. Quickly moving inventory, she flowed with a strange kind of grace that made E.J. smile. A few boxes down, a few boxes back up, with no hesitation. He looked at the canopy above the entrance: On The Run Shoe Store.

E.J. dialed Jeffery.

"Hey Jeffery, it's E.J... Remember the day that you came to work in tennis shoes? What did the editors tell you?"

E.J. listened as Jeffery told him the editors said it was out of dress code and not to wear them anymore, but didn't say much more to him. It was Press-Journal's policy: Professional dress.

"Jeffery, have you ever looked closely at the dress code policy?"

"No, can't say that I have," Jeffery answered.

"It's on page fourteen of the policies and practices book... I don't think it specifies anything about shoes. Can you look it up for me?"

Jeffery pulled the book from E.J.'s desk, thumbed through the book, and read the article about dress code. E.J. thanked him, hung up the phone, and went inside the store. The young lady smiled as E.J. scanned the hundreds of shoes on display.

"Can I help you, sir?"

"Yeah. I'm looking for some tennis shoes."

The young lady pointed to a display of tennis shoes and began her sales pitch.

"Well, we have some new Nikes that just came in..."

E.J. interrupted.

"No, I need all white tennis shoes. The whitest you have."

The young lady nodded and proceeded to show E.J. a half-dozen pairs of white sneakers, most of which had some other color minimally included in the design. He looked over to another rack and noticed a pair: all white leather, with a white tongue, and white shoelaces. They glowed white.

"What about those over there," E.J. said pointing to the shoes.

"Those are DVS skate shoes. Do you skateboard?"

"No I don't... I'm trying to get fired. They're perfect. I'll take those."

The young lady smiled whimsically, assuming it was a joke she didn't fully understand, and wrapped up the new shoes. By nine that night, E.J. had drunk a bottle of wine, taken a few shots, and danced for hours around the apartment in his new shoes. He was jumping on the sofa, on the kitchen table, and countertops screaming that he was "Fuckin' Tony Hawk," laughing as merlot wine splattered around on the floor, on the sofa, and on his shirt, but not one drop ever touched his brand new white shoes.

Chapter Thirty-Two

E.J. showed up to work wearing the usual attire: a dark blue dress shirt, black tie, and black Dockers slacks with one exception: The white DVS skate shoes. As he entered the lobby of the Press-Journal building, the security guard, the secretary, and the usual people milling around all greeted him the same way they always had, but the quick glances at his shoes were obvious. In the elevator, two colleagues took notice, asking him what he was thinking wearing those horrible shoes to work. E.J. just smiled, and with no eye contact, told them that he was protesting the privatization of Cochabama city's municipal water supply company, Semapa, by wearing white skate shoes. The entire elevator looked confused, and when someone asked where Cochabama was, E.J. put on his dark sunglasses and said Bolivia, assertively telling the people in the elevator to read a newspaper every once-in-awhile.

As E.J. walked through the newsroom, he got similar looks at his shoes. He went to his desk and called Walter, then called Noland, and asked for a meeting, which they both agreed to have immediately. E.J. looked over at Victoria, who was getting up to join the meeting, and told her not to bother, informing her that no one wanted her there. Skye made a comment about the shoes, which E.J. simply ignored. Jeffery looked over and laughed, wondering what E.J. was thinking. E.J. grabbed a post-it note and wrote: "Masturbating. Be back in twenty minutes," then slapped it on the screen of his computer before heading for Walter's office.

E.J. walked into Walter's office and sat down, moving one of the other chairs and propping his feat up so Walter could see his shoes clearly. Walter looked up from his desk, first a bit irritated at the relaxed attitude, then irritated by the white sneakers. Before he could say something to E.J., Noland walked in and sat down.

"Boys," E.J. said with a familiar tone, reminiscent of old friends. "I called you together to ask for a raise. I want the original amount that I was promised when hired to be the assistant city reporter. My best estimate is that it would be $150 more per week."

Noland chuckled.

"Mr. Lockhart," Walter replied. "We have never given a raise that high, and frankly, you're wasting our time with this... and take your feet off my chair."

E.J. dropped his feet and sat up straight.

Noland nodded his head in agreement.

"Look, I really would like a chance to argue why I deserve this raise..."

"Those shoes are not in dress code," Walter interrupted.

E.J. quickly looked at his shoes.

"Oh, these? It's a protest."

Walter and Noland looked at each other confused.

"I'm protesting the privatization of the Cochabamba municipal water supply... it's a city in Bolivia, if you haven't been keeping up with the news. It's about prices."

"What?" Walter said totally confused.

"Well, protest on your own time, not at work," Noland said.

"Noland, are you violating my free speech right? My right to protest peacefully?"

Noland attempted to respond, but Walter interrupted.

"Mr. Lockhart, you are out of dress code and this defiance will go on your permanent record. This is not about free speech or rights to protest."

"Well, you're wrong about that Walter. According to the company's policy, section 18, article 5, and I quote, 'Employees have the right to express their political views in any form as long as the expression doesn't interfere with work.' It's your policy. Would you like to call your boss Walter and see if I'm wrong? I've already dropped a line to the union, so they're aware of my protest."

Both Walter and Noland said nothing, both visibly aggravated.

"On top of that," E.J. added. "The dress code, section 4, article 13 addresses shirt, tie and pants, but says nothing specific about shoes. So, do we want to continue this discussion about my rights to protest and dress code under your company's policy?"

The two sat silently, goaded.

"I didn't think so."

E.J. quickly changed the subject.

"By the way, did you guys get the botanical gardens' story? Pretty good, wasn't it? I'll have both of my other stories in by five today."

Noland acknowledged E.J. indifferently.

"So, what about the raise? Are you sure you don't want to change your minds?"

"You're not getting a raise!" Walter said with authority, and then attempted to address the shoe issue again, but E.J. cut him off.

"Well then boys, I have a new request. Seeing how I have won an SPJ and CNPA award, I need to be acknowledged for that. Usually most newspapers would do so by a raise of some sort. So, if I cannot get acknowledged for my accomplishments financially, it will have to be verbally. From here on out, I will only respond to 'Award-Winning Reporter E.J. Lockhart.'"

Walter and Noland sat silent, then E.J. excused himself. As he got half way out the door, he stopped.

"By the way," E.J. said with a smile. "I'm wearing the shoes indefinitely and if you don't like it, you can fire me... I might file a lawsuit or complain to your bosses about violating the company policy, but maybe I'll just let it go and collect that unemployment until I find a new job."

E.J. slammed the door behind him. Walter and Noland looked at each other annoyed.

"Is this motherfucker really going to try to get his ass fired?" Noland asked.

"Sure looks that way."

"Why don't we just fire him then and be done with it. There are dozens of others we can hire in his place, probably for cheaper."

Walter shook his head no.

"The owners wouldn't like that, which means you and I wouldn't like that. Our asses will be on the line if he gets fired for anything other than cause. We can make him quit. We've done it before, we can do it again. Just make sure you give him every bad story, take away any good idea he has and give them to other reporters. He isn't going to be too happy with one bullshit worthless story after another or the pile of them we'll require each day."

"That's it?"

"For now, Noland. Let's see what happens."

Jeffery stopped E.J. as he made his way back to his desk.

"What the heck is going on with you?"

"What do you mean?" E.J. replied, seemingly unaware of what Jeffery was talking about.

"The shoes... and the note on your computer."

"The shoes are a protest... and who doesn't focus better after rubbing one out?"

Jeffery interrupted.

"I know, I heard that bullshit. What the fuck is really going on?"

E.J. pulled Jeffery to the side and went into a long narrative, a blow-by-blow of everything that had been happening. Jeffery hearkened intensely to E.J.'s doctrinaire as it unfolded before him. Jeffery verified much of what Warren had told E.J., sympathized with him because he was treated identically when he first arrived, but questioned if this was the best way to handle the situation. With a mild tone of trepidation and a calm disappointment fastened to his remarks, Jeffery advised that a more diverse solution be considered. E.J. nodded his head with respect, but confidently held steadfast in his undertaking, said nothing further, patting Jeffery on the shoulder hoping he'd eventually understand.

"What did the editors say about the shoes or the 'call me Award-Winning Reporter E.J. Lockhart' demand?"

"They didn't like the shoes, so I told them that any efforts to stop me were violating my freedom of speech and right to protest peacefully, plus it violates company policy. They didn't say anything about my new title... we'll find out real quick when I ignore them after they call me by just my name."

Jeffery laughed a bit.

"You know E.J., I've been exactly where you are... and just as mad... I thought about the thousands of things that I wanted to do to them, but I didn't do it."

"Didn't have the balls?" E.J. asked.

"Well, maybe, but I realized after awhile that I was here anyway, had an opportunity regardless of the beat or the shady shit they pulled on me, and like I told you on New Year's Eve, you have to take your opportunities and move out of this place or continue to climb that ladder. I realized they may have dicked me over, but they also gave me more than enough means to surpass this job and surpass the assistant city reporter gig. I'm going to get it. One day, I might even run this place. Fire all these editors. That, or get another gig running another major news outlet somewhere else. Either way, it's going to happen... and the ironic part is, I will still owe them some gratitude because they hired me, despite the underhanded shit they did to me."

E.J. smiled.

"I understand that… and I feel like I'm doing the same thing, just in a different way. I want more than this too and I'm taking this opportunity to make my statement. Your statement is just a slightly different direction."

"Well, I'm not sure I agree with you wholeheartedly, but it's clear you have a bigger goal in mind, something more important to you than this job, and I have to respect that, even if I'm not sure I agree with this thing you're doing. Whatever it is you're looking for, I hope you find it."

E.J. thanked Jeffery and left, knowing from here on out everything had to be perfect and on time for his plan to work..

Chapter Thirty-Three

E.J. sifted through his mail at work while the Hurston Newspapers Inc. Policies and Practices booklet sat open, mostly highlighted and marked up with post-it notes tabbed throughout. After dumping the junk mail and dealing with a few correspondences he needed to take care of, he went back into the booklet and continued to map out ideas.

"What are you looking for?" asked Jeffery as E.J. quickly thumbed through the booklet.

"Not sure yet," E.J. said, eyes still fixed on the pages he was flipping through.

"A good journalist always knows what he is doing, right?" Jeffery said with a quirk in his voice.

E.J. looked up and smiled, throwing his feet up on his desk, the bright-white shoes standing out like a beacon of light.

"Exactly."

Victoria walked over to E.J.'s desk interrupting the powwow between the two.

"E.J., you have four stories due today. What's the status? We need them all."

E.J. sat silent, ignoring Victoria.

"Hey, are you there?' Victoria said with frustration teeming in her voice.

E.J. sat silent refusing to acknowledge Victoria, who quickly became impatient.

"Award-winning reporter E.J. Lockhart, what's the status of your stories today?"

"Are they all running tomorrow?"

Victoria didn't answer the question because she didn't know the answer. She was just following Noland's directions.

"We need them today, do you understand?" she responded.

E.J. smiled.

"I got it boss... they'll all be in by five."

Victoria began to walk back to her desk.

"Victoria," E.J. hollered. "Four stories due in one day seems a bit much."

Victoria stood silent.

"Jeffery," E.J. asked. "Do you have four stories due today?"

Jeffery shook his head no.

E.J. stood up and shouted to get the entire newsroom's attention. Everyone stopped what they were doing.

"Does anyone here have four stories due today or am I the only person required to do this many stories in one day?"

No one said anything. E.J. looked over as Noland exited his office upon hearing the commotion.

"Let's get back to work. We don't have time for this. All of you, including you 'Award-winning reporter E.J. Lockhart,' have a lot to get done."

"Yes, I do… and more than others. Noland, you must have a lot of faith in me."

E.J. picked up the company manual.

"I wonder what the company's policy is on how many stories one can assign a reporter, because if no one else is doing four, it doesn't seem right that I have four due today. I'll have to read the manual a little closer to see exactly what it says."

Noland turned and began a trek back to his office without saying anything.

"Don't worry Noland, I'll have them done," E.J. said with a sappy disingenuous tone.

"You better watch your Ps and Qs around here Lockhart," Skye said without looking up from his computer. "You're making some enemies that I don't think you have the onions to contend with."

Jeffery looked over, saying nothing, waiting for E.J. to respond.

"Save your breath dickhead. You'll need it later to blow up your girlfriend."

"You think this is a joke? I'll report this," Skye snapped.

E.J. turned to Skye and rolled his chair close to the reporter.

"Explain to me Skye why it's acceptable for you to be a piece of shit, but not for me to point it out? I've been trying to figure this out for months. You're a disappointment to your family. You'll never be the man your mother was."

"Excuse me? What did you say about my mother?"

"I'm sorry. Skye, your mother loves you. It's everyone else that thinks you're a total asshole. Stay out of this... it's what's best for your health. Trust that."

Skye got up and made his way to Walter's office. E.J. swung his chair back behind his desk and began to aggressively organize the assignments in front of him, picking up the phone and drafting preliminary outlines for the four stories he needed to finish.

"These guys are going to try and break you with work, you know that," Jeffery said.

"Yeah, I know, but they have one flaw. These stories are all bullshit. They're easy, and I know they can't pile too many more than this on me."

E.J. picked up the employee handbook.

"It's in here somewhere."

"What about Skye?" Jeffery asked.

Both looked over into Walter's office.

"Do you think they're plotting against you E.J.?"

"Let them. I'll stay one step ahead of these clowns."

Chapter Thirty-Four

Walter, Noland, Victoria, and Skye sat at a table inside the Winston Pub, a popular bar and grill in Oakland. The place was well lit with pool tables and decor that could be described as classy, but it still held an atmosphere of a dive joint. It's long bar stretched the length of the narrow building. A few tables sat in the back and the walls were covered with neon bar signs. The sound of pool balls clanking, and mildly drunk patrons cheering on a game that was being played on the bar's television, provided enough background noise that Walter, Noland, Victoria, and Skye felt comfortable talking about E.J.

"So what do we do about stories? Just pile them on?" Noland asked.

"No, he is aware that if we give him too much, he is in his right to go to the labor union. We don't want that. Our bosses would have a field-day with us. We need to keep this in-house," Walter quickly answered. "But we can pile on four, maybe five each day, depending on what others are doing."

"The complexity and the length of the stories will also make a difference," Noland added. "I mean, in reality, we can only really give him four a day, if they are relatively easy, but what is determined to be easy is up to interpretation."

"Is this really necessary?" Victoria asked. "Can't you just fire him, or whatever? I mean, it's a huge corporation. Does unemployment really mean that much to the bosses?"

Walter looked at Victoria slightly irritated.

"Yes, Victoria, it does. We would be in some deep shit over that, especially now with newspapers struggling nationwide. You know how this company operates. You want your bonus to be affected? The policy is clear: If we fire the guy, and have to deal with unemployment, it's coming out of all of our bonuses, if we're lucky. It could be much worse. You want that, Victoria?

Victoria shook her head no meekly.

"In all my years as publisher for this paper, we have never fired anyone without cause. We have never paid unemployment. This asshole isn't going to be the first."

"I think we also are ignoring a key component in all of this," Noland said. "His girlfriend left him and he was already struggling to make his rent, even with her income. If we just wait him out, suspend him as we are legally allowed by law, he will get evicted eventually, and have to quit or get a better job… or something. We'll be rid of him regardless."

Skye remained silent for the most part, thinking E.J. was too good to fail simply by piling a bunch of work on him or by waiting him out financially. He mulled a bunch of different ideas and came to his own conclusion that sabotaging E.J. would be the only way to get rid of him.

"Look, this guy is smart. Too smart to underestimate," Skye said. "What about sabotage?"

"How would that work?" Walter asked.

"I'm not sure..."

Victoria shook her head and interrupted.

"I'm not sure we should be putting our careers on the line to run any kind of scam. If we get caught, we're all fired, possibly get in trouble legally."

"Victoria, no disrespect," Skye chimed in. "But we all understand how good E.J. is, and frankly, you're way out of your league here. You're underestimating him."

Victoria was annoyed, but sat silently, taking the abuse out of fear.

"I agree with Skye," Noland said. "We cannot underestimate him, but Victoria has a point. Running a scam, whatever that means, is a huge risk. I'm not sure I'm comfortable with that at this point."

Skye smirked with disappointment, convinced that he was smart enough to run a scam on E.J. and that he would out smart him at every turn.

"We're not doing any scams. Let's pump the brakes for a second," Walter said. "We pile stories on him, make him rewrite and rewrite. I want every flaw hammered on. We make him come up with his own stories as well and wait him out financially. We don't have to go to extremes. He will crumble if we put pressure on him."

They all agreed.

"This meeting never happened. You don't tell anyone. Not your wife, your girlfriend or anyone else. Is this clear?"

The group nodded, finished their drinks, and headed their separate ways.

Chapter Thirty-Five

The editors attacked E.J. at every turn, furiously, bouncing stories back to him constantly, asking for clarifications, demanding corrections and additions, regardless if they needed them or not. What started as a battle over E.J.'s shoes quickly fell into a battle over his new name, which took center stage. His first name was called time and time again, and E.J. simply acted like he couldn't hear anyone. Noland assailed E.J. while Victoria bombarded him, screaming. E.J. ignored them and fought back when his disregard could no longer be evaded, continuously demanding that he be addressed by his new name "Award-Winning Reporter E.J. Lockhart." The newsroom became a circus that Walter could no longer neglect, coming out to breakup verbal melees that were suffusing the Press-Journal. By the third day, Victoria sat silent, already having resigned herself to the reality that E.J. had created, while Noland, infuriated, continued his persecution, relentless in his refusal to address E.J. by his new title and name.

"Everyone in my office now!" Walter belted.

The mood in Walter's office was tense with most everyone in the newsroom looking through the big glass window. E.J. planned to say little, just what he needed to say to defend his rights. He knew the worst thing he could do was talk too much, to attempt to defend himself, and to allow the editors to twist his words around.

"E.J., this stops here, do you understand me?" Walter said sternly.

"I'm sorry, Walter. I have a right to be addressed how I want to be addressed and any other way, I think, is a violation of my rights."

Noland stood up, ready to speak, but Walter put up his hand to shut him down.

"Okay, E.J., if you want to play this game, we can play it too. I know by law, I can only put you on a five-day suspension without pay. That's what I'm prepared to do. Knowing that your girlfriend is back in Ohio, I'm not sure you can afford that week without pay. Is this the battle you want to fight?"

E.J. knew he was in a corner and reached in his pocket, rubbing the business card of the newspaper union's lawyer. He was ready to pull it out and threaten a lawsuit, but then something dawned on him and he took his hand off the card.

"No, I don't want to fight this battle. You guys can just call me E.J. from now on."

"Excellent. Now can we get back to work?" Noland said with frustration still in his voice.

E.J. looked over at Noland.

"Sure thing Bob, I'll have your stories in by five tonight."

Noland looked confused.

E.J. got up and headed for the door, turning around and addressing Walter.

"Thanks Bob for clarifying things. You're right... it's just a name. It's not that important."

E.J. slammed the door.

"Did he just call us both Bob?" Noland asked.

Walter was enraged, but kept a cool head.

"Noland, we need to get rid of this son-of-a-bitch. I want you to let him know he has been put on the weekend shift permanently and also will now be in charge of getting the obituary section in order. Everything he turns in, we trash it. If he thinks he can make us play his game, he's wrong, or my name isn't Walter Willieford."

Noland nodded his head blindly, still processing what had just happened..

"I get the feeling your name isn't Walter anymore."

Chapter Thirty-Six

E.J. arrived at work just as he had for the past few weeks: Wearing beaming white skate shoes, which he cleaned each night to maintain their uncanny brightness. He returned to the shoe store and bought an identical pair of DVS's as backups, just in case. He had been diligent in getting his assignments done on time and had become a strong enough writer and reporter to knockout every story thrown his way. He didn't flinch when they put him on permanent weekends, nor did he budge when they gave him the responsibility of obituaries. He knew those things, and more, were going to happen the minute he started this campaign to get fired. He just smiled the whole time, even when they ripped his stories apart; he just smiled, continued to do whatever he had to do to get the stories done, refusing to show any signs of dissatisfaction or dismay, even if deep down inside he was beginning to tear just a little.

E.J. exited the elevator and headed to his desk, passing several colleagues on the way, addressing all of them as "Bob" while he whistled an old snappy and upbeat Vaudeville tune.

"Hey E.J., the editors are asking me to give you a story that came across my beat," Skye said as E.J. sat down at his desk. "It's about the cutting of bus service in downtown."

Another shit story, E.J. thought, but he just smiled.

"Sure thing Bob, just leave the information on my desk. I have a quick meeting I have to go to with Bob. Are you going to have lunch with Bob and Bob today or is Bob requiring us to go to Bob's going away lunch? You know Bob got a new job and is leaving us right?"

Skye was visibly irritated.

"Whatever, man. I'll just leave the info on your desk."

"Thanks Bob."

In Noland's office, the mood was tense, but E.J. wouldn't let it show. He smiled, was cordial and respectful on all levels, except with the name. Victoria sat on E.J.'s left while Noland perched himself behind his desk and combed through two of E.J.'s stories, highlighting every possible mistake in them, insulting E.J., calling him lazy, stupid, and questioning his ability to do basic journalism. One mistake after another, he smashed on both stories. E.J. gritted his teeth, angry, but just smiled through it and nodded.

"Well, Bob, I'll correct these issues and have them nice and pretty for you by five. Thanks for the input. I really appreciate it," E.J. said, doing his best not to let his anger show.

Noland wasn't amused.

"You have taken this name thing way too far. I don't know what you hope to gain out of this, but it's not me you're only upsetting. There are people far beyond this little circle you live in that are pissed."

E.J. quickly became assertive, his tone stern, letting out a bit of the anger that had built up from the thrashing he had just received.

"Who is pissed off Bob!? Is Bob upset or is Bob upset!? I'm not afraid of Bob, or Bob, or Bob!"

Noland lashed out.

"Just stop! Stop calling everyone Bob!"

E.J. leaned back in his chair, smiling, and suddenly relaxed. The room silent.

"He hasn't called me Bob," Victoria said, trying to break the tension.

E.J. looked over at Victoria and winked.

"Bobett's correct about that."

"That's it," Noland belted. "Get out of my office! I don't want to see you or hear you anymore! Just get these stories done now!"

E.J. got up and cheerfully headed out back to his desk.

"Victoria, please keep your mouth shut. You're not helping."

"Sorry, I was just stating a fact... he never called me Bob."

E.J. returned to his desk to begin correcting the stories and noticed the message light blinking on his phone. He stared at it and focused on how fast it flashed. The faster it blinked, the more messages awaited him. He had never seen it flash this fast. He picked up the phone and checked his messages. One after another: Walter, Noland, Walter, Noland, Victoria, Noland, human resources, a few contacts, Noland, Walter, and it went on and on, most being bullshit tasks and other nonsense that Walter and Noland wanted, clearly a game to make his job harder. E.J. hung up after writing down the laundry list of shit that the editors wanted done. He gathered his things, ready to tackle every task dumped on him, and then stopped for a moment. He looked at the clock. It was 9:30 a.m. He looked at the San Francisco Press-Journal staff list of nearly 150 employees and thought to himself.

"I have thirty minutes."

E.J. took the list and looked at the first name: Aaron Anderson, support technician. He didn't have a clue who this guy was, but picked up the phone and dialed the extension. It rang a few times and went to voicemail.

"Just called to say I can't talk right now. Bye."

E.J. peered over to the empty offices of the editors. Each call he would make would show up on caller identification as "newsroom," likely resulting in return calls that would end up going to the editors' phones. Since it would only show up as "newsroom" on caller I.D., it wouldn't be easily traced back to him. The paper set this up so that no important calls would ever be missed if the reporter was away from his desk.

The next name: Billy Akers, printing technician. He dialed the number. Voicemail again.

"Just called to say I can't talk right now. Bye."

One name after another name, some E.J. knew, most he didn't, some straight to voicemail, some answering the phone. All the same type of comment.

"Just called to say I can't talk right now. Bye."

By the time he got to Walter's name on the staff list, E.J. had left so many messages, he lost count.

"Hey Bob, just called to say I can't talk right now. Bye."

"Hey Bob, I can't talk right now, but I wanted to touch base."

"Bob, I'm really busy right now, but I just called to say I can't talk right now."

After he was done, he walked by Walter's empty office and peered through the window at the light on the phone, flickering at an obnoxiously rapid pace. He stuck his head in Noland's office and saw the red light on his phone, flashing like a time bomb on the verge of exploding. Victoria noticed E.J.'s behavior and stopped him as he was heading out the door to do the chores that the editors had dumped on him.

"Are you looking for Walter or Noland?"

"I was Bobett, but I left them both a message or two."

Victoria smiled with the unaware blank look that summed up her life.

"Okay. Should I let them know you left them messages?"

E.J. smiled cheerfully.

"Please do... and let them know it's important. Also, let them know if they need to reach me, they can leave a message."

Victoria headed back to her desk, her phone beginning to ring from the return calls left to the dozens of random employees. E.J. watched in delight, smiling as she juggled the first call in confusion, and then the second, only to hang up and have the phone ring again.

"God, she has some nice tits," he said under his breath, watching her stupidly trying to figure out what was going on with each call. "I sure hope she develops a personality before she is thirty-five. She's gonna need one."

Chapter Thirty-Seven

The editors made mention of the messages and briefly addressed concerns about the acceptable phone use policy at a general staff meeting after dozens of people asked about the anonymous messages and odd calls they received that day. No names were used, but Noland sat eyeing E.J. the whole time while Walter talked about the issue. E.J. just smiled and gave an exaggerated two-thumbs up to Noland.

After the general staff gathering, E.J. strolled into the reporters' meeting, stopping by his desk first to get his sunglasses. As he sat at the conference table, thinking of his next move, he no longer worried about having to generate leads since the editors were laying every shit story they could find in his lap. One after another, each reporter talked about their leads as E.J. sat quietly and cool. When E.J.'s turn came about, he just regurgitated the stories that were assigned to him. This didn't sit well with the editors.

"Is that all you have?" Noland said coldly.

"It's what you gave me. What else do you want?"

"You have a beat and you need to be generating something."

"I'm the general assignment reporter... that's not a beat, that's a nice title for the reporter that gets all the shit no one else wants. You assigned me a nice stack today… and if I'm not mistaken, I don't think you can expect me to do anymore stories than I'm doing right now, per the standards set out in the Hurston Newspapers Inc. Policies and Practices. Enough said."

"That's not entirely accurate," Walter chimed in, extremely irritated. "Your job description states that you are required to produce story leads."

E.J. shrugged.

"You want something? I got something. Bobett, take this shit down."

Victoria got her notepad and pen. E.J. launched into a stream of phrases and ideas that had no connection, babbling incoherently with a collection of random words. Victoria attempted to keep pace for a few seconds until she realized that none of what E.J. was saying made any kind of sense. He continued talking as if she was still taking notes, only stopping when Walter and Noland quickly cut him off. The room was silent for a moment.

"Did you get all of that Bobett? I don't want to have to repeat it."

The editors were aggravated, and the rest of the staff looked equally annoyed. Even Jeffery, who seemed to understand E.J. to some degree, looked disappointed. E.J.'s eyes scanned the room and not one friendly face looked back. At the end of the table sat Warren, who smiled and laughed softly. E.J. grinned. At least he had one person still in his corner. That was enough for him.

"You know what? We all have been a bit tense lately and it's primarily my fault. I'm not ignorant of that," E.J. said. "What we need is a bonding moment. Everyone join me in singing the National Anthem."

E.J. stood up and began singing the song at the top of his lungs. Strong, and in key, he sang his heart out through the first verse. Noland's face turned beet red and many of the other reporters got up and excused themselves. Before Noland could go off, Walter stood up and screamed.

"That's enough! You're excused Mr. Lockhart!"

E.J. stopped and headed for the door.

"By the way, I'll have your stories in by five," he said happily.

E.J.'s antics at the meeting landed him a two-day suspension for his behavior and the lack of lead generation. E.J. defended that he had performed his job well and had yet to miss a deadline, but the editors had enough grounds to dissolve his services for a moment. The editors wrote him up and threatened termination again. This fell on deaf ears as E.J. simply smiled, knowing that he had done nothing to warrant termination with cause, and ever so politely, reminded them of that fact. He was more than happy to take the unemployment and leave if they wanted to fire him now. The knotted looks in their faces were absolute… that wasn't going to happen.

Chapter Thirty-Eight

Paul Belikov was a Russian immigrant who was raised in America. His parents brought him to the states in the late 1950s when he was eight and taught him the value of hard work, which never involved working for anyone, but rather making your own way to a fortune. His parents bought a small piece of land outside of San Francisco, and by the time they retired, they had parlayed the land into a sizable property empire that included apartment complexes in the city and Oakland. He was a nice man, patient with his tenants, knowing the struggles of trying to pay for apartments that could be half a person's monthly salary.

He liked E.J. and Kalea when he first rented them the apartment, even though he wasn't entirely sure they could afford the $2,000 a month. He was a jovial guy, tall and fat with a deep laugh that came with an honest sense of humor, sprinkled with a slight Russian accent that he never lost. Paul had done three things well: Managed the inheritance his parents left behind, invested most of it in safe blue-chip stocks, and lived cheaply himself, taking a less desirable apartment in one of his own complexes rather than living in a fancy house. His place was on the second floor, just under E.J.'s and Kalea's.

For the last two months, Paul had been after E.J. for the remaining rent he was missing. He was able to pay $1,000 the previous month, but it broke E.J. He had given a few bucks here and there: $300 on a good day, $100 the next week, but was falling behind severely. Paul was patient, but E.J. had fallen behind so much that he was always at his door. E.J. would just hide in a corner with the lights out, ignoring the knocks. E.J. was leaving before dawn and coming home really late as the editors pushed so much on him. The free moments E.J. experienced from his agitated landlord came courtesy of his editors that made sure he was up before the sun and never home early enough to be accosted by Paul. Avoiding the problem was not an ideal situation for E.J., but it worked for now.

E.J. was awakened on a Saturday morning by a knock at the door that wouldn't stop. He was exhausted, not getting home until well after midnight. The sun was just rising and peaking through his window. He tried to ignore it until shouting came for the other side.

"E.J., I need the rest of the rent," Paul's voice echoing into the bedroom.

E.J. dragged himself out of bed, realizing that he had to address the problem. He put on his robe and, like a zombie, made his way to the door, opening it as far as the security chain would allow.

"Hey Paul, sorry I have been lagging. I've been working long nights."

Paul smiled.

"Sorry to wake you, but you have been hard to get a hold of."

"I know."

"Do you have the rest of the rent... you're really behind."

E.J. tried to think of a quick comeback, but he was in a fog.

"Yeah... ummmm... I'll have the rest of it when I pick up my check today. Can I drop it off later?"

Paul's look was that of skepticism.

"Well, okay, but I have to have it today or we're going to have to talk about you leaving. I don't want to evict you, but this is getting to be a huge problem."

E.J. rubbed his eyes, worn out, and wanting to go back to sleep. He was willing to say anything to make Paul go away for now. He had no check coming in today and, in that moment, tried to figure out how he would cover the missing rent or buy himself a bit more time.

"Paul, I'm trying to adjust to Kalea leaving, but I guarantee you I will drop off the money today."

Paul seemed satisfied with the answer, for the time being.

"That's fine," he said. "But a check needs to be in my mail box by the end of the day."

E.J. nodded and closed the door. He stumbled back to the bedroom and laid down. His thoughts briefly were about how to get something to Paul by the end of the day, but passed out before any real solution even entered his head. He had no real options. A few hundred dollars sat in his bank account and he wasn't going to get paid for another week. Even then, he'd still be behind the full amount he owed. The suspensions from work were not helping either. Even with the long hours he worked when he was working, he was losing a lot of time overall.

The BART was virtually empty. E.J. wasn't used to riding the train at 9:00 a.m. on a Sunday. He had called Jeffery and asked if he could come over to watch the football game and have a beer. He was looking for a place to hide for a few hours until he could figure out what to do about the rent.

"Sucks being the only two guys on a train," said a little old Jewish man sitting in the seat across from E.J. "Makes me want to walk into another car to see if there are more people somewhere else."

E.J. said nothing, nodding, and smiling at the gentleman.

"Where are you headed young man?"

"Fremont… visiting a friend."

"Your friend expects you to take a forty-five minute ride at 9:00 a.m. on a Sunday to that shithole city? Doesn't sound like much of a friend to me."

E.J. and the old man laughed together.

"I had to get out of my apartment. I usually work on Sunday, but I got suspended and I'm a bit overdue on my rent, which I do not have at the moment. I needed to disappear for a minute. My landlord wanted the rent by the end of the day yesterday. Had to tell him I was working overnight and wouldn't get it to him until today. I can't pay, so I have to stall."

"Can't pay your rent? Suspended? It sounds like code for being unemployed to me."

"Sadly no... I'm a reporter for the Press-Journal."

The old man winced.

"Ouch. That's a real J. O. B... just over broke. I have known a few media guys. They always had cheap beer and Top Ramen. Not much else."

"Yeah, it is. I have a plan in place, but I just need to buy some time. A few more weeks and I'll be good."

The old man smiled with understanding.

"Well, if you want to buy some time, drop off the check today."

E.J. immediately assumed the old man was a bit senile since he had just told him he didn't have the money. He attempted to remind him of his situation, but the old man cut him off before he could respond fully.

"Just don't sign the check."

"What?"

"Drop off the check, but don't sign it. He'll call you about it, you tell him sorry that you must have forgot, and that you're now out of town. That should buy you a few days. Just need to find a place to hang out for awhile, or a way to sneak in and out of your apartment."

E.J. smiled as if he had found a missing piece to a puzzle. He knew with Paul living on the floor beneath him, that sneaking in and out would be difficult, if not impossible. He figured Jeffery might house him for a few days.

Jeffery's place was fairly big for a one-bedroom apartment. Fremont was a true suburb: Strip malls, tracked housing, streets as wide as the Mississippi River, and plenty of parking. Jeffery lived in a huge apartment complex called Fremont Ridge. It was newer, consisting of hundreds of units that all looked the same with perfectly manicured lawns, a playground, community pools, with tennis and basketball courts. It was the exact opposite of San Francisco. After living in old apartments in the city, having to park a mile from where he lived, and grateful that he found a spot that close, Jeffery packed his bags and moved to Fremont. He didn't like the commute, but said it was easier to swallow the pill of a sterile generic town for an apartment that was built in this century with a garage. In reality, he loved it, but would never say that out loud as nothing was more hated than saying you prefer Fremont to San Francisco.

Jeffery's place was like every other apartment E.J. had ever seen in suburbia. A medium-sized living room with tan carpets and a kitchen on the side. It had the stereotypical white walls throughout, and a short hallway that led to a bedroom and a bathroom, both of which were uninspired and square. Jeffery had made it home. Decent leather couches, a nice black glass coffee table, and Laurentii trees in two corners anchoring the living room. The apartment sported a 42-inch big screen Phillips television, with black and white nicely framed photos of Boston, New York and San Francisco, circa 1930s, on the walls. He also had a small liquor collection on the mantle above the unused fireplace.

"Would you like a drink? A beer?"

E.J. looked a bit puzzled, thinking it was a bit early to start drinking, despite the fact that he had been drinking excessively, morning, noon and night, the past few weeks. He looked at the television which was playing the first half of an Oakland Raiders and Cleveland Browns game. E.J. smiled.

"Sure, it's five o'clock somewhere."

Jeffery made his way to the refrigerator and grabbed E.J. and himself a beer. E.J. sat on the sofa and became fixated on the game.

"You're from Ohio. Browns fan?" Jeffery inquired.

"It's like a long marriage with an ugly wife... you love her, but can't stand to look at her."

Jeffery laughed, sat down, and handed E.J. his beer.

"Well, I'm a New England Patriots fan and they don't play the games out here, so I'll take what I can get. I'll watch any game."

E.J. sipped on his beer while the two made small talk about work, the football game, the state of journalism, articles Jeffery was working on, and the antics that E.J. was pulling at work. Part of him championed E.J., but the love he had for the profession began to override that feeling. He was now conflicted. In some ways, he felt like a defender and advocate of E.J., but had become fractionally disgusted at the mockery and the disrespect his behavior displayed to the job he felt was so important.

"Can I ask a favor of you Jeff?"

"Sure. What do ya need?"

"I need a place to crash for a few days... my landlord is after me for rent. With Kalea gone and these suspensions, I'm way behind and need a few days to lay low."

"Not a problem, as long as you don't mind my couches."

"Thanks, I really appreciate this."

Jeffery threw back another drink of his beer.

"Dude, not a problem, but what are you going to do in the long run? You can't dodge your landlord forever."

"Oh, I thought about this on the train over here. I have one or two ideas to buy more time. I'm going to break these editors before I get evicted, trust that."

E.J.'s tone was strong, but Jeffery had been working in the industry too long and could hear a bit of hesitancy in his voice, a slight fragment of uncertainty that resonated beyond his words.

"You sure about that?" Jeffery asked.

"I have to be... failure isn't an option."

Chapter Thirty-Nine

E.J. walked up the street from his apartment, unsigned check in hand. His plan was simple: Get into his apartment, pack a few things, quickly drop the check in Paul's mail slot, and hop the BART back to Jeffery's place. When Paul would eventually call, tell him that he had to go to Los Angeles for a story and wouldn't be back until the end of the week. Hunters Point's main drag, Third Street, was intimidating at night. There often were a lot of people hanging out, a lot of drugs, and a large collection of shady characters. E.J.'s apartment was off of Third Street, up a steep incline on Jefferson Court. On top of the hill, things were generally quiet, but if you got down to Third Street, things changed. As he made his way up to his apartment, he had an idea. Was there a way to access his place from the alley in the back of the building? He should be able to climb the fire escape. It was dusk and the sun was setting, but there was enough light that he felt safe checking the alley behind his own apartment complex. Out of the shadows, a young black man appeared. He had long braids, baggy jeans, and a Golden State Warriors jersey with a hat to match.

"You lookin' for somethin', bro?"

E.J. didn't see him coming and was startled, but did his best not to appear that way.

"No man, I live here on the seventh floor," E.J. said with confidence. "Who the fuck are you and what are you doing back here?"

"Chill out bro, I ain't no crazy thug nigga... I'm just a businessman out lookin' for business."

The young man pulled out a large bag of marijuana and held it up to E.J.

"You get high?"

E.J. was surprised.

"What? No man, I ain't into that shit," E.J. said. "Are you crazy trying to sell to me? You don't know me. What if I'm a cop?"

The young man smiled and laughed.

"Man, I've been working this neighborhood for years. Long before you and your woman moved in. You don't think I know who's a cop and who isn't around here? Nigga, please. I'm just trying to hook you up with some of the Bay Area's finest."

E.J. became relaxed and no longer felt threatened.

"The name is Blaze."

"Is that your real name?"

"Come on, man. That's what they call me around here."

"I'm E.J."

"I know who you are. You're the reporter. I've read some of your shit. I saw the story about Oakland's mayor. I pay attention to that shit."

E.J. was perplexed.

"What? You think us niggas can't read?"

E.J. laughed.

"No man, it's just you know more about me than I would expect."

"I'm slanggin' weed on the streets right around your neighborhood. To be successful means I know about you, you don't know about me... feel me?"

"It makes sense."

"So what's the deal? You smoke? I know that reporter job be stressin' you."

"No man, I told you I don't really smoke... just lookin' for an access point to my apartment from the back."

Blaze and E.J. looked down the alley. It was dank and dirty with a few trash bins along the building. The fire escape had a ladder, but on the first floor, it was raised up, too high to grab a hold of from the ground.

"You can go up that fire escape to whatever floor you're on. The landlord won't see ya. You can dodge that rent for a long time."

"How do you know I'm dodging rent?"

"Man, I just told you. To be successful, I need to know you, but you don't know me."

"If you know I'm dodging rent, why would you try and sell me weed? You should know I'm broke."

"Mothafucka', you're lookin' at the situation as the glass bein' half empty. I see it as half full. If you're dodging rent successfully, you probably have the money for a bag here and there."

E.J. laughed.

"That is one way to look at it."

Blaze put the bag away, led E.J. down the alley, and showed him how to get on the fire escape using the trash bins as a jumping point. The two climbed up the escape gingerly to minimize noise. Blaze explained that by keeping the latch on the seventh floor window just a bit loose, he can get in. E.J. snuck into his apartment and packed a bag for his stay at Jeffery's then quietly dropped off the unsigned check in Paul's mailbox. They both made it back down to the street and E.J. thanked Blaze for the help. The young man quickly rolled a joint and sparked it.

"I have a question," E.J. asked

"Sure," Blaze said, his lungs full of smoke.

"Why are you bothering with me? Out of nowhere, you just appear helping the random white guy? What is it that you want? This isn't a coincidence."

Blaze let out a thick trail of smoke and coughed a bit.

"You're in media. It's always good to have someone like that on your side, just like having someone like me around in this neighborhood is good for someone like you. Plus, your woman left you and you're strugglin'. I got a heart for that. I think you do too, from what I know. We ain't that different. I see a brotha strugglin', I'm gonna help... that's just me. I know you're the same. Are you sure you don't want some? Try it."

E.J. had smoked weed a few times in his life and wasn't into it, but grabbed the joint and took a long drag.

"Good shit, huh?"

E.J. shook his head yes as he coughed a bunch of smoke out his mouth.

"Hey," E.J. said. "How'd you know my woman bailed on me?"

Blaze smirked at the stupid question.

"What have I told you?"

"Yeah, yeah... to be successful on these streets, you need to know me."

E.J. made it back to Jeffery's house just before the late night news and set himself up in a small corner of the living room. Jeffery gave E.J. a blanket and pillow. He lied down on the long leather sofa, finally feeling rest upon him, until his phone rang. It was Paul. He answered, apologized for forgetting to sign the check, and sold the lie about being in Los Angles for a few days. Paul seemed content with the answer and E.J. just smiled, relishing the easy out. He thanked God that he didn't have to fight another battle that day.

"How long do you think you can pull this off?" Jeffery asked, eavesdropping on the phone call. "You can't stay here forever."

"I know... but I have found a way to sneak into my apartment. That should help buy me some time."

"So you didn't sign the check today, but you're going to have to sign that check eventually."

"No... I'm going to claim that I cancelled the check and then pull another little trick. I'll sneak around for another day or two, make up some excuse, and give him a bunch of cash when I get paid Friday. I'll tell him the rest is coming that same day and disappear again."

Jeffery laughed at the haphazard plan.

"Yeah, well you have until the weekend here."

"Gotcha."

Jeffery turned out the lights in the hallway and made his way to bed.

"Goodnight E.J."

"Goodnight... thanks again."

Chapter Forty

E.J. returned to work and nothing much had changed. The editors had remained steadfast and he wasn't budging either. The atmosphere remained tense. He still couldn't make full rent and batted away his landlord with a few dollars, buying himself a few days with each partial payment, but realized that he had to step up his efforts to command the dismissal he desired. He knew the eviction process was inescapable and slithering adjacent, gliding close overhead.

Noland emerged from his office and called E.J. in to see him.

"What's up Bob?"

Noland was curt and short.

"We need you to cover a huge story, the San Francisco Seven by Seven Marathon. It's a big deal that is going to happen next month. It's an AIDS charity run to raise a bunch of money... we need some preliminary articles and as steady stream of stories leading up to the race."

"What are you talking about... one a week?"

"One a week? What the fuck do you think this is? A weekly paper?"

E.J. knew what this was about. There is no way that a reporter could produce any real stories about some charity marathon every day without running out of things to write about. The editors were setting him up. He had been consistent with every bullshit story they had dropped in his lap and this was a move to make him fail to produce. This would be an excuse to fire him with real reason. He began to contemplate how he would pull this off as Noland rambled on. He nodded his head, as if he was paying attention, but was lost in his own thoughts, trying to figure out a way around this problem.

"By the way, this is a Hurston sponsored event, so make it good."

E.J. smirked while Noland smiled, a bit of retribution dancing across his face.

Skye looked on as E.J. scribbled down notes. He listed every person related to the marathon, read previous stories to figure out historical elements, and outlined the angles he could take. He called organizers and got names of participants, sponsors, past winners, past runners that came in last place, any celebrity that ever participated, searched for any oddity he could find, and any other minute weird story that could be exploited or angle that could be taken. He mumbled to himself as he drew up a dozen possible stories, but needing somewhere between twenty to twenty-five article ideas minimum... his pen stopped. Jeffery looked over.

"They might have you in a bind on this one E.J."

"It isn't over until the fat lady sings."

"You're killing yourself with this game you're playing. Is this really worth it?" Jeffery asked. "You're stressing over a job that if you died tomorrow would replace you in a week."

E.J. became slightly irritated.

"I thought you were in my corner on this?"

"I'm trying, but this cannot be good for you. It certainly isn't good for the profession either. When is it enough?"

E.J. put down his pen.

"Jeffery, I'm sorry if you're becoming uneasy with what I'm doing, but I'm doing all the stuff everyone in this newsroom wish they did at one time or another in their life, be it to a boss, or a corporation, or other oppressive and dishonest industry. There is a larger mission here. It's not about smashing the profession. I still love and respect media, good reporters, good editors, and good ownership. I'm trying to teach the others that have no respect a lesson. On the surface, maybe it seems as if I'm disrespecting the profession, but I'm not. I'm defending it against the practices that destroy it. Look at me, at Warren, at yourself, and every other reporter around you that bleeds the ethics and principals that led them here. Then look at the others and ask yourself: Who is really destroying it? Me? You? Or them?"

Skye leaned over, only hearing a snippet of what was said.

"When did you become the authority on media and ethics?"

E.J. swiftly spun his chair around.

"Well, I certainly would love to hear your opinion on this," E.J. sarcastically shot back. "I mean if you want to know about the people that crap all over media and ethics, get it from the piece of shit that sits next to me. Who the fuck are you to say anything, Skye?"

Skye sat silent for a moment and then got up and left, mumbling some inaudible obscenities.

"What do you want me to say?" Jeffery asked rhetorically. "The editors and the owners are the ones' destroying the industry? That you are the champion of the industry?"

"No Jeffery, I just want to give you some more perspective."

Jeffery nodded in acceptance.

"So what are you going to do about this marathon?"

"I don't know. You have any story ideas?"

Jeffery looked at the notepad, combing through every idea E.J. laid out.

"Wow, this looks pretty complete."

Jeffery thought for a moment.

"What about following the training of one runner? Each day you have a new story. That should easily fill in the last twelve or so stories you're going to need."

E.J. grabbed the notepad and wrote the suggestion down.

"This is a good idea."

"Who are you thinking of following? A favorite to win? Maybe a celebrity who's running?"

An thought popped in E.J.'s head and a wicked smile draped his face.

"No... no... I will follow myself. A personal narrative of someone running the race."

Jeffery seemed a bit confused.

"Are you talking about joining this race? When did you decide to run the marathon?"

"Right now," E.J. answered.

"Are you serious?"

"Of course," E.J. chuckled with a hint of evil sprinkled in his voice. "It is, after all, a Hurston sponsored event. How can I not support it? The editors have made it very clear that a Hurston sponsored news story is one of the most important there is, right? More important than anything else, right? Just ask Kalea. She'll tell you all about it."

Chapter Forty-One

"Do you have today's story for the marathon?" Noland screamed across the newsroom.

"Got it," E.J. said, trying not to use any proper names. He felt the "call everyone Bob" stunt had worn itself thin, but refused to revert back to using real names so as not to look like he had given into anything. He made sure to call someone "Bob" every so often to keep the tone set and the ball in his court.

"What do you have for the next two weeks, E.J.? I need to get an idea of what's going on. I'm only seeing enough stories to take us to the end of the week."

Both Skye and Jeffery stopped what they were doing; knowing that E.J.'s stream of stories was running out. Noland's face showed slight arrogance while Walter, who heard Noland from his office, looked through his window to see what was going to happen. The editors knew that E.J. had ran out of stories and they were ready to corner him.

"I've decided that I would follow a runner, each day, training for the marathon," E.J. replied.

Walter came out of his office while Noland thought for a minute, searching his brain for a reply.

"No, no, no... I don't like that idea," Noland said. "It's too weak and has no real legs to cover another two weeks leading up to the marathon. You have to come up with something better than that."

Walter smiled while Noland smirked pompously, both convinced they had finally painted E.J. into a corner with nowhere to go.

"Well, that's not exactly what I meant. I'm talking about a personal narrative. I'm going to run the marathon and write a personal story each day chronicling the journey. This is a Hurston sponsored event, so how awesome would it be that a reporter not only supports this wonderful company, but participates in the event itself? That Hurston sponsored event that you sent me to on my anniversary was so important to you, and I understand that now. I know you love this idea… just as much as your bosses at HQ. I let them know and I got a real positive response from them."

Before Noland or Walter could respond, E.J. turned to the entire newsroom to drum up support.

"Well, everyone?! What do you think?! E.J. Lockhart is going to run the San Francisco Seven by Seven Marathon! Who is with me on this story idea?!"

The newsroom erupted with cheers and claps. From the back of the newsroom, Warren was leading the ovation which cascaded across the entire floor, drawing everyone's attention. Dozens emerged from the offices and cubicles to see what was happening. Jeffery laughed loudly and clapped his hands. Skye sat quiet, a look of distaste for what was going on draping his face. E.J. turned back and grinned widely at Noland and Walter, both of whom said nothing as the entire newsroom continued cheering E.J. on.

"Bob!" E.J. screamed in the direction of the editors. "You'll have your first training story today! The journey to winning the marathon starts now!"

E.J. pulled his tie off and quickly unbuttoned his shirt, revealing a white tank top that read "Hurston's Ass Haulers" with a marathon bib pinned to his chest, number 52,000 scrolled across it, an homage to the salary he was originally promised. He dropped his pants, a pair of running shorts underneath. He threw the pile of clothes on his desk and donned a headband. He began stretching, warming up in the middle of the newsroom, while the inaudible chorus slowly turned into chants screaming E.J.'s name over and over again. Noland and Walter stood stunned while the newsroom started filling up with others that heard the commotion, adding to the melee of raucous applause as E.J. finished his toe-touches and began running in place.

"Thirty laps today! Fifty tomorrow! One hundred laps by the end of the week!"

E.J. started to run around the perimeter of the newsroom, counting each time he passed Walter's office, high-fiving coworkers as he circled his laps. One, he would scream. Two, three, four, and so on, until he hit thirty, while the newsroom cheered along the way. Walter and Noland quietly went into their offices, logged themselves into their computers, and sent E.J. an e-mail: Come see us after your "training" is done.

In Walter's office, E.J. sat, dripping of sweat and still breathing hard. Walter and Noland were ready to squash the personal narrative stories, but realized in that moment that the support he was receiving from the rest of the company might expose the editors' vindictive motives to get rid of him if they didn't allow him to pursue the assignment. Their only move was to attempt to stop the training that E.J. was clearly going to do every day leading up to the race.

"First of all," Walter said. "If you think you're going to run around this office every day, you're sadly mistaken. This is a disruption and grounds to be fired, with cause and without unemployment."

E.J. nodded with affirmation.

"I know this Walter, but I do have a lunch hour and you saw the support out there for me. Company policy specifically states that my lunch hour is mine, and another section states that I can do whatever I want during these times as long as I'm not distracting coworkers. I don't think people will mind me training. As a matter of fact, I think they want me to do this. You saw them. They loved it! It's not a distraction. I'm motivating everyone."

"If they cheer when you do it, it's a distraction. You'll be fired," Walter said.

Noland jumped in.

"I know this whole personal narrative story angle and the phony support for a Hurston sponsored event is some kind of get back for the assignment we sent you on, as if you give a shit about this company. We know exactly what you're up to and if you think for one moment you'll win this battle, you're wrong. Come Hell or high water, your ass will be on the street sooner than you think. You can't beat us at this game."

"It's easy to end this Noland," E.J. said with calm. "Fire me…. but you won't. Your bosses would bury you two if you fired me without cause. A million-dollar business that would drop a hammer on you two just because you had to pay one employee unemployment. Pennies to this business, but you two have no choice because you both are gutless cowards. Really, it does explain everything about you two. Y'all are just like the Tin Man from the Wizard of Oz… you act hard, but have no heart."

E.J. got up and headed for the door.

"You can try to get me to quit, but it won't work. You can try to sabotage my job, but that won't work either. I will make you two deal with me, just riding that line of the rules, until you can't take it anymore. In the meantime, I will train and unless you can prove it's a distraction. I won't stop."

Noland and Walter said nothing.

"By the way," E.J. said as he exited out the office. "This personal narrative is a legitimate series of stories, regardless of any motives, and you will take them. If you don't, you'll have to answer to a whole lot of people out there in that newsroom and to those at HQ, all of whom disagree with your take on the matter."

E.J. stepped out the office door. As it slowly closed behind him, he hyped himself to everyone in the newsroom one more time, cheers erupting. He turned back, smiled at Noland and Walter who sat looking through the window drenched in frustration.

"What now?" Noland asked.

"Let's write him up, but wait until after the marathon. Our bosses won't question us for doing that after the fact. Once they get their stories, they won't care, and because of this stunt, they'll understand and back us."

"So, you're going to put up with this training bullshit?"

"I'm not sure we have a choice," Walter replied looking out the window as E.J. schmoozed the newsroom, everyone congratulating him. "Looks like we're outmatched in this round of insanity, but we're not beaten by any stretch of the imagination. First thing we do is move him to the night shift until the marathon is over. Let's see how much training he does in a mostly empty newsroom. Let's see how he likes that. After this marathon, suspend him for five days. Keep him late, make him work every holiday, and tear his ass apart on every little mistake he makes. Make his fucking life miserable."

"What about the union?"

"As long as we stay within our rights, he can't go to the union for anything. This stunt is clearly too much, and they won't support his behavior if we suspend him. We won't be able to fire him for it, if he stays within those lines, which he will, but this isn't going away unpunished."

Noland nodded in agreement.

"Also, Noland, we need to get Victoria more involved in this somehow."

"Victoria?" Noland asked in a skeptical tone. "You think she can outwit E.J.? Gimme a break."

"No, it's not about that. We need to get all of our allies more involved. In fact, we need to get both Victoria and Skye to help us step it up. We need a bigger team to get rid of this cancer."

Chapter Forty-Two

Although the night shift left the newsroom virtually empty, there were still plenty of people around, mostly sports reporters, weekend feature reporters, and layout people that assembled the paper and weekend sections. Various middle-managers in circulation, sales reps trying to get paperwork done, copy editors, janitors, and security also meandered throughout the building. E.J. was meticulous with his stories. Every word carefully analyzed while sending continuous updates to the editors to make sure there were no surprises along the way. Every minute had to be accounted for, every second precise so he would never miss a deadline. Four stories a day, coupled with writing obituaries, while the editors attempted to throw every curveball they could to inundate him and derail his ability to train for the marathon at work. Even at night he would be picked apart. Readjusting his shifts to lessen E.J.'s antics in the newsroom and squash his visibility didn't allay tensions or weaken the editors resolve to extinguish E.J. The editors still identified every minute mistake, created holes to fill, and built obstacles at each turn. Even though nothing was ever good enough, E.J.'s approach diluted the editors' cleverness. Like a machine, all stories were filed by 2:00 a.m. They were then torn apart by the night editors, as directed by Walter, then kicked back to E.J., only to be returned to the editors, all corrections corrected, all mistakes fixed, and any vacancy sewed up. In the middle of all this back-and-forth, E.J. never stopped training openly in the newsroom and throughout the building.

He would write at home immediately after waking up, completing stories in the morning before arriving to work the night shift, focusing on his own training stories, which were easy for him to complete. Stories that were dumped on him the night before would be up next, mostly written in skeleton form and completed immediately when he arrived to the office. The first drafts of every story he had that day were turned in within an hour of walking through the Press-Journal doors. The editors' game would start shortly after his arrival. However, without fail, every night at 9:00 p.m., he would start his training routine.

E.J. would strip down to his marathon outfit, scream random generic gym phrases, and do pushups and stretches in the middle of the newsroom, trying to get the few people around to cheer him on. Most of the time they did, sometimes they'd just smile or chuckle and continue with their business. Each time the editors made his job harder, he made his training more involved and his laps around the building more methodical, running through multiple floors of the building and yelling a barrage of terms at no one in particular. "Push harder!" "Never die!" "Come on! One more lap!" "Don't quit on me now you pussy!" He jumped in office doorways, grabbing on the moldings above and doing pull-ups while the person in the office sat baffled. He sprinted, grabbing glasses of water out of the hands of coworkers and dumping it over his head or throwing it into his face as he traversed the hallways. He hopped onto desks to do jumping jacks, blocked hallways while doing squats, and made sure that Noland and Walter saw everything he could, and if they didn't see it, at least heard about it from those working the night shift. While some of this was a nuisance, the night staff loved it, praising E.J. for his spark and helping keep things upbeat at night. While the move to the night shift may have seemed like a good move at the time, the editors didn't realize E.J.'s antics could be amplified because there simply weren't enough folks in the building to disrupt, and the usually somber night-shift mood had turned into a cheerful environment everyone loved.

The editors met secretly again as they strategized. E.J. refused to budge; taking low-grade amphetamine pills to keep his energy up as sleeping became a rarer luxury between his shifts. The workload being dumped on him and the personal training was punishing. He refused to break as the onslaught of stories, edits, re-edits, rewrites, his own personal training narratives, the marathon, and his mission to get fired collided together into one endless loop of exhaustion.

The first two weeks of E.J.'s personal journey stories were gaining attention across the Bay Area as the public cheered for the homegrown runner. The e-mails were piling up, but E.J. was too busy to notice them. Stories began to emerge outside of the Press-Journal's newsroom as local television stations called E.J. to find out more about the reporter that was running in the marathon and writing whimsical stories about his journey. Although the stories often poked fun at the San Francisco Press-Journal, people took it as tongue-in-cheek, and E.J. began to develop a following. The city of San Francisco became enamored with E.J. as his quest for marathon glory began to take on a life of its own. E.J. was too wrapped up in his own worries and work to really even notice how big he was becoming.

"Good job making the front page of the East Bay Express," Jeffery said as E.J. walked up to his desk.

"What?" E.J. said, confused.

Jeffery threw the issue of the Express on his desk, a cartoon drawing of a marathon runner with E.J's head superimposed, pasted on. The headline: "The Running Reporter: One Man's Quest to Document Every Step in the San Francisco Seven by Seven Marathon."

E.J. laughed.

"What the fuck?"

"You need to check your e-mail and messages," Jeffery said. "It looks like you're becoming a bit of a celebrity from your stories."

"I know a few folks have ran pieces on me, but this is more than I expected."

E.J. walked over to Noland's office.

"Have a lot of people been calling about my marathon stories?"

"Yep," Noland replied flatly, turning back toward his computer screen and continuing to edit.

"Looks like I may have to go do some more interviews," E.J. said brightly, waiting to see what reaction Noland would have.

There was no reaction at all.

E.J. checked his phone and e-mails, dozens of local rags, local shows, and news stations across the Bay Area wanted to talk with him. Hundreds of messages from readers also clogged his inbox. The support was overwhelming. E.J. smiled as he realized this small wave of celebrity had enlightened him.

E.J. thought to himself, mumbled lightly.

"I haven't really thought about it, but they haven't been hounding me the last few days. It's been quiet… makes sense now."

He looked over to Jeffery.

"Hey, do you think that this following I'm getting is forcing the editors to back off of me?"

"Are you serious? You really are completely out of the loop. Your stories are blowing this paper up and ramping up sales. The owners are in love with us right now. You could be pissing on Walter while tonguing Noland's daughter and they wouldn't say shit about any of it. If you're making this paper money, the owners are happy and the editors will back off."

"I've been so wrapped up in my training and all my work I didn't realize I was getting all of this press. No wonder Noland didn't have any opinions as to whether or not I should interview for stories about my journey."

"Well, when you get this kind of action, they change their tune," Jeffery said. "This paper wants the sales, the positive publicity, and the boost in circulation. They're getting fat bonuses for all of this. Noland and Walter aren't going to say shit... no one is going to say shit."

"Wow, what a bunch of dirt bags."

E.J. threw himself into the spotlight, taking every interview he could get. In papers, on television, on the cover of local and regional magazines, his journey made for perfect public relations. The editors relented as the increase in his time spent working on his stories and doing interviews took over. E.J. ate it up, taking every chance to light-heartedly poke fun and passive-aggressively take jabs at the paper. Although on the surface it seemed that things were getting better for E.J., tensions between him and the editors subsiding, the unexpected turn of events only strengthened his tenacity. The shallowness of the industry was more exposed than he ever thought he would witness. He smiled, they smiled, both knowing that once the race was over, his personal journey forgotten, sales leveling out, that they would go back to war.

The day of the race, E.J. had his own camera crew behind him. He had partnered with a number of organizations and began to raise money for various causes, all awarded money based on how he would place in the race, assuming he could even finish it. He was in good shape, but in reality, he wasn't truly prepared to run the distance and had been burning the candle at both ends for weeks. The editors remained painfully quiet as the hype surrounding E.J. grew to levels that expanded out of the Bay Area. He never wavered on his enthusiasm in public interviews, nor did he stop jeering the Press-Journal in a continuous mix of being lightly sincere, but always sarcastic, with a tone that the public took as simply being part of his quirky and infectiously-cute personality. More support poured into the newsroom cheering him on, papers sold at record levels, and E.J. became a fixture for weeks across the Bay Area, the state, and even nationwide. His stunts got more outrageous, and although the editors hated every moment of it, they bit their tongues and said nothing. E.J. became more solidified in his resolve as he further realized how deep the paper-thin commitment to journalism the Press-Journal really held. No matter how outrageous E.J. acted during this whole stunt, the absolute hatred the editors had toward E.J. and his antics, all of it could easily be tamed by numbers, money, and sales.

During this time, he never realized or considered that his story had reached across to the other side of the nation. One night while watching the news, Kalea saw the story of the San Francisco reporter that was training for the San Francisco Seven by Seven. She was shocked and confused as the story repeatedly emerged on her television screen and crossed her path in the employee lounge at

Cleveland State University when the newspapers arrived in the morning. As the reports continued to unfold in front of her eyes, she smiled, laughed a bit, and quietly thought about the essences that made her fall in love with E.J.

Although he started near the front at the beginning of the race, he was easily outmatched by real runners, but never outmatched by the cameras that followed him in the crowd of the nearly 30,000 people that took part in the marathon. Fans stood on the side, signs held high, and cheers screamed loud as E.J. slowly ran the race. He finished near the bottom, but he finished. His body hurt as the realization that the phony training he was doing, although at least was some training, didn't prepare him at all. The colossal crowd at the finish line erupted when he ran the final feet of the race, the media waiting for him as he nearly collapsed across the destination. A few slightly incoherent interviews, repeated statements, canned responses, plugs for the charities, and the unwavering passive-aggressive attacks on the Press-Journal sprinkled the news that night as E.J. officially became one of San Francisco's darlings. The minute he came back to the newsroom and filed his last story about the race, he was quietly suspended for five days without pay for his initial insubordination. The journey that made the paper the most read periodical across the state, made him a beloved figure nationally, and both fattened the wallets of the publisher while lining the editors' pockets at the same time couldn't save him at the end of the day.

Chapter Forty-Three

Time off presented a real problem: It didn't sit well with his pocket book and he was running short with his landlord, robbing Peter to pay Paul for too many weeks. Now he was home all day and it was easy to find him. E.J. did catch up with his rent occasionally, but the landlord was becoming increasingly impatient as payments were constantly overdue and the spotty $200 here, $100 there, was starting to wear thin. E.J. had been working so much, he had been able to avoid him and keep up with some bills with overtime, but the suspension made him a sitting duck. He didn't answer the door the first day, ducked out the second day, but as the landlord became more persistent, he couldn't ignore the pounding and the screams.

"I know you're in there Lockhart!" Paul yelled.

He gave the landlord everything he had, but was told that if didn't pay his rent on time again, he would seriously consider eviction.

The high of his marathon run was over and he had spent a good portion of his suspension drinking, thinking of Kalea, and was desperate to talk with her. All alone in his apartment he had no distractions. Thoughts of Kalea consumed him more with each passing minute. He picked up the phone and called her. For the first time, after dozens of attempts to get a hold of her, she answered.

"Hey," E.J. said with a reserved tone, trying to hide his slight intoxication.

"Hey," Kalea replied with indifference.

There was a long silence, neither one of them knew what to say.

"How ya doin'?"

"Good," Kalea replied. "But not as good as you, Mr. Marathon. I must say, you've been busy since I left."

"Wow, I had no idea that would make the news in Ohio." E.J. said with a bit of shock, not ever considering that Kalea had known what was going on.

"Oh, I saw the coverage. I was shocked to say the least."

E.J. sat quiet for a moment, the low hum of the cell phone connection being the only thing audible.

"Why did you ditch me?"

"I could ask the same thing about you," she replied.

"Look, I'm not mad," E.J. replied. "I understand why you left. I just wish you would have said goodbye or took my calls. This killed me."

"I'm sorry E.J., but after our anniversary night I couldn't take it. I was upset. I should have handled it better. I just needed some space."

"I want you to know that I'm going to come home. I want to be with you. I lost the most important thing to me while trying to get something I thought really mattered when it didn't. I love you and will make this right"

Kalea smiled.

"Are you quitting? When are you coming home?"

"No. I'm not quitting."

E.J. sipped on the bottle of Jack Daniels and began a tirade about why the paper hired him, why his beat was changed, how they duped him into a lower-paying job, why people like Skye can get away with stealing stories, how they take the reporters' credit and never the blame. Kalea patiently listened as he continued about his plans, explaining the shoes, the name "Bob," the odd behavior in the newsroom, and why he ran the marathon. He rambled on, happy the woman he loved was on the other end and relieved that the one person he wanted to tell all of this to was finally listening.

"I can't believe you're doing this. It's ridiculous. Just quit and come home."

"Babe, I want to, but this is bigger than me. I thought the journey of life was about what you get and how fast you can get it, but now I realize it's about who you become. In the end, people only remember who you become, the type of person you are, and not what you achieved or what you have. Some people need to know what they have become, and that goes hand-in-hand with the person

I need to become as well. I need to show them who they are and who they have become, so I need to do this before I leave."

Kalea interrupted.

"I thought I was the most important thing. I guess this stunt you're pulling is more important than me too."

E.J. was silent. Kalea was frustrated.

"I can't talk about this. Call me when you decide to come home... hopefully after you realize how utterly stupid you're acting."

The phone went dead.

"I'm sorry Kalea," he said to himself. "One day you'll understand."

Chapter Forty-Four

The deal went through and the first edition copy of Raymond Chandler's "The Big Sleep" was sold to a collector. E.J. hated to part ways with the book, but the $5,000 he got for it covered all his rent as he could no longer dodge Paul. He owed $2,000 and in two weeks, rent would be due again. The last $3,000 he hid in an old shirt pocket hanging in the closet. At some point he would need it, he thought, as another stopgap to buy more time. His routine of climbing up the fire escape through the back was working well, for the most part. Paul never noticed, but neighbors did, and they started to talk. Blaze covered for E.J., telling people who became suspicious that it was other neighbors that were coming in and out, either because they locked themselves out or were sneaking people into their apartment. When residents claimed they were sure it was E.J., Blaze reminded them he was house-sitting and that it couldn't be E.J. because he was "out of town." E.J. worried that he would be exposed, but most of the apartment's residents were either too busy living their big city lives or simply too busy to care about the details. No one even realized that Blaze was a new face in the building, just assumed he had always been around because he acted as if he always was. Paul was oblivious to any of this.

Even though he had paid back rent, it was soon due again and he needed a few more days to ride out another suspension that followed the five days he received after the marathon. He picked up his next check and grabbed the $3,000 he stashed in his shirt pocket. Paul was coming over at odder and odder times to catch E.J. It was no different today, the knock at the door at 11 p.m.

"Hey E.J., just noticed that the rent is late again. Remember what I told you. No more late rent," Paul said, trying to be nice, knowing every bit of E.J.'s struggles.

"Sure thing Paul, ummm... I get paid tomorrow and I'll drop it off in full. I'm leaving for Oregon to cover a story, so I'll get that to you before I leave."

Paul nodded, thanked E.J., and began to walk away, before turning back around, just as E.J. was closing the door.

"Oh, by the way E.J., I know things are a bit tough, but I have bills to pay too. I cannot take partial payments anymore. You miss your full rent again, you'll have to go."

E.J. responded with acceptance and closed the door.

"Fuck... I better figure this out."

E.J. sat down and looked around his house. The television, the radio, the Playstation, the stacks of DVDs and CDs, the furniture, the handmade cherry wood coffee table his aunt gave him before he and Kalea came out to the Bay Area, and the throw rugs that decorated the apartment. He got up off the sofa and made his way to the closet. Inside was a bunch of miscellaneous household items. A hand vacuum, a small television, old duffle bags, an extra iron and ironing board, an old computer, his snowboard with bindings, and bunch of other small boxes that had old silverware, plates, and other kitchen and bathroom items. He pulled all the material out and began sorting it. In the back of the closet were two folding lawn chairs that were perfect for his next idea. E.J. stopped and stared at the chairs for a minute. He looked at the pile of stuff pulled from the closet and noticed a fairly large plastic storage bin full of old books and a few board games. He took the bin and quickly removed what was in it, then moved the coffee table off to the side of the apartment. He placed the empty bin where the coffee table was originally sitting. He then pushed the sofas out of the way and folded out both lawn chairs. He took the small television he found in the closet and set it on the ground, plugged it in, and turned it on. The reception wasn't half bad, he thought to himself. He took his beer and sat down. He placed the drink on the plastic bin as if it were a table and watched the slightly grainy late-night newscast.

"Perfect. This isn't such a bad set up for the apartment."

The next morning, with the help of Blaze, the entire front of the apartment building looked like a thrift store. Everything from the apartment that he absolutely didn't need was out for sale. The street was buzzing with people as E.J. and Blaze sold off items. Blaze, under the radar, dumped off bags of weed to those shopping for more than a good bargain on old stuff. Blaze was an amazing salesman working the crowd for every dime. Any item E.J. wanted $10 for, Blaze got $20. Everything for sale was systematically pushed and sold, even to people that really didn't want the items. Blaze had the ability to convince people it was a good deal, regardless if they needed it or not. As the sun began to fall, most everything was gone. Just scraps and pieces of trash littered the streets. The two cleaned up and went upstairs to E.J.'s nearly-vacant apartment.

Blaze sat in a lawn chair in the middle of the living room and crushed some weed on a Playboy magazine that was sitting on the plastic storage container nearby. He was meticulous, slowly breaking the weed up into a fine pile. E.J. could smell it from the kitchen as he poured beers in the only two glasses he had left. The apartment was baron.

"Smells good," E.J. said. "What is that?"

"It's called Purple Cush... San Francisco's finest."

Blaze rolled a faultless joint, perfectly round just like a cigarette, licked the glue of the Zig Zag, and then twisted it.

"Hey, thanks for helping me Blaze. You really came through."

E.J. sat in the other lawn chair next to Blaze and handed the young man his beer.

"No problem, brotha... I made a killin' out there too. Suckas that hit yard sales always be the biggest stoners."

E.J. pulled out a wad of money and began counting.

"How much you think you got?"

"Not sure... I didn't want to count as I got it."

Blaze sparked the joint as E.J. laid down the bills. What started as $20 quickly turned to $40, to $100, to $500, to $1,000 until the last bill was counted.

"Holy shit!" E.J. belted as he took a drag off the joint and handed it back to Blaze. "I made $3,430 off all that stuff."

Blaze smiled.

"That should hold you for a few more weeks in this place."

"Fuckin' A!" E.J. screamed.

The joint was passed back to E.J., who took another long drag.

"Blaze, why do you sell drugs? You're a smart motherfucker. Why this life?"

"Well, E.J., I'm not really university material. College wasn't my thing. Look at it this way, you use your brain to make something happen. I use my brain to do the same thing. We're not that much different, just working in two different fields."

"But what if you get busted... you can't do this forever."

Blaze took another drag.

"That's where you mothafuckas get shit twisted. I do my homework. Have you been following any of the marijuana law reform movements?"

E.J. shook his head no as he inhaled and choked off another hit.

"Lesson number one my brotha, not all of us street niggas is ignorant. I got real plans, and although they aren't the most practical plans, I see what's coming. It will be legal eventually… another few years. When it is, I'll be on the ground floor to sell it legally, for medical use or otherwise. Maybe I'll join with the media, but like an alternative media. You know, start my own media company to promote the benefits of marijuana and demand fair treatment for us smokers. Like the Martin Luther King Jr. of weed."

They both laughed, completely stoned.

"What if that never happens… or it's not until twenty years down the line?"

"I can't argue with that. But you'd be surprised what I know and where I've been."

The two high-fived and quickly supercharged each other with the remaining hit on the joint.

"What's your next move?" Blaze asked.

E.J. thought for a moment.

"I have to go big to get these motherfuckers to fire me. Look at my place. I've got nothin' left to sell. The marathon got me close, but I have to go bigger."

"Can you parlay the media attention you got from the race to get a better job? At another paper?"

E.J. nodded with indifference.

"Yeah… the offers are out there, but fuck that. These people are all the same. They're about themselves, the big story that will make them famous, the money that can be piled on because of others' misery... the sales... more stories that can beat the competition to sell more papers."

"What job isn't like that? I mean, did you ever really believe that the world of business was fair or concerned about ethics and morals. Moreover, when did you ever think they would care about you?"

"I'm not sure Blaze... maybe it was being idealistic... I still am, to a certain extent. I know this industry isn't all bad. Regardless of how shitty the industry is where I work, that doesn't mean every place, everywhere, is the same. I just need to find the good. That golden ring I was looking for is out there. There are good folks in this business. I think that golden ring is just a bit more tarnished than I originally thought... and even though it's tarnished, it's still a golden ring."

Blaze thought for a second.

"Then why won't you go to another paper and see if that's true?"

"Honestly, Blaze, I don't think it's at another paper. I don't think it's in the obvious location, where it should be. That's what's sad about it all. It's hidden and I have to find it. It shouldn't be that way... it doesn't have to be that way."

Blaze swigged the last of his beer and gathered his stuff.

"Well, let me know what's up and if I can help. Just holla at ya boy."

E.J. smiled and thanked Blaze. As he made his way to the door, E.J. stopped him.

"Hey," he yelled. "Why me?"

Blaze turned and smiled.

"Why what?"

"Why help me?"

"You really don't know why, do you? Fuck, why am I even telling you this? I already told you why."

"Yeah, yeah," E.J. interrupted. "All about hatin' to see a brotha struggle and helping him out. It was bullshit when you said it then as it is now Blaze."

"I would think if you were such a good reporter you would have figured it out. Okay, let's get real. A friend of mine needed your help and you put your ass on the line for him, and you didn't even know him. He is alive because of you. He asked me to keep an eye on you. To be honest, it was originally about seeing if you would crack, maybe talk about what happened with others, but it's not about that anymore. After I got to know you, I realized you handle business with loyalty, trust, and heart... and I only fuck with fools that handle business. You take care of shit and with the fuck-offs I deal with on the streets every day, loyalty and trust is priceless."

E.J. was silent, confused. Blaze just stood there waiting for the light bulb to illuminate above E.J's head.

"Heist?" E.J. said softly with puzzlement.

Blaze snickered lightly.

"Good work Woodward and Bernstein. You cracked another major story."

E.J. smiled, a feeling of joy mixed with surprise flooded him.

"You know I would have figured this out eventually," E.J. exclaimed.

Blaze smiled.

"My nigga. I know you would have."

E.J. laughed and shook his head in disbelief.

"E.J., you know I got your back. No matter where and when, because I know you got mine ten-fold."

"Thanks Blaze. That means the world to me... you need me for anything, ever, you know I got you."

"You know lawyers, right?"

E.J. chuckled.

"A lot of my family members work in law."

"I hope I never need you," Blaze quipped. "But I know if I do, you'll be there."

E.J. laughed as the door slammed.

He leaned back into the lawn chair, throwing back another swig of beer. His hand accidentally hit the power button on the remote control to the small television he had set up. A blast of unexpected volume startled E.J. as the screen lit up. It was an infomercial about Jamaican vacations.

"Ay mon, travel to Jamaica for just $500," the heavily accented voice on the television exclaimed.

E.J. sat up, stared at the television and smiled as the infomercial went on.

"Yeah... a trip to Jamaica is just what I should do with the few days of suspension I have left," he whispered to himself. "I wonder where the nearest tanning salon is around here."

Chapter Forty-Five

The tanning booth had turned E.J.'s hue into a dark brown with a slight tint of burnt orange, with the exception of the tan line that his Ray Ban sunglasses left behind. He looked like a raccoon, in reverse. The workers at the salon recommended that he not spend so much time in the booth, but let it go after their insistence that he remove his sunglasses fell on deaf ears. They thought he was either some performance artist or mentally unstable. He didn't want to explain it to them and the salon didn't want to ask. He looked like a fool, but that was the point. As long as no laws were being broken, they just smiled and made their comments privately. His credit card went through and that's all that mattered to them.

E.J. walked into the newsroom with the standard shirt, tie, slacks, and the white shoes, but there was a change in color and style. His shirt was green, slacks red, and he had a Bob Marley tie on, which was slightly tangled up into an Afro-centric necklace that donned a faux-leather pendant featuring an outline of the African continent, split into the three colors of the Ethiopian flag: Red, gold, and green.

"What the fuck?" Jeffery blurted as E.J. sat down at his desk.

"I just spent the last few days in Jamaica, mon." E.J. replied in a horrible Jamaican accent, a big grin stretching across his face.

Skye turned away repulsed, muttering under his breath something about being a jackass, which E.J. ignored. The rest of the newsroom within an ear shot looked over. Some laughed, some cringed, and the spectacle got the attention of Walter and Noland, both of whom became instantly distressed.

"Holy fuck," Noland said as both he and Walter peered through the large window of Walter's office into the newsroom. "What the fuck is this about?"

Walter said nothing and stepped outside his office.

"Lockhart! My office. Now."

E.J. strolled into the office with confidence.

"Can I help ya, mon?"

"Sit."

E.J. sat down, grin wide, bobbing his head as if he had a Reggae beat pulsing through him.

"I'm not sure where to start with this," Walter said. "The dress code issue or the fact that this is, at best, just slightly offensive to African-Americans."

"Hey mon, I got me a shirt and tie, no dress code violation."

Noland couldn't handle it.

"Oh, Jesus Christ!"

"Noland... let me handle this," Walter said in a diplomatic voice. "This is unacceptable, racist behavior, and I'm certainly not going to allow you to put this company in the firing line of some lawsuit."

"Hey mon, I took the time off to visit Jamaica and was completely enlightened. I'm a new mon... mon. I'm Rastafarian now, looking to Africa for the crowning of a Black King, he shall be the Redeemer! I found me-self and if you cannot handle me new religion and lifestyle, mon, you may be the one discriminating. That sounds like a lawsuit to me, mon. Have you checked the company's policies on practicing religion at the office, mon? I'm well within' my right, brotha, to practice Rastafarianism."

Walter and Noland sat silent.

"You cannot do anything to me, mon. You could fire me... maybe if you do that, mon, I will walk away quietly with no lawsuits and some unemployment, but if you decide to discriminate against me lifestyle while I'm here, we have a problem."

E.J. got up.

"Now, I have a stack of stories sitting on me desk, mon, so let me know what you want to do. Keep it irie brothas."

E.J. made his way back to his desk.

"Why don't we just fire him," Noland said defeated. "He finishes every story and stays all night to fix anything we throw at him. I cannot give him anymore stories or we will be looking at a lawsuit. He's already doing twice as many stories as everyone else.

Just fire him. That's what he wants and I don't care what the bosses have to say about it."

"No," Walter replied. "I know he is close to getting evicted. He's broke. Give him the required time back before we can legally suspend him again, then we get one black person in this office to complain about this Jamaica thing he's doing. That will end that. In the meantime, keep dumping everything on him and never stop complaining about the quality of work. We have a huge file piled up on him. Either he will end up homeless and go back to fucking Ohio, or we'll have enough on his file to fire him with real cause and not have to deal with any unemployment."

"What about the bosses?"

"They don't know much, for the most part. They know he has created some issues here, but he's obviously a good reporter too. With the marathon and Graham stories, they see his potential, but they have been made aware of his eccentricities, as I call them. They know what we need them to know about what's going on here. Let's keep it that way."

"How do we get a black person to complain?"

"We find one and 'ask politely' to file a complaint."

Noland smiled.

"Got it."

E.J. began running through the pile of stories that sat on his desk and opened his e-mail, typing up a message to Noland about which stories he wanted first. Within minutes, a message from Noland came back: "I want them all by the end of the day, mon."

"Fuck," E.J. said to himself, his voice dropping the Jamaican accent.

"Already out of character?" Jeffery asked.

"No mon, da bosses want me to do the impossible. But I keep it irie, ya know mon. We shall overcome," E.J. said loudly, raising his fist in the air and bowing his head.

"What did they say to you in the office about all this Jamaica stuff?"

"They thought I was offending African-Americans, mon. But I let dem know that me union might say that they be discriminating against me and me new found enlightenment and religion."

Skye returned to his desk visibly upset.

"You know Lockhart, I can't wait until you're fuckin' canned. You're an embarrassment and this Rastafarian shit you're pulling is what's going to get you sent back to Hicksville."

E.J. turned around and laughed.

"If the almighty Jah so makes it so, mon, then it will be," E.J. said. "As a Rastafarian, I must follow the enlightened path of love and forgiveness, so me soul is purified of hate. But Skye, me friend, you can bet that karma will be sure to visit you mon."

E.J.'s grin suddenly vaporized and his accent vanished.

"Do you think karma is getting what you deserve or deserving what you get? I've often wondered if you're upset at what the cosmic balance did to you, or just too stupid to realize you're the one that created it?"

Skye just stared into his eyes, fuming.

"So, if at all possible, keep your mouth shut. I have stuff to do."

E.J. worked until late night. Every story finished. Every criticism handled. Every adjustment Noland threw at him addressed and corrected. Every other tweak the editors wanted, he made. The sun was just coming over the skyline of San Francisco when E.J. awoke, just a minimal amount of sleep. He put on a pot of coffee and popped a few pills to carry him into the new day that was arriving. He grabbed the water bong he had bought with the new Jamaican outfit, opened up the top drawer of his dresser and pulled out a large bag of marijuana that Blaze left for him. He poured some of his coffee into the pipe's water chamber, loaded the bowl, and with the spark of the lighter, took a long, slow, drag. He exhaled a thick and rich plume of smoke and smiled wide, his eyelids drooping low. Slowly, the whites turned pink, then red, as he descended horizontally onto his bed.

"Mon, mon, mon..." he said to himself. "Keep it irie... We shall overcome, me brotha."

Chapter Forty-Six

The editors had generally remained quiet as E.J.'s Rastafarian persona became more pronounced, still working on finding a black man in the company to file a complaint. By the end of the second week, the dreadlocks he was growing became more noticeable as it was now clear he hadn't washed his hair in a long time. He had better perfected his accent to a point where it even became harder to understand him. He continued to pop pills to keep up with the demands of the editors as they dumped as much work on him as they legally could. He spent his days off sleeping and doing prep work on stories to keep up with the workload being placed on him.

Things had not improved with his landlord, so E.J. decided to use his new found Rastafarian pot-smoking side to buy more weed, in slightly larger quantities, and flipped much of it by selling small dime bags around his apartment complex. Blaze was reluctant to sell marijuana to E.J. for fear that he would land in trouble, but relinquished when he realized other avenues for capital had dried up. E.J. had successfully convinced Paul that a roommate was moving in and that his uncle left him an inheritance. In three weeks, E.J.

claimed, he would have a steady stream of income and he would no longer be late with rent. Even though he said he would no longer take late rent, as an immigrant who struggled, Paul's heart was forgiving despite the earlier threats. His landlord bought every bit of E.J.'s story and wanted to help.

At work, a young black man was hired in the circulation department as part of a secret deal. Walter had pushed human resources to bring the man aboard as soon as possible and on his second day, the paper's newest employee, Wesley Baker, filed a complaint about E.J. The complaint went on file and the paper suspended E.J. again. He was too tired to fight it. For another five days, E.J. would be at home. His tan had begun to fade. He put his Rastafarian clothes and his bong in the closet. He combed the dreadlocks out of his hair and dropped the accent. He took the half ounce of marijuana he had left from the large amount he had bought earlier and sold it off, dropping off some of the money to the landlord, and putting the rest in his sock drawer in case of an emergency. The Rastafarian E.J. had rattled a lot of cages at work, more than any other stunt he had pulled, but it still wasn't enough. The editors found another loophole and E.J.'s new found persona was to be put to rest. He sat down with a drink, a cigarette, and contemplated what stunt he would do next.

A knock at the door nudged E.J. out of his deep thoughts. It was Jeffery. The visit surprised E.J. since Jeffery had never dropped by unannounced and had only come by a few times since being hired by the paper.

"What's up champ?" Jeffery said as the door swung open.

E.J. stood there as Jeffery looked at the plain-clothed E.J., hair washed, dreadlocks gone.

"Hey," E.J. said in his natural voice. "Come in."

Jeffery followed E.J. into the living room, where he offered his colleague a drink.

"Sure thing," Jeffery responded.

Jeffery sat down.

"Dropped the accent, I see."

"I did... done with that."

"You really pissed off the editors with that act. I'm not sure this is true, but the guy that filed the complaint was just hired, and the rumor is the editors brought him in for no other reason than to file that complaint."

"Yeah, they've been quiet since I showed up in full Rastafarian mode. I figured they were stepping back because they were too scared to be the ones to complain... no surprise they hired a ringer to do it for them."

E.J. sipped his drink and offered Jeffery a cigarette, which he took and lit.

"I'm getting better at this," E.J. said. "The Rastafarian thing had them scared shitless... and the marathon had them so torn. Man, that was awesome. I pissed them off so bad, but they wouldn't do anything because of the publicity, sales, and circulation boost."

"Yeah, money makes any action look less heinous."

E.J. handed Jeffery another whiskey and Coke.

"That's even more of a reason to do this. They hate me and it's a fuckin' war, until my antics start generating money. Then I'm okay. I shouldn't be surprised. They have been using me since the day they hired me, so why would this be any different."

Jeffery laughed contently.

"So, Jeffery... you're there when I'm not. How close are they to firing me?"

"Don't hold your breath. Their bonuses, possibly their jobs, are likely on the line too. This Internet boom is killing print and things are just going to become faster and more streamlined in the future. The ship is sinking... but you know the deal. I think they're waiting for you to get evicted. They know you can't afford where you live with Kalea gone. They know it's only a matter of time before you get thrown out of your place."

E.J. nodded his head in agreement.

"Yeah, I kinda figured that. I guess I'm going to have to step up my game. You know, go big or go home, literally. I need to piss them off to a point where they are willing to swallow their bonuses, maybe risk their job, and their pride. I've got to throw a haymaker. I'm living here on borrowed time and I can't let them win."

Jeffery sat down his drink.

"That's kind of the reason why I came over to talk. I'm not sure this is good for you. This Rastafarian thing was way over the top. I thought the marathon thing was insane, but you surpassed that. I think you're going a bit crazy. Is this really worth it? You have an awesome girl back at home that loves you and I'm sure you can find another job in media that isn't this place... a place maybe more your personality and speed."

"What do you know?" E.J. said with a bit of bite to his tone.

"Hey, I was hired the same way. Don't act like I haven't been there, and I've backed you up on this, at least for the most part. I admit that I've gotten a little upset at your antics, but I believe in your cause... I'm just also a huge believer in this profession as well, regardless of the tactics involved. You have the fire and you're a great reporter, but rather than use that anger to be the best reporter you could be, you became this… this… well, whatever this is. You're not fighting the good fight. This situation has turned you into a petty little man. You are so much better than this, but you choose not to be, and I just think these antics, this war you're waging against the editors, is not good for you on any level and not good for this profession."

E.J. leaned back and thought for a moment.

"Kalea seemed to feel the same, in her own way, but I think you're both wrong. There is a mission here. A journalist rights wrongs, exposes corruption, and is a voice for the voiceless. I'm righting a wrong, exposing the shameless practices. Exposing the lies and the blatant abuse they have been practicing for a long time here, and probably practicing at other media companies across the country. If there was ever a more important mission for a journalist, I haven't seen it. They are wrong with what they did to me, to you, and to who knows how many others. You should be working with Warren... shit, you two should be running this paper. People like you and Warren are what this business needs and that's what I'm fighting to change."

Jeffery became a bit upset at how close E.J. cut to him, but inside, he knew a lot of it was true. He got up to leave.

"Well, I hope this all works out for you."

E.J. just sat on the lawn chair content as Jeffery let himself out, slamming the door.

"Well," E.J. said, addressing his empty glass on the table. "I have five days to figure out my next move and you need to be filled up to help me figure it out. Whada say? A bar?"

The glass sat still as E.J. looked at it, waiting for an answer.

"I'll take that as a yes."

Chapter Forty-Seven

E.J. sat at O'Brien's, an Irish bar on Howard Street in the Rincon Hill area near the bay. The place was fairly small, but had a nice upstairs area that made the place look larger than it really was. The bar was crowded, but not so crowded that it became an irritant. E.J. sat at the bar contemplating his next move. He started any conversation he could with anyone near him, all leading to the same question: If you could do anything to a boss to piss him off, what would it be? He got a storm of answers, all of which involved impossibilities that were nothing more than drunk fantasies far outside the realm of reality. One after another: Fuck his wife, plant drugs on him and call the cops, cut his car's brakes, infect the company's computer system with a virus, and dozens more that meant nothing. E.J. went back to his drink... alone.

"Think, E.J., think," he said to himself.

The loud quack of a bird echoed from behind him. A man walked through the door, a short, light-skinned Italian wearing a colorful blue sport coat, black slacks, and alligator shoes, He had a top hat and a perfectly waxed handlebar mustache. On his shoulder rested an African Grey Parrot. Its black beak looked poised, sharp, and the bright white that surrounded its eyes beautifully cascaded into its gray body, all the way down to the bright red tail feathers, which the bird periodically flared up. He was feeding the parrot small slices of zucchini and talking to the bird, each time the bird responding with a dozen phrases or so. E.J. watched as the man coordinated a conversation with the bird while onlookers smiled.

"Would you like to show the nice people a card trick Oscar?" the man asked the bird.

"It's not a trick, it's magic," Oscar answered.

The crowd laughed as the man nodded in agreement.

"Yes it is Oscar, yes it is," the man said laughing and smiling.

He pulled out a deck of cards and did a Hindu shuffle, with a quick riffle shuffle at the end. He asked Oscar to pick a card. The parrot's beak snatched a card and the man asked Oscar to put it back into the deck, which the bird did. The entire bar looked on. He did another round of shuffling. The man then fanned out the deck and looked intensely at the cards. He pulled one and placed the card, face down, on the parrot's back.

"Oscar, what card did you have?"

"Seven of diamonds," the parrot quacked.

"Reveal the card, Oscar."

The bird quickly reached over itself and snatched the card off its back, flipping it over, revealing a seven of diamonds. E.J. smiled and clapped along with the cheering crowd as the man took a bow, along with Oscar. E.J. stared at the parrot as the man told the bird to thank the crowd. Oscar listened to every command, every order, and no matter how chaotic the bar got, the bird responded immediately and never flinched. E.J. turned to the bartender.

"Excuse me, do you know that man's name?"

"Reynaldo," the bartender answered.

"Do you know what he drinks?"

"He usually orders and martini, extra dry."

E.J. reached in his pocket and pulled out a $20 bill.

"I'm buying Reynaldo a drink."

E.J. called out Reynaldo's name and waved him over. Reynaldo smiled and made his way to E.J., who introduced himself and handed the colorful man his martini. Reynaldo was eccentric, but kind and jovial. He thanked E.J. in his thick Italian accent. E.J. could not take his eyes off the bird, who sat patiently on Reynaldo's shoulder, as Reynaldo randomly talked about himself and his travels, even though E.J. didn't ask about any of these things.

"What's the bird's name? I didn't catch it during the act," E.J. asked during a brief moment in between Reynaldo's stories.

"His name?"

Reynaldo looked at the bird and asked the parrot to introduce himself.

"I'm Oscar," the bird quacked.

E.J. smiled.

"Nice to meet you Oscar, I'm E.J."

"Nice to meet you too," Oscar responded.

"Did you train Oscar yourself?"

"Yes, that's what I do for a living. Train animals for shows, circuses, and the like. On the side, I take some of them out and perform in bars and on the streets for some extra cash. It gets them used to crowds."

"How much would it cost to rent and train a bird to do something for me?"

"Depends on how long and what you want the bird to do."

E.J. began explaining the details of what he wanted. Reynaldo smiled and laughed. It was simple enough, Reynaldo said. He had a brightly colored Amazon parrot named Demetrius that he previously used in Las Vegas that could easily be taught and adjusted to meet E.J.'s needs. Demetrius was an especially easy bird to train. The two exchanged numbers and they met the next day. After a few hours of showing E.J. how to handle the bird, care for the bird, and helping teach Demetrius new sayings, Demetrius began responding to E.J.'s commands flawlessly. Demetrius responded so well that even Reynaldo was impressed, calling E.J. a natural with animals. E.J. could make the bird talk, fly away, and come back with a few commands. He taught E.J. a few sleight of hand moves to show him how to best control the bird and how he could easily make the bird react to non-verbal cues. E.J. used the last of the marijuana money he had stashed to pay Reynaldo for two weeks with Demetrius.

Chapter Forty-Eight

E.J. walked into the lobby at the Press-Journal, back to his normal attire of a blue shirt and tie, black slacks, and the white skate shoes, the only part of his uniform he refused to let go since the beginning of this journey. On his shoulder sat Demetrius, quietly fluttering around. Everyone in the lobby stopped what they're doing and looked over, a few of the female employees commenting on how cute the bird was.

"Ah, what an adorable bird," the front desk secretary said as E.J. walked by.

Before E.J. could respond, Demetrius spoke.

"Nice rack, baby."

The secretary was taken aback.

"Demetrius, please... show some respect."

E.J. reached in his pocket and fed the bird a piece of zucchini.

"Sorry, he has a bit of a horny streak in him," E.J. said to the lady.

"Don't cock block me," Demetrius cracked.

E.J. smiled to the secretary and continued walking toward the elevator. When the doors opened, it was crowded. E.J. squeezed in and everyone immediately became enamored with the bird, except for Skye, who was standing near the back.

"Oh Christ, Lockhart. What bullshit are you pulling now?" Skye said, more confidence in his voice than in the previous months following their fallout.

"Fuck off!" Demetrius cracked, the whole elevator laughing. "1990 called, they want their suit back, you homo."

Skye quickly examined himself as a reflex while the whole elevator continued laughing.

"Demetrius!" E.J. said, a slight sarcastic tone in his voice. "Be nice... they liked to be called 'gays,' not homos."

E.J. walked straight to his desk, everyone in the newsroom quickly staring. Skye went straight to Walter's office to bring his attention to the foul-mouthed bird. Jeffery stood up, shook his head in disbelief, unable to stop himself from smiling.

"Oh my God," Jeffery said to himself. "When he said he needed to go big, he wasn't kidding. What the fuck is he doing with a parrot?"

E.J. sat at his desk and fired up his computer. Noland stared and mumbled some obscenity to himself. Walter stood at his office window with Skye as he rambled on about what happened in the elevator. Victoria smiled, enamored with the beautiful creature.

Demetrius remained silent while E.J. whispered something inaudible to the bird.

"Nice parrot," Jeffery said. "Does it talk?"

"Like a sailor," Demetrius cracked, the whole newsroom giggling and laughing.

Noland got up and made his way over to E.J.

"What the Hell is going on? What is this?"

Before E.J. could say anything, Demetrius chimed in.

"I'm a parrot you moron... are you that fuckin' stupid or are you blind?"

Noland was shocked silent.

"Noland, I'm sorry, he is a bit rambunctious. I'm taking care of him for a friend and you cannot leave these types of animals home alone for long periods of time. It's just for a few days."

Noland didn't believe a word of it, knowing that this was another stunt. Walter came out of his office with Skye and approached E.J.'s desk.

"What is this?" Walter asked.

E.J. quickly pulled a piece of zucchini out of his pocket and fed it to Demetrius before the bird could answer the question. E.J. stood up and addressed the newsroom.

"Everyone, this is Demetrius. He is a friend's Amazon parrot that will be in my care for a few days."

"You can't bring pets to work," Walter belted.

"Oh, but I can, Walter... you should know this."

E.J. reached into his desk, pulled out the company's handbook, and turned to page thirty-four, reading the passage verbatim.

"Pets are allowed at work as long as they are not physically aggressive, are housetrained, are not left alone for substantial periods of time, and are cleaned-up after."

"This thing is a distraction," Walter shot back.

"Well, that isn't listed in the company's handbook, so, looks like you're out of luck."

"I think he's adorable. What's the big deal?" Victoria chimed in.

"Victoria, be quiet. This is not your concern," Noland snapped.

"I'm an editor too, Noland. You're not the only one that makes decisions in this room."

"Walter and I make the final decisions, and in this case, we don't need your input."

Victoria walked off upset.

Walter and Noland stood silent, trying to figure out what to say next, while Skye remained visibly troubled.

"Only in San Francisco... pet lovers," E.J. said with a huge smile. "Don't worry guys, Demetrius will be just fine."

"Can't you do something about this?" Skye said to Noland and Walter.

The two just shook their heads and walked away.

"Oh, by the way," Noland said, turning back around. "That stack of stories on your desk all need to be in by midnight tonight. Seeing how it's already past four, you best get on it."

E.J. picked up the heavy stack of assignments, research material, and previous stories.

"Fuckin' assholes," he said softly.

"Assholes!" Demetrius squawked, the whole newsroom bursting out in laughter.

Noland and Walter were irritated. Victoria laughing.

"Sorry about that," E.J. shouted out to no specific person.

The laundry list of stories were piled high as E.J. laid out each one, weighing which would be easiest to finish first. He started with the obituaries, his exclusive domain the last few weeks as the editors continued to punish him with tedious assignments. He had a story about an elementary school that got some grant to build a new playground, a story about road closures, a church carnival, the mayor of Alameda going to a conference of mayors in Washington D.C. for no specific reason, a community cleanup in Hyde Park, and sifting through the police blog since Robert, the paper's police reporter, was on vacation.

Demetrius sat silent on E.J.'s shoulder has he shuffled papers around, opened a few blank documents on his computer, and began to make phone calls. As E.J. left messages for each filler story, Skye would chuckle a bit, laughing at the rubbish that E.J. was assigned. He ignored the laughs as long as he could. He was under a deadline and didn't want to get involved, until Skye made a personally derogatory remark under his breath. E.J. leaned his head over to the side, brushing Demetrius.

"Go fuck yourself," the bird cackled, looking directly at Skye.

E.J. didn't flinch, continuing to work as if nothing was happening.

"What did you say to me you stupid bird?"

E.J. moved his finger in quick motion, cuing Demetrius to respond.

Demetrius let out a stream of insults at Skye, who retaliated back, first telling E.J. to shut the bird up, but eventually addressing the bird directly, falling into E.J.'s trap. Insults flew and the newsroom slowly began to catch wind of what was going on. After a minute or two, Skye stopped, realizing that he was in a heated argument with a parrot and the whole newsroom was watching. His face turned red, deeply embarrassed, as giggling and snickering could be heard across the room.

E.J. continued to work, saying nothing and ignoring everything around him.

"You think you're smart, don't you Lockhart?"

"Skye, I don't have time for your bullshit today. You want to argue with Demetrius, be my guest. I'm busy."

Skye laughed and tried to save face, refusing to let E.J. and Demetrius get the last word.

"Yeah, I can see you have some huge stories in front of you. You're pathetic. Look at you… obits, bullshit stories, and now this: A parrot. You're a joke."

E.J. continued to type on his computer, ignoring Skye.

"You kiss your mom with that mouth?" Demetrius blurted out. "I kiss your mom with this mouth."

"You better shut that bird up before I do it."

E.J. spun his chair around.

"Skye, I really don't want to hear you and neither does Demetrius. Would you like me to file a harassment charge against you? Stop bothering me and my parrot."

The rest of the newsroom watched from the corner of their eyes as the confrontation continued.

"Good luck with that, bird boy. Go to the editors and cry about it," Skye said in a sad baby voice and acting like he was wiping tears from his cheeks. "Let's see how much sympathy you get. You're the odd man out. You're the cancer in this place and I cannot wait until you are cut out."

"Skye, your asinine simian countenance alludes that your fetid stench has annulled the anthropoid ape species diversity."

Skye looked confused while several people laughed.

"I will leave on my own terms, not yours, nor the editors. I will make sure every second I'm here is Hell for all these pricks… yourself included, you degenerate douchebag. In the meantime, why don't you slip into something more comfortable, like a coma."

Skye sat silent, chewing his gum with a nonchalant attitude on his face.

"Eat shit and die you faggot!" Demetrius said.

"Exactly," E.J. agreed. "That's what I meant."

By 6:00 p.m., E.J. had finished the obituaries and was nearly done with two of the six stories due at the end of the night. Noland and Victoria began to complain from the start while E.J. juggled each concern and corrected them at lightning speed. The third and forth story were done by 9:00 p.m. and again, both Victoria and Noland complained incessantly about the stories, all corrected. By 10:00 p.m. the last two stories were complete. Walter watched as E.J. ran around the office with Demetrius on his shoulder, periodically calling in Noland and Victoria to see how E.J. was doing. He didn't like the answers.

"He's made every correction and every change we have thrown at him. He just doesn't stop," Noland said.

Walter stood stoic looking out his office window into the newsroom, Noland next to him while Victoria sat in the back of the office.

"What stories does he have left?"

"Well, he just submitted his last story, the one about the Alameda mayor's trip to Washington D.C.," Victoria said, "which is nothing more than a public relations trip. He basically interviewed the mayor about issues he plans to address in Washington... mostly jobs, business development, and some road issues. A bunch of bullshit, really."

"Well, can we push him to get something more relevant from the Alameda story?" Walter asked.

"We could, but what are we going to ask for? The mayor said his peace. What else can we grind on?" Noland replied.

Victoria got up and made her way to the window.

"What about getting him to quote another mayor on his visit? Make him go out and ask a couple of mayors around the Bay Area about the conference… you know, what do they think are the important issues that should be addressed? There is no way he could get a hold of two or three other mayors this late at night."

Walter smiled.

"Victoria, I like that idea. Let's do it."

She smiled, finally happy that they liked one of her suggestions.

Noland and Victoria made their way back to the deadline desk that sat in the middle of the newsroom, E.J. peering at them from the corner of his eye. He whispered to himself about the assumed conversation the editors were having, another correction or addition, he guessed. Demetrius just sat silently on his shoulder. Noland opened up the completed Alameda story and didn't bother to even look through it. Victoria beamed across at Noland and nodded her head, letting him know she had his back.

"E.J., come here," Noland barked.

E.J. sat still, ignoring Noland, deciding at this moment he wanted to be addressed as "award-winning reporter" as he had required weeks ago. Noland asked again, not changing anything other than the frustration level in his tone. He raised his voice again, calling for E.J. a third time, ready to unleash on E.J., but pulled back when Victoria quickly stood up and stopped him from screaming across the newsroom. She smirked at Noland with a look that told him to keep his cool. E.J. still sat as if he heard nothing, deaf to Noland's beckoning. Noland took a deep breath, composed himself.

"Award-winning reporter E.J. Lockhart, may I have a word with you?" Noland asked calmly.

E.J. jumped up and quickly made his way over.

"This story about the mayor of Alameda's trip to Washington is missing a few things, mainly some comments from other mayors."

E.J. was a bit perplexed.

"Why would I get comments from other mayors? They're not going. What would they have to say that has anything to do with what the mayor of Alameda is doing?"

"This is basic reporting, E.J.," Noland said with a condescending tone. "It's one thing to come here every day with your attitude, but another to fuck up basic stories that a first-year journalism student could complete."

"Well, I apologize if you feel I have short-changed this story... but that's what happens when you drop a bunch of work in my lap, with police blogs and obituaries. This is something a bunch of editors should have learned, but it's clear you didn't. You give me a lot of stories and assignments compared to others, so what result were you expecting?"

"Fuckin' prick. Don't you know how to do basic math?" Demetrius squawked.

"That's another way to put it," E.J. replied.

"Shut that fucking bird up!"

"Make me," Demetrius rattled off. "Your fat ass gets winded just thinking about throwing a punch, you walking gravy boat!"

"Demetrius, please," E.J. said in a veiled attempt to quiet the parrot.

"I said shut that fucking bird up or you're outta here!" Noland screamed.

The whole newsroom stopped as if they heard an explosion, gasps echoing from wall to wall. Victoria intervened and slid her tiny frame in between the two, attempting to squash the problem, but to no avail. Her infinitesimal interruptions were no match for Noland's booming voice. She was swallowed up between the two men as they locked eyes and barked at each other, dangerously close to throwing blows. Walter came out of his office in a flurry.

"What!? Am I fired Noland!? If I am, it can't be because of my stories and Demetrius has every right to be here! I think you just fired me without cause! Good job! Where's the unemployment line?!"

Walter squeezed between the two, pushing them apart and forcing Victoria to the side.

"You're not fired Lockhart... not because of that bird. We are on a tight deadline and I don't need this shit, so pay attention. We need comments from Daly City Mayor Michael Guingona, San Francisco Mayor Willie Brown, and another one... Fremont's mayor Gus Morrison. We need that by midnight. You don't get this done and you will be fired, with cause. So take your parrot and get to work."

E.J. stepped back and calmed himself down. Noland's face was red with frustration. He stood at his wit's end, ready to do something he would regret. Walter held his hand against Noland's chest motioning him to relax while E.J. collected his thoughts. He looked at the three editors, knowing each was out to derail him, neither of them showing any shame in their feeble attempts to make these changes to the story seem legitimate.

"It's past 10:00 p.m. There is no way I can get a hold of these three guys this late. This is a fucking setup. You don't need their comments to run this story. I've done five stories already! Who else has done that many fucking stories today?!"

E.J. turned to the rest of the newsroom's nightshift reporters, all transfixed on the situation that was unfolding.

"Anyone at all! Did anyone write five stories today?"

The newsroom sat silent.

"How about four?"

Silence.

Walter, Victoria, and Noland said nothing.

"Well, go ahead and fire me for failure to do my job, if you're confident that I failed to do my job. Unions always have a different opinion."

"You're treading on some seriously dangerous ground Lockhart," Walter retorted.

E.J. interrupted, realizing this wasn't the time to fight, being so close to the deadline.

"No worries, boss... I'll get those quotes, and you'll sit there wondering for the rest of the night how the fuck did he pull it off? You'll all go back to your caves and try to figure out another way to run me out, but you can't do it. Now, if you'll excuse me, I have some phone calls to make."

E.J. headed back to his desk.

"What a bunch of cock-sucking fuck-offs," Demetrius belted.

E.J. was up against the wall. He had to get a hold of three mayors. It was way after hours and he had no personal phone numbers for any of them, assuming they were even awake. He asked around the newsroom, but the only people that would likely have these personal numbers were gone for the day. Skye would have those numbers and was working late, but E.J. knew asking Skye was a dead end. Demetrius sat quietly on E.J.'s shoulder as he leaned back in his chair, contemplating his next move. He had less than two hours to get these quotes for the story.

"Looks like you're at the end of your run," Skye snipped. "The only person that has those guys' private numbers is me. Checkmate."

E.J. leaned forward, seemingly unfazed by Skye's mocking.

"Take that dick out of your mouth, I didn't catch that," Demetrius squawked.

"Cute... real cute," Skye said. "Let's see that bird get you out of this."

"You're right Skye, you are the only one that has those numbers," E.J. said introspectively. "You're a city reporter, so you would have all those contacts."

E.J. picked up the phone and quickly dialed.

"Hello, can I speak to Travis Taylor please?"

Skye smirked.

"Calling the Oakland Tribune's city reporter... nice idea, but he isn't going to give you any contact numbers. A competing paper would never help you out. Lockhart, you're an idiot. A desperate idiot."

E.J. stared at Skye emotionless, eyes fixated on him.

"Hey Travis, this is E.J. over at the Press-Journal... remember you interviewed me for the San Francisco Seven by Seven Marathon? Yes, that's right... lunch at Del Rio's. Good times. Hey, I need a favor. My editors are wanting me to add some comments from Willie Brown, Michael Guingona, and Gus Morrison for a story that's running tomorrow and I'm working on a seriously tight deadline. Do you have their personal phone numbers?"

Travis asked why not just get them from the Press-Journal's city reporter. E.J. answered as if Skye wasn't anywhere around him.

"Oh, he has them, but he's a piece of shit, so he isn't going to help me, unless he gets the opportunity to backstab me and steal a lead... yeah, a real douchebag."

"Real douchebag!" Demetrius blurted out while E.J. raised his middle finger in Skye's face.

Skye sat stunned as E.J. jotted down the numbers. The editors began to peek over as other neighboring reporters talked about what was happening. Walter quietly fumed from his office window while Noland and Victoria huddled, discussing the situation. E.J. immediately dialed the first number, the newsroom hanging on every dial tone, until Mayor Willie Brown answered. The interview was quick. Then Michael Guingona. Then Gus Morrison. E.J. hung up the phone, crowded his computer, and added the comments to the story. He looked up at the clock. It was 11:15 p.m. He had forty-five minutes. Plenty of time, he thought to himself. He stood up and looked at the editors.

"It will be done in ten minutes."

The editors said nothing.

E.J. dropped back down on his computer, hacking away at the keys and ignoring everything around him. Demetrius turned and looked at Skye.

"Did you hear that?" Demetrius said.

"What?" Skye said, confused that the bird was addressing him.

"That's the sound of my balls in your mouth as you gargle my nuts!"

"Demetrius!" E.J. interjected. "Skye is not gargling your nuts… he's gargling mine."

Chapter Forty-Nine

After a week of being punished by the presence of Demetrius, the editors felt they had won the battle simply by enduring the parrot, but that really wasn't accurate. Noland and Walter both started to show signs of breaking. Outbursts were more frequent and screaming matches became a more common scene. Elevated frustration from management saturated the newsroom where the normal stress of journalism was now amplified, becoming too much to bear. The sullen mood slowly turned against E.J. who had created this world that so many others had to live in.

That morning the editors' meeting completely revolved around E.J. The bird was gone, the stunt had ended, but the editors knew something else was coming around the corner and, admittedly, were embittered and teetering on the edge of giving in. Quietly, Victoria had long given up, but also was never that vested in backing Noland and Walter as they treated her poorly as well. She would take it only because it meant future promotions, so it was worth it to her to play along. Noland and Walter stubbornly fought, still wanting to battle until they won, but were having their doubts. E.J.'s two-week vacation was starting the following Monday, which worried the editors. They believed that it would be two weeks, paid, to plan against them. Each stunt had been more outrageous than the previous, and they were becoming increasingly alarmed at what may come next. The weekend was approaching and they had do figure out a plan.

"Look, he isn't going to pull anything with just a few days left. It's going to be during this vacation time that he'll come up with some other fucked-up plan. However, if we take away his vacation and move it, keep him here, we can go on the offensive. This gives us time to come up with something and beat him at his own game... something to end this now."

"We can't legally take away his vacation," Noland replied

"Not true, technically," Walter said. "We can move it for a serious and compelling reason. It's in the employee handbook and part of the job agreement."

"Okay, so what then? What's a serious and compelling reason?" Victoria asked. "All we give him are shit stories and obits. That's not grounds to keep 'em here."

"How about an actual story that is difficult, complicated... like some big hitter-type story? One that requires some real time?" Walter suggested.

"He has yet to fail on any story we have given him," Victoria reiterated. "In fact, he has busted open more huge stories in the last year than anyone else."

"I mean, let's be real, what huge monumental story is going to fall into our laps? What story is going to be too big for him? Victoria has a point," Noland said.

"There is a lot of corruption in the Bay Area," Walter replied. "There has to be something. Skye must be sitting on a thousand rumors in Oakland alone. That improbable story is out there."

"We have dumped a lot on him, and he comes through every time. I have zero faith in the strategy that he'll fail if we go the opposite direction and assign him a difficult story," Noland held.

"I don't think this is a bad idea," Victoria said. "We get a rumor from Skye that is the most outrageous and make E.J. chase it."

"And what if he proves it's a rumor?" Noland questioned. "He is too good to get sideswiped by a rumor story. He'll either get the story or prove it's just a rumor and then we're back at square one."

"So what if he does fail to get the story, saying it's just a baseless rumor, then we send Skye out and he is able to get the story?" Walter suggested. "Skye is the Oakland reporter. He knows everyone. If E.J. can't get the story, Skye can get it and then we have him dead to rights, with cause."

"If E.J. can't get the story, Skye won't be able to get it either... or if it's a rumor, Skye too will find the same result," Noland said. "Both are that good."

"I think you're wrong Noland," Walter responded. "Skye is not only more than capable of outdoing E.J., this is his beat on top of that. We get the most insane rumor coming out of the city of Oakland, and if E.J. can't get it, send in Skye. I guarantee you Skye will get the story that E.J. cannot."

"If E.J. fails to get the story and Skye somehow does, we would have grounds to let him go with cause," Victoria answered.

"And there is still no guarantee that Skye can get the story either, or that the rumor is true," Noland said. "What's the point of even doing this?"

Walter didn't address the question.

"I think the bigger concern is getting E.J. to actually take on a serious assignment at this point. We need to pull him back onto our side for this."

Chapter Fifty

E.J. worked furiously at the new stack of stories dumped on him, his desk a complete mess from the previous day. The editors had been quiet and things had calmed down since Demetrius was gone. The editors were correct that E.J. hadn't thought of his next move, and they also were correct that he was looking forward to his vacation to create another scheme. He was planning on calling Kalea, possibly going back to Ohio for two weeks to connect and talk with her, if she would let him. That would never happen. The editors called E.J. into Walter's office. He assumed they were going to discipline him, or throw more stories his way, or some other nonsense.

"What?" E.J. said coldly to the group as he walked in, shutting the door behind him.

"We have a story for you... and it's huge."

E.J. instantly became suspicious, his brow curled.

"A huge story for me?"

Walter motioned for E.J. to have a seat in the semi-circle the editors were perched in, telling him that despite their problems, the needs of this story outweighed any of the animosity between them. This was about business, nothing personal. E.J. brought down the mayor of Oakland and he was their best hope of figuring out what was going on. E.J. said very little, figuring this was another ploy, and he was right about that. They couldn't break him by piling a lot of bullshit stories on him, so they'll try the other direction: A difficult and involved story. He cautiously accepted with little argument, knowing that he really couldn't refuse because that would be cause to be fired. He also was sick of the nonsense stories. If this was as big as they claimed, this would be another victory for his career, and another "fuck you" to the editors.

"Okay, but we have to come to an agreement. For this story I'm off night shifts, no more bullshit stories, and no more obits until this is done."

All the editors agreed.

"What's the story?"

The editors, already having discussed all the various rumors and story possibilities with Skye, kept it vague for now.

"We have word that Oakland City Councilman Tom Seville is involved in some corruption... maybe connected to Oakland mayor Russell Graham. It's unclear as to what this corruption is, but it seems there are some credible rumblings that something is going on. That's all we know."

E.J. was confused.

"You know, Skye is your Oakland city reporter. He would have many more contacts than me. If this is really going on, he would have a much better shot at figuring it out," E.J. said with honesty.

The editors expressed their understanding of E.J.'s point.

"We know, but if something is going on, it might be tied to Russell Graham, so you actually are better suited for this. Maybe whoever tipped you off about Graham, we don't know. We're going to talk with Skye about this so that he doesn't get bent out of shape. Who knows, maybe he'll help you if he can."

"Right... Skye help me? Doubt that."

Victoria leaned over with a serious tone in her voice.

"You let us worry about Skye. You get to work. We need this story and it's imperative that you come through. This is why we have one other piece of criteria: We're suspending your vacation until this is done."

"There it is!" E.J. extolled. "Now I see your game. Give me a complicated story to see if that breaks me, and it's also a reason to suspend my vacation. A twofer, as they call it. Newsflash assholes: You cannot take my vacation from me."

Walter quickly grabbed the employee handbook and threw it in E.J.'s lap.

"According to article fifteen, we can move your vacation if the story warrants it for serious and compelling reasons. In this case, it does."

"I'm not sure a rumor falls under 'serious and compelling,'" E.J. replied.

He paused, ready to argue this point, but then an idea entered his head. He smiled.

"I'll admit, you guys are, well, tenacious. Guess I have no choice. I'll be here next week and I'll get this story..."

E.J. trailed off and thought for a moment, then openly commented, to no one specifically.

"Yeah… A story this big has to be more important than my vacation."

E.J. got up and headed for the door.

"Oh, by the way E.J.," Noland said. "Send Skye in here so we can talk with him."

Chapter Fifty-One

E.J. called in sick on Friday, the last of his sick days, to do a little shopping. He went to Walmart and picked up everything he needed. A long folding pool chair, a medium-sized umbrella that had every color of the rainbow, swim trunks, Bermuda shorts, five of the ugliest and loudest Hawaiian shirts he could find, an oversized beach hat, flip-flops, sunglasses, zinc sunscreen, and a dashboard Hula dancer figurine. As he spent his day shopping, the editors spent their day nervous. They knew he wasn't sick. They waited, unsure of what was going to happen when he returned Monday. Their only comfort was in their own plan. So far, everything was lined up as perfect as they could get it. They held a sliver of faith that whatever storm came into the newsroom on Monday was something they could weather.

E.J. strolled into the newsroom around 9:00 a.m. The light brown Bermuda shorts he was wearing hung a bit low and the bright yellow and red Hawaiian shirt, covered with toucans, almost blinded anyone that looked in his direction. His flip-flops made a whipping noise as they crashed against his heels. His large beach hat jiggled back and forth, his sunglasses tight around his eyes. A small amount of zinc was settled across his nose. Under one arm was the beach umbrella, under the other, the long folding beach chair.

"Holy fuck me," Jeffery mumbled to himself as E.J. began setting up the umbrella and folding chair next to his desk. Skye picked up the phone to quickly call Walter's office. Noland and Victoria were in the staff lounge and hadn't witnessed any of this. The rest of the office giggled, smirked, and made comments to each other as E.J. made himself comfortable under the umbrella, sitting in the folding pool chair. He grabbed his laptop and affixed the dashboard Hula dancer next to the touchpad, settling in to begin work. He grabbed his cell phone and made his first call of the day in an attempt to uncover whether Oakland City Councilman Tom Seville was involved in some corruption.

Walter came out of his office at nearly the same time that Noland and Victoria returned from the staff lounge. The editors looked over at E.J. in astonishment, and then looked at each other with immense irritation.

"What the fuck is this?!" Noland shrieked as he darted toward E.J.'s desk.

Walter grabbed Noland and motioned him to calm down while Victoria, who smiled and lightly laughed at the spectacle, was disinterested in a confrontation and allowed Walter and Noland to deal with E.J. Walter quickly silenced her giggling.

"Mr. Lockhart, this is not a resort and if this is going to be another one of your fucked-up games, we are not interested in playing it. You have one of the most important stories we have seen in a very long time and this isn't acceptable."

E.J. looked up from his laptop.

"Walter, I'm on this story, so you don't have to worry," he said politely. "You took away my vacation, so I decided to bring my vacation here to work. You can't fire me for dress code, only suspend me. However, you need this story, so I don't think suspending me is going to work for you. If you do suspend me, that's fine too. It essentially gives me my vacation as planned. However, if you decide to let me stay, I'm going to enjoy this lovely office while I work on the Seville story."

Skye sat silently, along with the rest of the office as they eavesdropped. Noland and Victoria remained hushed as they waited to see what Walter would do, all knowing that the rumored Seville story may be the white whale that sends E.J. home.

"You're right, Mr. Lockhart. We cannot fire you for dress code and we want you to get this story... just get it done."

Walter motioned for the editors to leave and graciously ordered everyone to get back to work. The editors and Skye looked at each other, knowing that they had to deal with E.J. turning the office into his private beach vacation to get him to take the story on. It was a disruption, it was distracting, and in poor taste, but they grinned and dealt with it knowing that it would be short-lived. In his office, Walter let the editors know that this would help their case. When E.J. fails to get the Seville story, and then Skye pulls the story through, they will point to his failure and his continued stunts as an ironclad cause to fire him. Walter reassured the editors that they needed to deal with some pain to win the game.

Chapter Fifty-Two

E.J. headed out to snoop around the Oakland City Council meetings and to start talking with people. He didn't change his attire and stood out like a sore thumb at the meetings. He had his beach hat tight on his head and his press pass dangling from his neck, lost inside the absurd design of the Hawaiian shirt he was wearing. People stared and snickered. Others would ask about the getup and he would tell them it was crazy Hawaiian shirt day at work.

Tom Seville was an older man, in his late sixties with a thin frame, thin gray hair, and a long, cut jaw and nose. He smiled a lot and was well-liked. He had been in Bay Area politics most of his adult life. E.J. pulled up every story he could find about the guy, dating back to his first run at public office in 1955, and outside of a bribery charge in 1985, which was discovered to be unfounded, he had no baggage. E.J. didn't know what he was looking for, so he started at the bottom, asking the local gadflies about Seville and other low-level city employees if they knew anything. Nothing came up. As far as E.J. could tell, the man was clean. Even in the eyes of those that differed with him politically, he was respected. Every question about Seville being involved in any type of bad behavior or corruption was received as odd by everyone E.J. approached. He was good at reading people and nothing anyone said seemed forced or out of the ordinary. After three days of poking around, he concluded there was nothing to the rumors and prepared to return to his editors with those findings.

Skye and the editors sat in Walter's office discussing E.J.'s progress. Skye had made a number of phone calls to his contacts to see what he could find out about E.J. and the Seville story. The calls were off the record rather than professional, so none of Skye's inquiries would get back to E.J. His contacts let him know that nothing seemed too out of the ordinary and that no one in the city or in Seville's camp seemed to be reacting to E.J.'s inquiries. The editors were delighted.

"This is great," Walter said with a huge smile. "He isn't getting anywhere and no one is paying him any mind."

"Is there a time frame for me to start working on this story?" Skye asked.

"No, not yet. We have to give him the full opportunity to get this story before we send you in," Walter replied.

"What about the specific information regarding Seville trying to fix the mayoral race? Do we want to give him that information?"

"Yeah... we'll give him that information."

E.J. had returned to the office. He laid down in his beach chair, adjusted the umbrella, and picked up the phone to call into

Walter's office. As the phone rang, he looked through the glass window and saw Walter motioning for him to come into the office. Skye exited as E.J. walked in, both of them stared at each other with indifference.

"E.J., let's talk about what you got," Noland said.

E.J. sat down as the rest of the editors joined, slightly surrounding him. He felt uncomfortable with the seating arrangement, but was not letting it show.

"Well, Noland, this guy is clean. I don't think anything is there. I've done my research on this guy, back and forth, asked every gadfly and employee, on and off the record, and no one seems to think Seville is involved in anything corrupt."

The room sat silent for a moment, the editors waiting for Walter to make a move.

"Well, we got some new info from another anonymous source," Walter said. "We have good reason to believe that Seville tried to fix the mayoral election that Russell Graham won... and won barely I might add. Skye got some info through an e-mail. We need to find the person that sent this e-mail."

E.J. looked perplexed, frustrated, and confused. Noland and Victoria sat silent.

"Are you sure this is a legit lead?" E.J. asked. "I've been all over everyone that's anyone and I can't find one person who thinks this guy is crooked. Even the crazy gadflies that think every politician is involved in some conspiracy had nothing bad to say about Seville."

"Skye seems to think this is legit... he poked around a bit and I trust his instincts," Walter said.

Noland nodded in agreement while Victoria, trying to show her importance, cut in with her own thoughts.

"Maybe it's your approach," Victoria said.

Walter looked at her with an expression that suggested she be quiet.

"Like I said before," E.J. replied. "Skye has contacts I don't. He is the Oakland city reporter. I think you should really give him this story."

"No. We need you to do this. Skye has one random e-mail and that is fine, but this is something you have proven to us that you can do. This is your story. You took down Russell Graham and if Seville is part of some fraud that helped rig Graham's election, you would have the inside track. This is your territory."

E.J. was bewildered. His pessimism was getting the best of him, clouding his judgment. He assumed this was some sort of ploy. He kept coming back to the only two conclusions he could fathom: One, they couldn't get him to stumble by inundating him with work, so they go the other direction and give him an important and complicated story to see if he fails to come through, or, two, the greed of this company knew no bounds, and if they thought he had the best chance of breaking a huge story for them, they would swallow their pride and any self-respect to get it done.

"I'll talk with Skye and see what I can do," E.J. said.

The e-mail was to a dead address that was shut down shortly after it was received. The message claimed that Seville was involved in a plan to rig the mayoral election and that a man named Fred Tanner was involved. E.J. became a bit frustrated with himself. He couldn't turn up any information working public meetings or the corridors of city hall for three days, while Skye got a lead for doing little more than opening his e-mail... and he wasn't even involved in this story.

"Do you know this Fred Tanner guy?"

"No, I have no clue who he is," Skye replied.

"I guess this is where I'll start. He can't be that hard to find."

E.J. started by combing the phone books and website directories. He also accessed the paper's online archives searching the name Fred Tanner to see if he had ever appeared in any article. He found four men in the Bay Area named Fred Tanner, one of them deceased. With one guy eliminated via death, he contacted the other three, but none of them were the Fred Tanner he was looking for. He began to branch out, calling every Fred Tanner near the Bay Area, then any Fred Tanner in California. He gave up after he contacted more than twenty men. He was frustrated. After six hours he had hit nothing but dead ends.

E.J. headed out to a meeting of the Concerned Citizens of Oakland, a conservative group that was known to fight local government corruption and always had a pulse on the inner-workings of the city. Still dressed like a horrible tourist combing the beaches of the Pacific Islands, he sat through the meeting and networked with everyone there. Some of these people had been involved in Oakland politics for more than thirty years, while others had served in high-level government positions at one time or another. They organized rallies, stormed meetings from the county supervisors to the school board, and just about every other government agency that had tax-payer dollars to spend, making sure that whatever they did was watched closely.

"Fred Tanner?" one man contemplated. "No, never heard of the man... and as far as Seville is concerned, I have heard nothing about the rigging of any election."

E.J. dealt with this type of response all night. The more he pried into Seville and his cronies, the more dead ends he ran into. He hopped back into his car, pulling into the Press-Journal parking lot at 10 p.m., exhausted. After a short meeting with Noland and Walter, who were clearly upset that nothing had materialized, even with a name, E.J. headed home. The drive was long. He couldn't understand how he had a full name and still was coming up empty. He thought back to the Union City High Hills Shopping Center story and Donald Tate. Even with limited information and a crazy gadfly like Tate leading him in weird directions, he was still able to find T. Wayne Hammett, despite not having anything more than part of a name. He became more irritated and bothered with the situation.

He cursed and babbled to himself as he flew down the freeway. Over and over again, going through the steps he took in hopes of finding a lapse. He repeated every move in his head as he thought out loud in dissatisfaction. The midnight San Francisco air was cold and clear, the traffic soft and open. As he drove down Third Street, Blaze was exiting a corner liquor store and noticed E.J.'s car flying past him. He yelled as E.J. breezed by, but the man was too deep in his own world to notice. Blaze did a quick jog up the hill and caught E.J. coming out of his car.

"What the fuck are you wearing?" Blaze said with a bewildered stare.

E.J. looked at his outfit, totally forgetting what he had been wearing the last few days.

"It's a long story..."

E.J. looked at the twelve pack of Samuel Adam's Boston Lager in Blaze's hand.

"I didn't know you brothas' drank Sam Adams."

"Looking at the shit you have on right now, which mothafucka' here really looks out of place?"

E.J. chuckled.

"You got one of those for me?"

"I certainly do," Blaze said, reaching into his shirt pocket and pulling out a bag of marijuana. "And look, I brought her sister to the fuckin' party as well."

E.J. and Blaze sat in the empty apartment and passed a bong back and forth, smoke filling up the living room. E.J. explained why he was dressed like a man that couldn't find his way back to a Beach

Boys' concert and the story that he was assigned. The high was swarming him as he continued to take hits, rambling on until Blaze interrupted him during the brief seconds that E.J. stopped talking to hit the bong.

"So wait, I'm confused. Why are you pursuing this story so hard if your goal is to get fired? I mean, look at you... one minute you're turning your cubicle into the Bahamas, and the next you're all over this story. They're not going to fire you if you produce good material."

E.J. collected his thoughts.

"Assuming I get the story. That may be their move here. They couldn't get me to crack by piling on a bunch of shitty stories, so they go the other direction and give me a complicated one like this. I'm sure they are hoping it falls through. If that happens, I'm probably done, fired with cause. Or maybe they're just that greedy for a good story. They don't care about anything that's gone down, as long as they get it. I just don't know, but regardless, I think they may be able to fire me if I don't get the story and someone else does."

E.J. looked around his empty apartment, the stack of notes left by his landlord for overdue money and the spot on the wall where a nail sat pounded in. The spot where the picture of him and Kalea was hung before she left. He wondered how it ended up this way.

"I don't know Blaze... It's all fucked up. This game to prove it was always them, and not me, is getting complicated. Look at the mess I'm in. I don't know if there is a story, if I can even get the story, or why I'm trying to break a big story for them."

"Do you think it was all on them? Or do you think it was partly you too?"

"I'm not sure anymore. I know I could have played it differently. I just thought I made all the right moves in school and professionally, thought I did what I was supposed to do... and now I'm not sure how I got here."

"You don't know how ya got here?" Blaze laughed. "Come on, man. This country and its system is fucked up, and you walked blindly into it with too much idealism and no realism. No wonder mental issues are on the rise. Folks walk into the real world believing what school teaches them, then they learn this world isn't like that at all. Suddenly, they're living a life without focus or meaning. That's you right now, brotha."

"It's just not fair."

"Of course it's not fair, mothafucka! You college boys are all the same. Y'all think just because you went to school and did all the shit everyone was telling you to do, that the world would respect that. It ain't fair out there. Never was. You just walked out in the world not knowing that, and when you found out what's really goin' on, you ended up here. Look at you. Dressed like some beach faggot, in an empty apartment, with your woman on the other side of the country, and your sorry ass about to get thrown out this mothafuckin' apartment."

"You think I'm a punk, huh?"

"Nah man, you ain't no punk. This isn't about bein' a punk. Knock that shit off. You fuckin' almost put yourself into some serious shit with Heist, the cops, the black mafia, and a bunch of gangstas. Not to mention what you're doin' right now. You got some serious fuckin' balls to pull the shit you be pullin' at work… and I gots to respect that across the board. No punk would even come close to doin' what you've done. I wouldn't be here if I didn't respect you, bro'."

E.J. smiled. Blaze packed another bowl while E.J. grabbed two more beers from the fridge. Blaze took a long, slow drag, filling the entire chamber and blowing out a head of smoke that added another layer to the one already settled throughout the apartment. E.J. handed him the beer.

"You know E.J., I went to college... two years. Had a basketball scholarship and everything. Wanted to go pro..."

E.J. was taken aback. He never bothered to ask what kind of education Blaze had and just concluded Blaze didn't do much past high school. He assumed that because of what he did... where he lived.

"What happened?"

"Dropped out as soon as I realized I was never going to make it to the NBA. What the fuck was I going to do if I didn't get to the NBA?"

"How did you know that you wouldn't make it?" E.J. said, a bit encouraging. "Come on. Work harder, practice more."

Blaze chuckled.

"I just knew... you know when you know."

"That's bullshit."

Blaze shook his head lightly and posed a question.

"Let me ask you somethin'. Do you think you could have made it to the NBA? If you practiced enough... tried hard enough... gave it all you had?"

"You serious, Blaze? I've never played a game in my life. I couldn't make it onto a high school team."

"You sure about that?" Blaze asked. "What if you tried hard? Practiced every day?"

E.J. acquiesced, understanding what Blaze was trying to indirectly illustrate. The distortions of fancy that institutions planted in him, he was now imparting to Blaze. E.J. knew he could never had played professional basketball and recognized that Blaze at some point realized the same thing. E.J., for the first time, understood that life was not a road paved easily for him to travel and the world was not built to fit perfectly into some design that he was taught. The lesson that life is fair and the life you wanted was a guarantee if you just made the correct moves was technically accurate, but not in the way he perceived growing up. It was as fair to him as it was fair to everyone else. It wasn't fair at all... to anyone.

"You should have stayed anyway. It's a free education, at least."

"And do what? End up where you're at?"

E.J. was perplexed.

"That's right mothafucka'. I was majoring in broadcast journalism. Even did an internship at WTDZ radio in San Jose calling high school games."

E.J. busted out laughing and Blaze followed.

"My man!" E.J. yelped, fist bumping Blaze.

The two spent the next few minutes laughing hysterically, tears rolling down their faces, while they made fun of each other. E.J., the dank-smoking, beach-wearing, beat reporter for the Jamaican Pot Head Daily, and Blaze, the evening news sports' reporter straight from the mothafuckin' streets.

After they calmed down, E.J. took another hit and blew a thick cloud toward the ceiling.

"You should have stuck with it Blaze. Radio isn't the NBA. Not that hard to get into… and its honest work."

"I know… just wasn't my time."

Blaze took a drink and continued.

"E.J., remember this. Just because you quit doesn't mean you lost. It means you're smarter than the bullshit around you. You only lose when you abandon your game, and end up playing theirs."

"I think it's still my game. I'm making my decisions and making my moves… moves no one else has the balls to make."

"Yeah, I see that," Blaze replied. "But I also can stand on the other side of that mirror and see how close you walk that line of playing their game too. The question is this: When does it become their game, and will you be able to notice it when it does?"

Chapter Fifty-Three

"Fuck!"

E.J. slammed the phone down so hard, his beach hat tipped over.

Skye looked over gingerly and smirked.

"What's the problem?" Jeffery asked. "Still getting dead ends on whatever story you're working on?"

E.J. lightly bobbed his head yes, saying nothing.

"Considering how frustrated you've been the past week, it must be huge... but I also see that you're still... how do I say... dressed like a man wishing to piss off a few people. What's your deal?"

"No deal, Jeffery," E.J. said curtly. "I have done every assignment the editors have given me and this assignment is no different."

Skye got up from his desk and moved around to the front of the room, gazing at E.J. and motioning him to meet in the employee lounge. E.J. turned away and picked up the phone, dialing another person on his thinning list of contacts and leads, which had a growing number of names crossed out. The familiar soundtrack of a disconnected line blasted in his ear as the recorded voice repeated, over and over again, the number was no longer in service. He looked at Skye standing across the room, hung up the phone, and followed him into the lounge.

"What do you want Skye?"

"Just a head's up. I have heard some rumblings about Seville."

"Who?" E.J. asked with contempt. "I have combed all through the city of Oakland and no one seems to know anything. Who have you've been talking with?"

"Well, no one in particular, really. Just some rumblings."

"Right," E.J. said sarcastically, walking out of the room back to his desk.

"Hey, I'm trying to help you out here."

"You? Are you serious right now? Not that I doubt you, because you have been nothing but help since I arrived here," he replied sarcastically. "But let's just get real. You're all hoping I fail so this place can be rid of me. That's why I have this story... but all evidence says there is no story here. This is all rumors and zero facts, so pardon me if I find it hard to believe you have any leads. You're playing some game to make it seem like something is there, maybe to use it against me if I fail to get the story. Use it to get me fired. The reality is this: I can't be fired for cause if the story doesn't exist."

"Are you sure there's no story? I'm not sure you're correct about that." Skye questioned. "I have leads that you don't. I hear things on my beat that you don't. Maybe you should put your hate for me aside for a second and listen for once. I don't care about what happens to you. The editors asked me to help, and I'm doing what they ask. That's my job. I'm a professional."

"Yadda, yadda, yadda... Whatever Skye... you're a lot of things, but professional isn't one of them. Do you have any clue who you're talking to?"

Skye said nothing.

"Are we done here?" E.J. asked coldly. "I have to get back to work."

Skye followed E.J. back into the newsroom as an eavesdropping Victoria looked up from her desk. Noland drifted out of his office while Walter looked on through the window of his office. All could feel E.J's frustration with the Seville story.

At his desk, Skye opened his e-mail with a message from Walter telling him to begin working on the Seville story behind E.J.'s back. Walter was now confident that he had finally beaten E.J. with a story he could not get. Skye opened a new file on his computer and titled it: Seville story. E.J., unaware of what was happening around him, continued to make calls, eventually heading out into the field, determined to find the story. He would find nothing. The next three days were one dead end after another.

After two weeks past, every road had led to nowhere. E.J. was called into Walter's office for an update. All the editors were present. E.J. sat down with a stack of notes resting on his lap. He didn't allow anyone to start, but rather simply took control of the conversation. He was not only ready to drop the story, but ready to defend himself and the fact that there was no story about Tom Seville or the rigging of any election. He had mentally organized his argument, expecting to put the editors to task if they blamed him for his failure to produce any story or any real evidence of malfeasance.

"This story is a complete lie, as far as I can tell. Total rumors," E.J. said with an air of confidence.

The editors said nothing while E.J. dumped each piece of paper on Walter's desk. He went through a list of names that went nowhere, dead ends at every turn, the universally positive comments made about Seville, evidence that showed the election was not rigged, and not one piece of evidence that suggested otherwise. E.J. explained in detail how every person, from staff to gadflies, and all his own underground contacts, both in power and on the fringe, had nothing and never heard of any rumors about Seville.

"It's like every time I brought this up to anyone I talked with, they looked at me as if I was the only person that had even heard of this story, both on and off the record. There's nothing there. Everyone, including Seville's opponents, were dumbfounded by these accusations."

The editors looked at each other and said nothing, all silently agreeing it was time to pull E.J. from the story. Walter stood up and retrieved a folder from his desk and handed it to E.J. He opened it slowly and saw a few sleeves of paper, Skye's name draped across the top. The papers contained a rough outline, some rough paragraphs, and quotes from sources about the Seville story. The quotes were there, but tagged with cryptic notes as to who said them. One quote after another, all claiming that Russell Graham's election was rigged and Seville had been involved. E.J. was shocked.

"What is this?" E.J. asked rhetorically, knowing exactly what it was. "This is impossible."

"Apparently not impossible," Noland said a bit coldly. "We had Skye drop in on this story to see what he could find when you started to struggle with it. This took him a few days to dig up. You, on the other hand, have been on this story for nearly three weeks."

"We were ready to drop this whole story when you kept coming up empty, and I'm glad we didn't," Walter said. "I'm really disappointed. I mean it would be one thing to not get certain aspects of the story, but to get absolutely nothing while Skye comes through with some serious evidence. It makes me think it was wrong to put you on this story."

E.J. was a bit confused, but he knew Skye had something serious to prove.

"I think what Walter is saying is that maybe you didn't try as hard as other times you went after the big stories," Victoria said. "Probably do to your new found attitude over the last few months."

"Victoria, I don't need you to speak for me," Walter said.

"You think I fucked this story off? Are you serious? Assuming that I'm dumb enough to blow this off and get fired under conditions that would warrant my termination with cause, which I would never ever do, I'm simply not that lazy. I have come through with every story, on deadline, without fail since I've arrived. You think I would fold that all up now?"

"Slow down," Noland said sharply. "I don't care whether you simply failed to get the story or did this on purpose as part of your stupid game. The fact is you didn't come through and we're at risk of having another newspaper scoop us on this. You can be let go for this failure."

E.J. thumbed again through the papers in the folder. All the info and quotes had no names attached to them, just weird markings that looked like shorthand notes.

"What story is going to be scooped?" E.J. lashed back. "There isn't a story here. Looking at Skye's work, all I see are a bunch scribbled and cryptic sources. Who said these things to him, because it doesn't say? Are these sources reliable? What are all of these stupid markings?"

"This isn't the first rough draft he has turned in with his own markings. This is a big story and he is just protecting it from being stolen," Noland clarified. "It's going to be in 'Skye language' during early stages."

"Well, he would know about stealing stories..."

Walter walked over to his office window and called Skye into the meeting. Skye looked across the room and smiled, gathered his thoughts, and walked in, standing tall and confident with a huge grin on his face. E.J. sat sternly.

"Skye," Walter asked. "These sources... tell us about them. E.J. seems to think that it's an impossibility for you to have gotten legitimate information while he got nothing. Please ease his mind."

"Well, E.J. did approach many of the same sources I did, but he missed on a key person: Fred Tanner. This is the guy he couldn't find who supposedly had sent that e-mail. I found the guy. He's dead. Actually, E.J. found him too, but he assumed it wasn't the right Fred Tanner, which makes sense. Dead men don't send e-mails. However, I looked into it a bit deeper. His wife had sent that e-mail using his account and the information comes from the journal he kept. She immediately shut down the e-mail after that because she didn't want it to be traced over the Internet. I had to track her down in person. So, technically, it wasn't him, just his information and a small list of a few contacts he left behind. Easy to overlook. It was a small misstep on E.J.'s part. He also missed a few key people that I thought maybe would have some inside information. Talking with them led me to a few other people that verified the rumors, but they did make it clear that no smoking gun has surfaced. These folks are seriously connected and investigating. They have strong evidence and are ready to come out with it, on the condition that we only quote them on exactly what they give us on the record. They think our story will break this investigation wide open."

E.J. said nothing.

"I mean, don't take this as a knock on E.J. The same misstep could happen to anyone."

Skye smiled big.

"A dead guy? E.J., you missed a dead guy?" Noland asked rhetorically. "You're telling me that you didn't bother to check into this guy because he was dead?"

E.J. ignored the question.

"Well, I would like to see the final story when it is done because I'm curious as to which key people I missed, be it Fred Tanner, no Fred Tanner, dead Fred Tanner, or anyone else," E.J. said getting up from his chair. "I assume I'm off this story and your boy here is now on it? Let me know what else I can do for you."

E.J. walked out and slammed the door, the editors saying nothing.

"Well," Skye said as he turned to watch E.J. walk back to his desk through the window. "It looks like you finally got the failed story you wanted. He wants to see a final draft of the story. Is that cool?"

"Of course it is. Why wouldn't it be?" Noland said intensely.

"Do you know everyone E.J. talked with?" Walter asked.

Skye thought for a moment.

"I do know most of the people. E.J. keeps a list of everyone on a notepad. I've seen it."

"Good," Walter answered. "We'll need that list, just to be thorough and to make sure we don't cross our wires. No mistakes can be made."

"We have him dead to rights now," Noland said with glee.

Walter smiled in victorious fashion.

"Of course... He didn't get the story, so let him go. Finish the story Skye. Make it seamless. His sorry ass will be back in Ohio once the paperwork goes through in a few days. Congrats everyone. We won."

Chapter Fifty-Four

The neon lights glared into Warren's eyes as E.J. and him sat at The Argus, a hole-in-the-wall pub that if you sat far enough in the back, you could smell the urine from the bathrooms. Warren didn't know what exactly was happening, but knew that E.J. was struggling with his story. He tried to steer the conversation away from work, but E.J.'s third shot of whiskey, coupled with the two drinks he already slammed, made it hard to change the conversation. Warren rarely went out, but knew that the last few months had been hard on E.J., so he couldn't say no when E.J. invited him out for a drink.

"I have to tell you Warren, I have never failed to get the story."

"It has to happen sometime... even to the best reporter."

"It's more than that. You see, what happened is..."

Warren quickly cut him off.

"You know the rule. You don't talk about stories you're working on. Did you not learn your lesson from Skye?"

E.J. withdrew. The two sat in awkward silence for a minute and sipped their drinks.

"I thought you were on the road to getting fired. Does it matter if you don't get the story?"

"Well, it does in terms that now they could fire me for cause. Failure to get this story, and it's a big one, is a legitimate reason, so I wouldn't get what I want. Regardless, beyond that, they figured out a way to beat me. That's what's eating at me. They won."

Warren leaned back in his chair and laughed at E.J.'s stubbornness.

"You have put yourself through hell trying to get fired. For what? So you can collect unemployment? A few hundred dollars here and there? You're ridiculous."

"Warren, we talked about this... it's more than just being about money. They need to learn a lesson."

Warren thought for a minute, having witnessed everything.

"Funny, you have constructed every insane stunt that a man could possibly pull off in an attempt to teach them a lesson. However, I haven't seen any evidence that they learned any lesson. They're the same dumb-fuck asshole editors they were when you started your mission... what lesson have they learned?"

E.J. sat quietly, pondering Warren's statement. He had no response.

"I think, E.J., the only lesson that has been learned is what you've learned. Do you know what that is?"

"I'm not sure anymore," E.J. said a bit deflated.

"You have learned that they don't give a rat's ass about you, your career, or your humanity. They want production and expect nothing less. In return, they will expect more production. You can't win. Even if they fire you and you get that unemployment, you've still lost. You wanted to hold these people accountable, but no matter what you do, even if you win, you've still lost because you never succeeded in holding them accountable. Nothing changes, except you no longer work there. They'll continue to operate as they always have. I get it. I understand the feeling. You're a reporter. It's in your blood to want to hold people accountable, but in this case, it doesn't work. That's life. Not everyone is held accountable."

"That's basically what Blaze was talking about," E.J. mumbled, while floating in his own head for a split second. "Life isn't fair."

"I'm sorry, who is Blaze?" Warren asked confused.

E.J. snapped back into the conversation.

"I'm sorry Warren, just thinking out loud. Blaze is a friend of mine. He asked me whose game I was playing, and if I would recognize which game it was: Their game or mine? I think it's clear now. You're right. This game I'm playing, even if I won, would still never hold them accountable. It was never my game. It was always theirs. Considering all I've been through and all its cost me, I'm the only loser here. I never could hold them accountable, regardless of what I did. I was playing their game the whole time, and never knew it."

Warren smiled.

"I think you're right. I wish it was different, but I just don't see it any other way."

"Here I am with my woman walking out on me, I'm being evicted from my apartment in a matter of days, I have no career, nothing left, and the editors haven't changed a bit. They will be rid of me and the best I could have ever hoped for is their bosses bitching for a day or two about having to pay me unemployment. Hell, after failing to get the Seville story, I don't even have that."

"Your abrasion count is like a ten," Warren said.

"My what?"

"You know, abrasion count?"

E.J. sat bewildered.

"In the old days, when a delivery boy would throw a paper, sometimes it didn't make it all nice and neat. Newspaper companies fielded complaints from customers ranking the damage from one to five. This was termed abrasion count: One being minimal, five being destroyed or totally lost. My friend, you're at a five."

"So, what am I suppose to do now? It's just a matter of time before they file the paperwork for my termination."

"Fix it," Warren said.

"How?"

"On your terms. Stop playing their game and finally start playing yours."

Chapter Fifty-Five

E.J. swayed as he tried to shove his key into his apartment's deadbolt. A piece of paper hung in front of him, pinned to the door, but he stumbled as he tried to straighten his vision out long enough to read it. He caught a few words: OUT, EVICTED, FINAL NOTICE. Even in his intoxicated state, he understood what the note said. He just ripped the paper off the door and shoved it in his pocket. As he dumped his bags on the floor, he picked up the phone and called Kalea.

In a drunken rant, E.J. spilled out what had been happening and his realizations about what he was doing. He was angry, embarrassed, and in many ways feeling defeated and lost. Kalea sat silent as his rant died down... he waited to hear her speak.

"What happened to you? This is beneath you. Who gives a fuck about these people? You used to be someone that would never lower yourself to this level. This isn't you, it's become you. You think you can beat these guys at some game, but look at you, how you're acting, what you're doing... even if you get what you wanted, you've let them get the best of you."

"I know, I realize that now... but I can fix it. I know how to win. Kalea, nothing has changed about me. I'm still the guy that wouldn't let anyone get away with anything. I will always try to hold people accountable, but now I understand that not everyone will be held accountable, no matter what I, or anyone else does. Life isn't fair, and all I can do is try to make it so, but it doesn't always end right. I only thought I was holding these people accountable, but I wasn't, and I realize now that I'm not sure I ever could."

"What are you going to do?"

E.J. smiled.

"If I can't hold them accountable, the least I can do is fix it by finally playing my game, not theirs."

"What does that mean?"

"It means finally taking control of my... and it's... making my call..."

E.J. slowly trailed off. The phone went dead as E.J. passed out.

Chapter Fifty-Six

E.J. stood in front of his mirror wearing nothing but a plain white T-shirt and underwear. His hair was still wet, with the bathrobe and towel from that morning's shower lying on the floor. On his bed was his suitcase, packed fully, resting next to a few other bags with miscellaneous things ready to go. In his closet hung a lone dress shirt, slacks, and a tie, all of which were dangling from the last hanger he had yet to pack. He took them all down and put them on. Pants, then shirt, tucked it in, and then wrapped the tie around his neck. Winsor knot… his favorite.

On the floor, next to the night stand, were his black dress shoes. They looked brand new and shined perfectly since he hadn't worn them in months. Next to them were his white DVS skate shoes. Pure white and clean, as he always kept them. He looked at the sneakers for about a minute, then grabbed the dress shoes and slipped them on. He dumped the white sneakers in the trash and proceeded to pack the last of his things.

As he shoved a random pair of jeans into one of his bags, a card slipped out of the pocket and onto the ground. The card was that of Eagle Eye CEO Art Bechtel, the media watch-dog group that offered E.J. a job shortly after graduation. E.J. looked at it and put it in his wallet, throwing the rest of the trash away that was found in that pair of jeans. He went down to the street and loaded up his car with everything that was left, closed the trunk, and headed to work. On his way out, he pinned a note on the door of his landlord. It read:

I'm sorry for not keeping up with rent. You can stop the eviction process. I'm out of the apartment. Keys are under your mat. Be well.

He made his way down Third Street to a part of Hunter's Point that he was unfamiliar with, but knew it was where Blaze lived. It may have been early in the morning, but he felt that Blaze would be around. As he turned the corner at Ninth Street and Bayview, he saw his friend. As he pulled up, Blaze smiled.

"Mothafucka," Blaze belted, as he saw E.J. slow to a stop. "What ya doin' in my hood?"

Blaze looked at E.J.'s outfit.

"What happened to the beach look? You look like someone getting ready to go to work, or someone that wants to get jacked cruising down my street."

E.J. laughed.

"Naw man, I'm just getting ready for my final day."

"Seriously? You finally got them to get rid of you?"

"Not exactly... I'm ending this on my own terms, just like you said. I'm quitting before they can fire me, with or without cause. I'm now playing my game, not theirs. You probably won't see me again and I wanted to say thanks for being there, when I know you didn't have to even deal with this mid-west white boy."

Blaze leaned into the car and hugged E.J.

"I know good people when I meet them, brotha… and I knew you wouldn't go out like a punk. Man, I got mad love for ya. You let those bitches know what the fuck you want. That's real."

A car pulled up behind E.J., a brand new BMW with dark tinted windows. Blaze pulled back and looked at the car.

"Hold up, bro," Blaze said. "I got to handle business."

Blaze made his way to the car while E.J. watched through the rearview mirror. The man handed Blaze a wad of bills, and Blaze reached in his jacket and handed the man a bag. A few words were exchanged and the man drove off. E.J. shook his head with a bit of reservation as Blaze made his way back to E.J.'s window.

"What are you doin', Blaze?" E.J. asked.

"Business, man… business…"

"You can do better than this, Blaze. I'm not the best example of the model working man, but what are you going to do? This shit the rest of your life? You saw what happened to Heist."

"What are you suggesting? Become a CEO of a Fortune 500 company?"

E.J. chuckled.

"Well, there is going to be an opening at the Press-Journal… you have some studies in media, some college, some experience. Why not apply?"

"After all the shit I saw you go through and this is the job you recommend? Your next job should not be in recruiting, E.J."

"Well, regardless of my situation, it's a good start in a legitimate job. It made me a better man. Maybe things would have worked out differently if I would have recognized that earlier."

Blaze nodded in agreement.

"I'm just looking out for ya Blaze.... stop slangin' drugs on the street. I just want to see the forty-year-old Blaze doing well and not sitting in a prison, or dead. You have to start somewhere and, frankly, it will give you a launching pad for something real... not the bullshit you're doing now."

Blaze smiled.

"Thanks man... I'll think about that... now get to work and tell those pieces of shit to go fuck themselves."

E.J. laughed and they shook hands. E.J. quickly realized that Blaze was palming him a bag of marijuana for the road. E.J. slid his hand down and pocketed the drugs.

"I don't know what you're going to do after you leave today, but figured this would help end the evening tonight in a cool way. Stay real brotha and don't be a stranger."

E.J. grinned and drove off to his last day of work.

Chapter Fifty-Seven

The editors waited patiently in Walter's office. A small stack of papers sat on the desk: E.J.'s termination papers. All the necessary "I's" dotted and "T's" crossed. They chatted about E.J., reassuring themselves that this was just business and that E.J. dug his own grave considering all the stunts that he had pulled. E.J. brought this on himself. Next to the termination papers was Skye's story. Perfectly assembled. Perfectly edited. Perfectly finished.

E.J. walked up to the San Francisco Press-Journal tower and looked up the side of the building for the last time. It seemed higher than it ever had, as if it touched the heavens. He just stood on the sidewalk for what seemed like hours as dozens of people drifted by him. He smiled and the sound of the city slowly disappeared as he thought about the first time he walked into this building.

"I guess it's time," he said to himself.

He smiled and greeted everyone cheerfully in the lobby, as if it was just another day. Everyone noticed that for the first time in months, he was wearing the typical professional dress of a newspaper reporter, even down to the polished black dress shoes. As the doors of the elevator opened, Jeffery appeared. He looked at E.J. and then directly at his shoes.

"Well, aren't we a bit overdressed for work," Jeffery said jokingly. "What's up with the clothes?"

E.J. smiled, said nothing, and hugged one of the few people at the paper that he always respected; one of the few reporters that would not only get the story at all costs, but one that would do it with that cost in mind. No matter what he did, he did it with class and respect. E.J. marveled at how Jeffery trekked through the shit-field of journalism and always came out smelling like roses. He did it with purpose, the way E.J. wished he would have. In truth, he was jealous of Jeffery because he was the reporter he wished he could have been, but happy knowing now what type of newsman he could be. He had Jeffery to thank for that.

"I'm heading home."

"Really?" Jeffery said skeptically. "Did they finally cave in?"

"No," E.J. said smiling. "I just decided to win this game on my terms... the way I think you would have done it: With class and dignity. You are the type of journalist that makes journalism work and there are too many fucked-up people in this business that work against people like you. I realized I had become one of those people too, even if I couldn't admit it."

Jeffery smiled and assertively shook E.J.'s hand.

"You are one of a kind E.J., and I'm a better man for knowing you. It's been a pleasure."

"Jeffery, if anybody is the better man for knowing one of us, it's me."

Jeffery walked away, down the lobby, and out into the sea of people swarming the city. E.J. never broke his smile as he made his way up to the newsroom. He reached in his coat pocket and pulled out an envelope with Warren Lippman's name on it, dropping it off in his mailbox. The letter was a simple thank you to Warren for all he had taught him and for the time they spent together. Warren would pin this letter on his wall where it would stay until he retired nearly a decade later.

E.J. walked briskly to his desk, smiling, and saying hello to everyone he passed. They all looked at his clothes with wondering stares, always ending their gaze with a quick glance at his shoes. The editors stared through the window of Walter's office and prepared to call him in as E.J. grabbed a small box under his desk and threw a few things in it.

"Going somewhere?" Skye asked arrogantly, assuming the editors already had given him the bad news.

"Not just yet," E.J. said jovially. "I have to tell them a few things I've been meaning to let them know."

Walter walked out of his office and called E.J. over to meet with the editors. The newsroom went silent as everyone waited to see E.J.'s reaction. He nodded. Nothing else. No scene. No white shoes. No Jamaican accent or parrot on his shoulder, nor any beach clothes. Just E.J. as he had arrived a year earlier, only a little wiser.

"Got to talk with the editors," E.J. said to Skye as he began to walk away, but he stopped in mid stride.

"Oh, Skye," E.J. said with calm and manner. "I just want to say goodbye and let you know you're an embarrassment to journalism… and I hate to admit this to you, but I was no different either. However, I figured that out about myself. I don't think you ever will... and for some reason, that makes me happy in one way, but sad in another."

E.J. sped off before Skye could respond, strolling into Walter's office. The editors sat quietly for a moment. E.J. looked over at Walter's desk and could see the finished story that Skye had written. He smiled a bit, feeling okay with the fact that Skye somehow got the story he couldn't. He drifted to the desk and picked it up. All the info was there: The quotes, the evidence, and the slick style that made Skye an award-winning reporter.

"This is it?" E.J. asked.

"That's the story," Noland replied. "All there… and he got it all in just a few days. We know the Oakland and San Jose papers are on this story as well. You know what this means, right?"

E.J. looked at Noland and then glanced at Walter and Victoria, both still silent.

"Save it Noland. I may have been born during the day, but I wasn't born yesterday."

"This is a serious lapse in duty, you understand E.J.," Walter attempted, but only to be cut off by E.J.

"You too, Walter. Just save it. I know why you called me in here. But before you go on some long, drawn out speech about mission statements and professionalism, and whatever prefabricated crap your bosses tell you to say to justify this whole move to fire folks like me, and to do it with cause, I need you guys to know something."

The editors sat quiet, contemptibly, glaring at E.J., waiting.

"I quit... and I win."

The editors looked at each other with a slight attitude of victory.

"Is that it?" Walter asked.

"No, it's not. I thought this rebellion I was doing was for some larger purpose. To teach you bottom-feeding rats a lesson in accountability, but I learned something. You weren't going to change, even if I got what I wanted. The only person who changed was me, and I didn't like what I had become."

"I don't need to hear this shit, just get the fuck out of here," Noland chimed.

"No, you will hear this. You need to hear this. You see, Noland, I did win. You are still the same hypocritical piece of worthless garbage you were the day you hoodwinked me into coming out here and taking this job. You, Walter, and that airhead you call an editor haven't learned a thing either."

"Excuse me!" Victoria shouted, insulted.

"No! No!" E.J. belted, his voice drowning out Victoria. "You have nothing to say Victoria! You haven't had an original thought in your entire life, so this has nothing to do with you. Every last one in this room should be ashamed of themselves, myself included."

The editors were confused.

"Yes, I have been just as much of a scumbag this whole time as you folks, but I'm the only one that realizes this about myself."

E.J. paused for a second.

"But this ends today. I'm killing off the side of me I'm ashamed of and keeping the side that operates from a position of strength... the side I wish I had enough courage to operate from a long time ago."

E.J. threw Skye's story down on the table.

"Great story."

E.J. exited Walter's office, head high and with a sensitivity and elation that he had never thought imaginable, or even thought fundamental to him. He strolled straight through the newsroom, down to the lobby, into the elevator, and out the front door. He didn't utter another single word. He quickly made his way down to the street, into his car, and headed for the Bay Bridge. Gratified with a conquering sense, he expedited his way east to head home. Within minutes, the backdrop of San Francisco was seen only through the rearview mirror between the cracks of stacked boxes in the back seat.

Chapter Fifty-Eight

The falling snow was something E.J. still disliked, but it didn't stop him from smiling as he entered Cleveland's city limits. It was cold and E.J. didn't have the clothes necessary to handle an Ohio winter, nor did his car have a working heater. His phone kept ringing, but he refused to answer any of the return calls that he had placed earlier. He left messages, letting everyone know he was coming home and it would be a few days before he arrived. He also made sure to let everyone know that he didn't want Kalea to find out he was coming back. He wanted to deal with her in a different way.

Cleveland seemed different to him as he passed Cleveland State University on Euclid Avenue, before making a right onto 18th Street, heading down toward Superior Avenue and into the parking lot of the Cleveland Plain-Dealer. He stepped out of his car and looked at the large curved building, much different than the tall historic Press-Journal tower. People were going in and out the facility while E.J. just stood there watching.

"Can I help you?" a voice from behind called out.

E.J. turned to see a middle-aged man, a bit scrawny with horn-rimmed glasses and thinning hair.

"Maybe," E.J. replied. "Do you work here?"

"Yes," the man replied. "I'm Harold Yates, education reporter."

E.J. shook his hand.

"E.J. Lockhart."

"Can I help you with something, E.J.?"

"No, not really… I left my job at the San Francisco Press-Journal and just got back into town. For some reason I wanted to come by and see this place."

"Looking for a job?"

"I was offered a job here last year, but decided to head out west."

"Oh, I see… just decided to come by and see if that old job is still available?"

E.J. smiled a bit and chuckled.

"No, I don't think so."

A confused look danced across Harold's face.

"So, where are you looking for work?"

E.J. reached into his pocket and pulled out Art Bechtel's card, Eagle Eye stretched across the top. He couldn't take his eyes off of it.

"I'm looking for a job at a place where I can hold people accountable for what they do."

"Well, it's journalism. It's what we do here," Harold replied.

"Yeah," E.J. said with skepticism, knowing that was the same line his editors gave him when he first arrived in San Francisco.

"Quick question, Harold. Do you think the job I was offered a year ago is available?"

"I thought you said you weren't interested in working for the Plain-Dealer?"

"I'm not… just curious if maybe the person that took that job after I turned it down still has it… or if they quit?"

"Yeah, a young lady from Grambling took it. She lasted about eight months," Harold replied.

E.J. nodded with assurance, still staring at Art Bechtel's business card.

"Whose card is that?" Harold asked, transfixed on E.J.'s unwillingness to pull his eyes away.

E.J. looked up.

"The CEO of Eagle Eye. You familiar with them?"

"Yeah, they're a media watch-dog group. They did a piece on us about the accuracy of one of our stories. It's the reason why that young woman quit after eight months."

E.J. smiled with a bit of validation dancing across his face.

"You should talk to the editors. We may have a job open."

"No thanks. You answered my question. I thought maybe I was going to be able to compare apples to oranges by coming here, but it's still apples to apples."

Harold dismissed the comment, not really sure what E.J. was talking about.

"Well, I bet they would at least be interested in talking with you. The San Francisco Press-Journal is a huge paper. Are you sure you don't want to come inside? You can talk with my editor."

E.J. took Art Bechtel's card back out of his pocket and stared.

"I don't think so."

E.J. walked away dialing the number on the card.

"Hi, can I speak to Art Bechtel please?"

Art was unavailable.

"Sure, I would love to leave a message."

Chapter Fifty-Nine

The Silverstone apartment complex consumed almost an entire block of Cantner Avenue. Hundreds of units, two-stories high, laid out on a lush landscape with a medium-sized golf course, swimming pool, and perfectly manufactured green space with faultless trees lined around the property. It was strategic in maximizing space while attempting to look inviting, but it only really accomplished looking like a large-scale model. Every apartment was identical, mirror images in one, two, and three bedroom units. It was hard to tell the difference between this complex and any other similarly-sized apartment complex in Midwest America, but E.J. wanted an apartment here and nowhere else.

The driveway to the complex's office stretched, weaving around, signs every few feet offering deals, move-in specials, and amenities, like a gym, recreation room, and an on-site laundry room. E.J. pulled up to the office and gathered the few pieces of paper he downloaded from the Silverstone website. He had already filled out an application.

"Can I help you?" the old man at the office desk asked as E.J. walked up.

"Yeah, I want to rent an apartment."

E.J. handed over his application with all the necessary paperwork needed.

"And here is my deposit," handing over a check.

The old man looked through the application, slowly turning each page and checking off sections one at a time. E.J. watched carefully, hoping he would glance over the section about current employment, but the man stopped when he got to the section that was left blank.

"Current employment isn't filled out. You have a job, correct?" the man asked, handing the paperwork back to E.J.

"No, I don't at this minute, but I will have one shortly. I have the deposits and good credit… A job is on the way. I'm just waiting on something."

"We'll run your credit, as standard practice, but that isn't my concern. I'm sorry Mr. Lockhart, we cannot rent a place to you without a job, or some source of income."

"Look, I understand, but I'm not really unemployed, just waiting for a call to come through. I wouldn't be here doing this if I didn't have a job ready to go. I wouldn't waste my time or your time filling this stuff out."

"I understand, but the rules are the rules. There are apartments in this town that will rent to you. I suggest you check those places out."

"You don't understand," E.J. said frustrated. "I need to be here. This is where I need to be. I could go into it, but…"

The old man took off his glasses and interrupted.

"I'm sorry Mr. Lockhart, I cannot help you."

E.J.'s pocket began to vibrate and his ringtone, the song "Mr. Brownstone" by Guns 'N Roses, echoed from his phone.

"Hello."

On the other end was Eagle Eye CEO Art Bechtel, the man E.J. had blown-off after graduation, leaving his business card buried inside a pair of old jeans for over a year. Art was now the call E.J. needed. The old man sat quietly as the two conversed, E.J. pacing up and down the lobby of the office. He turned and headed back to the front of the desk, handing the old man his cell phone.

"Here," E.J. said. "Talk with him."

The old man took the phone.

"Hello?" the old man inquired, confused.

"The man you're talking with is the newest member of my news team," Art said. "If you need any proof of his employment, I would be happy to send that."

"Sure… fax it to 215-555-7435."

The old man hung up the phone and handed it back to E.J.

"Would you like to view a few of the apartments before we complete the lease agreement?"

"No, I want apartment 216."

The old man seemed confused.

"Have you been in that apartment before?"

"No, but It's the one I want. Can I have it?"

"Sure," said the old man, pulling a few pieces of paper out of a filing cabinet. "Do you want to see it first?"

"No, I don't need to see it. I know what's there," E.J. said smiling.

"Okay. Fair enough. When would you like to move in?"

"Today… right now."

Chapter Sixty

E.J. dumped all of his belonging on the bedroom floor. He stood there looking at the pile, all that was left of his entire life. He made his way back into the living room, glancing into the closets and the bathroom as he passed them. The apartment was barren, a huge empty space. He smiled. Surprisingly, he felt at home. On the counter was his grocery bag, inside the ingredients to make champagne shrimp and pasta, with a bottle of Owen Roe Slide Mountain merlot. He had stopped by Target and bought some decent plates, silverware, candles, cloth napkins, and wine glasses. A few pots and pans were left behind from the previous tenant, which he cleaned up before prepping dinner. Every so often, he would look out his window and then look at his watch. He was worried that five o'clock would come too soon and he didn't want to postpone his dinner plans or have to hide out inside his new apartment all night.

As the prep work for dinner was being completed, a faint sound of someone walking up the stairs could be heard. The door bell rang and then a huge thump echoed through the walls as something heavy hit the ground. E.J. smiled and quickly made his way to the door. Outside was a huge box. He took a quick look at his watch: 3:30 p.m. He scanned the apartment complex grounds and saw no one else, just the delivery man disappearing into the parking lot. He dragged in the box and immediately got a blade to cut it open.

A few basic tools were included and the table took less than thirty minutes to assemble. The chairs, although not too fancy, looked good and were easy to put together. He moved the new piece of furniture to the middle of the room. As he set the table, moving napkins, plates, and candles, a knock hit the door. E.J. looked at his watch: 4:15 p.m. The voice of a young man standing in the open doorway, holding an expensive tuxedo gently wrapped in plastic, echoed through the room.

"Are you the guy that ordered this tux?"

"Yeah, that's me."

E.J. took the tux and hung it in the closet. He removed the plastic, ran his hand across the fabric and smiled. He headed back into the kitchen to finish up cooking. While the food simmered, he completed the table settings, lit the candles, and poured two glasses of wine. It was 4:45 p.m. and he headed for the bedroom to put on the tuxedo. At 5:00 p.m., he walked outside onto his porch, holding a single rose he had cut from one of the bushes out in front of the apartment complex. He stood there, the sun beginning to go down as a cold breeze dusted the city of Cleveland.

In the distance, the figure of a woman appeared. Her head was down as she dug through her purse looking for keys, her arms struggling to hold a few file folders. E.J. stood still, smiling as he had never smiled before, looking directly at the woman while she made her way up the stairs to apartment 215. The apartment that was right next to his.

"Can I help you?" E.J. asked as the woman continued to scrounge for her keys, still making her way upstairs.

Kalea's head snapped up to see E.J.

"What the fuck!?" she blurted. "Oh my God! What are you doing here!?"

Her keys and folders hit the ground. She drifted back, almost falling, but E.J. quickly swooped in and wrapped his arms around her, pulling her toward him.

"Be careful… I don't want my new neighbor to fall and hurt herself."

"New neighbor?" she said, grasping for air as she noticed the front door of the neighboring apartment wide open. "You're here?"

She peered through the open door at the lone table sitting in the middle of the room. Candles burning, wine poured, and a beautifully set dinner. E.J. picked up her keys and her folders.

"Let's go. I don't want dinner to get cold."

Chapter Sixty-One

The first month at Eagle Eye was a type of revenge for E.J., who took out his anger on just about every story he got his hands on. Sometimes it was bad reporting, questionable angles, or bad editing. Sometimes the stories were just victims of space in the paper. Either way, E.J., and the team of five working underneath him, systematically dissected all major stories from all major news outlets in the Midwest. Eagle Eye had become the premier watchdog of news accuracy and E.J. consumed their mission wholeheartedly. Sometimes they did their own original reporting to fill in the half-truths left out of stories, sometimes corrected misinformation, and sometimes they would run the same stories covered by different outlets side-by-side, pointing out inconsistencies. For the first time in his career, he was doing exactly what he set out to do: Hold people accountable.

"Hey E.J., I have a phone call for you."

"Who is it?" E.J. asked, still banging away on his keyboard while juggling the dozen or so stories his crew had been following.

"Marcus Greenbury."

"Who?" E.J. asked, still completely focused on his computer screen. "I don't know any Marcus Greenbury? Is he with the Associated Press or something? They've been pissed ever since we shredded their coverage of the Brownsville-Macklin Warehouse shooting in Wisconsin."

The secretary asked a few questions of the caller.

"E.J., he says he is with Hurston Newspapers Inc. in San Francisco."

"What?" E.J. said, pulling himself away from his work.

"Blaze," shouted the secretary. "He told me to tell you 'Blaze.' Is that some kind of code word?"

"Holy shit! Blaze? Yeah, transfer him over."

E.J. picked up his phone.

"Hey Blaze, what the fuck's up man?"

"Hey E.J., I wanted to call and congratulate you on the CNN interview last night. I saw that shit. My man! Always doin' it big."

"Thanks... what the fuck is this about you calling from Hurston? I don't get it."

"Shit changed up here. I took your advice. I'm legit. I'm workin' with your old company and also got a spot in their radio division."

"What? Are you fucking joking me?"

"No man. That's why it's no longer Blaze... It's Marcus. Put that dealin' shit behind me."

E.J. smiled.

"No shit? Wow… What are you doing for them?"

"Fact checking stories for the various papers, but I also got the company to give me air time overnight on Sundays WBSF. I'm doing a sports show. Hopefully it goes well enough, you'll be hearing 'Marcus On The Field' nationally, right? We can all hope. Like you said… use this place to my advantage."

"Nice… Man, I'm fuckin' so happy to hear this."

"Yeah, I decided to take my own advice. I realized after our last conversation that I wasn't playing my game. I was playing somebody else's. It's funny how when I asked you if you were playing your game, and if you could even recognize when you no longer were, that I was in the same situation. I didn't realize in that moment I was always playing someone else's game. I wasn't going to ever win, just lose."

"Looks like we both figured it out in time. Glad you made the move."

"How about you, man? How's Eagle Eye?"

"Shit, this job is awesome. The people are great. I got a great team. The pay is solid. Kalea and I got back together. Things have been amazing since I left Hurston and the Press-Journal."

"Word! That's what I want to hear…. I felt weird taking a job with the company you were working for, but I couldn't pass up the opportunity. I'm gonna go back to school next semester to finish my degree. I figure I can hang with these cheap slave-drivin' motherfuckers until I'm done."

"Cool man…"

E.J. paused for a moment wanting to ask about the paper.

"Do you have any contact with the Press-Journal?"

"Sometimes. You know how it works. I get a few stories through the Visiontron system, so every once in awhile I'll have to fact check something from Jeffery or Skye. Always laugh when I see their names."

"What's the flavor like up there since Skye busted that Seville story? I haven't bothered to check. I'm doing the Midwest region out here, so I don't really deal with west coast news."

"What story are you talkin' about?" Marcus asked with curiosity.

"The Tom Seville story. He is the Oakland city councilman that was involved in election fraud with the former mayor of Oakland. You know, Russell Graham, Heist's story?"

Marcus thought for a second.

"I haven't heard anything about that."

"What? That story should have ran a month ago."

"I'm not sure E.J. Tom Seville is still an Oakland city councilman as far as I know. I haven't heard anything about him at all. He certainly hasn't been in the news."

E.J. paused, confused as to why Marcus hadn't heard anything. A dozen possibilities as to why it hadn't run coursed through his brain.

"It doesn't make sense. Are you sure nothing has been published in the paper about Seville?"

"I'm sure. If the guy committed election fraud and a story ran, I would have seen it. Shit, his ass would be blasted out of office. Maybe the story never panned out, or maybe they ran into a problem and are holding it?"

"Maybe… maybe…" E.J. mumbled as he tried to figure out what was going on. "I need to take care of something, Blaze… I mean Marcus. Can I call you back later?"

"For sure, man. Anytime."

Chapter Sixty-Two

The office was completely empty. E.J. had combed the news wire, trying to find any trace of the Tom Seville story or any indication that something ran somewhere. Every story on the news wire about Seville was run-of-the-mill generic stories about policy and ribbon-cutting events. Time was flying by and E.J. had lost all track of it. His phone rang.

"Eagle Eye. Lockhart speaking."

"It's Sunday night. Do you really need to be at the office this late?"

"What?" E.J. replied, his mind in a different space.

"Helllllloooo … Are you there? Earth to E.J."

"I'm sorry babe, just doing some research. Something's going on with my former paper and I'm perplexed."

"What is it?"

"Well, the last story I worked on, the one I couldn't get, was about an Oakland city councilman named Tom Seville. He was supposedly involved in election fraud. I worked on it for weeks and came up completely empty. Then Skye, that dickhead, somehow got the story."

"So what? 'E.J. The Great' can't always win."

"No, no, it's not that," E.J. replied. "The paper never ran the story that Skye wrote. It was done. I saw it. They just didn't run the story."

"Why wouldn't they run the story?"

"That's what I'm trying to figure out… it just doesn't make sense."

"Maybe something happened after you left that somehow negated the story? Maybe they changed their minds? Maybe Skye's story had problems they couldn't fix?"

"No, that's not possible. I saw the story. It was covered from all angles and verified up and down. It was as solid as a story could be. I've never seen anything like this."

"Can't you just let this go? Who cares what they do or don't do?"

"I know, but it's just that they pinned this story up against my job. I was basically canned for this story falling through… and here we are today with the story never running."

E.J. paused for a moment and began to think.

"E.J., are you there?"

"Yeah," E.J. said, snapping back to reality. "I'm heading out in a few minutes. I'll be home within the hour."

E.J. hung up the phone and looked at the clock. It was 10:10 p.m. He picked up the phone and called WBSF radio.

"Can I please speak to Marcus Greenbury?"

The call was patched through.

"This is Greenbury."

"Hey Marcus, it's E.J. Can you do me a favor?"

"Sure man, what's up?"

"Can you access the Press-Journal's files in Visiontron for me? I want to find that story about Seville."

Marcus pulled up Visiontron, the company's main storage system for stories, and typed in a few key words. Hundreds of articles popped up, all containing Tom Seville's name. Marcus adjusted the search to include Skye's name. Hundred's turned into dozens.

"I'm still looking at fifty stories here," Marcus said. "What's another key word I can use? Fraud? Election?"

E.J. thought for a moment.

"No, look in the dump file."

"What's the dump file?"

"In the upper right hand corner of the screen you'll see a link tagged DF. If a story never runs, it ends up in there."

Marcus clicked the link and within seconds, the story appeared.

"Yeah, I found it."

"They dumped the story… what is the time signature on the story?"

Marcus scrolled down to the bottom to see the electronic time stamp.

"It says January 13th at 11:36 a.m."

"Those motherfuckers," E.J. said angrily.

"What? What does that mean?"

"I saw Noland upload that story into Visiontron just before I walked out of my job. I saw it on deck to run in the paper. That was around 11 a.m. that morning."

"You're telling me they sent the story to run at 11 a.m., but then dumped it a half-hour later?" Why?"

In that moment a picture formed out of a thousand scattered pieces that were spread across a landscape. An image appeared as if to answer a stack of questions that were left pulling at E.J. each time he came up short on the Seville story. The improbable scenario had never entered his mind, nor did the idea that a setup this underhanded was even possible. He couldn't believe this level of deceitfulness was such an ingrained tradition at the Press-Journal, or that the editors would go to such lengths to violate the core principles of the profession. E.J. never would have imagined, even with the stunts he pulled, that people would go to such dangerous lengths to get rid of one man they didn't like.

"The story isn't real… it never was. That's why I kept hitting all those dead ends. They set me up. They faked this lead about Seville being involved in election fraud, made me chase a ghost, and then they got Skye to fabricate the story so I would believe I fell short. It's the perfect excuse to fire me with cause, but they knew me too well. They knew by that time what I was thinking. They knew I would quit before I would let that happen. Once I left, they just dumped the story. They figured I would come home to Ohio, never see the story, and I would never look back."

"Those motherfuckers," Marcus cursed. "I should take this story and put it in the run file, watch that story hit the newsstand. Fuckin' ruin all their careers."

"No, Marcus," E.J. interrupted. "You're signed into the system. They'll know you transferred the story to run it. You'll get fired. Plus, it will cross Victoria's desk... it's possible she would miss it during deadline rush, but not likely. She's naïve, shallow, and clueless a lot of times, but she isn't that stupid. Odds are she would catch it. Even if you moved it into the run file, it's still not likely to go through."

"Fuckin' dicks! What now?"

E.J. thought for a moment.

"I would love nothing more than to run that story, but we cannot do it without a user identification being stamped on it. That would not end well for the person that has their named tagged to that story. That's assuming it slips past Victoria."

E.J. began to become bitter and angry again. He thought of the last moments in Walter's office, where he took control and stopped playing their game and began to play his. It wasn't real. The editors at the Press-Journal not only beat him at his own game, but also made him believe he had won the game. For the first time since those last days in San Francisco, E.J. wanted revenge. He clinched his teeth, closed his eyes, and lowered his head. As Marcus rambled on about payback, E.J. thought quietly to himself that there was nothing he could do. He lost his game, as well as their game, all in one big wave, never seeing it come and never seeing it go.

Chapter Sixty-Three

Across the Eagle Eye newsroom was a banner that read "3,000,000+" in big red letters with a caption underneath: "How many more can we get through the looking glass?" The place was buzzing non-stop with everyone in high spirits. E.J. smiled politely as he made his way to his desk, greeting only those he had to actually talk with. He was still thinking about the other night. He couldn't shake the feeling of being beaten and humiliated.

"They probably are still laughing about this, somewhere," he muttered to himself.

"Did you say something E.J.?" Bradley, an intern at the office asked, overhearing him.

"What?" E.J. replied blindly, not realizing Bradley was near him. "No, Bradley, I didn't say anything… just thinking out loud."

Art Bechtel came out of his office dressed casually with shorts and flip-flops on.

"We have a meeting in the conference room," Art screamed across the office. "That means everyone, including interns and anyone else on my payroll. Let's go!"

The large conference room had two primary sections, custom built for the many news teams that worked at Eagle Eye. A huge conference table sat in the middle of the room while long, sectional-style sofas, lined the west walls all the way around to the south-end of the room. On the east side were several individual stations where teams could gather for small meetings. At capacity, it could sit 100 people easily, which came in handy on days like these. A day that Eagle Eye surpassed performance goals, and a day Art Bechtel expected to happen more frequently.

"A couple of things before we get into why I called you all in here: First, Team Baker. Great job on hitting that New York Times piece about the Bush/Gore follow-up, Team Castro on the Florida school incident, and I would also like to thank Team Lockhart for the Wisconsin shooting and the great job E.J. did for us on CNN during the interview. E.J., absolutely fucking fearless. You did an awesome job representing Eagle Eye on the national stage. We're not only doing work here that is unlike anything else in journalism, we're setting the new standard. Everybody that reads a story is coming here to get the truth about that story... and no one does it better than us. We're absolutely untouchable and all of you make that so."

Everyone clapped and cheered while E.J. smiled. For a moment, a brief moment, he wasn't thinking about the Press-Journal.

"A few other things. I know you all saw the banner this morning. It's because of you folks that I'm happy to report we have passed one-hundred million website hits and over three million subscribers."

Cheers erupted, briefly stopping Art from finishing his comments.

"Okay, okay, calm down," Art said loudly, waving his hands to bring the crowd back to him. "I'll be very brief. Quit working today. We're cutting out early and having an office barbecue out back. Also, we're celebrating a five percent raise for everyone… so, congratulations. We're officially a massive success as of today."

Everyone began cheering again, high-fiving, hugging, and pumping their fists in the air. E.J. joined in the chaos, embracing his team of reporters and researchers, caught up in the celebration.

"Oh yeah, one other thing," Art chimed in as the noise died down. "We have just signed a deal with Visiontron to store all of our stories automatically online, so soon, we'll no longer have to file them into your computer and transfer them over to the active file with editors. We'll simply write the story and everything is managed through the system. Don't worry about Visiontron right now. I don't want to go into a huge training session on the system since it's not up and running yet at Eagle Eye. We'll have plenty of time for that later, but I just wanted to let you know that's coming down the pipeline. Anyone familiar with this system?"

Everyone looked around silently or mumbled their ignorance of the system to each other.

"I have," E.J. said, his festive mood suddenly broken. "I used it at the Press-Journal. It's a good system. It's easy to keep track of stories, where they are, if they ran, if they've been dumped, and everyone can access any story to see everything about it. Full text, individual electronic tags to see who made edits, what edits they made, who moved a story from one file to the next, and so on. It's very streamlined."

"Yeah, our investors and IT guys loved it," Art said. "So you will all get usernames and passwords to access the system."

"When are we getting those usernames and passwords, and when will we be trained for it?" an employee asked from the back of the room.

"Well, I'm not going to sugarcoat anything… I've talked with reps from Visiontron and they have been in the midst of a huge overhaul of their system for a massive update, so they are a bit behind schedule. You're looking at a few weeks before they get back up to speed. I'm just letting you guys know about it now so you're not surprised. Just keep filing your stories the same way we have been until notified. So, enough of this. Let's go drink!"

The room filed out as people went to their desks, shut down their computers, and headed out to the back of the building where Art had built a small park-like setting for just these types of occasions. E.J. stopped Art and pulled him aside.

"I'm sorry sir, I don't mean to harp on this… I'm curious about Visiontron. What is this deal with the delays again?"

"They're just overhauling everything, so it will be a few weeks before they finish these updates. Is this a problem, E.J.?"

"No, not at all, I was just curious," E.J. said with a genuine smile. "I'm going to get back to work."

"Work? We're not working today, in case you didn't catch that at the meeting. I'm your boss E.J. and I'm ordering you to go outside, relax, have a beer, and some food. That's your new assignment."

"I will be out there soon, but I have a huge lead that I just got," E.J. said.

"What is it?"

"I'm not 100 percent sure, but it could be major. Just give me a few minutes to check a couple of things out."

"Okay, whatever you need to do, but I want to be personally notified as soon as you find out anything solid. You understand?"

"I understand completely Mr. Bechtel," E.J. said with a smile that he couldn't hide.

"I also want to be notified when you crack a beer and have a burger," Art said jokingly. "You have until noon. After that, I better see you eating and drinking something."

"Will do, Mr. Bechtel."

Art walked away, but suddenly stopped and turned around.

"One other thing, E.J. Stop calling me 'Mr. Bechtel.' That's my dad's name. It's Art, for crying-out-loud."

Chapter Sixty-Four

The smell of food permeated through the walls of Eagle Eye's office and the sounds of staff members could be heard as well from the party outside. E.J. sat alone in the office, the only person coming by was a janitor who periodically wheeled out kegs of Heineken beer to the celebration. He had spent the last twenty minutes working on a short critique of a Lancing State Journal story about a former policeman. He waited until the office was completely clear.

"Well, let's see how backed-up Visiontron is," he said to himself as he went to the Visiontron website.

The home screen opened up exactly as it had a thousand times at the Press-Journal. E.J. glided his hand onto the mouse and moved the pointer into the sign-in box, clicking it. Typing as if every character carried its own weight in gold, he entered in his old Press-Journal username: ejlock. Underneath that, he clicked the box, and slowly typed in his old password. He then pressed enter. The hourglass appeared and E.J. closed his eyes, sweat beading on his head, his breath held tightly. He waited for what seemed like hours before he lifted his eyelids. On the screen, in big blue letters: Hello, E.J. Lockhart. Welcome to Visiontron.

"Yes!" E.J. belted loudly as his fist hit the desk.

He still had access to the system.

The phone rang at Marcus' desk.

"Hello, Marcus Greenbury speaking."

"Hey Marcus. It's E.J. Listen... I just found out my username and password are still active in the Visiontron system. I can run the story."

"Wait.. What? How is that possible?" Marcus asked.

"Apparently, Visiontron is going through some kind of update and they're behind in that process. I'm assuming this delay is the reason they haven't cleared out my old credentials yet. I still have access."

Marcus jumped up, excited, but then remembered the other problem.

"What about Victoria?"

"There's nothing we can do about that. The story will be put into the run file, and if she catches it, she catches it. After that, we're done. All we can hope for is that she slips up or misses it, for whatever reason. It's kind of a long shot, but it's possible. I'm running this story before I leave here tonight."

He signed out and then closed Visiontron before opening a new document in the Eagle Eye system. The slug for this new story: How The San Francisco Press-Journal Fabricated a Story. For the next three hours, as the rest of the office celebrated their success out back, E.J. hammered out a scathing article critiquing the Tom Seville story, acting as if it had already ran. He never mentioned the scam they pulled on him, or that at one time he pursued the story too, or that he had any connection to the piece of fiction he hoped would be in the paper by the next morning. He just offered his opinion as to how something so egregious could happen. When he finished, he saved the work, but didn't file it into the Eagle Eye system just yet. It was 2:00 p.m., 11:00 a.m. Pacific time. He simply turned off his screen and joined the rest of his colleagues in a celebration outside, all the while trying to figure out the right moment to tell his boss that one of the nation's most well-respected newspapers might publish a completely fabricated story the next morning.

For the next few hours E.J. drank and ate with colleagues, continuously looking at the clock. Deadline at the Press-Journal was 5:00 p.m.. Pacific time, and that's when he planned to run it. He knew by that time, Walter and Noland would be gone for the day, with only Victoria still at work: The lone editor that could recognize the story and block it from running. As the crowd thinned and people headed home, E.J. drifted back into the office. Art was packing his things and leaving.

"Are you going home, E.J.? It's getting late," Art said.

"I need to finish something," E.J. replied as he fired up his computer.

"Is this about that lead you were talking about earlier?"

"I think so," E.J. replied. "I won't know exactly what's going on until tomorrow, but I'll be here by 7:00 a.m. and I will let you know what's happening."

"Can you give me any details?"

"I think a major newspaper is involved in the fabrication of a story. I mean the whole thing completely made up out of thin air."

"Wow, " Art said stunned. "That's as big as it gets. Are you talking about a Stephen Glass-type of fabrication?"

"I'm not sure of the details… yet. If this is true, we'll know by tomorrow."

"Tomorrow? You're telling me this story will run tomorrow?" Art asked, a bit of reservation in his voice. "Are you sure about this?"

"Trust me, Art. If my hunch is right, the minute that story hits the news, I will have a reply ready to go."

"Well, ever since you got here, you have been on point, so I trust you. You just better keep me informed."

Art pulled out his card and wrote a number on the back.

"This is my personal cell number. I don't care when, what time, or what you think I'm doing, you call me immediately when you figure this story out."

"Of course," E.J. said, taking the card.

"And don't stay here all night!" Art shouted as he left the building.

E.J. looked at the clock. It was 8:05 p.m., Eastern time. He quickly re-logged onto Visiontron, moved into the system's dump file, and accessed the Seville story, still sitting there, mocking him. He clicked the story, moved it into the "run" folder, and tagged it "read and edited." At the bottom, he wrote: "Priority. Must run tomorrow." He clicked finalize and sent it to the main printing center at the Pleasanton office, while simultaneously entering it into the Press-Journal system where Victoria could possibly see it slated for publication. All he could do was pray Victoria didn't catch it.

"Now it's time to play my game."

E.J. leaned back and finished what was left of his beer.

Chapter Sixty-Five

E.J. arrived at the Eagle Eye office at 7:00 a.m., going into the empty conference room for privacy. He immediately logged into the San Francisco Press-Journal's website, which hadn't been updated with any new stories yet. He set his watch to Pacific time, knowing that updates happened between 4:00 a.m. and 5:00 a.m., then set his computer to refresh every five minutes. He said nothing of his plan to Kalea, who was simply enjoying the new honeymoon period the two were having. He opened his story about the Press-Journal's fabrication, did some editing, and waited.

At 4:15 a.m.: Nothing.

At 4:25 a.m.: Nothing.

At 4:50 a.m.: Nothing.

"Damn!" E.J. cursed to himself. "Victoria must have caught it. Fuck!"

E.J. kicked the table and furiously walked off toward the bathroom. Suddenly, out of the corner of his eye, he saw his computer screen flash. Even from a bit of distance, he could see the bold headline at the top of the Press-Journal website: "Oakland Councilman Tom Seville Involved In Election Fraud."

"Ahhhhhhhh!!!!!!" E.J. screamed at the top of his lungs, jumping up and down. "She missed it! She missed it!"

E.J. immediately got on the phone and called Art. He sent his story out and notified the rest of the editors about what was going on. E.J. quickly began making phone calls to every major news outlet on the East Coast, e-mailed other major outlets on the West Coast, and sent messages to all of his contacts in the Midwest. Within minutes of the initial surge by Eagle Eye and E.J., the phone began to ring. CNN, MSNBC, FOX News, and a host of other media outlets called wanting to talk with him. The news spread fast, but wasn't fast enough to allow the Press-Journal to stop the newspaper from hitting the streets. E.J. made one more phone call, leaving a message on Skye Langevin's voicemail. Professional and courteous, he introduced himself, but never saying he was from Eagle Eye, and simply asked Skye to call him back with a comment about the fabricated story he wrote. E.J. would never receive a return call from Skye, which was okay with him. He just wanted the last word... and he got it.

By 8:00 a.m. in San Francisco, the Press-Journal was erupting. Walter, Noland, Victoria, Skye, and the rest of the editorial staff at the paper were in a meeting, while other personnel batted away the flood of phone calls coming in: Everyone from Tom Seville's camp threatening lawsuits, to those that were falsely quoted in the story, and from upper-management in Denver, the headquarters of Hurston Newspapers Inc. The walls around them were crumbling.

"Explain to me how the fuck that story landed in the paper!?" Walter screamed at his editorial staff.

All remained silent.

"Well!? None of you know how this happened!?" Walter yelled. "Noland, this is your responsibility. How the Hell did this happen!?"

"I don't… I don't know…" Noland replied timidly with a streak of fear in his voice. "Fuck, we're all going to burn for this. I have a mortgage and a family. We'll never work in this industry again."

"Look, let's not go overboard," Skye said. "It's a mistake. Media makes mistakes. We'll just run corrections. I mean, there has to be a way to correct this."

Walter sat down and put his hands over his face in frustration.

"Skye," Walter said. "This isn't a mistake. We didn't get some facts wrong or misquote someone. We just ran a completely fabricated story, and one that accuses one of the most powerful men in Oakland of election fraud. There is no correction for this. I want answers and I want them now, or you're all fired, immediately, while I still have the power to do so! Understood!?"

Noland excused the rest of the staff from the meeting so the four involved could discuss the matter in private.

"Why is this story in the system in the first place?" Skye asked. "I think we made a convincing argument to E.J. that the story was legit. You didn't have to put it into the system for show. Why the fuck would you put it in the system?"

Walter looked at Noland.

"Did you put it in the system, Noland?"

"Yeah, I did, just before E.J. left… but I had to do that to keep the appearance up. I mean, he would have known something was up if I didn't do that… but once he was out the door, I put it in the dump file. There is no way that story would have accidentally been pulled and put in the paper. Not from the dump file. That's impossible. That's why I don't get this at all. Someone would have to intentionally go into the system and move it from the 'dump file' into the 'run file'."

"Are you sure it was in the dump file?" Walter asked.

"Yes, it was!"

"Fuck!" Skye belted, his voice shaky. "I can't believe I let you fucking retards talk me into this scam. I'm fucking ruined!"

As the group continued to argue, Skye's brain clicked, realizing the voicemail E.J. left was not an unfortunate coincidence.

"Wait, this Eagle Eye. They're the ones that broke this story. Whose byline is on that Seville story they published?"

"No byline," Noland replied. "They don't use bylines at Eagle Eye. I already looked."

Skye stepped back, frustrated, still trying to piece it together.

"I got a message from E.J., left just after 5:00 a.m.," Skye said. "I didn't think about the time he called. I had so many other messages when I got into work. His was the first. That's just minutes after the system would have posted the story online… the paper was in the middle of being thrown onto doorsteps."

The three looked at Skye perplexed.

"Does he work for them?" Skye asked. "Do you know where he went to work after he left here?"

"Wait a minute," Walter said. "What the fuck are you talking about? You think E.J. broke this story for Eagle Eye?"

"I got a message this morning from him within minutes of the website posting it. No one could have figured this out so fast?"

Walter turned on his television. E.J.'s face appeared, being interviewed by CNN. He was talking about the Seville story, about working for the Press-Journal, and how the reporter, Skye Langevin, and the editors, had not returned his calls. They watched as E.J. played the perfect neutral reporter, but with a slight smile of victory showing up periodically. E.J. knew that somewhere in San Francisco the editors were watching him.

"That son of a bitch," Walter belted.

Noland jumped on Walter's computer and logged onto Visiontron. He went into the system's history and pulled up the

Seville story. On the bottom right hand corner of the screen it displayed a username: ejlock, with a timestamp from the previous day. The rest of the editors came over and stared at the screen, E.J.'s voice echoing in the background as the CNN interview continued.

"They never deleted his access," Walter said. "He somehow figured this out, pulled it from the dump file, and ran it. Jesus-fucking-Christ!"

Noland got up, panicked. He looked for a scapegoat.

"Okay, so he ran it, but that doesn't fall on us. First of all, Victoria was running the night shift. This is her responsibility. How the fuck could you have let this story slip by you!?"

Victoria, who had said very little this whole time, just shook her head in disappointment.

"Goddammit, Victoria! I've always known you were stupid, but not this grossly incompetent! How could you fuck up this bad!?"

Victoria pulled a piece of paper out of her folder and handed it to Noland.

"What the fuck is this!?" Noland barked in angry confusion.

"My resignation. I accepted a city editor position at the San Diego Union-Tribune last week."

Walter looked shocked.

"How...?"

Victoria cut Walter off.

"Oh, I have no doubt you're surprised, considering what you told the editors at the Union-Tribune about me. I guess you still needed me to be the assistant city editor punching bag? I know no one else wanted this job working underneath you two. It's the only reason you hired me, so maybe you couldn't find a replacement? Whatever the reason, I don't care."

Noland and Walter were fuming.

"I spent years here enduring your disrespect and the insults because I thought, one day, I'll get my chance. I always thought this was part of the job. You know, I have to pay my dues, right? But when that chance came up, you tried to ruin it. Luckily, it didn't work. I still got the job, but the editors over there were concerned about what you said, so we had a talk."

Victoria got up and adjusted her skirt and blouse.

"And to answer your question, Noland. Why did I miss the Seville story last night? Maybe ask Walter..."

Victoria looked toward Walter.

"What was it you said to the Union-Tribune? 'I would get lost in a supermarket if someone wasn't holding my hand?'"

Walter put his face into his hands, defeated. Victoria turned her attention back to Noland.

"I guess you have your answer, Noland. I got lost in the supermarket."

Noland seethed with rage.

"I can't believe you did this to us! We're all fucked here!"

"First of all, I didn't do anything. I just made a mistake. It happens when you're just a dumb girl, right? Oops… and you're the ones who are fucked, not me. I don't work here anymore."

Victoria excused herself. As she exited the building, she grabbed a copy of the paper with the infamous headline as a memento.

Chapter Sixty-Six

Kalea had just finished preparing dinner, even though it was past 10 p.m. E.J. had been making the nightly news rounds doing interviews the last three days, so Kalea just accepted that he wouldn't be home until late. She had watched every one of them with joy, the first time since E.J. entered journalism that she felt that way. She was proud of him, but also was suspicious. She found it odd that the biggest break of his career came at the expense of his former paper.

E.J. could smell the food as he unlocked the door.

"Wow, you cooked dinner?" he asked as he put up his jacket.

"Well, I was watching the news and knew it would be another late one for you. I'm not happy with the notion that you're eating pizza every night when you get home, so I made a real dinner."

They sat down at the table. Kalea poured two glasses of champagne and took a few sips while E.J. ate. There were a few moments of silence.

"So, what happened with the Press-Journal?" Kalea asked.

"They were all fired, as I understand," E.J. said in a nonchalant voice that was muffled with food.

"Can I ask you a question?"

E.J. said nothing.

"Did you have something to do with this? It's odd... we had just talked about this story."

E.J. shrugged his shoulders.

"Yeah, but you know how this business works. People get leads, and sometimes things don't really pan out, then editors push the issue, stories get manipulated, then things get published. It happens."

"And you expect me to believe that?" Kalea belted with a bit of doubt in her voice. "None of this seems a bit odd to you at all?"

"Like I said, honey, the media business sometimes..." E.J. replied, trailing off.

The television, which was running the nightly news in the background, suddenly reported an update on the story. The two abandoned their conversation for the moment and watched as the reporter gave an update:

"Following the scandal, the Press-Journal fired its main editors Walter Willieford and Noland Slade, and let go of reporter Skye Langevin. Assistant City Editor Victoria Cipriani, who also was implicated in the scandal, escaped backlash as she had accepted a job at the San Diego Union-Tribune the week before. Although still working at the Press-Journal up until the story ran, she said she had spent her last days getting her affairs in order for the move, claiming

she had no knowledge of the Seville story, when it was written, or how it landed in the paper."

"What? She got another job? A week ago?" E.J. said to himself, stunned.

"Well, it looks like one of your editors got away with whatever happened," Kalea said.

"Holy shit... I was wrong. She didn't miss the story."

"I'm sorry, what are you talking about, babe?"

"Just... uh... Looks like Victoria has paid her dues," E.J. said smiling.

"It was announced today that the paper will be turned over to a new staff of editors that Hurston Newspapers Inc. officials say will restore the paper's credibility and make moves to repair the damage caused by this scandal."

Suddenly, a picture of Jeffery appeared on the television next to a picture of Warren.

"Long time Press-Journal Education Reporter Jeffery Corbett was appointed the new Executive Editor and will be advised by Pulitzer-Prize winning San Francisco City Reporter Warren Lippman as the overhaul begins, officials announced. Corbett, in his first public address, said that changing the paper's practices and culture is his top priority and is looking forward to working with Lippman."

E.J. smiled.

"My man," E.J. said happily. "He finally gets the job he was originally promised: Working with Warren."

E.J. raised his glass and toasted the promotions with Kalea. She chuckled and asked again what happened with the Seville story. E.J. said nothing revealing, just suggested that life is unfair, but with a little luck, it works out in your favor... and that just wasn't the case for the editors. She knew better than to simply believe that E.J. had nothing to do with what was going on, but she didn't care anymore. For the first time in their relationship, she was the only one that wanted to talk about journalism and decided that was a good place to be.

"Okay, I'm not going to bring it up again."

E.J. smiled and continued to eat. Kalea poured another glass of champagne.

"Oh by the way, I was offered a job as a regular contributor to CNN and MSNBC."

"Seriously?" Kalea mumbled through her drink.

"And I was given a raise at Eagle Eye. Between these two, I'm looking at an extra $100,000 a year. Can you believe that? With your job at the university, we can now buy that big-ass house you are always talking about, and afford someone to clean it."

Kalea got up to hug E.J., nearly tackling him out of his dining chair. He cringed hard.

"Ow! Ow! Ow!"

Kalea pulled back a bit, her arms still around him.

"What's wrong? Are you okay?"

E.J. smiled and adjusted himself, the diamond engagement ring he was planning to drop into Kalea's champagne glass when she wasn't looking, finally shifted into a comfortable spot off to the side of his back pocket.

"I'm fine darlin'... just... ummm... some loose change in my back pocket grinding into my ass."

He smiled awkwardly.

In the background, pictures of Walter, Noland, Victoria, and Skye appeared again on television. A lovely young reporter continued to discuss the situation, E.J.'s discovery, the shakeup at the paper, and the state of journalism after such an embarrassing incident. E.J. and Kalea paid no attention and held each other. For the first time since they met, E.J. had no interest in the biggest news story of the week, even if it involved him.

END